The Ghosts of Antietam

The Ghosts of Antietam

By

John Grissmer

ISBN 1-58500-805-2

1stBooks – rev. 01/20/00

ABOUT THE BOOK

> Just received a telegram from Halleck stating
> that Pope and Burnside are very hard pressed __
> urging me to push forward reinforcements & to
> come myself as soon as I possibly can . . . Now
> they are in trouble they seem to want the
> "Quaker," the "procrastinator," the "coward" &
> the "traitor."
>
> George B. McClellan to Nelly, August 21, 1862

Abraham Lincoln dies only a few days after becoming
President. Vice President Hannibal Hamlin takes over the office
and then hastens to Charleston, South Carolina, in a desperate
attempt to avert civil war. Accompanying him as military
advisor is a brilliant young general.

The Ghosts of Antietam is an adventure in alternate history
which takes a fresh look at the Civil War through the eyes of one
of its most maligned characters, General George B. McClellan.

The novel poses questions. Was the bloody conflict truly
inevitable? Was McClellan a traitor or a hero? Would Hannibal
Hamlin have made a better President than Abraham Lincoln?

At Charleston George McClellan saves Hamlin from death
at the hands of a rabid secessionist and enjoys a vexing flirtation
with the beautiful Mary Chesnut. After seeing a tragic example
of what civil war would be, McClellan urges Hamlin to make a
courageous political maneuver which lures Jefferson Davis back
into Union and dooms the Confederacy.

But later McClellan is shocked into the realization of an
alternate world in which the war actually did take place. George
McClellan now relives his wartime odyssey of conflict with
Lincoln and the devious, vindictive Secretary of War, Edwin
Stanton.

The Ghosts of Antietam is an adventure of conflicting realities in which President Hamlin ends slavery without war, and George McClellan attempts to save Lincoln from assassination with surprising results.

Or as the ghost of Edwin Stanton says to Vice President Richard Nixon: "It's not the same old bullshit they put in the history books."

Cover: "The Ghosts of Antietam" by Sal Catalono

Central Figure: George B. McClellan
Lower left: Hannibal Hamlin
Upper left: Abraham Lincoln
Lower right: Edwin Stanton
Bottom right: Richard Nixon

PROLOGUE

By jinks, he was going over!

His quick mind instantly nailed the cause. The tall, stiff hat had been pulled down too tight on his brow. A warm day for March, and sweat had caused it to stick to his head just enough so that when a low hanging branch caught it, the hat stayed firm, pulling him off the saddle. Damn, but his hands had too tightly gripped the reins. The horse trotted right out from under him as he toppled.

Going over backwards.

Would Lamon, who rode on ahead, notice? He could call out to him, but that would be undignified and to what purpose?

He was a man who collected facts and insights about things and people, and now he analyzed his own reactions to this dismounting. Would it make a funny story for future use? Probably not. He seldom made himself the butt of his own wit. He preferred to be the teller of the laughing tale but not a joke himself.

The pearl gray sky turned in lazy motion as his body floated for an eternal instant above the ground. He decided he would tell no one of this incident. His old friend Lamon would keept the secret.

Time to hit the ground. Everyone who rides will eventually be thrown. That's the way with men and horses. He let his body go slack. Take the bump in a manly way and climb back on.

His last thought was: Sure hope I hit soft dirt.

Part One

The World of Charleston

"On the 4th of March next a sectional party will take possession of the Government. It has announced that the South shall be excluded from the common territory, that the Judicial tribunal shall be made sectional, and that a war must be waged against Slavery until it shall cease throughout the United States. The guarantees of the Constitution will be lost. The Slaveholding States will no longer have the power of self-government, or self-protection, and the Federal Government will have become their enemy."

From South Carolina's Declaration of the Causes of Secession

CHAPTER ONE

Cincinnati, Ohio, March 15, 1861

"So you met Lincoln?" George smiled the question at his supper guest as he refilled their wine glasses.

Cump Sherman's head jerked down as he took a quick pull on his cigar. His answer billowed forth in smoke. "I did, sir. I did indeed meet the President. And I have my doubts."

Ellen Marcy McClellan shifted in her chair. Sherman had been holding forth on "matters and things" as he put it, for well over an hour, long after the mince pie had been cleared from the table. Now the waves of smoke from two cigars were bringing on sour nausea.

"George," she said, "perhaps you and Mr. Sherman would enjoy sitting outside on the porch. There might be a breeze off the river."

George McClellan met her eyes. "But, Nelly, don't you want to hear about Cump's meeting with the President?"

She nodded. An expression of open radiant affection bloomed on George's face. George made time stand still when he looked at her like that. For a moment she forgot all about blustering Cump Sherman sitting there at their dining table. She could bear a little more cigar smoke.

Sherman launched into his story. "I hadn't even gotten my things unpacked at Willard's, when bang, bang on the door. It's my brother, John, the newly minted big wig."

"Cump's brother, John, was just appointed United States Senator from Ohio," George said, then cast an inclusive glance across the table at his mother-in-law. "Were you aware of that, Mother Marcy?"

"I read about it just today in the Enquirer," Nelly's mother said, her voice low pitched. "You must be quite proud of your brother, Mr. Sherman."

"I am indeed, Mrs. Marcy, very proud of my baby brother." Cump inclined his head toward the older woman. "Anyhow, John promptly announced that he was taking me over to the White House to pay my respects to the man of the hour, none other than A. Lincoln himself."

As their visitor spoke, Nelly studied his face. Mr. Sherman's right eye lived a life of adventurous independence. The more excited he got, the more that right eye turned inward as if to make a close inspection of his nose, while his left eye stuck to its stern duty, staring full front. So that's why people said Cump Sherman sometimes looked half crazy.

"It's a fast cakewalk from Willard's over to the White House," he said. "My brother just rolled in the front door and up the stairway to the President's office. Him nodding and waving to everybody like he owned the place."

Nelly turned her head slightly so that Sherman wouldn't notice, and gave her husband a slow wink of her right eye. Half hidden in a blur of cigar smoke, George winked back. Nelly put a napkin to her smiling lips. They had been married less than a year.

"Well sir, we walk in without a by-your-leave, and there's Lincoln sitting at the end of a long table, in conversation with three or four men. He gives my brother the high sign that we're to wait. That room, by the way, was nothing to write home about. It had the ugliest green wallpaper. Well, anyhow, after the other men left, Lincoln invites us, very courteously, to sit at the table with him. My brother introduced me, told him I had just come up from Louisiana. So then Lincoln says to me, 'Mr. Sherman, how are they getting along down there in Louisiana?' I said: 'They think they are getting along swimmingly. They are preparing for war.' I said it straight out to him, just like that."

"And what did Lincoln say?" George asked.

Sherman scanned the table. "He said, and I quote exactly because I wrote it down, 'Oh, well! I guess we'll manage to keep house.' Can you beat that? The country tottering on civil war."

George smiled. "Lincoln," he said, "always was an odd bird, or so it seemed the few times I've been with him. Always

4

that joshing, country-style speech. His legal writing, on the other hand, can be quite well wrought."

Cump Sherman tapped an inch of ash onto his pie plate, looking a bit deflated. "I wasn't aware that you knew Lincoln."

"We're not close friends," George said. "But he did represent us in some court cases when I was with the Illinois Central. He was never at a loss for words, full of jokes, some of them quite funny, if not so refined." George stroked his bushy mustache, and stifled a laugh. "One of them I remember. He called it: The Man of Audacity."

Nelly clapped her hands lightly. "Oh, do tell it, George."

George's cheeks colored with splotches of pink. "It contains a vulgar word, and unfortunately the whole point of humor hinges upon it."

"Oh, no," Mary Marcy exclaimed, "a vulgar word?" She looked straight ahead, sternly facing her reflection in the mirror that hung above the sideboard, but the corners of her mouth twitched. "Nelly and I have lived twenty years on army posts, so of course we've never heard a vulgar word."

Sherman turned to gaze at her in mock astonishment. "Hmm, I wonder, ma'am, if we were in the same army."

Nelly giggled. George let out his own distinctive, barking laugh, and Cump joined in, his right eye rolling gleefully.

Nelly pushed away from the table, gathering herself, the thick folds of her hoop skirt and her lurching stomach. George jumped up making a tardy grab of assistance with her chair.

"Thank you, dear," she said. "Now you men folk go on outside and finish your cigars while Mother and I clean up."

* * *

Out on the pouch George sat in his favorite rocking chair. He placed one high-laced, polished shoe on the rail and pushed off against it, enjoying the rumble of the rockers on the floor boards. Cump took the wide porch swing opposite. He sat enthroned in the center, his arms draped across the top rails, cigar cocked up to the corner of his mouth.

"Excellent view you have up here," Cump said, appraising the vista of the city now washed by the setting sun. "Takes in the hills and the river."

"Good ground," George said, using the soldier's term in praise of high terrain.

He picked up a small spy glass from a nearby wicker table and put it to his eye. A river boat was making for the third street docks, paddle wheels churning white water.

"I'm going to write a letter to Governor Dennison and tell him that Cincinnati will be a strategic point if war comes. Should I be placed in command of its defenses, perhaps I can direct operations right here from my own veranda."

Cump lifted both arms. "Of course your neighbors might protest when you have to tear down their houses to clear you fields of fire and observation."

George laughed. "Never have a soldier for a neighbor." He swept his spy glass down the curve of the Ohio River. "I think I would place two key forts over there on the Kentucky side at Covington and run telegraph wires across the river." He lowered the telescope. "That's how we'll manage our communications you know, telegraph lines. No more couriers being shot off their horses. The battle field will be wired up from one end to the other."

"Sounds plausible." Cump cleared his throat, then brushed a hand through the stubble of red hair that seemed to grow in all directions atop his head. "I did want to discuss certain matters and things with you, Captain McClellan."

George settled back in the rocker. Cump had shown up unannounced that afternoon at the offices of the Ohio & Mississippi Railroad. Though they had not been especially close friends over the years, both men were members of the small, prideful fraternity of West Point graduates. Still it had been some years since George was 'Captain McClellan.'

"My friends call me Mac."

Cump leaned forward. "A man needs to know who his friends are these days. I just wanted you to know, Mac, that, like yourself, if war comes I'm going to stand by the old gridiron flag."

"I never doubted that for a moment, Cump. Though I can guess that Braxton Bragg and the rest of those Louisiana Secesh must have put some big temptations in your way."

"Oh, sure they tried to get me to join their damn tin pot army. No, I told them. I stand by my oath to the Constitution."

George scratched a match on the sole of his boot, and lit a fresh cigar. "I heard from our mutual friend, Si Buckner, that you were well satisfied with your position down there in Louisiana."

Cump sighed and laced his fingers behind his head. "I figured I'd found my place on earth at last. Superintendent of *The Louisiana State Seminary of Learning and Military Academy.* I did love that school and the young men in it, even if they were a little wild, as southern boys will be. By the way I must thank you again for those French text books you sent us. We made good use of them."

"Happy to hear it, Cump. I brought too many books back from Europe. You can see how my house resembles an overflowing library."

Cump looked wistful. "The trustees were building a fine new house for me. I was going to have Ellen and all the kids together in one home."

"Too bad."

"Damn right, too bad. You know that school was built with a federal land grant? Carved in stone above the door, it said: *The Union, Esto Perpetua.* Now I hear they took hammers and chiseled out those words. The fools."

"I've always liked Southerners," George said, "but they've been sadly victimized by their leaders. If we have a war, it will be the greatest tragedy this country has ever seen."

"If there's war, Mac, there won't be any more country as we know it. A whole section has gone criminally insane, and I have no confidence in Lincoln or any other politician to get it back on track."

Cump rose from the swing and began pacing the porch, his hands clamped behind his back. "And all for what? Slavery! The Southerners have gone lunatic just because some wild-eyed Boston abolitionists call them names and hurt their feelings. You read Lincoln's inaugural speech, he offered them no threat. Yet they're all pissing in their boots that somehow he's going to sneak down there in the night and take their slaves. But under the Constitution he's not free to interfere at all with their property rights. Damn, but I hate Abolitionists, all those long haired men and short haired women with their anti-slave agitation. They ought to be horsewhipped."

George stood up. Cump's riled up energy was infectious. "I've always said there are two trouble-making states that ought to be detached from the Union. Massachusetts with their abolitionists, and South Carolina with their secessionists."

"Yep," Cump agreed, "they can go to hell together."

"And leave us all in peace."

Cump walked up to George and looked him square in the face. "Of course we know that ain't likely to happen. Which brings me to the point of my visit, Mac. I am enroute to Saint Louis to accept the presidency of the Fifth Street Railroad Company. I hope to establish myself there and send for the family. The trouble is, what's going to happen if Frenchy Beauregard starts shooting at Bob Anderson down in Fort Sumter?"

"But, Cump, you have Lincoln's word on it. He'll manage to keep house."

"In a pig's ass. I just can't figure which way he's going to jump. Lincoln, I mean. When I was in Washington nobody was taking this crisis seriously. It is a Southern town you know, and I saw much snickering behind fingers at the embarrassment to the general government. If Lincoln takes hold and wants to seriously build an army, then I want you to be sure to remember to call on me. Everybody knows you were one of the up and comers before you left the army, Mac. If war comes you're sure to be called back to high rank."

George settled in his chair, and pulled deeply on his cigar. If war comes. Yes, General Scott would be certain to champion him for major command. Who else was there who had observed the great armies of Europe in action and studied their techniques down to their horseshoes? The Federal government would use him at the highest level, and after the inevitable victory, well, what then? Politics? At age thirty-four his life spread before him like one of those great Western landscapes he had explored as a Second Lieutenant. Full of potential.

"There's one other thing you ought to know about me, Mac. Though it's embarrassing, I'm just going to come out with it."

George nodded.

"While you and Bragg, and Lee, and all that bunch were down there with General Scott, shooting up Mexico, I was stuck high and dry in California filing out supply vouchers and delivering mail."

"Supply vouchers are a very important element of army administration."

"Yep, okay, it's funny to you, Mac. But I want you to know something. I've done a lot of things in my time, been a merchant, a banker, a farmer, a teacher. I'm even a lawyer now."

"I didn't know that."

"Well, I've dipped my toe in too many professions," Cump said, striding around the porch. "I tell you, Mac, there is only one true calling for me. The one I was educated for. There's a term my Catholic wife uses about their priesthood. Vocation. My vocation, sir, is to be a soldier, to stand up in the smoke of battle, and lead the troops. I have it in me, I know it." Cump's blue-gray eyes searched George's face for encouragement.

George sighed. He understood what Cump was feeling. Six months after resigning from the army he had himself been tempted to become a 'filibuster,' a soldier of fortune for hire in the wars of South America. Hard not to scratch the soldiering itch once it gets at you. But he had been right to overcome his restless boredom and stay on at the railroad. His long years of courting the elusive Mary Ellen Marcy had been rewarded with an idyllic marriage.

Now the daily uncertainty about Fort Sumter in Charleston Harbor was beginning to grind on everyone's nerves, and not just frantic Cump Sherman. Even his normally unruffled Nelly was not quite herself these days.

The question was, would the South Carolina fire-eaters unleash their cannon on Fort Sumter? And if they did, what would be Major Bob Anderson's orders? Return shot for shot? Evacuate? Surrender a United States fort? What would Lincoln do then? Did Lincoln himself know? Let the South go, and good riddance, or send the army and navy to teach them a lesson of respect for Union and the Constitution? Thank God it wasn't his worry.

All he had to do was meet Cump Sherman's emotional plea for a position of rank in an army that didn't exist, which George didn't command, in a war that had not yet started.

George placed his hands on Cump's shoulders. "Sherman, I have no doubt as to your prowess as a soldier. I would be proud to serve with you in any capacity." He stepped back. "But right now our only duty is to press on with our everyday pursuits. You go back to Lancaster, and join your family and then take that good job in Saint Louis. I'll keep running my railroad. Let's pray there is no war."

Cump nodded, the attack of near hysteria evaporated. He turned and looked out over the hills of the city. "Mac," he said, "we both know the South. We know their people. I've concluded we're probably going to have to fight them. If we relax one bit they will ride over us roughshod. Whatever happens, when the bell rings, don't forget about me."

George grinned. "How could I forget any man named Tecumseh?"

* * *

Nelly folded clean white cloths over the leftover food dishes and placed them in the cold storage box. One of the advantages of living in a sizable city like Cincinnati was that ice got delivered twice a week.

"Well, mama, I'm quite pleased with myself, even if I do say so."

Her mother stood at the stove brewing a pot of dark Irish tea. "You have every right to be proud, my girl. That chicken and biscuits was very good. You've tinkered some with my recipe though haven't you? An improvement, mind you."

Nelly was careful in her reply. "I was looking at some of those French cookbooks George brought back." She sat at the kitchen table. "They do things with what they call herbs."

Mary Marcy laughed. "What we would call weeds."

"Well, I couldn't have done it without your help, mama. The mince pie was wonderful as usual." Nelly studied her mother's face with its taut and polished sheen of aged marble, and was pleased to see it relax and glow as the deeply etched lines softened.

"Of course, I do hope that George will not make a habit of this, bringing guests home on such short notice."

Mary Marcy spooned several heaps of sugar into her cup. "You're a knock-about Army child, Nelly. You can handle surprises. What did you think of Mr. Sherman?"

"He's certainly a man of opinions," Nelly responded, and decided to say no more. In that small, inbred and often contentious family that was the Regular Army, reputations, gossip, and scandals, real or imagined, circulated widely and easily. Nelly was not sure what she thought of Sherman or what she was expected to think. "He seemed to like my chicken. I counted three helpings he took."

Mary Marcy made a humph sound. "Mr. Sherman appreciates a home-cooked meal any time he can get it. His wife, being of the ultra society in Lancaster, Ohio, thank you, doesn't know what a kitchen's for."

Nelly smiled. "He seemed to think we may have war soon."

Mary Marcy waved a hand. "Wishful thinking," she said. "All these old army boys are chomping at the bit to fight. Never mind their solemn protests. It's just too bad they'll have to shoot at old friends and classmates. It'll be the only war we're likely to have in this generation, so they'll just have to make do with it."

Nelly smoothed her skirts, and strived to compose herself. "Why, mama, do you really think George is looking forward to war?"

Her mother nodded. "In his own gentlemanly way, yes, whether or not he admits it to himself. Daughter, I have known and lived among these men for twenty-seven years. They were trained for war. It's in their blood, and some of them are good for nothing else." She sipped her tea. "Naturally I do not include George and your father. George could be anything he wants to be in the world of affairs if he just applied himself."

"Don't you think he applies himself?"

"Oh, my yes. Now don't look that way and have a hissy on me. It's just that I sometimes see in George a little bit of the, oh, I don't know, artist or the schoolmaster. He'd rather be home with the latest book from London than out --"

"Making war."

Mary Marcy considered before she spoke. "Making war is a special skill, Nelly, and it calls for a certain kind of man. I'm just not sure George is mean enough, to be blunt about it."

"Mama, when were you ever not blunt? Mercy, but I don't know whether to laugh or feel ornery at you."

"Oh, Nelly, you know how I run at the mouth. I love George near as much as you do."

Nelly stared at her mother. George not mean enough? In order to defend him she would have to prove he was mean. Which of course was not true. He was the kindest most loving man she had ever known.

Ah, well, think on it later. She pulled in a deep breath and twisted in her chair against the twinges in her lower back and abdomen. Unknown forces and strange momentums surged in waves throughout her body. She wished she could lie down and sleep. Then she became aware that her mother was still speaking on. Nelly gathered herself to listen to the familiar, confident voice.

"I pity those poor boys with Bob Anderson hung out to dry down there in Charleston Harbor, not knowing whether to surrender or fight. It's the worst kind of witches brew, daughter, politics and war. It smells like a buzzard stuck down the chimney. Sooner or later Mr. Lincoln will have to take a recess from telling vulgar stories and call out the army and the militias and then..." Her mother stopped short, smiled and said, "Wasn't George a dear, the way he blushed at that awful old Man of Audacity story?"

Nelly glanced up. "Do you mean to tell me you know it?"

"The Man of Audacity? Good gracious, Nelly, that joke's so old it has whiskers."

"I've never heard of it."

"And that is quite as it should be for a proper lady."

Nelly tittered and covered her mouth with her fingers. "Oh, go on and tell it, mama."

"There's nothing much to tell," Mary Marcy said. "It's all about this Man of Audacity who passes wind while carving a turkey."

"What's funny about that?"

Her mother rolled her eyes. "That's the point. It's not funny. It's very common, and not worthy of conversation between a good Presbyterian mother and daughter. I'm sorry I even brought it up,"

Then she burst out laughing.

"Tell it, mother."

"All right. The Man Of Audacity is carving the turkey and he passes wind. The guests, observing the rules of decorum, pretend not to notice."

"Very polite of them."

"Yes, well, anyhow, the Man Of Audacity takes off his coat, rolls up his sleeves, spits on his hands, takes up the carving knife and makes a general announcement to the table. *Now then, let's see if I can carve this turkey without farting.*"

Nelly laughed until a sharp pain went zinging through her middle. It forced her to regain control.

"What an awful story," she managed to gasp. "It's not the least bit funny."

Her mother reached across the table to clasp her hand. "Yes, yes, deplorable. Now can we change the subject? I want to talk to you, seriously."

"Yes? What about?"

"I'm just a might concerned for you, child. Your face is white. I noticed it at supper. Are you feeling unwell?"

Nelly weighed her response. She could blame the cigars, but no, perhaps it was time. "Well, not really," she said.

"Uh huh. Your tummy way down below feels a little kattywampus does it?"

"All right, mother, I've been meaning to tell you." Nelly got up and peeked down the hallway to make sure George and Sherman were safely out of earshot. Then she went around the table to where her mother was seated, bent over and whispered.

"I've missed my last two monthly miseries."

Her mother's face lit up. "Oh, Nelly..."

"And I guess I'm in fashion, because sometimes I feel like my insides want to secede from the rest of me."

"Oh, Nelly..."

"I've been making some inquires after a doctor."

"Find one who's studied medicine," her mother said. "One who knows how a woman functions." She stood up, clasped both arms around Nelly and hugged.

"Have you told George yet?"

"I'm getting ready to."

"Tell him soon. Men like to be told."

"Yes, mama." Nelly felt a warm, prideful confidence overflowing and calming her. She had been right to tell her mother.

"We must face reality, daughter, if the baby is due in..." She tapped out her fingers on Nelly's shoulders. "October or November, George might be in the thick of the fight by then, and your father as well. Cincinnati may be too close to the war. I want you further North."

14

"I was thinking perhaps Philadelphia, with George's family."

"Yes, maybe. Wherever it is, I'll be with you then..." Mary Marcy's voice trailed off, her eyes dreamy.

Nelly smiled as she imagined the goings-on in her mother's mind, the cascade of ideas, memories, warnings, advice to come. She hugged her close. "Everything in good time, mama. It'll be all right."

"Nelly! Mother Marcy! Come in here!"

Nelly pursed her lips. She had just heard the parade ground bellow of Captain George McClellan. It rang of command and drawn swords, of whipping flags and drumrolls.

George shouldn't yell like that in the house. She would have to have a little talk with him about this.

"My goodness, what's all the fuss and feathers," Mary Marcy muttered as they made their way to the front parlor. George was standing in a loose triangular formation with Sherman and a third man.

Nelly felt her nostrils tighten at the sight of Allan Pinkerton or E. J. Allan or whatever name he had chosen for himself today. It wasn't the black, grizzled beard or the beady, lump-of-coal eyes or his rasping Scottish brogue she found so distasteful. It was simply the man himself and his identification as 'detective,' a term she suspected he had invented to give some respectable coloration to his occupation which was, after all, snooping on people.

There was something odd about Pinkerton today. Two glistening streaks ran down his cheeks. Tears?

"Nelly, you know Allan, of course," George said.

She inclined her head.

"Mother Marcy, may I present an associate of mine, Mr. Allan Pinkerton."

"E. J. Allan, ma'am. I prefer to be known as E. J. Allan."

Nelly shot a glance at her mother who stifled a smile.

"As you wish, Mister E. J." Mary Marcy said. "Makes no difference to me."

Nelly studied Pinkerton's pruney little face and felt a wave of hot annoyance beyond her usual scorn for the man. Whatever news he brought with him was bound to be unpleasant. He was like a smelly old Tom cat who had dragged a gashed and bleeding mouse into the house and deposited it here on her fine front parlor carpet. Why couldn't George have kept him out on the porch?

"Mr. Pinkerton is a detective, mother. He scurries around and discovers secrets for George and the railroad or whoever hires him."

"Mrs. McClellan..." Pinkerton tried to interrupt.

"Now don't be modest, Mr. Pinkerton. Tell mother how you saved Lincoln's life. This is fascinating, mother. Mr. Pinkerton discovered a plot against Lincoln as he was traveling to Washington for his inauguration." Nelly avoided George's eyes. She had started and would finish. "Anyway Mr. Pinkerton shifted Lincoln around to a different train and rolled him right through Baltimore in the dead of night. Baltimore was where the assassins lived, but it was after their bedtime."

She heard her voice trail away. The atmosphere of the room was weighted with ponderous, masculine silence.

"Nelly," George said, "Mr. Pinkerton has just come from the telegraph office. You'd better sit down. There is shocking news from Washington."

"Thank you, George, but I have no need to sit down."

"I thought... I thought you weren't feeling well..." George stammered.

A white hot flash of anger. How did George know? Pinkerton! That man had spied out her most intimate secret and reported.

"I am perfectly strong and able, George, now what is the news?" Nelly hated the hurtful bite in her voice. Poor George, pink splotches were rising in his cheeks. Her mother looked at her with disapproval. Well, she would apologize later, when Pinkerton was gone, and after she had criticized George for shouting at her. Be good, she told herself, you can take a nap soon.

Nelly's mother sat down in one of the carved wing back chairs, and addressed herself to Pinkerton. "I'm afraid Nelly and I can guess the import of your news, sir. Hostilities have begun at Fort Sumter?"

Nelly sat down in the chair opposite and closed her eyes, grateful that her mother had taken over.

"No, ma'am, there has been no news of Fort Sumter," Pinkerton began. "But there has been a tragedy. President Lincoln was pronounced dead this afternoon at twelve minutes past one."

Nelly caught her breath.

Pinkerton's voice grated on. "According to the telegraph dispatch, it was an accident, not an assassination. Mr. Lincoln was apparently riding on horseback out to the cottage at the Soldier's home on the Northeast outskirts of Washington City. Marshall Lamon, his bodyguard, was with him. It's not clear from the dispatch, but somehow the President fell or was thrown from his horse."

Nelly looked around the room. Her mother was staring at her, wide eyed. Pinkerton stood as if at a grave site, head lowered, hands crossed at his waist. Sherman coughed and consulted his pocket watch. George seemed lost in some private contemplation.

"The poor Man of Audacity," Nelly said. "Got to be President for only eleven days, then fell off his horse." She felt laughter rising in her throat and covered her mouth.

"He was a good man." Pinkerton glared at her, "I came to know him."

"Oh, mercy, yes, I'm sure he was a good man," Nelly said quickly. "Such a blow to our country. George, what do you think will happen now?"

She sat back, closed her eyes, and clutched her stomach. Let George deliver his opinion. It's what men love to do.

"These are troubled times, my dear," George said, his voice seeming deeper than usual. "What effect this will have on the situation at Fort Sumter, I can't venture to say. I presume through that the word has reached Charleston."

Mary Marcy said, "Is there any news of the Vice President?"

Of course, the Vice President. How sensible her mother was. Nelly drew a blank. Who was the Vice President? He came from somewhere in New England she remembered, and had a very strange name. But what was it?

"The end of the dispatch mentions the Vice President," Pinkerton said. "Fortunately he was at Washington City, and had not yet left for his farm in Maine. He took the oath of office this afternoon."

"Well then," George said, "may I suggest we all spend a moment in silent prayer, both for President Lincoln and for our new President, Hannibal Hamlin."

George bowed his head in perfect timing as church bells began to toll throughout the city.

"Amen! Hannibal Hamlin," Nelly exclaimed, relieved to have the name. "God help him!"

"God help us all," said her mother.

CHAPTER TWO

Letter from George B. McClellan to Ellen Marcy McClellan, Washington, D.C.   April 6, 1861

My Darling Nel,

   I trust my cryptic telegrams have kept you advised that I am well, and in good spirits. Now at last I find a few private moments in which to write to you in some detail as to the events of recent days and the grand adventure ahead of me.

   Ah, Nelly, who would have thought last year when we were married that I would so soon find myself back in the Army with the brevet rank of Major General, and called upon in the effort to save our country. I still can hardly believe it myself even when I glimpse the stars on my spanking new shoulder boards.

   One reason I am here is that poor old overweight General Scott is in such a state of ill health that he is unable to hoist himself to horseback. He has been the soul of helpfulness and courtesy to me for I believe he sees me as his young surrogate in the coming mission.

   It is really quite a straight forward plan President Hamlin has conceived. He, along with Secretary of State Seward and certain others of us, will embark on a coastal steamer to sail to Charleston harbor. The President goes under the theory that no state has leave to secede, and that as President and Commander in Chief of the Army, he has a perfect right to visit Charleston to inspect our coastal defenses at Fort Sumter. This theory supposes of course that the lunatic secesh will refrain from firing on our flag during the President's visit. On this I am less than optimistic for when have the fire-eaters of South Carolina ever behaved with rational civility? In short, dear wife, anything can happen. We will not know the outcome until it is upon us. I say this only to prepare you for any possibility, as the brave Army child you are.

Remember the time when you and your mother were in Saint Louis and it was mistakenly reported that your father and I had both been killed by the Comanches? How sad those days must have been for you Nel. Although I think your father enjoyed hearing his reported death mourned.

I have had several meetings with President Hamlin already, and we have struck it off swimmingly well, as Cump Sherman might say. Mr. Hamlin looks right in his role as President. He is a big man, measuring well over six feet in height. But unlike Lincoln who was such a bag of bones all poking out at unlikely angles, Mr. Hamlin's form is solid, and well filled out. We have heard that he was an accomplished wrestler in his youth, and I would reckon him to be still quite strong.

His face is oblong, topped by a thick thatch of curling black hair. His eyebrows are aggressively bushy, and from beneath them his dark brown eyes seem to bore right through you. Altogether he presents an attitude of dignity and importance. Were you to enter a room not knowing his rank, your eyes would be immediately drawn to him, and you well might surmise correctly that his was the position of leadership.

As to the matter of Mr. Lincoln's death, I have been advised of some of the details, but will save them for a future letter. Suffice to say that it truly was an untoward accident. There was no foul play. However the repercussions of this shocking event continue to accrue. On one of my visits to the President's mansion I was an unwilling witness to a most distressing scene between President Hamlin and poor Mrs. Lincoln. She has gone quite crazy, shouting and ranting at our President using unladylike language that would shock even Mother Marcy.

There is much more to tell but my fingers grow numb and I must catch a few winks. We sail tomorrow for Charleston, Capital of Secessionia. Pray with me that our efforts there will meet with success and will deliver our country from this tragic crisis.

Always your devoted,
George

ON A SEPARATE SHEET OF PAPER
A Very Private Message from George to Nelly

Dear One,

Who knows but that someday our papers and letters may become the happy hunting ground for historians or other scurvy snoops. Therefore I must caution you to burn this after reading.

Oh my Nelly, what can I say of your parting gift to me, when you awoke me all unexpectedly in that small hour of the morning before I had to leave for my train? I had thought that because of your delicate condition all such joys were to be denied me for a good long while. But voila! There you were, and oh, what a delightful gift was bestowed upon me by my darling, the gift of 'Nelly Herself' in all her glory just as God made her! I assure you the sweet memory of our last fervent "good-bye" will warm me through the lonely and difficult days ahead.

I must close now as there are urges stirring within me that as a good Christian Soldier, I must not yield to.

Your Most Ardent Lover,
George

CHAPTER THREE

Hannibal Hamlin sat up, wide awake from a frightening dream that vanished in the morning light. He reached out for Ellen's comforting body but she was not there. There was a noise and a sense of motion. Then he realized was alone in a rich man's cabin aboard the steamer Vanderbilt, its paddle wheels relentlessly chugging on a voyage to Charleston.

He closed his eyes. This trip would either be the supreme accomplishment of his life, or his most fatal blunder. The newspapers were already divided in their opinions. Yet he was President of those states still loyal to the old Constitution, and this spur of the moment voyage, this offer to parley with the secessionists was his sacred duty. He would give them every opportunity to rectify their folly so as to avoid fraternal bloodshed.

To avert a civil war he would do anything short of dishonor.

He swung out of the bunk and placed both feet on the floor and then, curiously, a procession of his past life's occupations marched through his mind. He had been a newspaper editor, teacher, farmer, lawyer, judge, Congressman, Senator, and the first Vice President ever to run on the Republican Party ticket. Now he was President.

He would need the wisdom of those Hannibal Hamlin's of the past to win at this chancy venture.

He wiped away a drop of sweat that had dripped from his nose to his chin. Already the heat of the new day was building in the tight little cabin. He sat on the edge of his bunk and pulled on his socks and shoes, both still slightly damp from the salt air. He hoped Ellen had packed enough clean linen. Next came trousers and shirt, leaving off the collar. He splashed water on his face and played his fingers over the overnight growth of beard.

Shave later.

His black, claw-hammer coat hung neatly in the stateroom closet. He flicked some stray cigar ash from its back collar.

Let it hang. He would dress as he chose.

He stepped out of his cabin and felt the refreshing sweep of sea air, not as cool or brisk as the breeze off the Maine coast, but good feeling all the same.

"Good morning, Mr. President."

A boyish looking navel officer had popped up out of nowhere to startle him with a salute. A very sharp salute. The youth's arm quivered with contained energy, the fingers stiff as rails, the elbow held frozen at an acute angle. Hamlin vaguely waved his right hand in return, and a memory crossed his mind.

"What is your name, young man?"

"Ensign Harold Filmore, President Hamlin, your servant, sir."

"I was just thinking, Mr. Filmore, that when I was your age I was all full of beans about attending West Point to make a soldier of myself. I suspect had I done so they would have taught me there how to salute properly."

"Yes, sir. They would have tried at least."

"My father talked me out of it." He paused and smiled. "But despite that setback, Mr. Filmore, I have managed to achieve military rank as Captain in the Maine Militia. Of course the men in our company are not much for saluting. A little bit of drilling and shooting off their muskets and a lot of getting drunk is more their program. So perhaps on this voyage you can school me in the fine art of saluting."

Doubt clouded Ensign Filmore's face.

"Oh, I'm serious, Mr. Filmore. I perceive saluting to be a big part of the job of being President. I would be much obliged if you would see that I do it correctly, young sir."

Ensign Filmore was quick with a smile. "I would be honored to assist you, Mr. President."

"That's settled then." Hamlin leaned out over the ship's rail and breathed in the salt air. The new morning sun, rising from the opposite side of the ship, cast a pink wash over scattered, fast dissolving night clouds. It would be a fair day's sailing.

"Have you any idea where we are, Mr. Filmore?"

"Yes, sir. We're near the bottom end of Chesapeake Bay, nearly abeam Yorktown. With the Captain's compliments, he estimates we will make Fortress Monroe by four-and-a-half this afternoon."

Hamlin continued to gaze out over the water toward the faint, gray shoreline.

"Is he a competent Captain, Mr. Filmore?"

"Captain Blackstone? One of the best in the Navy, Mr. President."

Hamlin was full of questions unspoken. Was the Captain as good as Filmore said, or was he merely hearing the expression of the expected loyalty to a commanding officer? And what of General McClellan who looked nearly as fresh minted as Ensign Filmore? Were they all the same, these brass buttoned military men? Would they all lie and disclaim and blather and dance a jog trot of equivocation according to what they thought the President might want to hear?

He would find out for himself soon enough.

"Sir, Mr. Seward is having breakfast on the Salon Deck. He asked me to convey an invitation to join him."

"Hmm, and how is the Secretary of State dressed this morning?"

Filmore considered for a moment. "Why, he is in shirt sleeves with collar and string tie."

"I'll trump him then, Mr. Filmore, by going as I am, with neither collar nor tie. There are advantages to being President you see."

Advantages indeed! As Hamlin fell in step behind Ensign Filmore, he sensed that the young man wished to ask the same question he'd heard so often of late from old comrades of the Senate and House. They would squint up at him, dart a sideways glance, and then demand in a half whisper, "Tell us, Han. How does it feel? How does it feel to be President?"

He would put them off with some humble pie about doing his duty to his country and the memory of Lincoln, for if he could not give them an exact and honest answer, at least he would not lie.

He could answer the question to himself with no trouble though. It felt perfectly fine and natural to be President, as if at long last he had found the one place in the world where he fit. Hannibal Hamlin fully expected himself to be acclaimed an excellent President.

If all went well in Charleston.

Too bad about Lincoln, of course. People called it a 'tragedy,' but he knew that to be an improper use of the term as understood in dramatic literature. A tragic figure such as a Hamlet or Lear fell by succumbing to some fatal interior flaw, or 'hubris' as the Greeks of old would call it. Poor old Lincoln merely had an accident that dashed the ambitions of a lifetime. Aside from their one sided competition at the convention, he had liked Lincoln, the real man Lincoln, the crafty railroad lawyer from Illinois, not the clever actor who liked to play backwoods bumpkin. Lincoln had been first off the mark by many months, quietly gathering up delegates on the sly, so that by the time Hamlin's friends had awakened him to the idea that he could be nominated, Lincoln had the prize all sewed up.

Hamlin had accepted second place on the ticket to give the infant Republican Party much needed strength in New England, but only after being assured by Lincoln's agents that "he would not be a mere figurehead, that his abilities and experience would be utilized fully in the service of the country." That was a promise that may or may not have been kept, but it was a moot point now. His abilities and experience were on their way to Charleston.

On the salon deck he found the Secretary of State happily spreading butter on a puffy, golden biscuit. Gentle sunlight filtered through the huge canvas awning flapping above the deck and reflected up from the stark, white linen tablecloth, casting a flickering glow over Seward's peculiar features. There was no getting around it, Bill Seward with his curved beak nose, wattled cheeks and absent chin, did look like a chicken. A very brainy chicken. Seward glanced up at him. "Good morning, your Excellency."

Hamlin smiled. "Morning, Mr. Secretary. You can drop that Excellency business when we're in private, you know."

Hamlin sat down at the table.

"Looks to be a beautiful day," Seward said with his gravely New York accent. "Have some breakfast. They've got a jim-cracky cook. The boy says he can even whip up a French omelette."

Hamlin stiffened. "I'm not much for fancy food."

They were sailing for Charleston to take on the most dangerous national emergency of the century. They should be talking of something more important than French omelettes.

"May I serve ya some breakfast sar?"

Hamlin's head jerked around. Close at his shoulder, much too close, was a gangling boy, a doleful example of the Irish race.

"A cup of coffee, please, nothing more," Hamlin said too gruffly, then tried to compensate by baring his teeth in a forced smile.

"Nuthin ta eat fer ya, sar?"

"Not just now, thank you."

The boy ambled off. Seward grinned. "Map of Ireland eh? All over that lad's face. His name is Patrick, wouldn't ya know?"

Hamlin hunched his shoulders. He was never comfortable with the Irish, ever since his student days in Boston where they swarmed the streets with their jutting monkey jaws, ugly pug noses, freckled faces and watery blue eyes. Most distasteful of all was their Papist-cult religion which would forever block them from being true, loyal Americans.

As a politician he had learned to meet them, to shake their hands, to simulate a proper if cool friendship. Because, for all their failings, the disorderly Irish voted. Early and often as the saying went.

"Ah, but is this not a high-flautin way to travel?" Seward carefully placed a morsel of ham on yet another biscuit. "A pleasant springtime cruise to the land of the palmetto and the citrus tree, and on our own government steamboat."

"I'm glad you're enjoying it, Bill. I hope you'll be just as pleased when we get to Charleston. I don't mean to ruin your breakfast, but have you given thought what we'll do once we get there?"

Seward chuckled and cocked his head. "Why your Excellency, I thought you had that all twigged out."

Hamlin allowed a frown to pass over his face.

"Perhaps I have been remiss," Seward said quickly. "In the bustle of getting this trip underway we've hardly had a chance to consult. If you don't mind me offering an obsequious compliment, Mr. President, it was a smart idea on your part, this voyage to Charleston. We are making the gesture of effort, taking bold action at long last."

Hamlin cupped his chin in the palm of his left hand. "And we may even be doing the right thing, Bill."

"That's always possible," Seward said, "but at least we are, that is you are providing leadership, demonstrating a strong tailbone, something missing in our chief executive until now. The country has been in suspense since December when the Gulf states seceded, and that buffoon, Buchanan, let them get away with it."

"He should have been impeached," Hamlin said.

"Or at least tarred and feathered. For all his hemming and hawing on whether to give up our forts or not, his most grievous mischief was in allowing the Southrons to believe they are independent States."

Hamlin gave a firm nod. From November of 1860 when Lincoln had been elected, until March fourth, 1861, when he took office as President, the secessionists had been allowed to run free in setting up their Confederate States of America.

The thought of former President Buchanan filled him with sour disgust.

He said, "I'll always believe that Buchanan made a secret deal with the slave states to facilitate their secession."

Seward's long fingers fluttered up in a gesture of agreement. "Wouldn't put it past him. He always was in their pocket, don't ya know."

"I thought that Lincoln should have..." Hamlin stopped himself. It would not do to criticize his dead predecessor.

Seward's eyes crinkled. "Lincoln should have what?"

It was pointless to talk of might-have-beens. "Who can say? Lincoln's not here. We are. Give me your thoughts, Bill."

"Well sir, with all due respect to our late lamented rail-spliter, I was becoming more than a little bit unhappy. In fact, I was composing a letter to him communicating my complaints when tragedy struck."

"What were you going to say in you letter, Bill?"

Seward leaned forward and lowered his voice. "Affairs of state were waywardly drifting, sir. We had no policy whatsoever, either domestic or foreign. The President's time was too much taken up with applications for Patronage. I felt those matters could be postponed and that we needed to get down to business."

"He wasn't moving fast enough for you?"

"Oh, he was moving with great dispatch in questions such as who shall be the Postmaster of Indianapolis. He enjoyed that kind of thing. I felt there were larger issues. Namely, were we going to let eight States of the Union walk out on us without a fight or were we going to make some sort of effort to get them back?"

"Were you for war then?"

"Well, yes and no. Mostly no. You see, I believe that Lincoln wasted months of opportunity after his election. Letters could have been exchanged with Jeff Davis who you must agree represents the moderate wing of their asylum and a secret meeting in a border city could have been arranged. In fact I proposed the idea and even offered myself as a go-between."

"What did he say to that?"

"Nothing beyond an acknowledgment. He stayed on in Springfield, complaining that his views were well known and that his hands were tied until he became President. So the

Confederacy was given time to grow and thrive and believe in its own invincible destiny."

"Things have been allowed to get out of hand," Hamlin said. "But there's no use blaming Lincoln. What would you have had him do if he had met with Davis?"

"Two possibilities." Seward made a V with his fingers. "He could have offered to give in just a 'leetle' bit on slavery in the territories, a line of demarcation, a compromise, or go the whole hog, let 'em invade Cuba and set up their slave patch there, anything Davis could take to his people that would get 'em back in the Union."

"Have you ever read our party platform, Bill? There's no going back on slavery in the territories. They should have damn well been satisfied we weren't going to interfere with it where it was already established."

Seward shook his head. "Oh, I know where your heart lies. If you had your way, the niggers would all have ten votes each and sleep on featherbeds."

Hamlin made a grumping noise. "You exaggerate more than slightly there, sir."

"Well, you know me, Han. I must always exaggerate. How else shall I ever discover what I think?"

"You held up two fingers," Hamlin said. "What was the second possibility?"

"Read him the riot act. Threaten to give him a fair trial for treason. Then hang him."

"Now, that's more to my liking. I swear by the Almighty, Bill, the time to nip this thing was when these malcontents were going about boldly holding those conventions of secession. Had I been President, I would have dispatched Federal Marshals to arrest and detain every single one of them." Hamlin sat back and sighed. "Of course," he added, "that might have started a war."

"Oh, don't you worry, Mr. President, we still may manage to bring one off." Seward slapped his knee.

"Very funny. What else did you have to say to Lincoln?"

Seward leaned forward, again hunkering down to business. "In order to get this secession thing cleaned up, go right to the heart of the sticking point and remove it from the picture."

"And the sticking point is what?"

"Your favorite hobby horse, slavery."

"Ah ha."

"My idea was, and is, that we should change the whole question before the public from slavery to the question of union or disunion." Seward spoke now in a near whisper, "Slavery, damnable as it is, counts merely as a political party question. It can be addressed later at our leisure. Our foremost duty right now is to save the integrity of the union by taking slavery off the table!" He made a sweeping gesture that nearly toppled the coffee cups.

Hamlin stroked his chin. "How do you propose to do that, Bill? It seems to me the whole crux of the argument between us. 'An irrepressible conflict,' to use your own words in the Senate. It's what must be threshed out at our meeting with Davis in Charleston, should he grace us with his presence. By the way, what faith do you have in those so-called commissioners of the Confederacy?"

"I still believe them, with due reservations. They assured me that if we launched on this voyage, Davis would just happen to make a tour of inspection of the fortifications in Charleston harbor, coincident with our visit."

"Well, we're doing our part," Hamlin said.

Seward nodded absently. "Davis will welcome the chance to talk with us I think. He may want a way out of this conundrum as much as we do. Perhaps he sees they went too far, and he's looking for a way out with honor intact."

Hamlin snorted. "Oh, yes, honor is so important to the Southrons. They talk of it much, and practice it little."

Seward shook his head in mock concern. "Say that to Jeff Davis and he'll call you out to a dual."

"Fine, as long as I am allowed to choose my weapon."

"Which would be?"

31

"Why, the arms of an honest Maine farmer. Pitchforks at a hundred paces."

"Hah," Seward barked, then waved to the mess boy. "Sir Patrick, son of the old sod!" Patrick knocked over a chair getting to their table.

Seward's face lit up in a politician's grin. "Would there, by any slim chance, be another biscuit loose in the galley, my gallant young knight of the plates and cups? And didn't I see a platter of fruit go by?"

While Seward interrogated the boy as to the exact disposition of every last bite of food on board the ship, Hamlin leaned back and surveyed his environment. At a far table, handsome young General McClellan shoved glasses and cups over the tablecloth, his thick auburn hair glinting, his resonant voice bristling with authority, demonstrating tactics of some famed battle while Ensign Filmore and John Hay looked on.

Hamlin liked Johnny Hay, a young man with sharp, rodent like features, who had been Lincoln's personal secretary, even if he was a bit of a Brown University smart-aleck at times.

There was a fourth man at the table, and Hamlin flashed the image through his memory. Though he was remarkably adept at the politician's skill of linking names to faces, the man's identity eluded him. Hamlin frowned and strived to connect a name to the tall domed forehead, the stringy gray streaked hair, the busy, darting eyes behind wire framed spectacles. And the beard, what a seedy, hopeless looking thing. It put Hamlin in mind of the tangled bramble bushes that grew wild on his farm.

He leaned toward Seward. "Who is that bearded man seated with General McClellan?"

Seward pretended to scratch the back of his neck, to turn his head in the proper direction. "Why, surely you know? That's Ed Stanton."

"Edwin Stanton? Buchanan's Attorney General?"

Seward's eyes narrowed. "I am perplexed. Surely you knew he was aboard this ship?"

"I've never laid eyes on him until now," Hamlin said, perversely enjoying Bill Seward's sudden discomposure.

"Well, I am at a loss..."

"What in the world is he doing here?" Hamlin felt his tone of voice to be politely reasonable.

Seward wiped his mouth with a napkin. "He gave me to understand last night, or at least that was the impression he left, that you had invited him."

"Do tell?"

"Yes, he said that he was feeling unwell and retired to his cabin shortly after boarding, so he was not present at the dinner last night. I spoke with him briefly at the time."

"And he gave you to understand that I had invited him?" Hamlin said, deliberately repeating Seward's locution. "A member of Buchanan's administration, and a Democrat? Didn't you think that passing strange?"

"Well, no, not really, Han." Seward spoke earnestly. "A Democrat he may be, but he is also most strongly for the Union. Surely you've heard how he went against Floyd and the other traitors in the cabinet. He was for holding on to and reinforcing our forts. He propped up Buchanan when that old nancy-boy was ready to bend over and drop his trousers for the Southrons."

"He is with us then?"

"Oh, indeed, yes."

"He is also a liar."

Hamlin pushed his chair back, stood up and walked over to Stanton's table.

"Good morning General McClellan, Ensign Filmore." The two officers rose hurriedly. "Oh, do sit down, gentleman, please, and you too, Johnny." He winked at the relaxed Hay who had remained seated. "I merely require a word with Mr. Stanton. Would you come along with me, Mr. Stanton?"

Hamlin moved off at a fast clip down a stairway to the main deck. He leaned his back to the ship's rail, folded his arms and faced Stanton, who had followed along after him, his face a misery of doubt.

Hamlin reached out. "I have not yet had the pleasure, sir." His fingers enveloped Stanton's hand which had the texture of cold bread dough.

"I am Hannibal Hamlin, President of the United States."

"An honor, sir. I am Edwin Stanton, former Attorney General of the United States, presently unemployed." He breathed out an uneasy twitch of laughter.

Hamlin waited to hear what he might say next.

Stanton cleared his throat. "It was a short term of office, as you must know. But in those few days, I am proud to say Jeremiah Black and myself held the fort for the Union. At least we did not permit Buchanan to give away the remaining loyal states to the traitors of Charleston."

"Yes," Hamlin said, "you performed patriotic service no doubt. However, sir, I have some questions to put to you."

Stanton shifted his weight from one foot to the other.

"Do you have a call of nature?" Hamlin asked.

"Why, no, Mr. President." Stanton cleared his throat once again, then reached up his right hand to fiddle with the strands of the tangle that grew from beneath his chin.

"How is it that you are aboard this ship?"

"Why... well, I was invited, you see, or so I thought..."

"Who invited you?"

"Who invited me? Well, I might say that the Secretary of State invited me. I might say that, however, I was given the impression that you, Mr. President had invited me."

"Who gave you that impression?"

"Why, Mr. John Hay intimated that you had expressed an interest in seeing me. I was unable to obtain an audience with you before you left. So I assumed..."

"Mr. Hay said I wished to have you aboard?"

"Not in so many words." Stanton spoke faster now. "Perhaps I was mistaken, but I was caused to be under the impression that such was the case. If I have presumed incorrectly, I beg your forgiveness. I would gladly lie in the gutter and allow you to stand on me before I would incur your displeasure."

Hamlin caught a sharp breath. The man was half cracked.

Stanton stifled another mirthless laugh, turning it into a cough that sprayed beads of moisture over his beard. "Please be assured, Mr. President Hamlin, that I stand ready and willing to render any service that you may deem necessary. I am, sir, four square for the Union and an eternal enemy to the Slave Power."

"So are we all." Hamlin tried to follow Stanton's jittering eyes.

"Floyd was the worst of the lot." Stanton said, his voice taking on a new harshness.

"Oh, yes, Floyd, the Secretary of War."

"One day it was discovered that his accounts were missing very nearly a million dollars while at the same time he was going hard at it to persuade the President to surrender Fort Sumter. I told the cabinet that no administration could afford to lose a million of money and a fort all in the same week." Stanton beamed proudly as Hamlin chuckled.

"Yes, I heard about that one."

"Floyd was the chief mischief maker," Stanton said, "by the end he wasn't even pretending loyalty. As Secretary of War he made sure that fresh arms and munitions were shipped South and that our navy was scattered to the four winds just before the secession movement broke on us."

Hamlin nodded pensively. "If I arrested and imprisoned all the federal officials in Washington who had given aid and comfort to the South, there would not be a prison in the land big enough to hold them."

Stanton gave a snort. "Don't waste prison cells on them. They should all be put in chains and thrown in the Potomac." Hamlin saw that all signs of nervousness were now gone. Stanton's dark gray eyes met his and held firm. Anger, it seemed, fed the man's energy.

"Well, Mr. Stanton, I look forward to further conversations with you. I'm sure you have some opinions as to our chances in Charleston."

35

"That would depend, sir, upon what you are seeking in Charleston."

"Why, I am seeking peace, Mr. Stanton. Peace with Union."

"The Union as it was?" Stanton asked, in a sneering, accusatory manner. Hamlin was dumfounded. What manner of man is this who transforms himself from blithering coward to a bully all of an instant? He recognized the term of the day, "Union As It Was" which referred to the country under the old Constitution with slavery legally intact. It was a popular phrase with the Democratic party.

"Sir, I wish to recall to you the fact that you are addressing the President of the United States. You may have taken such an insulting manner of speech in your dealings with President Buchanan. Perhaps he deserved as much. But my name is Hannibal Hamlin, a founding member of the Republican Party. I bow to no man in my opposition and loathing of slavery."

"I would never deny that, sir," Stanton said, his lips twisted in a strange, contorted smile.

"You have an unfortunately abrasive manner of speech, sir. I would look to correct it if I were you."

Again Stanton danced from foot to foot. "A point well taken, Mr. President. I'm afraid I am too much a veteran of the combative arena of the courtroom. Ha."

Hamlin pondered a reply. He himself was a veteran of the courtroom 'arena.' So was the good humored Seward and that natural gentleman Lincoln. No, being a lawyer did not excuse rudeness of manner. But still he would be cautious in his dealings with Stanton. He could not rule out the possibility that there might be a use for him.

Time to mend fences. He placed a comforting hand on Stanton's shoulder. "These are troubling times for us all," he said, deliberately using what his wife called his jolly-old-uncle voice. "We must all make allowances. As to our mission in Charleston, before I put slavery on the way to extinction, and that is indeed my larger purpose, I must first find a way to preserve this Union of States. If that means some horse trading with Jeff Davis, well, so be it. I can hold my own candle in that church. And I tell you, Stanton, I want to avoid war if humanly possible. The thought of Americans killing each other is repugnant to me. As Lincoln said in his inaugural, 'we must not be enemies.'"

"I thank you for confiding in me, Mr. President," Stanton said, with seeming respect. "But I hope you will not deem me presumptuous for offering a word of advice."

"Go right ahead."

"Far be it from me to speak ill of Mr. Seward. I would never think of doing that, however I am of the opinion that the Secretary of State leans perhaps a might too strongly in the way of conciliation. Naturally we want a fair settlement of this trouble, but a settlement with honor, sir. Distasteful as the idea of civil war may be to us all, I notice that your have brought General McClellan with you, presumably as a personification of the threat of cold steel. As well you should, sir."

Hamlin assumed a neutral expression. Let the man go and see where he ended up.

"I have heard on good authority," Stanton said, "that Mr. Seward has led the Southern Commissioners to believe that Fort Sumter might be given up. That must not happen, Mr. President. It would be a national disgrace."

"I have made no decision regarding Fort Sumter," Hamlin said. "As you may well know, on the very day he died, Lincoln was entertaining the idea of evacuating the fort, as he so stated at the cabinet meeting."

"Well, we should certainly not criticize the dead," Stanton said, "but I for one am comforted that it is you who have assumed the high office. Lincoln was quite a whimsical character, no doubt, but I for one was never quite satisfied as to his seriousness and general level of intellect. I recall the first time I met him, at a court case in Cincinnati back in '54. I was defending John Manny who had invented a grain reaping machine. He was being sued, most unjustly, by Cyrus McCormick for patent infringement. Lincoln was one of a party of lawyers on our side of the case. I remember that first day he shambled into the courtroom. I took one look and said to my associates: 'Who let the gorilla out of the zoo?' Well, sir, Lincoln heard me and started laughing at my witticism. You know that shrill, yelping laugh he had."

"Yes," Hamlin said, "you must excuse me now."

He turned his back sharply and walked off. Why, that man Stanton is a venomous swamp. Imagine referring to Lincoln in such an insulting manner, and then boasting about it to boot. Lincoln had been a good man, a little given to double-talk at times, but he often had a way of saying things that stuck in the mind. Hamlin remembered how he had quoted him on one occasion at Bridgeport, Connecticut, one of a number of stops along the way on the journey to Washington for the inauguration. He had addressed the big, cheering crowd that greeted his train.

"Our next President, my good friends and neighbors of Connecticut, had this to say in Pittsburgh the other day, and I proudly quote:"

There is no crisis, except such a one as may be gotten up at any time by turbulent men, aided by designing politicians. My advice to them, under the circumstances, is to keep cool. If the great American people only keep their temper both sides of the line, the trouble will come to an end.

Hamlin felt a smiling calm envelop him.
Good advice, that was.
Keep cool.

CHAPTER FOUR

Letter from George B. McClellan to Mary Ellen McClellan
April 8, 1861

My Dearest Little One,

I am pleased to announce the safe arrival of our ship and the President's party at Fortress Monroe, this ancient pile of brick and granite that commands the sea lanes to the Chesapeake Bay from the tip of the James River peninsula.

We have stopped here for a day in simple but clean accommodations, where I have even been able to take a bath. Tomorrow it's on to Charleston to whatever fate awaits us. To help stack the odds a bit more in our favor we are taking with us from this place some one hundred regular troopers, fully armed and equipped, as well as provisions for our gallant comrades in Fort Sumter. This re-supplying of our very own fort is what the Southrons in their nincompoop logic refer to as "aggression."

As I made mention in my last letter, I now have some of the details of President Lincoln's death. The simple fact is that he became entangled in some low hanging branches that extended out over the roadway of the Seventh Street Pike, causing him to topple over backwards. His head struck a sharply pointed rock which inflicted fatal injury. I am told that the doctor who examined the skull post mortis believed death was instant.

Ah, but it makes you stop and think, Nel. After achieving the high office he sought, and after being President for a mere eleven days, his life was extinguished in a split second. What a blessing that Divine Providence masks the future course of our lives. While I grieve for President Lincoln, I believe that the Divine plan which carried him off has also given us our upstanding President Hamlin.

I met today with two Army officers who put on civilian clothes and sojourned a week in Charleston. They have been able to give us detailed reports on conditions in that city, as well as drawings of the harbor defenses.

As for the mental state of the population, I fear from their account that we may be facing a crazed mob who shout great blasts of bravado about the defense of their "rights," while on the other hand they tremble at the threat of coercion by the central government. They have mounted a great banner over one of the principal streets which reads: "Only The South Shall Rule the South." They march about singing "La Marseillaise," seeing themselves as heroes of a new revolution. Let us hope that they don't haul out the guillotine in our honor.

I must close now, darling companion. The mess call has sounded.

A quick post script. My information on the details of Lincoln's death came from a fascinating individual. He seems to have the inside story on everything. He is an odd sort of duck who has for some unknown reason, taken a liking to me and offers to be my mentor in matters political. His name is Edwin Stanton.

Your faithful George,

CHAPTER FIVE

Charleston Ship Channel, Tuesday, April 9, 1861, 6:30 a.m.

George stood on the bridge of the Vanderbilt, his legs braced against the roll of the waves, his telescope trained over the port bow straining to catch a glimpse of land through the dawn's fog.

"It's hopeless." Captain Blackstone's voice boomed in his ear. "I'm not moving another foot until this here fog burns off." He yelled over his shoulder to the helmsman in the pilothouse. "Full stop."

George approved. No use blundering ahead when it was impossible to see.

"By all my reckoning" the Captain said, "we ought to be sitting dead in the middle of the ship channel just to East of Morris Island, but I'm not going to gamble my ship on it."

George recalled the report from the two officers who had reconnoitered Charleston. Morris Island, the outer reach of the city's defenses, was manned by a strong company of infantry reinforced by some fifty cadets of the Citadel Military Academy who were busy constructing batteries of 24 pounders on the North point.

"They're calling it Star of the West Battery," George said aloud.

"A fitting name for it," Captain Blackstone said, "marking as it does their first victory of this war."

George steadied the telescope and slowly traversed from left to right. He could see nothing but opaque gray.

"Victory? Well, sir, it was hardly that." He flashed a patronizing smile at the Captain, hoping it was visible in the dim light from the pilothouse lamps.

"They fired on our flag, did they not, General?"

"They fired on a civilian vessel," George replied, "that had been contracted to deliver supplies to Fort Sumter. The Star of the West turned tail and Major Anderson withheld his fire. It takes two sides shooting to make a battle."

"No battle, but it was indeed a towering insult to our Nation's honor. I only hope, General, if I may speak frankly, that we are not about to become another Star of the West. What are we to do if they fire on us, hurl tea cups at 'em?"

George stretched to his full height and aimed a hard glare up at Captain Blackstone. "They would not dare fire on the President of the United States," he said, wishing he could be sure.

"It seems to me we're making the same mistake they did in January. Here we are again, another unarmed ship, and this time with no escort even, sailing right up under their guns to do something which they view as an act of war."

George made his voice cold. "We are following the direct orders of his Excellency the President," he said.

Captain Blackstone locked his hands behind his back, and stepped off a few paces, then turned. "Stupid orders."

"I find that remark most offensive to the President, Captain Blackstone, and I will tolerate no more such talk. It is your duty to bring us into the harbor and up to the dock at Fort Sumter. Do so."

Blackstone stepped back and raised his right hand in an extremely slow and disdainful salute.

"Aye, aye, sir. It's been challenge enough to get through forty years in the Navy. If I manage to survive this here sockdologer, I'll retire next month to my farm in Maryland. Where I will say any God damned thing I please to say, any God damned time I please to say it, and with all due respect, General, you can get your fancy ass off my bridge."

George recalled the advice of his father-in-law, Major Randolph Marcy, that old iron-backed explorer. "When lost in the wilderness, George, never get into a pissing match with your Indian guide. Wait until you get back to the fort before you kill the sonofabitch."

George blew off the angry tension that had constricted his chest. Captain Blackstone was nothing more than a kind of

42

watery Indian guide, and they were, after all, stuck in a fog bound wilderness off the coast of a hostile city. So there would be no pissing match. He cleared his throat and spoke with measured authority.

"Captain I am hard of hearing. Therefore I missed your last remark, although I doubt if I missed anything very intelligent. Now I bid good morning to you, sir. I shall be with the President. Proceed only when you have satisfactory visibility, and keep me advised."

George spun on his heel and hurried off the bridge before the Captain could get off another insult.

* * *

On the lower deck, George could barely make out the looming form of President Hamlin with the thinner form of the Secretary of State at his side. Both men leaned out over the ship's rail, squinting to see through the pearly, enveloping mist. George stayed back, unwilling to intrude. Their voices sounded unnaturally close in the thick air.

"Seems like we've stopped," Steward said.

"So we have Bill. Always best to stop when lost in a fog."

Seward sniffed. "Say, have you noticed that smell? "

"Ah, yes, the effluvium of a great city," Hamlin said. "We're smelling Charleston before we see it."

George tasted the air. Yes, there was a scent, sweet and rotten at the same time.

Seward spat out a glob of tobacco juice into the nothingness that surrounded them. It plunked distantly in the water below.

"Tell me something, Bill," Hamlin said. "Do you ever entertain any regrets?"

Seward bit off a fresh tobacco plug. "About what?"

"The way events turned out at Chicago last year. We went into that convention convinced, most of us, that you would be our nominee."

Seward snorted a laugh. "Yup, and I was one of those convinced ones too, until I ran up against that gang of inland

43

pirates from Illinois. They stole the whole thing right out from under my nose while making me dance a jig trot."

"You've got to hand it to 'em," Hamlin said. "It was politics at a high level of art. Me and my people saw we were overmatched right off."

"Art you call it? Hell's bells, they promised the sun, moon and stars ten times over for any delegate vote. I heard they even promised Mary Lincoln as a prize, but there was no takers!"

Hamlin put a hand to this mouth. "Shame on you, Bill, for such talk."

"Well, whatever might be said, we did pick us a right likely Vice President."

"Good of you to say so, Bill."

Neither man spoke further. Gentle waves slapped against the hull of the ship, and from somewhere in the fog a faint bell could be heard. George felt the need to make his presence known. He cleared his throat.

"Good morning, your Excellency."

"Good morning, General McClellan," Hamlin said. "How long do you estimate we are to remain stopped here?"

"Only until the fog burns off, sir."

"Yes, I know that," Hamlin said with an tinge of impatience. "Does the captain have an estimate as to when that might be?"

"He did not say, sir. He's reluctant to proceed ahead until he can see where he's going."

Hamlin laughed. "Why, how sagacious of him."

Seward could be heard snickering to himself.

George tightened his jaw. It had not been a good morning thus far.

"I'll report as soon as I learn more, Mr. President."

He felt his way along the rail searching for the commander of the infantry company that had come on board at Fortress Monroe, and bumped into the very man he was looking for.

"Steady there, General." Sam Grant's square head loomed in his face. "We don't want you falling overboard."

"Good morning, Captain Grant. Are your troops out on deck? I can't see a thing."

44

"Both platoons are awaiting orders, sir, Each man has been issued forty rounds."

"Have they had their coffee yet?"

"Coffee and a mighty fine breakfast, sir. The Navy sure knows how to feed a man."

"Very well. Now Sam, here's the situation." George reached into his coat pocket and produced a hand drawn map of Charleston harbor. "We're here just to the east of Morris Island. Can you see this?"

Sam grunted a yes.

"Our aim is to head Northwest up channel to the granite wharf that juts out of the back wall of the fort. If they take us under fire, we can expect it at these three positions. First, Cummings Point off to our immediate left, then as we get close, Fort Moultrie across the way will come in with bow shots. Then, to cap the climax, we might get fire from the James Island batteries on our far left flank." George squinted at Sam Grant through the fog. "Your comments, Captain?"

Grant sighed. "I'd sooner keep my comments to myself, Mac. Excuse me, I mean General."

"Go on."

"The way I read this map, we can't even bring any of those batteries under effective musket fire. We're looking at ranges here of at least a thousand yards. All I can tell my boys to do is to angle their pieces at forty degrees or so and pray when they pull the trigger. If a ball makes it that far, it wouldn't have enough spunk left in it to kill a sparrow."

"Yes," George said. "I think that sums it up."

"Why the hell, sir, haven't we got the gunboat Brooklyn with us? It's there at Fort Monroe, all ready to go. It could sail right into this harbor and blow the whole city of Charleston to blue blazes, and I guarantee you sir, that would be the end of secession."

"You may be right, but having the Brooklyn with us would have been seen as too provocative. That was decided at high political levels, Captain Grant."

45

"Well, it's sorta nice to know that if those high political levels got it wrong, we'll all be swimming together. "

George gave a wary chuckle. "That is indeed a cold comfort, but I don't think they'll fire on us. They talk big, but Jeff Davis wants to parlay."

"I hope you are correct in that assumption, sir."

George hoped so too. "You'll see, he said. "I'll buy you a Kentucky bourbon julep at the best hotel in Charleston tonight."

A pause while Sam Grant licked his lips. "That sounds mighty tempting, General, but let's make it a cup of tea."

Tea? What had gotten into Sam Grant?

"This fog will burn off soon," George said. "Ready your men, one platoon to each side. If they fire on us, we fire back. Make it a good show as the British would say. Aim high."

"I'll have 'em aim for the moon," Sam Grant replied. "For we have as much chance of hitting that as we do the enemy."

George was startled to see Sam's face suddenly brighten out of the mist. He looked up to see pale patches of blue through the quickly dissolving fog. He felt the deck began to vibrate under his boots as the ship's engines rumbled into life and the paddle wheels began to churn.

George could now see the crisply blue uniformed troops lining the deck and experienced a stirring, galvanic thrill. They were Sam's men, but they were his men as well. For the first time he felt himself to be a true general.

He would address the troops!

"Soldiers of the United States," he shouted, "there is danger here present. What the Charleston Secesh will do remains in doubt. But there is no doubt in my mind or heart but what you men of the Grand Old Army will do your duty! Gloriously, bravely..."

George strained to think of a conclusion for this extemporaneous rally cry. He was relieved to hear an old sergeant shout:

"Three cheers for General McClellan!"

While the soldiers were hip hooraying, George said to Sam Grant, "Join me in the bow when you can."

They exchanged salutes, and George went off to find the President.

Then he saw it, dead ahead through the mist, a reddish mass floating on the blue waves.

He called up to the bridge. "Do you see it, Captain?"

"I'm a long way from being blind, General! I've had that pile of bricks sighted for the past five minutes."

"Very well. Carry on."

He found President Hamlin and Secretary Seward on the bow, their heads bent close in conversation.

"Underway at last, Mr. President. Fort Sumter straight ahead."

"What was all that cheering back there," Hamlin inquired.

"Oh, it was nothing." George uncased his field glasses. "The troops were giving me a cheer."

"And well deserved at that I'm sure," Hamlin said, kindly.

Seward coughed.

George put the glasses to his eyes, and twisted the focus knob to study the beach now visible to their left. He saw golden sand, splashing waves of surf, palmetto trees, waving strands of high grass, and suddenly, the white, freshly baked look of an artillery earthwork. The cold barrel of a cannon poked out, then another and another. Troops in a variety of quasi military dress scrambled around the guns in the old familiar drill.

Preparing to fire?

George continued to sweep the scene until he came upon a figure standing calmly on the earthworks. The man was looking directly back at him through a large, tripod mounted telescope. George felt the hair crawl on the back of his neck.

"Mr. President. Mr. Seward. They have us under close observation. They are manning the guns. I strongly advise that you both retire below!"

"Can they see us, General?" Hamlin asked.

"Yes, sir, they can."

"Then they shall not see me scurry below like a cornered rat." Hamlin removed his broad brimmed straw hat, held if aloft and waved it expressively from side to side. Seward cackled and joined in, pumping his black bowler up and down in the manner of a comic stage Irishman.

"Let's give them a bow, Billy my boy" Hamlin said, laughing. "One, two, three."

The President and the Secretary of State bowed deeply in unison toward the Carolina shore.

George snapped the binoculars to his eyes again. He was amazed to see the man with the spyglass waving his red military cap and the troops around him jovially bowing up and down in return.

"Now let us give 'em a thumb at the nose," Seward shouted, sounding like an impudent adolescent.

"None of that, Billy," Hamlin said with light severity. "We're here to prevent a war, not start one." Then the two statesmen clutched at each other in a laughing fit.

George looked on, bemused. Then from above and behind came the croaking voice of Captain Blackstone, sounding off from the bridge, singing:

There was a young gal from Nantucket,
She would dance with her head in a bucket ...

Sam Grant strolled up and inquired, "Has he taken a drop or two?"

"More than a drop or two," George said, recalling the Captain's breath. "He apparently required some brace-up to make this run today."

Grant sighed. "Well, I know how that feels."

George looked out at Fort Sumter which was now a little over a thousand yards away. "We're closing fast. Looks like we're going to make it."

"Sure is big."

"You ever been stationed here, Sam?"

"Nope. I would've remembered if I had been."

"What I find amazing," George said, "is they've been working on it since 1830, and it's still not completed."

"Not surprised to hear that," Sam said, "considering the way Congress squeezes out the funds."

The two officers watched Fort Sumter loom larger by the second. The fresh morning sun glowed warmly off the stark, red brick walls. Their destination, a long granite wharf, jutted out from the main entrance which was flanked by pilasters topped by a flat triangular pediment, Greek temple style. George burned the scene into his memory for his nightly letter to Nelly. He would poetically describe the fort as resembling the red brick mausoleum of an ancient giant.

"See up there on the ramparts," Sam said. "They're waving at us."

George was struck with sudden inspiration. "What irony."

Sam Grant raised his eyebrows. "That they're waving to us?" Irony wasn't an everyday word with him.

"No, Sam, what I mean is that here we have a two acre, artificial island made up from seventy thousand tons of granite from New England. I see it as the symbol of all the states of the Union, against the forces of disruption here at Charleston."

It was a pretty thought. George was considering ways to expand on it when he noticed a blue uniformed officer who had dashed out of the main entrance of the fort, waving his arms and shouting.

"He sure is agitated," Sam Grant observed.

They were moving up to the wharf.

"I know that man," George said, "and so do you. That's Dynamite John Foster. Remember he was with us on Scott's staff in Mexico? Loved making explosions."

"Why you're right, General. That's old Dynamite John his very self. Can you make out what he's saying?"

Now more soldiers came running from the fort. They carried long white strips of engineer's tape, and under the direction of Dynamite John they began stringing it in patterns over the wharf.

George chuckled. "Oh, that's what it's all about. The wharf is mined. Looks like they laying out safe paths for us."

"The least they could do," Sam said. "Would be a mighty embarrassment to blow up the President after he went to the trouble of coming here."

49

George nodded. "Didn't they teach you at West Point that you earn a very bad mark on your army record for blowing up the Commander in Chief?"

Sam Grant bent over with a whoop of laughter.

George clasped his hands behind his back and looked off to the blue-green waves of the Atlantic in the distance.

"At ease there, Captain Grant! Prepare to disembark your troops."

* * *

Major Bob Anderson had always thought of himself as a serious and honorable man who possessed that quality his schoolboy Latin texts defined as 'gravitas,' a weighty dignity befitting his responsibilities.

As the U. S. Army commander of the harbor at Charleston, Anderson and the seventy men of his command at Fort Sumter were a vexatious scab of embarrassment to the secessionists, a blatant reminder of the Federal power in Washington symbolized by the brazen red and white striped flag that fluttered above the fort. How could South Carolina be seen as a sovereign independent state when there was the military presence of a "foreign" power sitting smack dab in the middle of Charleston Harbor?

Anderson had been wildly unpopular in the city of Charleston ever since Christmas eve, 1860, when he evacuated the dilapidated Fort Moultrie on the shore, and occupied the more seriously threatening Fort Sumter in the harbor. His actions had been seen by the Carolina red-hots as somehow unsporting.

"Not what we might be led to expect of a true gentleman," huffed an editorial in the Charleston Mercury.

Bob Anderson had rattled the paper and shook his head in disgust when he read that one.

"No, I suppose a gentleman is expected to meekly await their attack and surrender without a fight," he remarked heatedly to his adjutant, Captain Abner Doubleday. He had been able to read the editorial denouncing him in those balmy early days of the crisis when there was still daily mail and grocery delivery to Fort Sumter from Charleston.

All that was over now. Mail and food had been cut off, and rations ran low. His outlook had been bleak, but no more. This bright day, April 9, 1861, was a well deserved triumphal climax to his thirty-five years of Army service. He was puffed with honest pride as he strolled over the upper battlements of Fort Sumter with his three honored guests, the President of the United States, the Secretary of State, and the acting commander of the Army. They had come here to Charleston to support him with fresh provisions, munitions and even a handsome company of regular infantry. Much relieved now, Anderson was no longer the worm on a hook.

He looked over to tall President Hamlin who shaded his eyes and gazed out over the sun-lit blue of the harbor.

"Such a beautiful aspect," the President remarked. "The beaches, the palmetto trees," Hamlin's voice was mellow on the sea breeze. "It's hard to believe there could ever be war here."

"They've got guns all around us," General McClellan said, "plus that floating battery down near the city."

General McClellan's field glasses slowly swept from the battery at Cummings Point on their left across the expanse of harbor to Fort Moultrie on their right.

Ah yes, McClellan, who must announce the obvious for all to hear. As a long time observer of army officers, Anderson saw in McClellan a familiar type. Full of piss and vinegar they were, these ambitious young strutters, but if you knew how to look you could always catch the flicker of uncertainty on their faces in an unguarded moment.

For some odd reason he had immediately liked William Seward, that shrewd old political buzzard who shambled along, his hands locked behind his back. So far the Secretary of State was playing "shut-pan," as they said in Kentucky, keeping his thoughts to himself.

Anderson took in a breath of sea air and recalled with satisfaction the welcoming ceremony he had so carefully staged.

51

His brushed and polished troops had stood at rigid attention and looked quite spiffy, comparing favorably to the newly arrived regulars. The rendition of the Star Spangled Banner by his band had been marred only by one shrieking sour note of the clarinet, but the President had not seemed to notice. Indeed Anderson had admired President Hamlin and the way he had stood with all the perfect self-assurance of an experienced officer. He liked this new President. But was there ever a politician you could fully trust?

Hamlin turned to him. "Major Anderson, you look quite contemplative."

He would feel his way here. "It occurred to me sir, what an astonishing thing has happened today. Provisions and troops were landed without a battle breaking out. It was the action that would have lit their fuse and set them off, had you not been along. You made all the difference, Mr. President. They must have some residual respect for your office, not to open fire."

Hamlin gave a faint smile. "Well, that may be."

Seward spoke up. "What if Lincoln had come down here? What would they have done then, Major? Knowing them as you do."

"With all respect to the late President, sir, I believe they would have blasted him clean out of the water."

"Hah. Well and good that it never occurred to him to make the trip."

"They still don't know what to make of you, your Excellency," Anderson said with new found confidence, "although the newspapers try to make you out to be just as much a devil with horns as Lincoln was. Still and all, you've caused them to stop for a time and catch their breaths."

"It is flattering," Hamlin said, "to think that they didn't shoot today out of respect for me and my office. I suspect however that the real reason is Mr. Jefferson Davis ordered them to stay their hand. Don't you think that's it?"

Anderson blinked. "That too is likely, sir," he said, feeling the fool. Of course it was likely. Davis was coming to meet the

President tomorrow. The war had been postponed at the highest level, simple as that.

"What plans have you made for defending Fort Sumter, Major?"

It was General McClellan asserting his rank, but instead of annoyance, Anderson felt an unexpected surge of relief. He could talk to this pompous little brass-banger about what he knew best. "If you will follow me, sir, I will be glad to point out to you the features of our defense."

"Before you do that, "President Hamlin interjected, "I want to ask you a question, Major."

"Yes, sir?"

Hamlin took two steps forward and raised his right hand, palm down, indicating the City of Charleston. "What do you make of these people, Major? You've been here since when? Last November wasn't it? What makes this fort of such almighty importance to them that they're willing to risk war over it?"

Anderson rubbed his chin, not ready with a quick answer. He recalled that Secretary of War Floyd had placed him in this position in the sinister hope that he would surrender to the secessionists without a fight. It was easy to see how they might have misjudged him since he was a native of a slave state, Kentucky. Indeed he felt no shame in owning slaves which were rightful, legal property. He often defended this belief in spirited argument with his abolitionist adjutant, Captain Doubleday. He would explain how the Bible itself sanctioned slavery, so it was a system approved by God, if not the Republican party. Yet Anderson would not surrender a fort entrusted to his care, which left him feeling unfairly abandoned during the confused and blundering final days of the Buchanan administration. Secretary Floyd had ordered him to resist a secessionist attack, but between the lines was a clear suggestion not to resist too much. Only enough to "satisfy the demands of military honor."

And so, after considering all this Bob Anderson could only offer the plain truth as he saw it. Hannibal Hamlin, rampant anti-slavery politician, could make of it what he would.

"Mr. President, they believe rightly or wrongly that their property rights are threatened by the general government, especially with a Republican administration. So they have seceded, or at least they damn well think they have. I leave the pros and cons of that debate up to you statesmen."

Hamlin's face suddenly drained of its friendly aspect. "Property rights is it? I'll be happy to debate property rights with them, the damnable criminals." He produced a sheet of paper from his coat pocket. "Here, Major Anderson, is a full list of Federal property that has been illegally appropriated by these robber States, upwards of a million dollars worth of our property rights violated, without so much as a howdy-do or by-your-leave."

"I understand that, sir."

"Now they want this fort. Well, they shall not have it."

"No, sir."

"How should I deal with them, Major? I ask your advice as a student of these ..." He searched for a word. "These Carolines."

Anderson, closing in on his sixtieth birthday, was done playing politics. He had been asked. He would state his views.

"Mr. President, these people of Charleston are not criminals or devils or anything of that kind. They are Americans who are frightened enough of the aims of the general government to take up arms, if need be, against that government. They have banded together with other Americans to form the Confederate States, believing as they do that there is safety in unity."

"Go on," Hamlin said, his tone neutral.

"I have no further advice, Mr. President, except to say that you should go into Charleston, show yourself among the people, converse with them. They are your fellow Americans. Show them that you don't have horns."

"I was intending to stay here at the fort as your guest," Hamlin said, "horns and all."

Anderson sighed. He was out on a limb now, might as well saw it off. "That would be a mistake, in my opinion, Mr.

President. Your going among them might help to cure them of their lunacy."

McClellan spoke up sharply. "Yes, but would it be safe for the President to be ashore in Charleston?"

Anderson turned to him. "This is an inherently unsafe situation, General McClellan, for all of us. I cannot deny that."

McClellan countered with a scowl. "Then I would recommend against your going ashore, Mr. President."

Hamlin rubbed his chin. "I'm going to have to go ashore eventually to meet with Jeff Davis. Tell me, Major, what's the best hotel in town?"

"That would be the Mills House, sir, and Colonel Chesnut tells me they're saving their finest rooms for you should you honor them with your presence."

"Chesnut? James Chesnut, the former U.S. Senator?"

"The same," Anderson said. "He is an excellent gentleman, comes out here most every day to talk things over and put me up on the news."

"Must have been quite a strain on you," Seward said with sympathy "isolated all these months out here. I see how it might unnerve a man."

Anderson was dismayed to find tears welling in his eyes. Seward's words had triggered memories of the grim months since December, of the frustration of being trapped out here on this rock, object of the rage of Charleston, and subject to vague and contradictory orders from Washington. Since Lincoln's inauguration Anderson had received two secret messages from the President, one telling him to prepare to evacuate Fort Sumter, and another a few days later ordering him to "defend to the last." President Lincoln had neglected to say what the 'last' was, and he was dead before Anderson could seek clarification.

"It has been hard times for all of us," Anderson said, his voice under tight control. "But we have done our duty."

"Indeed you have, sir," Hamlin said, "but tell me now, Major Anderson, what is your recommendation for the fort? Where should duty lead you now?"

"If it were up to me, Your Excellency?"

55

"Yes."

"Oh, that's easy. I would evacuate this fort, move the whole command up to Fortress Monroe, leaving only a color sergeant to haul the flag up and down each day."

Hamlin dropped back a step, then glanced at Seward who offered only a minimal shrug.

"They have guns on three sides of us," Anderson want on. "They outnumber us ten to one. It would be foolish of us to bring on a fight under these conditions. And all for what? I tell you, sir, my heart would not be in a civil war."

Hamlin's cheeks colored. "Were you ordered, Major Anderson, to engage in such a war, I trust you would obey."

"I have stood to my duty for some thirty-five years, your Excellency, and will continue to do so. I believe, with all due respect, that you asked for my recommendation."

"That I did," Hamlin said, "but I may not be able to accept it." He turned to Seward. "Can you imagine the outcry in the North, Bill, if we gave up this fort? Of course," he added quickly, "I can't rule out the possibility."

"All things are possible," Seward said, beckoning to Hamlin with a tilt of his head. The President joined the Secretary of State in close conversation while young General McClellan, his right leg thrust forward in an actorish pose, continued to sweep the harbor with his binoculars.

Anderson sighed, discouraged, and suddenly tired. He had spoken his piece. Hamlin and Seward would do whatever they deemed most opportune for themselves. For at the end of the day, and for all their fine words, they were still nothing more than politicians, that contemptible breed that might very well blunder the nation into a tragic and unnecessary civil war.

Bob Anderson saw no beauty in the late afternoon sun that glittered over the waters of Charleston Harbor. He was still the worm on the hook.

CHAPTER SIX

"Dixie!"

George knew he would despise that damned song for the rest of his natural life.

"Dixie," that cheerful old minstrel show walk-about tune had been appropriated by these infernal people, and now their ragtag band of musicians was blasting it in the ears of the Presidential party, following close on their heels as they walked the cobblestones of Meeting Street on their way up to the Mills House Hotel. The blaring trumpets, shrieking fifes and rattling snare drums blended into a raucous musical insult that fit well with the nasty catcalls of the crowd.

"Dixie" wasn't the worst of it. Sam Grant jogged up alongside George and said, "I don't mind the music. It's these damn fruits and vegetables!"

Just then a tomato splattered George dead center in the back of his neck. He felt the cold, squishy pulp and seeds dribble down the gap between skin and tight wool collar. He marched on, eyes disciplined ahead, anger flushing his cheeks. He would not touch his neck, would not give this pack of yelping pug-uglies the satisfaction. He double timed to catch up to the President who was marching a few paces ahead in the middle of the formation.

"Just a few more blocks, your Excellency."

Hamlin gave him a hard look and a crisp nod. "Remind me to convey my gratitude to Major Anderson for his splendid suggestion that I come ashore to enjoy the acclaim of my people." Just then someone lobbed an egg at them. George reached out and swung at it with his sword. Of course it was rotten, and bits of it splattered in President Hamlin's face.

"Well, this is a new thing," Seward said, his legs swinging along in a high stepping lope. "Instead of throwing a banquet for us, they throw the banquet at us."

Hamlin acted as if the egg had missed and yellow droplets were not streaming down his cheek. His smile was vulpine as he waved his hat at the crowd, exactly as he would if the reception had been friendly, simulating expansive affection.

"Say, Bill, don't you detect any cheers among the jeers? There must be at least one Union man left on all of Charleston."

"They probably hung him from a magnolia tree this morning," Bill Seward called back. "Oh, oh, look up ahead."

George saw it now. A large banner had been hoisted by ropes anchored to buildings on either side of Meeting Street, creating an arch over their intended path.

It said, in fresh red paint: NIGGER HAMLIN GO HOME!

The smile left Hamlin's face. "Oh, happy day."

George jaunted out a few paces ahead of the President hoping to intercept any more incoming produce. He shouted back at Sam, "Tell your men to swat at these missiles with their weapons if they can. Let none break through to the President!"

George noted with satisfaction that his orders were not needed. A tall sergeant marching just ahead dealt two lightening blows with his rifle butt, knocking a demonstrator flat in the gutter. The sergeant marched on impassively and the mob parted before him as the Red Sea parted for Moses.

George grinned down at the man as he passed by.

"Greetings from the U.S. Army, ya all."

On they went through the slanting light of the late afternoon in The City of Flowers, the troopers grimly lock-jawed, the two politicians feigning a desperate good will they did not feel, and the rolling crowd, freshly energized by the brass band and the "Dixie," went on spewing cheers of honor to the sovereign state of South Carolina and the Confederacy, along with a lot of "kiss our rosy ass you goddamn fuckin' nigger lovin' black Republican!" and "Go join Lincoln in hell!"

And through it all the band played "Dixie."

The party finally made it to the Mills House and drew up on the wide, colonnaded porch, or "piazza" as the locals called it. Sam Grant's men, on his orders, crisply snapped into ranks surrounding the main entrance to the hotel, the points of their bayonets forming a glittering steel tipped porcupine that threatened all who might dare to take them on.

The scruffy band tooted into silence while the crowd muttered and melted away to resume their everyday pursuits, having accomplished their civic duty of welcoming the visitors from the North and giving a them a jagged chunk of South Carolina political discourse.

The President and his people moved through the elegant framed glass doors from the bright street into the welcoming coolness of the hotel's main parlor.

"Make sure the back entrance is covered," George told Sam Grant.

"The order's been given, sir. I've posted a squad there on the double."

"Well, done."

"If you ask me, we ought to have killed us a few of them," Sam said. "That would've changed their opinions some."

George thought it over as he unbuttoned his tunic. "I was tempted to give the order, I don't mind saying."

A squat, little man pushed by them, leaving in his wake a powerful scent of English cologne. "Mr. President, Mr. President, which one are you sir?"

Hamlin stepped forward, his face expressionless as he looked down at the intrusive speaker. "I am Hannibal Hamlin."

"Your Excellency, I am Alexander DuBott. It is my privilege as resident manager to welcome you to the Mills House."

"Why, thank you kindly, Mr. DuBott."

"The prime suite on the second floor awaits your inspection, sir. My humble apologies, your Excellency, for the behavior of those ruffians."

Hamlin laid a consoling hand on the manager's shoulder. "Now, that was none of your doing, Mr. DuBott. All cities have a low element, even beautiful Charleston. I understand that political feelings run high."

George simply stared as Hamlin the old politician instinctively smoothed things over. Was he dreaming or had they not just confronted a murderous mob?

DuBott, at ease now, said, "I have a fine supper set out in your suite, your Excellency. If you will follow along with me."

"Yes, yes, well and good" Hamlin said, with an impatient edge, "but the service we most require is that of a laundress. I have bits of what should have been somebody's breakfast on me, and poor General McClellan there has been hit in the back."

DuBott's eyes widened. "Oh, my, should we have the doctor?"

"It's not that kind of wound," Bill Seward said as he came up to lightly touch George's back and put a finger to his lips. "Um, tomato sauce. Needs seasoning."

George removed his coat and handed it to DuBott. "I am wounded only in my dignity, sir, and that readily heals. Please do have this cleaned as quickly as possible." He then turned to address the President and abruptly realized he was wearing only stained white shirtsleeves and the red braces that were Nelly's favorites. Dignity indeed. He held himself at rigid attention, "Will you be needing anything else, sir?"

"No, not at all, General. My compliments to you and to Captain Grant on your conduct in that unpleasantness. I felt mighty well protected out there."

"Thank you, your Excellency."

"We should've killed a few of them," Sam Grant said.

Hamlin managed to frown and smile all at once. "No, Captain, that would go counter to our cause. We seek peace with these miserable, wretched misguided ... um ... fellow Americans."

"Yessir."

"I see there is a bar room, "Hamlin said. "My order to you gentlemen is to adjourn there and refresh yourselves. I'll let you know when I need you next. Mr. DuBott, lead on, sir."

George watched as the President, Seward and DuBott mounted the stairs to the second floor.

"You heard our orders, Sam," he said, with an easy wink.

The bar room smelled about right. It was a place of dark paneling and heavy, carved tables with chairs to match. Wispy blue gas flamed from polished brass wall sconces. An aged Negro attendant was wiping glasses and pretending to take no notice of them. The place was otherwise empty except for one man who sat leaning against a far wall, his head down, writing. George squinted in the dim light.

"Ho there, Sam. I believe I know yon gentleman."

The man looked up with a happy chuckle. "I believe you do indeed, General McClellan."

George and Sam walked up to the table. Yes, he had recognized the round head topped by a tangle of curls, the sleepy eyelids above the heavy brush mustache. The chins had multiplied and the body was a bit more given over to embonpoint than when last they had met nearly four years ago, but the man was none other than Sir Billy Russell himself.

George held out his hand. "I should have known you'd be somewhere about, you old fire horse."

Russell stood up with unusual agility and spoke with a mellow English-Irish lilt. "General McClellan, a pleasure, sir, to renew our acquaintance, and congratulations on your advancement in rank. I saw both of you men marching bravo under that rain of catcalls. Upon my word, you put me in mind of stoic Roman Centurions." He cast an approving eye at Sam Grant. "And you, sir, made your company parade like a regiment. Well done indeed."

"That's right, Sir William, nothing fazes us," George said. "We survived four years at West Point. May I present my fellow graduate, Captain Sam Grant."

Handshakes. "An honor, sir," Sam Grant said with a shy smile, "but regarding our adventure out there, it puts me in mind of the man who was going to be hung. They asked him if he had any last words, and he said, 'Well, if it wasn't for the honor of the thing, I'd just as soon miss it.'"

Russell chuckled cordially and waved them to be seated.

"Sir William here is famous in a certain way," George said. "He is the military correspondent for the London Times. What

61

the dramatic critic is to the theatre, Sir William Russell is to the art of war."

Russell's deeply dimpled cheeks cracked in a grin. "You flatter me, sir, with but simple truth, and please drop that Sir William falderol. You used to call me Bill when we were plugging around the guns and earthworks and I say, isn't this a pleasant contrast to that place of our last acquaintance?"

"Indeed so. You see, Sam, I first met Mr. Russell when he was a correspondent on the war in the Crimea. I was with our observation team inspecting the Russian trenches at Sevastopol. By the way, we were sent over there by none other than Jefferson Davis."

"When he was Secretary of War," Sam said. "Yes, I've heard about that Grand Tour you made. Must've been some big doings."

"It was," George said. "And Mr. Russell here was our gracious host, introducing us to the British officers."

"I was just thinking on that, old boy," Russell said. "You are probably the only soldier in this country who has ever actually seen fifty thousand armed men on a field of battle."

"Not only did I see them, I brought a hundred books and manuals home with me, on everything from artillery to horse shoes. Then I had to translate them for my report. The French and German were simple enough, but I had to teach myself Russian."

"The thought of that makes my head hurt," Sam Grant said.

"Ah, George Washington." Russell looked up at the old Negro who had quietly approached their table.

"Gentlemen, may I present George Washington, the best barkeep in Charleston." George glanced up, expecting to see the old ritual shuffle of a Negro serving man, the sparkle of white teeth, the good natured, rumbling chuckle, the soft words of respectful banter. George Washington was silent, his shining, deeply lined blue-brown face a blank, his eyes distant and hooded.

Russell didn't notice or care. "What will you have, gentlemen? They have a rather good Baltimore lager-beer on ice, or more ardent spirits if they are to your taste." He beamed a host's questioning look.

"Baltimore lager sounds fine to me," George said. "Sam, what about you?"

"I'll have me a cup of tea if you've got it, and all the fixings," Sam replied softly.

George flinched. For some years it had been widely predicted that Sam Grant would booze himself out of the Army and into an early grave.

"I see I owe you an explanation," Sam said.

George held up a palm. "Not at all, old man. I enjoy a cup of tea now and again, myself."

"No, I want to speak my piece." Sam Grant hunched over and addressed the Englishman. "You see, Mr. Russell, I was once the worst drunk you ever saw. General McClellan knows that. He himself warned me about it when we were both posted in Washington territory, but it did no good. I went on drinking, was near ready to give up on the army and go back to Missouri and work my father-in-law's farm."

Russell glanced a bemused query at George who was just as taken aback. One didn't often hear an infantry officer bare his soul in confession.

"Then, lo and behold," Sam said, "in San Francisco one day, an old army mate picked me up out of the gutter and took me into his own home to sober me up. He was a banker, and rich from it, but he and his good wife, they nursed me along and made me believe I could mend my ways and make a fresh start. That man is the reason I'm here still in the Army. There is no better gentleman on God's green earth than Bill Cump Sherman."

George raised the frosted glass of Baltimore lager that had just been placed in front of him. "Heartily agreed," he said. "Here's to good old Sherman."

Russell solemnly raised his glass. "To the noble Sherman," he said. I hope I may have the pleasure of meeting him someday."

"I saw him recently at my home," George said. "He's in Saint Louis, president of the street railway, but he'll come running should war break out."

"Ah, the question of the day," Russell said, obviously relieved to get down to the meat of things. "And what is your forecast, General?"

"I was about to put that very question to you," George said.

"Well, I could have given you a most definite answer two weeks ago, but now?" Russell lifted both hands. "I am adrift in a sea of dubious speculations."

George sipped his beer and dabbed the foam from his mustache with a tomato stained handkerchief. "I find it quite unusual, Bill, for you to be adrift or doubtful about anything."

"Ah, well, there you have it. Truth to tell the openings lines of my communiqué were already writ. 'Beauregard opens bombardment on Fort Sumter after Lincoln sends warships to relieve the garrison.' I've met with Lincoln, dined with Beauregard, discussed the situation in some detail with Jefferson Davis. In short, I knew my dramatis personae. I fully expected war. Both Lincoln and Davis were looking for any likely excuse to go at it, to thrash out the issue as they say hereabouts. Sooner or later the cannon would boom. But now?"

George cocked an eyebrow. "Now you have doubts?"

"Indeed. Your President Hamlin has changed the game," Russell replied smoothly. "You, after all, know him far better than I."

"Which is to say I hardly know him at all. What about you, Sam, do you have any enlightenment as to what our big wigs are likely to do?"

"No, sir." Sam Grant stirred his tea. "I'm just here to follow orders, but I still say we should have shot a few of them."

"Oh, then I would have had a tip top dispatch for London," Russell exclaimed with relish. "'The great Charleston massacre, opening shots of civil war.' None of you would have escaped with your lives. They would have reduced Fort Sumter to rubble. They would have hung your President by his heels after cutting off his ears and God knows what else."

Sam Grant frowned thoughtfully. "Well then maybe it's a good thing we didn't shoot."

Russell leaned forward and spoke in a stiff whisper. "This city is an armed camp. You are outnumbered at least ten to one."

"I saw no troops except on the batteries around the harbor," George said.

"Oh, the troops are here, General. They were ordered to remain out of sight. You were allowed to march in here with only a minimum of street rabble insult, by courtesy of General Beauregard and Governor Pickins. Look about you. This room normally abounds with the high-blood of Charleston. They are not here because they lurk behind closed doors, awaiting directives. Indeed, the whole city of Charleston is holding its breath."

George sipped his beer, his tongue savoring the crisp, cold tingle. Would he ever see Nelly again? After a moment, he said, "Give me your estimate, Sir Bill."

"It all depends on your President. If he is prepared to evacuate Fort Sumter, there may be a chance for peace."

"Would honor permit us to do that?"

"That would depend upon what is most important to you, General. It has been my experience that a loose definition of honor is always best in that it allows much more room for maneuver. Of course, this is not so in the South, where they take a very narrow view in the matter and are constantly going after each other with guns and knives. I'm very careful with my conversation in the South."

George nodded. "It's the way to survive down here. How long have you been in the country, Bill?"

"I arrived in New York March third, spent some time with your great men in Washington, spoke with Lincoln just two days before the poor man's fatal mishap. I liked what little I saw of him. Then I lit out, as they say, for Dixie, so I missed meeting President Hamlin when he took office.

"Where did you go first?" Sam Grant asked.

"New Orleans, where I found very strong Secessionist sentiment. All the men were going to be solders, preferably Colonels or Generals. 'Gonna whup you Yankees, boy ah tell you, yes suh!' I've seen plantation masters drilling the neighborhood troops on their great front lawns, a copy of Hardee's tactics in one hand and a frosty mint julep in the other."

"What's the quality of these troops?"

Russell shook his head. "They cannot march worth a ha'pence, have no discipline, no uniforms to speak of and are drunk at every opportunity. They are armed with a glut of rusty, old, unrifled muskets with mismatched ammunition. While observing their artillery practice, I determined the safest place to be was on the target. However, they have horses and ride them well, and their war spirit is remarkable. They are prepared to 'bodaciously exfluncticate' you pasty faced barbarians of the North every day of the week and twice on Sunday. I quote directly. I heard no voice in support of the Union."

Sam Grant grunted. "They know what happens to 'em if they do. I heard about some poor Irishman in Richmond who accidentally said a kind word about Abe Lincoln. They stripped him, whipped him and doused him with hot tar."

"Then the most awful punishment of all," George added with cool sarcasm, "They banished him from Virginia."

Russell smiled easily and nodded. He was clearly in his most satisfying element. Whatever happens, war or no, he would have thrilling stories to retail in London after his hobnobbing with all our "great men." George wondered if he himself would be included among them.

"So now tell me, General," Russell said, "as a hypothetical question, what if there were to be a war? Started here or perhaps Fort Pickens in Florida. Shots are fired in anger. Further, what if you retained your command of the army? General Scott is decidedly on his last legs you know. What would be your overall plan, or have you decided yet?"

George chuckled uneasily. "What a question for a public bar room. And in South Carolina."

"We are alone, sir, except for George Washington who is no threat to reveal your secrets. Isn't that so, Uncle George?"

The old Negro mopped the bar and looked unhappy. Russell reached into a pasteboard folder and produced a map showing the Eastern half of the United States.

"I had the foresight to bring some maps from London," he said, pleased with himself. "They are a rarity in these parts."

George agreed. "If we have a war, procuring decent maps will be my first priority. Getting them out to the fighting commands will be the trick. I've been looking into ways of reproducing maps with photography."

"Indeed possible," Russell said, approving. He spread the edges of the map, and waved a hand over it. "Well, anyhow, General, see here, the key to the whole thing is first the Mississippi. Control that channel down to New Orleans and you've won the whole shooting match. Yet there is the Eastern half of the country as well. Here is Washington, and here a hundred miles to the Southwest is Richmond."

"A key city," George said.

"The crucial city," Russell said. "Do you know it is to be the new capital of their Confederacy?"

"We have heard that."

"It is a blessing. I have, of course, visited their current Capital at Montgomery, Alabama. There are more flies there than anywhere else on earth, and I do not exclude India. The flies however, are more appetizing than the food. But look here on this map, General. Study it. Suppose you were given the assignment to take Richmond. How would you go about it?"

"Well," George replied, "first I would light up a cigar."

He peered down at the map, pretended to study it, but he was really pondering Bill Russell. War was all a hop-jolly game to him. Had Russell ever closely studied the dead bodies of soldiers in all their grisly contortions, or did he simply prefer to see war on a neat chessboard-like map such as this one, where it was all so bloodless.

"Well, General," Russell broke in impatiently, "do you see what I see on that map? Do you see the grand opportunity?"

67

"I'm not sure I do, Bill, but I can tell you this. If I am ordered to advance on Richmond, I'm going to be sure to take one little thing along with me."

"What, pray tell?"

"An Army of two hundred thousand men, trained, armed and well officered."

Sam Grant snorted and slapped his knee. "Yep, that one little thing might come in handy."

"Yes," George said, "and assembling that one little thing would take time and a lot of it." He continued scanning the map, now really seeing its implications for the first time. Washington, Richmond, the Potomac, Chesapeake Bay. Suddenly he saw it, a great swooping arc of attack, over water, south out of Washington down the Bay to Fortress Monroe and then into the narrow Peninsula that divided the James and York rivers. Strike out to the West over that peninsula and you are on the high road to Richmond. But where to find transports enough to move such a huge army?

"You see it now?" Russell asked, nudging his arm. "Any General worth his salt would, I daresay."

George looked at him with narrowed eyes. "You mean the water route?"

"Of course," Russell said, delighted as a child at a circus. "Why bloody your head in direct battle on the overland route when you can swoop down by the water route in a swift attack?" He radiated self-satisfaction. "By the by, I have not breathed a word of this to your Southron countrymen."

Sam Grant's stubby fingers waved over the map. "Yes, the water route would be dandy, but looky here! What if you could go both ways, overland *and* by water. A two- pronged attack, put the pressure on 'em, keep 'em guessing which is the main effort."

Bill Russell puffed his cheeks and looked at Sam Grant with new interest. "Hmm, yes, possibly I should have seen that."

George declined to discuss grand strategy with a mere Captain. It was all theory anyway. It would depend on so many contingencies, mainly what the Secesh would do, and who would be commanding them. It would take much more thought and study. Wars were not to be planned over beers in a barroom.

"I think it's time we look to our duties and report to the President, Captain Grant." George stood and offered his hand to Bill Russell. "I trust we will be seeing more of you, Sir Bill, as events develop."

Russell laughed. "I'm a hound dog with a treed possum, General. You can't shake me."

George couldn't resist another glance at the map. "Of course if I came down here by your water route, I would also take with me more rifle bored artillery than has ever been seen on the face of the earth. Have you visited our steel foundries in Pittsburgh? They can make all the guns we need."

Sam Grant nodded. "You can never have too much artillery."

George paused a moment, then pronounced a belief that he held with near religious faith. "You can never have too much of anything."

* * *

George to Nelly   April 9, 1861

My Own Dear Little Wife,

I find myself in the deranged state of South Carolina, which thinks itself a sovereign nation, in the perfumed city of Charleston, which is inhabited by the most eccentric, charming, yet rudely overbearing and pride cursed people. By now you have heard of the 'unusual' ovation that greeted our arrival in this place and you may fear for our safety. Well, never doubt your good old husband's ingenuity should we be forced to retreat Northward. I'll be the one stepping off the train in a Paris gown with roses in my hair!

From the viewpoint of my window here at the hotel I can see dim glowing lights in the harbor at Fort Sumter, which Major Anderson will either evacuate or defend. (The chimes of St. Michael's church nearby have just rung two. They must keep a slave up all night to pull the rope.) The next few days will tell the tale, as we await the widely advertised but much delayed arrival of Jefferson Davis.

Despite the delicate situation we did manage to have a pleasant dinner tonight with our Charleston friends(?).

"Colonel" James Chesnut, late of the United State Senate who knows as much of military science as an infant, was our host. The "Colonel" and his wife, Mary, occupy an apartment suite at this hotel on the floor above us. Present among the dignitaries was Governor Pickens, a portly man with a head to match who loves to hear himself talk.

Ye olde Crafty Pierre Beauregard was also at table, perfumed, waxed and uniformed to a fine edge as you might expect. (I got him to give me the source of his French scent.) You'd like it. We talked old army gossip and our mutual interest in the tactics of Napoleon. Nothing at all about the near and real prospect of us blowing each other to atoms. Such élan! Sa va, ya all!

There was a quaint old gaffer known to all as "Judge" Petigru, who it seems had once been in law practice with our host the "Colonel." The judge claimed to be the only remaining Union man in the whole city of Charleston, says South Carolina is a "lunatic asylum," and hopes that they will recover sanity short of armed insurrection. He has the oddest looking face, all pushed in from forehead to chin, like a squashed pumpkin head. But not pumpkin for brains I should add.

We dined, by the way, on an acceptable fish salad, a very fresh and tasty oyster pie, assorted sweets, and a capable champagne. The china was good English stock but bland.

Speaking of English, Sir William Russell, the war correspondent of the London Times is here on the prowl. You've heard of him from my days in Europe. He plays the lofty critic but does have a good grip on things. After dinner we had cigars on the roof of this hotel discussing "big war science."

Spoke only briefly with the Colonel's lady, Mrs. Chesnut, but found her quite a stimulating character. She speaks little, but always with measured wit and her keen eye observes all. She has a jolly flirting way about her and enjoys an innocent(?) friendship with old Judge Petigru. She claims she has met you, "my pretty little wife," while in Washington a few years back, and sends her best regards. Do you remember her at all?

Must close now, and try for some sleep. Tomorrow President Hamlin insists on visiting the batteries out on Morris Island, which promises to be a tedious trip by ferry boat to a dangerous destination. (My protests were in vain.) For some reason he must see Fort Sumter from the seceshers view point.

The day after we expect J. Davis and Company and then we will get down to business.

Your Devoted George

Entry from Mary Chesnut's diary April 10, 1861

Dined last night with our would-be conquerors from the North___So clever of Mr. Chesnut (Oh, but I must call him Colonel now) to have issued the invitation. Told Mr. DuBott to prepare us some kind of fancy supper and that silly goose served us the same old smelly fish salad and oyster pie that never fails to "grace" the menu every night here at this hotel___ La! So much for my powers of influence.

I don't care what anyone says, I like President Hamlin___Had only met him in brief passing once when "we" were in the Washington Senate, so had no expectations con or pro___He is a gentleman of graceful dignity. I asked him outright why he is rumored to be a Negro when it is perfectly plain that he is no more tinged with the tar brush than I am___ Told me it was all his father's doing. He has brothers named America, Europe, Asia, and AFRICA. So of course according to The Charleston Mercury, anyone with a swarthy skin, <u>and</u> a brother named "AFRICA" has to be etc. etc. etc.___ That idiot Bob Rhett will print any nonsense if it suits "the cause."

Mr. Hamlin told me how he had boyhood dreams of being an actor, but of course his father put the quash on that. A political man is a actor or so I've observed. He would not sparkle in any literary exchange, and no bon mots escape his lips, yet there is something about him, a comforting strength, an honest dignity. I do believe that he must be a kind husband and father. This for a man who may well be our sworn enemy tomorrow. Such are the days of doleful dumps we live in.

Spoke also with General George McClellan who is a jumpy, anxious sort of young man who (I think) feels the great responsibilities thrust upon him___But he grits his teeth, grins and blushes and is often charming. We had a short teté de teté, and Colonel Chesnut whispered that I should take him on a promenade tomorrow and "talk sense at him." As if I would have any influence, but "my country calls" and I must obey. (I had met his wife in Washington, pretty little Miss Marcy, who had a very high opinion of herself___perhaps justified.)

The rest of the President's party___ young Mr. John Hay, smiling widely, but with the face of a rat, not to be trusted___ Bill Seward of course I had met many times before in Washington___Sad to report his manners have not improved and he still talks out of three sides of his mouth at once. Yet we hear, and can only hope it true, that he secretly preaches reconciliation.

The clock of St. Michael's has struck two. Charleston dozes, yet J. C. stays up writing mysterious documents. I hear

72

him in the parlor his pen on paper making the scritch-scratch sound of and it warmly comforts me somehow.   My eyelids droop to the floor___and so to bed.

I pray there will be no war.

CHAPTER SEVEN

The sun blasted beach of Morris Island reminded Russell of the coasts of India. Nowhere near as hot of course, and thank God there was a moderating moist breeze that flipped back the broad brim of his straw hat. He squashed it down and set about recording his impressions with a stub pencil on the back of a used envelope. Somehow people found it easier speaking their true minds to a jolly, envelope-writing Englishman.

First he would set the scene. He was standing only a few yards off from a group of four batteries of mixed artillery, eight-inch and ten-inch mortars, plus a fine new Blakely gun, an English-rifled cannon with side mounted optical sights that pointed out over sandbag ramparts toward Fort Sumter. He gazed at the target, and scribbled *squatting tiger-ready in the harbor; its red brick walls warmly colored by the late morning sun.* Close enough. He would edit later, but he knew that "tiger-ready" would have to go, though he rather fancied the metaphor. Ah well.

President Hannibal Hamlin and Secretary Seward were working their way through the gun emplacements, jovially shaking hands with the puzzled and often sullen soldiers of the Confederacy.

"What do you suppose he thinks to gain by all this?" The voice at Russell's side evoked a petulant little boy, the accent silky South Caroline. He turned and looked into the face of last night's dinner host, James Chesnut.

"Why, I declare, Colonel Chesnut," he said. "I believe he must be running for Governor of South Carolina."

Chesnut gave a restrained laugh.

"More to the point," Russell continued, "I suspect he wants to regain some dignity after that reception on Meeting Street yesterday."

"Yes, I don't reckon he enjoyed that much," Chesnut said. "Must've rankled."

"I say, your troops are notably well behaved this morning. They are, at least, being civil to him."

"They better be," Chesnut said. "This morning General Beauregard told them that any disrespect to the President would be rewarded with severe punishment."

"Namely?" Disciplinary matters interested Russell.

Chesnut laughed softly. "Nothing serious. A rough ride astride a gun tube, a session with the hot tar brush."

Russell approved. "Soldiers respond to discipline, sir. It is a true rule throughout the world." The praise was a bit disingenuous given the wretched camp conditions of the secessionist troops. It had disgusted him to see tattered tents pitched every which way, chicken bones and feathers along with human filth strewn about impromptu. Many had been drunk at that early hour of the morning. Still as a guest of these people, he would be agreeable to a point.

"Hah! I suppose President Hamlin thinks it his power of personality that has won them over," he said, soliciting Chesnut's amusement.

"Well, we must never reveal the secret of his charm then."

Russell weighed his words. Perhaps he should consolidate himself further with Chesnut whom he judged an influential man of the regime. "May I compliment you sir on your wife, a most accomplished and elegant hostess. I thoroughly enjoyed my time with her last night."

The words caught in his throat.

Chesnut took no notice of the frightful double entendre. "Well, it's something she has been doing most of her life," he said, dismissively. "After twenty years of practice at anything, why I suppose you are bound to get good at it."

Russell rejected the jaded husband's appraisal. Indeed, he relished thought of Mrs. Chesnut and of how he could enjoyably endure some more time with her.

Hamlin, ever the politician, had mounted the earthen rampart, and launched into a speech to the troops. Snatches of it drifted on the wind, and Russell was lazy in making notes. Words, merely words ... fellow Americans ... not enemies ... no tampering with ... institutions ... must be friends ... Americans ... fellow Americans ...

"He might as well be speaking to a brick wall," Chesnut said.

There was movement among the throng of soldiers, someone with wild looking gray hair and carrying an ancient iron pike was pushing his way up to the Blakely gun. "Who, pray tell, is that crazy looking old coot?" Russell asked, then blanched. For an awful moment he feared Chesnut might reply: "Why that is my honorable old father, sir, and I demand satisfaction for your insult."

Chesnut laughed easily. "That crazy old coot, sir, is Edmund Ruffin."

Relieved, Russell wrote on his envelope. *A tangled mane of silvery white hair sprouting in all directions, eyes burn and radiate hatred, (even madness?). Repugnant fellow, the other soldiers step out of his way.*

"Old Edmund is the best hater we have," Chesnut said. "He gained some small fame for himself years ago as a planter who advocated scientific farming methods. Published a periodical on the subject. But his real obsession has always been Southern nationalism. He will gladly tell you at length how much he despises the accursed 'Yankee race.'"

Russell could easily believe it. Old coot Ruffin was now standing next to the Blakely gun looking up at President Hamlin with a fixed glare of obvious loathing.

"He has joined our militia in hopes of firing the first shot at Fort Sumter," Chesnut continued. "Our men treat him as a sort of mascot. You see that spear like device he carries?"

"Yes," Russell said, "an infantry pike. Our troops used to jab you rebels with them during the revolution. It's a good job they do to kill a man."

"It might be of interest to you the way he obtained that pike," Chesnut said. "It used to belong to none other than John Brown."

Russell turned in amazement, then busied his pencil. Here was a story. Mad John Brown, that demon enemy of slavery, had tried to invade the South with a small band of followers. He had been captured at Harpers Ferry, Virginia, and was promptly tried and hanged in December of '59. The Boston abolitionists who had backed him, considered him a saintly martyr. There was even a song: *John Brown's body lies a molding in the grave.* Unconsciously, Russell began to hum it as he wrote.

Chestnut's fingers squeezed his arm. "That is not a good song for South Carolina."

"Oh, yes, yes, of course," Russell recovered, "but tell me Ruffin's connection with John Brown."

"Well, that old boy traveled all the way up to Harper's Ferry to witness and cheer on John Brown's hanging." Chesnut chuckled. "Just wanted to see it for his own satisfaction I reckon. Now, as you may know, Brown had an army of twenty-one with him, mostly his sons and relatives. They carried those long pikes. Brown was going to issue them to the slaves so they could rise up and kill their masters. After the hanging I suppose the pikes were just lying around, free for the taking, so that's what Ruffin did. He took 'em. He sent one to each Southern governor as a warning of what the North had in store for the South. Of course he kept one for himself, the one you see there."

Russell's mouth opened to speak words which never left his lips. Amazing how something could happen in an instant and yet be slowed down in perception to pour through the brain like cold molasses. He was about to eyewitness an American President blown to smithereens by a cannon shell. It was all inevitable. Hamlin, meandering about and lost in the self-importance of speechifying had chosen to stand before the deadly mouth of the Blakely gun. What would be the most likely thing for Edmund Ruffin to do? Why to pull the white cord of the lanyard of course, which would set off the cap, which would set off the propellant charge in the breach, which would send the shell blazing up the tube to obliterate Hamlin. Russell had seen enough of the results of artillery explosions to imagine it happening in the time-space of a bolt of lightening. Perhaps he himself would be killed by a stray fragment. Bloody

78

parts would fly all over. Hamlin's half digested lunch would form a wet mist in the air. Oh, well, to be killed was an ever present risk of his vocation. Then the thought came in anger, to be killed by the shenanigans of that scruffy maniac, Edmund Ruffin, what horrible glory.

It was merely an exercise in logic. There could have been no other outcome. Ruffin had crept up to the Blakely gun and smartly pulled the lanyard, just as General McClellan, sensing his intent an instant too late, went crashing into him, knocking him to the ground.

Ah well, game try, McClellan. See you in hell.

* * *

George's strong legs drove him right into the old man's waist, puffing out his breath, knocking him down into the sand. As they fell, he looked up to see the lanyard cord stretched tight, then heard the metallic click of release. Terrified, he waited for the explosion. It didn't come. Instantly in the elongation of time he knew what had happened. There was still a chance. He struggled up on his knees, fighting to free himself from the entanglement with the crazy old man who was all sputter and rage and smelled like rotten meat. He gained his footing barely and launched himself through the impeding sand toward the front of the gun, where, oh that fool, Hamlin still stood in stupefied bewilderment, his oration frozen in mid syllable.

One chance in a hundred. Something had gone wrong inside the breach. A faulty cap, damp powder bag, thank God for defective military skills. He had nearly reached the President when he heard the hissing sizzle from inside the gun. Powder burning! Could go off at any moment! He reached the President, knocked him down and fell on top of him. As they tumbled in the sand the gun went off in an ear blasting explosion.

George rolled over, coughing in the enveloping black smoke.

"Beg your pardon, sir," he said, "but there was danger."

Hamlin lay sprawled on his back among the sandbags looking up at the smoking gun tube, his mouth open, his lips quivering, sand in his hair and eyebrows.

Through shocked eardrums, George could still make out old Ruffin's voice as he was led away screeching at the top of his lungs.

"I curse you all, toads of the vile Yankee race!"

The fort! They might return fire!

George scrambled up, grabbed a red signal flag, ran down to the water's edge and began whipping the red cloth back and forth, while yelling at the top of his lungs, "Misfire, misfire! Don't shoot!"

* * *

Major Robert Anderson stood on the granite wharf of Fort Sumter with his second in command, Captain Abner Doubleday observing the Presidential party on Morris Island.

"Now tell me, Doubleday, what in tarnation does President Hamlin hope to accomplish visiting the guns at Cumming's Point? Is he looking for further insult?" He made a sound of disgust. "I tell you, sir, I feared Lincoln, but had some hope for Hamlin. Now I see he is no better than the rest. Mark my words, these politicians will somehow blunder us into a shooting action."

"I can't think a war to end slavery would be such a bad thing, sir."

Anderson snorted. Trust Doubleday, a stocky West Pointer of forty-one years, to speak his feelings without reservation. "Ah, there you go again, declaiming from your Black Republican heart. Why, pray tell must we have war to end slavery when the whole history of the century shows it on the decline? Slavery is merely an excuse for hotheads."

"I trust you do not consider me a hothead, sir," Doubleday said, his eyes intense, his lips hardly visible from behind a black bush mustache.

Anderson enjoyed twitting Doubleday. He was spinning up a sarcastic reply when the cannon went off on Morris Island. First the flash and powder smoke, a second later came the deep resounding "thump." His experienced artilleryman's eye instantly caught sight of the shell arching toward Fort Sumter, a clear miss.

"Short a hundred yards and to the right," Doubleday called it. In artillery matters Doubleday was sound as a ripe apple.

The shell whined into the water, splashing harmlessly as predicted.

"Shall we return fire, sir? Doubleday shouted, transformed now with new impetuous energy. "Shall I give the order?"

"Steady now, Doubleday. I judge that to be a misfire." Anderson raised his glasses with slow deliberation. "Notice there is no concerted fire from other batteries. See, look for yourself, Captain, that man waving a red flag. They are afraid we will construe that shot as an act of war."

"Well perhaps it is," Doubleday said, all stirred up now. "How do we know they haven't taken President Hamlin prisoner? That could have been their opening shot and the red flags are in celebration."

Anderson squinted at him. "You have quite an interesting mind Captain Doubleday." He continued to study the scene on the beach, shaking his head. "What a bunch of raw yahoos to go calling themselves soldiers. Look at that fool rolling around under the gun tube. Good way to get himself killed."

CHAPTER EIGHT

Late that afternoon George, Bill Russell and Sam Grant stood three in a row at the Mills House bar with frosty mugs of Baltimore lager. George reached for his and was alarmed to see his hand tremble.

Russell, back in top form now, patted him on the back. "A very close thing indeed it was, General. You played the hero today as you will see from the story I am about to write."

"Hear, hear and second the motion," Sam Grant raised his mug. He had announced that saving a President was an occasion to go off tea just once.

"We were all lucky today," George said, inspecting his image in the bar's mirror. "Thank God for that misfire." His voice was controlled and his face looked all right, though his insides still felt like bread pudding. "That shell would have certainly killed Hamlin on impact. Had the fuse gone awry, it could have blown up any number of us." He wiggled his toes still feeling sand in his boots.

"That crazy old gaffer," Sam Grant exclaimed with overblown scorn. George noticed Sam's mug was already half drained. His own was still untouched.

Russell turned and studied him. "Aren't you going to drink your beer, General?"

George smiled at the Englishman, then carefully arranged the fingers of both hands around the slippery wet mug and willed steady hands. He was rewarded with a gulp of the cold Baltimore lager.

"That will cure what ails you, old son," Russell said amiably.

John Hay came in rustling a newspaper. "Ahoy there, shipmates, have you seen the editorial in the Charleston Mercury, that great journal of moderation? It is entitled: Welcome To Charleston."

"Ah," Russell said, with a loud sigh, "you are about to inflict it on us."

"Indeed I am," Hay said.

"Then we shall need another round, George Washington. Southern newspaper editorials make my mouth dry and my brain ache."

"I say there, General," John Hay said to George. "I hear you fired on Fort Sumter today."

George nodded soberly. "Didn't hit anything. My gunnery skills are a bit rusty."

"Hear, hear," Sam Grant said, plunking down an empty mug. "You should've been there, Johnny. Boom!"

John Hay cocked an eyebrow at Sam Grant, then began to read:

Beware of Yankees who come all smiling and bearing gifts.

Yesterday, that renowned hound, Hannibal Hamlin, that darky in white man's guise, and by stroke of fate, President of the late unlamented United States, had the gall to sail into Charleston harbor. He first paid respects to his menials at Fort Sumter, unloading materials of war for the faithless Major Anderson. Later he landed his pompous self at our steamer wharf. He and his party of armed rascals then marched up Meeting Street where they were given a hot welcome by a wide-awake band of Charleston citizens. It is rumored that Hamlin and his partner, the occasionally honorable William Seward, are here to confer with our President Davis. We will not presume to advise that capable statesman as to how to deal with Insignificant Yankee trash, but we fully expect our visitors from the North to shortly depart our fair Charleston at full yelp with their tails between their legs. Let the South Rule the South!

Russell held up both hands. "George Washington, a beer for this gentleman to stop him from reading more."

"For shame! For shame!" Sam Grant muttered to himself.

Startled, John Hay said, "His name is George Washington? Any relation to ...? Oh, well, of course not."

"Oh, you never can tell," Russell said. "I've seen many a light skinned 'servant' on my travels. What about that, George Washington? Are you a descendant of the great man of Mount Vernon?"

The black man gave him a heavy look.

"Oh, well. Say, chaps, after touring these semi-United States I have conjured up a definition of Americans. Care to hear it?

"I do," Sam Grant said, too loudly.

"Ahem," Russell declared, his hand to his chest. "American: A biped mammal, nearly as intelligent as a horse, who believes himself to be God's gift to creation. Who dotes on ice to cool his beer and oysters, and military titles to feed his vanity."

"Sounds about right to me," Sam Grant said.

"Captain." John Hay spoke sternly. "He just insulted your countrymen. Are you going to allow that?"

"My countrymen need insulting now and again, Mr. Hay. Ain't that the truth General?"

"You had best stick with tea, Sam."

Russell drained his mug. "I shall miss iced beer when I go home," he said wistfully.

"Mr. Russell," John Hay said, "I have not had the honor of conversation with you."

"That is because you have not had the honor of my acquaintance. I am Sir William Russell of the London Times. So there."

John Hay bowed low. "And I am John Hay, a biped mammal, nearly intelligent as a horse."

Sam Grant slapped his knee with a lusty hoot while Russell grinned easily.

"But seriously, sir," Hay went on, "may I inquire as to your impressions of the Southern States?"

"The Southern States." Russell assumed a purposeful frown. "How shall I put it, Mr. Hay. It is a land of illusions, the chief of which is that England and even France will come in on their side for the sake of the cotton supply. How could I dare inform them that the British government will never side with a state supporting human slavery when we have been battling the African slave trade for most of this century."

The Englishman paused, then leaned toward them with quiet intensity. "I can say this now, being as it were, among friends. It is a monstrous system. These planters let their very own children slave away in the fields, the paternal image shining darkly in their faces. They are so puffed up with their own know-it-all, hubris defending slavery, life or death, that you must agree with them or they will get annoyed and cut out your liver. I must have heard the phrase a thousand times. 'Oh yes, happiest people on the face of the earth they are.' Then one looks into those long suffering eyes. Something like yours, George Washington. Tell me, George, are your people the happiest creatures on the face of the earth?"

"Yessir, Mr. Russell, if you says so."

"Now, now, George Washington, do I detect a tinge of bitterness in your demeanor?" The barkeep looked directly at them for the first time George could remember.

"I's a free colored" George Washington said, glumly. "Got's nobody to look out fo' me. Whatever happens it'll go bad. You has a war, it'll go bad wif me. You don't has a war, it'll go bad wif me. It's all the same bad wif me. Though Mr. DuBott is kindly. I lets's on I belongs to him, and he let's me let on."

"Your terrible secret is safe with us," Russell said, his tongue having some trouble with the "s."

"Yes," Sam Grant said, ponderously. "Safe with us."

John Hay searched his pockets. "Oh, by the by, General McClellan, I have a card from a lady for you here somewhere. Ah, here it is."

George inspected the card. "Mrs. James Chesnut?"

"Our dinner hostess of last night," Hay said. "She awaits your attendance in the reception room. Sorry, it slipped my mind."

George turned on his heel. Damn Johnny Hay. How long had the woman been awaiting him? No wonder Northerners were accused of rude behavior. He found Mrs. Chesnut alone in the reception room writing in a small notebook. Her face lit with an open smile as he entered.

"Forgive me, Madam, for my tardy appearance."

She stood and offered her hand. For a desperate moment George was uncertain whether to kiss or shake it. He touched her fingers. The other might be too European for Charleston.

"Your servant, Madam."

Mary Chesnut beckoned to him. "Come, promenade with me, General. I declare, you are in for one delicious treat down at the battery."

"I marched up Meeting Street yesterday, Mrs. Chesnut, and I assure you it was no treat." He hesitated for a moment, then offered his arm and they began to walk.

"Why, you only lacked for the proper chaperon to guide you, General."

"Ah, then they would've have thrown breakfast at you as well."

"Oh, nonsense." They stepped from the shade of the piazza into the late afternoon sunlight. She snapped open a flouncy pink parasol and propped it at an angle over her left shoulder. George took her right arm and they began walking East on Meeting Street toward the wharf.

"People here know how to respect a lady," Mary Chesnut said. "It's visiting Yankee Presidents who bring out the worst gumption in 'em. May I ask, do you see any threatening developments along our way ahead?"

George surveyed the few people on the street. "I see dirty looks," he said.

"Oh, pish! Ignore them," Mary Chesnut said, as she nodded to some startled passersby. "Maude," her voice fluted at a woman who seemed frozen on the sidewalk opposite. "I so look forward to our tea tomorrow. Right now I must show General McClellan our lovely Charleston!"

"I trust you won't be made a social outcast," he said, "for being seen in company with the enemy."

Her smile was confidence in a gilt frame. "Whomever I am seen with is, by definition, no enemy. Don't you know I'm a big pumpkin in the patch around here?"

"I am forming that opinion, Madam."

87

He glanced sideways at her. In daylight, he saw that she was older than Nelly, well into her thirties he guessed, and not nearly as beautiful as she had seemed by candlelight. Still, there was a vibrant air about her that made up for the square, plain face with its heavy dark brows. What was her game in this little saunter?

"I heard we nearly went to war this afternoon, some silly man shooting a canon ball at your President? And you played the gallant hero?"

"Well, the old fool made the effort, Mrs. Chesnut, but it's hardly worth mentioning. He missed both the President and Fort Sumter."

"Hah! The cannon blast was heard clearly from the hotel. All of us ladies sallied up to the roof to see the war start." Her arm tightened on his elbow. "Tell me, just between us, don't you in your soldierly heart of hearts hope there will be a war?"

He paused. She had hit on a question he had asked himself often in the last weeks. He would be good at war, he knew that, and the future of a successful general could be rosey indeed. Still he remembered too vividly what he had seen in Mexico and Europe, the wholesale death, the mutilation and stink of modern war. Did he want to bring that down on his own country? He looked at her expectant face, and tried to make light of a heavy subject.

"I am not allowed by my oath of service to have personal wishes."

"Oh, pish."

They arrived at the Battery, the curved street that bordered the harbor. Mary Chesnut led the way to a red, barn-like structure that was labeled 'Bath House.'

"This is a convenience for those who are fool enough to bathe in Charleston Harbor, but here now is our destination."

George blinked. "The ice cream stand?"

"You like ice cream don't you?"

Under her supervision he bought two helpings of peach ice cream with Yankee coinage which the serving boy readily accepted, then sat with her under a broad red and white striped awning while they ate from crystal dishes.

"Most scrumptious ice cream I've ever tasted," George said. "Better flavor than Roman gellato."

"Why of course," Mary Chesnut said beaming. "This is Charleston, after all. Although I've never been to Rome. It is a place I've always wished to visit, but there are so many places." Her voice died on the wind.

"Delightful vista of the harbor down here," George said, squinting into the shimmering water.

Mary Chesnut stared at him, her eyes unblinking, her head slightly cocked. "Yes, it is indeed a pleasant aspect, our harbor, the intersection of our worldly commerce." Her voice fluttered brightly once again. "I used to stroll here with my dear James when I was fifteen years old and my name was Mary Miller, but that was forever ago." Her tone changed. "The only thing spoilin' the view now is that awful old pile of bricks out there astride the ship channel. So ugly, don't you think? You have dribble on your mustache."

George hastened to wipe under his nose.

"Fort Sumter is a tool of war, Mrs. Chesnut," he said, resonant in the way of a man gently guiding the thoughts of a woman. "Such things are often ugly as you say, but they can possess a certain utilitarian beauty all their own."

She gave a pretty sigh. "Oh, ugly is ugly, and that's all I have to say about it."

"Now I sincerely doubt that, Mrs. Chesnut. I reckon you're just getting started."

"Well." Her fingers floated down to smooth her skirts. "I must admit that I am here with you at the instigation of my husband, who specified this very place for a nice little social meeting." She nodded and smiled at an inquisitive looking man and woman who glided slowly by.

"Why, Mrs. Chesnut, you wound me." George pressed a hand above his heart. "Here I thought you had sought out my company for myself alone."

She tittered. "I declare, you would fit in well around here at dinner party season. Your Mama or someone taught you very nicely how to flirt."

George shifted in his chair. Best not to bite on that one. Mary Chesnut picked up her spoon with thumb and forefinger, clinked it gently against the glass dish. "I love that sound, don't you? Tinkle tinkle. Anyway, Mr. Chesnut, the Colonel I mean, thought it would be uncommon good if I could convey some ideas to you, which perhaps you in turn could convey to your President Hamlin."

"Why doesn't he speak for himself?"

"Oh, that would not do," Mary Chesnut said, matter-of-factly. "No, no, indeed. He could not be seen as ... well, I don't know how to put it since I am only a prattle-brained woman without understanding of these matters, but it seems to me that Colonel Chesnut would not wish to approach your President directly, since then there would be possible misunderstanding." She leveled her dark liquid eyes at him. "On the part of some people, I mean. Or worse, rejection, and with rejection would come an end to talk, and well now, you understand that don't you? We must keep talking? Must keep the telegraph wires all connected?"

George stroked the stubble of beard that he had begun to let grow on his chin. "Those people are still staring at us."

Mary Chesnut waved her parasol and called to them. "Elise, Sam, let's have toddies this evening at the hotel?" The woman nodded dreamily, took the man's arm as they ambled on.

"Elise and Sam will want to know all about me," George said.

"And I shall tell them that you are the most brutal of the Unionist Generals, come to work your masculine will on poor, feminine Charleston."

George snorted. "Madam, you astonish me. How can I work my will on poor feminine Charleston when she outnumbers us here ten to one."

Mary Chesnut pushed out her lower lip in a mock pout. "Oh, there you go, being reasonable, just like a man. We can't ever get along if you persist so."

George was truly puzzled now. "Do we want to get along?"

Mary Chesnut pulled her white gloves tighter on her wrists, then inspected them for fit. "Of course we want to get along, but on terms we can live with." She glanced at him. "We may flap our wings a lot, make loud crowing noise about war and such, but don't you know we want peace as much as you do? We merely wish to be left alone."

"That is your message for our President? Leave us alone?"

"Why, yes. Respect our independence. Give up that awful old ugly fort. What do you care about it anyway? What good is it to you? Just leave us alone and let our fate befall us."

"And what will that fate be, Mrs. Chesnut?"

"As for the Confederacy? Oh, if you don't unite us by doin' something foolish, I daresay we'll all split off from each other in a plague of little secessions, such prideful men as we have. States will declare independence, and, who knows, counties may break from states, cities from counties. Where it will all end I don't pretend to know. We'll all probably eventually get tired of all this secessionism, and come crawling back into the Union, if you just have a little patience with us."

"Is this what Colonel Chesnut wished you to say?"

"I have added some elaborations and conjecture of my own."

George warily wondered how to reply. Was this in any way an unofficial message from the State of South Carolina, the Confederacy, or even Jefferson Davis? Or was he hearing merely the larky meanderings of a charming feminine mind?

"Mrs. Chesnut, it's not as simple as all that. People in the North are troubled. They see your secession movement as deliberately chopping away a rather large portion of their country. They see your politicians, to speak bluntly, as criminals and blackguards. I'll admit there is a difference of opinion. Some say: 'Let the erring sisters go in peace.' Others say, we should make war and use military coercion to bring you back."

"Well, yes, but now that you see how alluring and lovable we are, how can you ever think of making war on us?" Her eyelashes fluttered.

George smiled. "Mrs. Chesnut, you are a corker."

"Leave us to our fate, General." Her eyes were now firmly fixed on him. "That is the message for your president."

George looked away from her persistent gaze. "If only it wasn't for the nigger question," he said, finally. "It complicates matters."

Mary Chesnut's eyebrows shot up and her forehead crinkled to her widow's peak. "Please, sir, refrain from using street language in my presence. Polite people say 'Negroes,' or 'coloreds,' or 'servants.' But we hardly ever use that ugly word."

"Excuse me," George said wryly with a glance around. "I believed myself to be in South Carolina."

Mary Chesnut clicked her tongue. "Do I detect an ever-so-slightly patronizing attitude, General? Oh, my, poor us, burdened with the 'nigger' question? There would be no such question if those busybodies up North would stop moralizing and lording it over us."

"Whatever they are," George said, "and whatever you may call them, I notice you seem to have got a lot of them down here, and many people are in disagreement as to what is to be done about them."

"Oh, do we have a lot of them? I hadn't noticed. 'Slaves' I believe you call them in your parts."

"No need to become testy, Madame."

"Oh, there is every need, sir. I get so sick and tired of hearing your moralizing, literary ladies and gentlemen safe in their cozy libraries, telling us all about how to reform our domestic institutions." She opened her blue-beaded reticule and extracted a silver pill box. "May I offer you an opium pill, General?"

"No, thank you. Opium only makes me sleepy."

She poked a pill in her mouth and swallowed it with a spoonful of ice cream. "Honestly, I do get so vexed with this whole subject. I assure you, sir, there is no one who hates slavery more than a Southern woman. We are not such heathens as you might think."

"You hate slavery? I am surprised to hear that from you, Madam. It seems to me you are quite comfortable with your arrangements."

Mary Chesnut shot him a sidelong glance. "Oh, indeed? Well, you can go back to Cincinnati and be content with your sweet little wife. We are the ones who have to live down here among 'em. We own them and they own us. We fear them, so we spoil them, which just makes them that much more arrogant and feisty. Do you know, sir, that I had a distant cousin, a dear old saint of a lady, murdered in her bed by her 'servants?' God spare me from such servants. I do believe the only good that could come out of a war is that slavery would be a goner."

George had brought up the Negro slavery issue as an artful tease. Like most Northern Democrats, he thought the whole issue was merely a trumped-up political excuse promoted by fire-eating secessionists. He could easily envision a war over state's rights and integrity of the Union with the institution of slavery unthreatened, and surviving into the next century when moral force would gradually do it in. The last thing he had expected to hear out of Mary Chesnut's mouth was anti-slavery talk.

"So then you are opposed to slavery, Mrs. Chesnut?"

"As any moral and sane person would be, General. Aren't you?"

Once more taken aback, George searched for a reply. "Well, I suppose I am," he said. "I know my wife is."

Mary Chesnut's eyes fixed on him, dark haunted liquid pools. "I may not like them much, but I do believe they are human beings, sir, even as we are, having souls even as we do. We have no right to keep them down and even more disgusting, our men-folk have no right to use their women as they do. You do catch my drift, sir?"

George felt his cheeks go warm. "It's not hard to catch your drift, Mrs. Chesnut."

He looked at Mary Chesnut with a new respect. Yet, he wondered if she, as a Southern woman, was capable of grasping the finer points of politics and the affairs of men. "Do you realize, Mrs. Chesnut, that there are some men in the North who would view a civil war as a grand opportunity? There are many in Congress, the so-called Black Republican faction of that party. They would make sure that your prophecy would be fulfilled, that war would kill slavery. But in so doing they would seek to financially ruin the South as punishment for making all this trouble. Your lands would be forfeit to them, for they would not compensate you for your slaves. They would simply declare you immoral for owning them in the first place and declare them free under new laws they would pass."

Mary Chesnut blinked in amazement. "Not compensate us? End slavery, but not compensate us for our investment? Why that would ruin us! That would be nothing more than stealing."

"They would not see it that way," George said, oddly pleased that he had scored a disturbing point with this fine woman. "They would see you as immoral, worthy of punishment."

Why had he chosen that word? The mental image came, uncalled for, of Mrs. Chesnut being "punished" by that arch Vindictive, Edward Stanton, her pale wrists tied with chains to a tree branch, Stanton with a bull whip, ripping at her lacy dress ...

"General McClellan?"

"Yes, madam?"

"You seemed lost in thought, a thousand miles away. You said they would seek to punish us?"

"Yes," George licked his lips. She smiled up at him. Could she somehow read his unworthy thoughts? He rose awkwardly, feeling an unwanted pressure.

"Perhaps, Mrs. Chesnut, we should return to the hotel."

CHAPTER NINE

Mills House, Charleston April 11, 9:25 a.m.

In the grand ballroom of the Mills House, George strolled over the polished wood floor to inspect the jam-packed food serving table. It was something to do while their party awaited the arrival of Jefferson Davis, and a suitable excuse to get out of range of President Hamlin who was flagrantly ill tempered this morning.

DuBott, the manager appeared at his side. "May I serve you something, General?"

"Hmm? Oh, no, thank you Mr. DuBott. I'm just admiring your fine presentation. A most impressive spread, sir."

The manager beamed and rubbed his hands. "Thank you, General. I think everyone will enjoy it."

Lavish might have been a better word. There were oysters, cooked and raw, pineapple glazed hams, roast turkey and chicken, a variety of wines and fruit juices, biscuits, rolls and nut breads with jams and compotes, many kinds of pies and cakes, all flanked by gleaming pots of coffee and tea.

DuBott's fingers flicked out to realign a stack of crisp napkins.

"I suppose you go on the theory that discussions of high national affairs must make men hungry," George said.

DuBott smiled, enjoying the appreciation. "I must say, your uniform looks as good as new today, General, very spiffy."

"An excellent laundry service you have, Mr. DuBott. Thank you." George backed off a step, somehow apprehensive that DuBott was about to touch him, then nodded cordially to the manager and moved off to the corner windows. A damp zephyr fluttered the freshly starched curtains. Looking out he could see that fog still gripped the harbor, but there was pale sunlight above that would burn through by midmorning.

"I wonder what can be keeping Mr. Davis?"

"Who can tell? George said, startled. DuBott had followed him. The man must have the silent feet of a cat. How should he know what was keeping Jefferson Davis? He turned back to the window and breathed in the fishy flowery breeze, willing for DuBott to go away.

Exactly what was he doing here in this contradictory place? What was his mission? Hamlin had been good to bring him along, and to actually attend this first meeting was an unexpected gift. But Hamlin had told him nothing else. Of course he supposed the President was using him as a symbol of military power, there to intimidate Davis. He hoped he could look suitably grim and menacing. Practicing, he turned the corners of his lips down. Mean and serious.

Would Frenchy Beauregard be at the table with Davis? Funny prospect. Would they sit there making warlike faces at each other?

He was feeling oddly ambiguous. Trying to explain it to Nelly in a letter he told her he felt 'split in two.' A part of him wanted Hamlin and Seward to succeed in their mission, to thrash out a peace agreement. Yet an everlasting part of him was a soldier. Bill Russell's exciting ideas of war and strategy had stirred the old juices. He had been tempted to try to tell Mary Chestnut about it yesterday. But why? It was not her business.

Yes, hard to be rid of that old soldiering itch. But a civil war? Politics to the extreme, deadly battles with old comrades?

Horrible.

They must dodge it if at all possible. He walked back over to the food table, selected a small cube of yellow cheese and nibbled at it. Still if war came, and Hamlin asked him to take Richmond, he would do it with pride and honor, and a hell of a big army.

There's a thought.

An army sufficiently large and powerful could win the war without firing a shot. Take it to Richmond, show overwhelming muscle and make peace. Yes, that would be the best kind of army, and the best kind of war, where no one dies. He pleased himself with the idea, the famous McClellan theory of war, fabled in song and story ...

"May I interrupt your deep thinking?"

He turned around, looked up and there was President Hamlin glowering down at him like a thundercloud.

"I hear you had quite a nice little chat-chat with Mrs. Chesnut down on the Battery yesterday."

George felt like the victim of an ambush. Indians gave more warning. "We had ice-cream."

"Ice-cream? I was given to understand that you held some political discussion as well."

"That is true." Tread softly now.

"When did you propose to inform me of it?"

Surprise. He hadn't planned to inform Hamlin at all. "Mrs. Chesnut had very little to say that we have not already heard from other sources, sir, except for one surprising thing. She is opposed to slavery."

"Oh, indeed? Hamlin scoffed. "She and her husband have a peculiar way of showing it. Was there nothing else?"

"Her 'political message,' if you could call it that, was to 'leave us alone, and allow secession to run it's course.' I didn't think it worth troubling you."

"Yep, same old refrain," Hamlin said, dismissively. "Still, you should have reported the conversation."

George pondered a moment, then said, "May I inquire of Your Excellency from what source you heard of my contact with Mrs. Chesnut?"

Hamlin gave him a blank look, then said, "Mr. Stanton told me yesterday evening."

"Mr. Stanton? But he never leaves the ship. How could he know anything of what I do?"

"I can solve that puzzle, General," John Hay popped up. "Mr. Stanton, out of boredom perhaps, has taken to haunting the Captain's deck. Since he is afraid to go ashore, he surveys the city with a telescope. It is his main occupation these days. When you had ice-cream with Mrs. Chesnut, I guess you were within eye range of him."

"The man is a coward," George said, "and now we know him to be a liar. He could not have heard our conversation."

"Be all that as it may, General," Hamlin lectured like the school master he once was, "it is best to leave the politics to us."

George's cheeks burned, but he took it as his duty to remain mute in response to the President. 'Brace and take it,' as they said at West Point. He would have some savory words with Mr. Stanton who had professed to be his friend and political mentor. Enough of that horse shite.

Hamlin clicked the silver lid of his pocket watch. "He is late now by a full half hour. They get us down here, then make us wait two days. Now they make us wait some more. I will give him until half past nine, then we will be but a memory in this place."

No one said anything. Hamlin tapped his foot. George thought about Stanton. Everything he had been told by the man was now suspect. Stanton had fumed that Hamlin, not sure enough of himself, had come under the sinister influence of Secretary Seward.

"They will be too soft," Stanton had told him with a sneer. "They will give away the store to the secessionists."

"So Mrs. Chesnut wants us to leave them alone does she?"

George's lips tightened. Hamlin was back. Why the devil was Hamlin picking on him? "She framed it so as to be a message from Colonel Chesnut," he said.

"Ah, yes," Hamlin said, the Colonel, that great moderate. Where have I heard such talk for the last twenty years? Why, I know! In the Congress from that poor picked-on minority of Southerners. They get to count three-fifths of their slaves for congressional districting and then complain of ill treatment. What a mistake that was in our constitution. It will be changed if I have any say about it."

"Change what you can when you can," Seward interjected. "Let's not forget that our goal here is to glue up the Union."

"Oh, you can stop preaching that sermon to me, Bill. I'm in your choir. But I have faint hopes, the more I see of these people. That trip to the island yesterday was a futile gesture that could've got me killed but for the bravery of General McClellan here." Hamlin looked at George, curiously, as if seeing him for the first time "By the way, General, pardon my testy manners. I am not in a happy disposition today."

"There is nothing to pardon, sir," George said, not quite meaning it. But at least the President understood who saved his life.

Hamlin thrust his hands in his trouser pockets and began a short back and forth pace.

"We just may have to come down here with guns blazing," he said, side-glancing at George again. "Perhaps I should order Anderson to open fire now, get it over with. We'll all die heroes." He eyed his group with an uncertain grin.

Seward said, "Count me out of that program, old sport. I have a few good years left to enjoy as a live coward."

"I was speaking in jest," Hamlin snapped.

Seward pursed his lips, then ambled over to the food table, calling over his shoulder, "Say, boys, is anybody hungry? I think you could use a bite to eat, Mr. President. It'll soothe your nerves."

Hamlin had resumed pacing. "My nerves need no soothing, thank you."

George heard floorboards squeak in the main entranceway. He turned and saw that two men, Jefferson Davis and Judah Benjamin, had entered the ballroom.

Hamlin, Seward, Davis, and Benjamin had last seen each other only a few months before as fellow members of the U.S. Senate. Now there was a significant silence as their eyes met.

"Ah, well now," John Hay behind him whispered, "let the games begin."

George joined in the series of formal handshakes and stiff introductions, looking once again into the face of Jefferson Davis, the man who as Secretary of the Army had dispatched him on his grand study tour of Europe. Davis, his breath slightly tinted with wine, greeted him with small teeth framed in a thin lipped smile.

"I am most pleased to see you again, General McClellan. My goodness, it's been all of four years hasn't it? I note you have come up considerably in rank since last we met. My congratulations. Nothing like impending civil war for advancement in our profession, eh?"

"A regrettable fact, sir."

George wondered if Hamlin had caught the reference. Davis, a proud West Pointer, still considered himself a soldier. It was rumored that he would take the field in command of the secesh army should war come. Now he stood stiffly erect, looking fit enough for such duty, though George noted that the fine lines that etched his face were deeper. His head was still a model of high patrician pedigree with the full forehead, square and high, and the jutting cheek bones, contrasting with sunken, shadowed jaws. The only feature that marred the face of Jefferson Davis and threw it lopsided was the sickly, clouded left eye.

"Gentlemen, please be seated." Alexander DuBott, playing the role of host to the hilt, gestured to the long mahogany table.

"Sir, I am pleased to inform you that we shall be seated only when we choose to be seated." The words, soft and sweet as creme brulee,' came from the mouth of Judah Benjamin. George had heard of Benjamin, the so-called "Jew of New Orleans," successful attorney, planter, U.S. Senator, and now Attorney General, of the Confederate States of America. With a plump torso shaped like a pear, Benjamin's round, chubby face normally wore a perpetual inward turning smile. But not now.

"Who in hell are you, sir?" he said to the hapless DuBott.

"Why, I am Alexander DuBott, sir." The manager made a last desperate clutch at his toppling dignity. "I have the honor to be the manager here at the Mills House."

"Go do your managin' somewhere else, and don't be tellin' us when we should sit down. Get me a cup of tea, three sugars."

DuBott's face bloomed pink as he hurried off, snapping fingers at the serving boys.

"Do I have your permission to sit, Mr. Benjamin?" Hannibal Hamlin asked with a cool quirk of an eyebrow.

100

"By all means, Mr. President Hamlin," Benjamin said with a broad grin. "By the way, congratulations on your recent promotion, sad as the circumstances were."

Without further comment Jefferson Davis sat opposite Hamlin. George and Johnny Hay quickly found places for themselves. Secretary Seward strolled up munching a sandwich he pronounced as: "Turkey salad. Uncommon good."

Hamlin gave him a strained look. "Can't you wait until lunch, Bill?"

"No, I can't. Meetings like this always make me hungry."

Bill Seward slouched down in his chair, grinned broadly across the table at Davis and Benjamin, and took another giant bite of his sandwich.

Someone coughed. Seward chewed. George cleared his throat and was about to make some harmless social remark, but thought better of it. Hamlin would likely take his head off. Don't mix in politics. Don't speak until spoken to.

Be careful.

"Interesting you should say that, Bill." It was Judah Benjamin. "Meetings like this, ya say? Gives one to believe this is old hat to you. Here I was under the assumption that we were doin' something by way of being historical here today."

"What's old hat to me is history itself," Seward said, with chipper self assurance. "Before every war, usually, some arbitrators like us sit down at a table like this and try to twig things out."

"Usually what happens then, Bill?" Hamlin asked. George saw he was relieved that words were at last crossing the table.

"Oh, they either have a war or they don't," Seward replied. "Whatever happens, we all escape with our lives." He cackled a laugh.

"Ah, well," Davis said, "let's us proceed then." He fixed a stare above Hamlin's head. "To whom it may concern, I am Jefferson Davis, President by act of Congress, Confederate States of America."

George felt sweat bead on his forehead. He looked at Johnny Hay who grimaced back at him. Yes, let the games begin. He noted the time on his pocket watch, 9:34a.m.

Hamlin sat unmoving for a silent minute, then leaned forward. "I do not recognize your Congress. How can I recognize you as officials of a government whose existence I deny?"

Jefferson Davis shrugged and gazed around the table. "Yet, here we are, Mr. President Hamlin, living and breathing men. How do you account for that? Moreover, how do you account for your presence here among us?"

Score a hit. Could the grouchy Hamlin muzzle himself? George waited to see.

Benjamin joined in. "Yes, how do you propose to view us then, Mr. President?" There was a hint of a lisp. "Are we but ghostly figments of your imagination?"

"I view you, sir, as what we all are, and can agree that we are, Americans." Hamlin's reply was as calm as if they were discussing crop prospects.

Hamlin nodded gravely to Davis and continued. "I recognize you sir, as a distinguished gentleman from the state of Mississippi, who has served his country honorably as a U.S. Senator and Secretary of War." He inclined his head toward Benjamin. "You, sir, are an accomplished New Orleans attorney and former Senator, but you hold no official title I am obliged to respect."

Benjamin put a hand to his mouth. "Oh, dear, no respect? My feelings are hurt."

Seward stuck a finger in his collar and pulled. "Say, it's getting hot in here already. How about something cool to drink?"

Davis waved to one of the servants hovering near the entrance.

"Lemonade for all."

"Put some ice and orange juice in mine," Seward said.

The servant went to the food table and conferred with DuBott who was staying well out of the way.

Hamlin gave Seward a stressed smile. "Are you quite comfortable now, Mr. Secretary? Ice is on the way."

"Why, I am always comfortable in Charleston, Mr. President. How could I not be in the company of such a fine and noble citizenry? If I am not mistaken, Mr. Benjamin, didn't you originate here?"

"Close on to it. My parents brought me to Charleston when I was ten. They were dealers in fruits at the dockside market here. I can still tap up a melon right smart." George looked at the hawk-nosed Secretary of State with bemused admiration. The man was all but breaking his neck to maintain a gracious atmosphere at the table to keep them talking. He caught Seward's eye, and got a quick wink in return.

Jefferson Davis glanced at Benjamin, then placed two fingers to the bridge of his nose, and closed his eyes.

"I will accept your perplexity about official recognition of our government, Mr. President. Yet we are here to talk," Davis said. His neck arched back and he focused on Hamlin with his one good eye.

"Yes, we are here to talk," Hamlin came back swiftly, "as good and concerned Americans."

"Well," Davis said, "I can accept that characterization. We meet with honorable intent to search out some common ground of agreement, if such be achievable."

"Well, then," Seward bounced in. "The job's half done, since we are all men of reason and good will." He beamed a confident smile around the table.

George was beginning to like the Secretary of State.

"If it's peace we're talking," Davis spoke in a low tone, almost as if to himself. "Why is the distinguished General McClellan here, much as I admire him personally." He flicked a thumb at George. "You will notice that I have no military advisor present. General Beauregard is not a party to this conference."

"I am sure General Beauregard is most actively engaged in sighting in the forty-eight guns that surround Fort Sumter,"

Hamlin said. "How does the computation go, General McClellan?"

"We count thirty cannon, and eighteen mortars aimed from four different directions," George told him, relieved to hear his own voice at last.

"And I believe, Hamlin said, "that you have upwards of seven thousand men stationed all around the city, facing down our Fort Sumter garrison of some seventy men. Strong odds, sir. Strong odds. I need sound military advice, therefore General McClellan stays."

George touched his mustache. Thank you Mr. President. All is forgiven.

Davis pursed his lips, then spoke deliberately. "We are," he said, "assembling military force for our defense because we fear, sir, that the President and the Congress of the United States may be disposed to exert military coercion in opposition to our rights of secession. After all, we ask no more than to be left alone, to live in peace, but we fear that the fire eaters of the North, to use the word you have coined to describe some of our public men, will seek to march into the South and spawn servile rebellion in the spirit of John Brown."

Seward chuckled. "I believe, Mr. Davis, that the last servile rebellion you had down this way was when a mad-drunk preacher named Nat Turner cut loose back in the thirties."

"And killed sixty people." Davis threw a hard look at Seward. "There is nothing laughable about it."

Hamlin rose from the table and clutched at the satin lapels of his coat. "I agree, sir, but Turner was a unique and isolated incident. I assure you that I was not an advocate or supporter of John Brown. Justice was served by his hanging. Let that be an end to it."

Davis and Benjamin remained silent.

Hamlin cleared his throat and seemed to search for his next thought, even as he spoke. "So you seek to go your own way," he said. "To be left alone, as you put it."

"That fact has been public knowledge for many months now," Davis said with a nudge of sarcasm.

Judah Benjamin spoke in a loud mock whisper. "We are about to be informed, I fear, that we have not the right of secession."

"Be cautious in your assumptions, Mr. Benjamin. You may yet be surprised today." Hamlin strolled to the corner window where the shimmer of Fort Sumter could be faintly discerned in the brightening morning haze. "I have been cracking the books of the founding fathers, Madison especially, and in his opinion this union of states was founded by the American people and not by the individual states themselves. If so, it would be absurd to recognize a right of secession. The constitution would require unconditional adoption, 'in toto, and forever.'"

"My dear sir," Benjamin said, with centered self assurance, "nothing is forever."

"Agreed, Mr. Benjamin, if you choose to be so literal. But I think you take my point."

"Of course, I take your point, sir. You're telling us we have not the right of secession. I said you would say that, and now you've said it. *Fait Accompli.*"

George studied the animated face of Judah Benjamin, who, as a young man, had been thrown out of Yale for reasons publicly unknown. It was publicly known that he was married to a wife who made her residence in Paris. Prickly, agreeable, yet bizarre was this Judah Benjamin. A bad man to face in court.

Davis rose and squinted with his one good eye at Hamlin as if measuring and matching himself with the other man.

"I believe," he said, "in one of his speeches, Mr. Seward here made reference to what he called 'A higher law,' meaning as I take it, a law higher than the Constitution. I must voice my profound agreement, sir. That higher law grants us the God-given right of revolution for our political self-determination."

He strolled up to Hamlin face to face. "Now sir, I submit to you that all seven states of our Confederacy have acted in concert, and I am their duly chosen executive. We have acted in good faith and in good cause, namely the protection of our rights of property as well as political and personal security, and I submit to you that we have the power to enforce our revolution, exactly as our ancestors enforced their revolution against King George of Great Britain."

"Suppose we leave off higher law," Hamlin responded, "and get back to the plain old law of the Constitution. Will you grant me the floor now, and let me have my say."

Davis bowed his head, looked over to Benjamin and winked with his one good eye. "The floor is all yours sir, but seven states are missing." Davis kept straight faced as he resumed his seat.

Hamlin nodded sharply and pulled some crumpled pages from his coat pocket. "There is in the Constitution," he said, glancing at them, "no right or power residing in the states of unilateral secession. The writers of that document intended no such contingency and made no such provision. Accordingly, I adhere to President Lincoln's theory of the case, that no States have in fact left or resigned or seceded from the Union, because no due process of law has run its course. You can make all the speeches you like, proclaim whatever revolution you like, and wave your banners and sing your songs til you're blue in the face, South Carolina and the other six are still member States in this Federal Union."

Jefferson Davis' face was blank. Judah Benjamin studied the back of his right hand.

"That being said," Hamlin pressed on, "I will confound your expectations by affirming that under certain circumstances one, some or all of the several States could in fact secede from the Federal Union. Isn't that correct Mr. Seward?"

A wispy smile played over Bill Seward's lips as he sat back comfortably, his fingers laced behind his head. "Right as rain, in my opinion Mr. President."

Davis looked at Benjamin. "What did I just hear, Mr. Benjamin? Are my ears failing me?"

A servant arrived with glasses of iced lemonade and a tea for Benjamin.

Seward snatched one and took a gulp, "That sure hits the spot. Nothing can daunt us now."

Hamlin fingered his frosty silver cup but did not drink. "Three of us here are lawyers," he said, "although I'm not certain about you, Senator Davis."

"I have consorted enough with lawyers," Davis said, "to mark me as an accomplished amateur."

"Ah, we will deem you an honorary lawyer then for this discussion. Now then my theory is this: View the constitution as a partnership contract between the States."

Davis interrupted. "But I thought you just claimed it to be an agreement of the people of the several States, and not of the States themselves."

"Well," Hamlin paused, brought up short, "yes, but for discussion's sake, let us say it was an agreement between the States as well. That better reflects your thinking anyway does it not?"

Davis smiled. "As the old Greeks would say, we are merely speculating in cloud cuckoo land."

Hamlin took a breath and ploughed on. "Due Process of Law. That's my point, Senator Davis, the constitution is a binding agreement between States, between peoples, of the States, however you want to see it. So let us call it a partnership between the States."

"Very well," Davis said.

"But we are not agreeing to anything," Benjamin cut in.

Seward laughed, "Oh, damn and perish the thought. We couldn't abide seeing you agree with us on anything! Why we might keel over in a faint from the shock of it."

Hamlin took a quick sip of lemonade. "Now then," he said, "as true in any partnership, all parties to the contract, or at least a majority, must agree as to the general course of action of the partnership. Who are your partners in our Federal Constitutional Partnership? They are the States, sir, States every bit as sovereign as Georgia or Alabama or your own Mississippi. The State of Wisconsin for example, is party to this agreement, and has standing in this meeting because I represent the people of Wisconsin, also of Ohio, Pennsylvania, yes, and even Massachusetts, sickening as that may be to you."

"That's why we seceded," Benjamin said. "We could not stand the sanctimonious stink of Massachusetts."

"Well, they can't stand the flowery stink of South Carolina," Hamlin shot back. "Furthermore they are mighty disapproving of seven States gamboling off on their own hook with no by-your-leave from their partners. Gentlemen, don't you realize you have just gouged a huge chunk out of the United States of America and you expect us to roll our eyes Heavenward and accept that with saintly passivity? What if Great Britain tried to do that to us? What would our recourse be?"

Davis sighed heavily. "No, sir, we do not expect you to accept our action, rightful as it may be. We fully expect you to make war on us, thus the troops and guns gathered here for self defense. Or at least," he said, with a severe stare at Hamlin, "I expected Lincoln to make war on us."

"Speaking of Lincoln," Seward said. "I am reminded of some advice I was about to give him before he died. You recall, Mr. President, that letter I was writing to him? How I told him not to let the political issue of slavery break up the Union. I had another idea as well."

Hamlin winced. "I don't think we need to hear that one right now, Bill."

Benjamin jounced like a delighted child. "Oh, do tell us. Let us have no secrets here."

Seward looked at Hamlin who was glowering. "Oh, it was just an idea I had that might extract us from our difficulties." He hunched forward. "Now, I warn you, it may seem like a sort of desperate, radical kind of thing."

"We shall try to control our astonishment," Benjamin said.

George shot a questioning look at Johnny Hay. Got a shrug in return.

Seward stood up and looked around the table. "My thought was to demand explanations from France and England."

There was a long pause. "Explanations?" Davis said, his face a cloud of bewilderment. "Explanations for what?"

"Why anything or everything. We'll accuse one or both nations of some vile insult to the honor of the United States. It don't matter what. We'll trump it up."

Benjamin nodded as he caught on. "Ah, yes," he said, "and if we trump it up ourselves we can be assured the offense will be sufficiently vile."

"I don't believe I understand," Davis said.

"War, sir," Seward said, resounding with pride of authorship. "War to unite the country. A war crisis that gets us all pulling on the same wagon team again. The UNITED States of America! Why, my friends think on the opportunity. We are about half organized for it already. Just consider, war with Great Britain, a huge national Army marching up through Canada which we conquer with ease and then break it up into three or four new States before the British Lion can bite back."

"Free States no doubt," Davis said with a grunt.

"Oh, never mind that," Seward said. "Or, say we head further South, kick the French out of Mexico, net ourselves three or four new States down that way."

"Slave States?" Benjamin asked, his eyebrows arched innocently.

"Well, who knows? We'll see. Perhaps we could attack both countries simultaneously, with General McClellan going north and General Beauregard going south."

Hamlin had heard enough. He reached up to tug at Seward's sleeve. "Very well, Bill, you've presented your idea."

Seward sat down, eyes blazing.

George squinted at the Secretary of State. Had he heard right? Seward would unite all the States in a war against a European power? Or Mexico? Or Canada? What an astounding scheme, brilliant or appalling. What an army that would take! Should he offer comment? Hell, no!

Hamlin puffed out a sigh. "If we declare war on Great Britain there will be Canadian troops marching right down through Maine. The first stop they make will be at my farm to burn it." He gave a strained laugh.

109

"Not if we strike first and fast enough," Seward said, deadly serious.

Hamlin lifted both hands and spoke with a ring of mockery. "Well, what do you say? Shall we put differences aside and unite in a war?"

Davis frowned then smiled tentatively "It is one of those ideas that perhaps sounds intriguing," he began, "but, I just don't see how, practically, it could be achieved."

"It is a worthy daydream," Benjamin pitched in. "Possibly when our current matters are settled, why I for one wouldn't object to a joint attack by our two nations on Canada. There's more than enough territory up there for all of us and there's nothing on it right now but trees and bears."

"Yes," Seward, said, straining with frustration, "but to do it, we must be one Nation. Don't you see? That's the whole point." He sent a pleading look at Hamlin. "That's the whole point."

"Very well, Bill, you've offered us all much food for thought," Hamlin placated. "Now here's a proposal of my own." He stood up.

"I certainly hope it will be just as interesting," Benjamin said with an expectant look around the table. "I didn't expect to have so much fun today."

"No fun," Hamlin said, "just some plain old practical politics. Suppose we have a constitutional convention in, let's say, three months time? Place it in a border State such as Tennessee for convenience of travel. Memphis has some fine hotels I hear."

Davis and Benjamin listened.

"In the intervening three months I would suggest you have a referendum among the citizens of your seven States. Ask them if they wish to leave the Union? That has yet to be done, you know. If, at that time, it is still the will of your people to set up shop on your own terms, then let us reason and grind it out properly, under due process of law, and not as you have acted so far, in criminal conspiracy."

Davis snapped a sour look up at Hamlin.

"Let us be guided by the words of George Washington who said:" Hamlin read from one of the note papers he had been holding: "'The Constitution binds us, until changed by an explicit and deliberate act of the whole people, it is sacredly obligatory upon all.' Therefore, I am merely suggesting that which is implied by the Father of our Country. If we are to split apart, let it be under due process of law, not by the gun and the sword."

"Criminal conspiracy, sir," Benjamin said, "are harsh words, indeed." He looked at Davis. "Very harsh indeed."

"It is harsh actions they describe, Mr. Benjamin. When the legal property of the Central Government is appropriated by force, unlawfully and against the will of its rightful administrators, I call that thievery, which was called criminal when I studied the law. And when such criminal action is brought about by the will, cooperation and direction of State officials, I call that Conspiracy, sir. I know no other term for it."

"Yes, but there is sound legal theory for our actions," Benjamin replied, primed to argue. Jefferson Davis laid a restraining hand on his companion's arm.

"Let the President go on," he said.

George thought on Stanton's words. Was Hamlin giving away the store? Didn't sound like it so far.

Hamlin shuffled through his papers some more. "I have a list here of all the Federal properties that your people have stolen from us." Hamlin cleared this throat, then began to read: "January 5th, this year, Fort Morgan and Fort Gaines, seized at Mobile. January 6th, Federal arsenal seized at Apalachicola, Florida. January 7th, Fort Marion at St. Augustine, Florida, January 9th, Fort Caswell, North Carolina ...."

* * *

Jefferson Davis' bad eye had begun to pain. He squeezed the bridge of his nose for relief, guessing now that the essential business of the meeting was over. Hannibal Hamlin would continue droning on from his list. Davis searched his memory.

111

So far the Confederacy had taken over a hundred Federal properties. Was Hamlin going to read the entire list?

Yes, he probably would. Some kind of a ploy designed to unnerve.

Davis put a hand to his lip, resisting a smile. He would allow Hannibal Hamlin to ride this rhetorical hobby horse to the last. He had always liked the man from their days in the Senate, through they had been constantly at odds on all the slavery issues and most everything else as well. Some newspaper writer, he recalled, had once compared Hamlin to a sturdy old oak. Well, Davis thought, the image did fit, this stern New Englander who lived and breathed superior moral certainty.

Yet, he had always liked New Englanders, the Bostonian Democrats and the others he had meet on their vacation tour in 1857. Varina had loved New England as well, the strolls along the beach, the camping in the cool, sweet-smelling woods. It had been most pleasant, but not as successful as he had hoped. The Presidential nomination would not be his, they told him, those jolly narrow-eyed Boston Democrats. Jefferson Davis, they said, was perceived as too much of a fire-eating anti-Union Southerner. He had made several speeches strongly supportive of the Union while in Boston, enough so as to get him criticized in Mississippi. He knew that for this reason the hard line secessionist were suspicious of him, afraid that he might turn out to be a sell-out Union man in wolf's clothing.

Hamlin was going on now about some obscure fort in Alabama that Davis had never heard of.

His wistful memories drifted back again to the New England trip. It had been a testing of the waters of course. He had wanted to run for the Presidency, but it was not to be. The party in 1860 split into three contentious factions, "a three-way mutual crucifixion," someone had called it. By their collapse of unity, they had allowed Abraham Lincoln to have the office fall plop in his lap.

Lincoln. He never would have made this trip to Charleston. He would have remained in Washington, puffed up with the honor of the presidency, making proclamations about his "oaths registered in heaven" to preserve the Union. Varina always said Lincoln reminded her of a camp meeting preacher, always on the job to correct each and every one of our faults. His beautiful, Varina. She had been so pleased last night to see her dear friend, Mary Chesnut. The women greeted each other at the railroad station like long lost sisters. Davis always felt comfortable with the smart talking Mary and her husband as well, a man of breeding and honor.

Hamlin was still reading.

Davis forced his mind back to the business at hand. What was the real reason behind Seward's silly proposal to incite a war with Britain and France? They had played that one like two black-faced minstrel comedy men, with everything but a song and a dance. What was behind it? He was anxious to chew that one over with Benjamin. And did McClellan know? Would the young general even be allowed to speak with him outside this room? Bright man, McClellan, and ambitious. As Secretary of War he had seen that early and thus chose McClellan to study war making in Europe. He might live to regret that choice.

More to the immediate point, what about Hamlin's proposal for a national convention in three months? Be careful here. That was no comedy. It could be a dagger thrust at the very heart of the Confederacy. For time was against them. Every day that passed without war or some new outrage would deplete the secessionist spirit. Hamlin was on strong ground when he argued against illegal appropriation of Federal property, but not a mention of the Republican cause of honor, slavery in the territories. Seward's influence there, no doubt.

Seward was not the harmless jester he made himself out to be. Beneath all the gruff was a kind man. Davis recalled the terrible time when his eyes had pained him to distraction. The doctors had required him to spend his days in silence in a darkened room. No one had visited him except Seward, who came every evening to report the doings of the Senate, with wildly funny parodies.

Hamlin was still reading from his list.

Davis glanced at Benjamin who raised his hands in a shrug. He's trying to unnerve us, Davis concluded, make us feel guilt. New Englanders are good at that.

Well, let it go, he would give Hamlin his time in the sun to express his outrage. Then tomorrow they would reject the national convention and reiterate the demand for the immediate evacuation of Fort Sumter. They would give Hamlin a deadline. Then the meetings would break up on the rocks of impossible differences. Hamlin and Seward would sail back to Washington and Davis would do what he had intended all along, find some excuse to open fire on Fort Sumter and give birth to the long talked about, long sought after, irrepressible conflict.

For he had been told, and well believed it, that in order to hold the Confederacy in line and to confirm the integrity of his infant Nation, he must, as the phrase was put to him, "throw blood in their faces." Yes, Davis told himself, we had better get this damn war going fast as we can.

Peace and too much talk will do us in.

CHAPTER TEN

George paced the deserted bridge of the Vanderbilt and took in a deep pull from his after dinner cigar. Late sunset glow played across the gentle lapping waves of Charleston Harbor. An offshore breeze came heavy with sickly sweet fragrance.

He could retire this evening with a sense of duty well done. After the meeting broke up, he had braced himself to attention and made a formal proposal to President Hamlin.

"Your Excellency, I recommend, in the interests of security, our whole party change its base from this hotel to the Vanderbilt."

"A capital idea," Seward had chimed in, "just in case we have to get out of town on the hop. We don't want a reprise of what happened when we landed. I'm still picking fruit out of my hair."

Hamlin, long faced and worn down from the meeting, had thought it over for a moment and tacitly agreed so they had quickly packed and moved back to the ship.

"Good evening, General." Sam Grant joined him at the bridge rail with a loose salute.

"Evening, Sam." The salute was returned with interest.

"That's a fine smelling one, sir."

George reached in to his inner jacket pocket and presented Sam with a Cuban cigar.

"Thank you, sir. Don't mind if I do."

George leaned over the rail and squinted down the Battery. "The town seems quiet enough."

"That's good." Sam fired up the stogie.

"Your men are posted?"

"Yes, sir, we're patrolling five blocks to the West, and up and down the Battery, disguised as civilians."

"Our uniforms tend to provoke these people. Each man has a pistol?"

115

"As you ordered, sir, to be used only if life is threatened."

"Very well, Sam. Perhaps we can enjoy a peaceable night."

"Sir, begging your pardon if it's none of my business, but can you tell me what went on at the conference today?"

George faced Captain Grant. "I would advise you to get your affairs in order, Sam. Make out your will if you haven't done so already."

Sam sucked a puff and chuckled. "My will is a mighty scrawny document, sir, not much white meat on it."

"Your family is still in Saint Louis?"

"At her father's place, yes, sir."

"Look to their safety. This war could reach Saint Louis. We may be fighting up and down the whole damn Mississippi before it's over."

Sam Grant shook his head. "What a shame."

"A shame and a tragedy. We'll be fighting our own friends."

"You were feeling more optimistic before the meeting, sir."

"Before I saw those men today, Sam. They've got ramrods up the backbone. President Hamlin tried legal arguments on them with no effect. They sat there and smiled, and made their sneering remarks. I don't see how we'll move them. They want a war for whatever reason, and they're primed for it."

"I reckon we may be headed for home very soon and sudden then."

"That's why we're on this ship. I feel like the good shepherd who just got his lambs back in the barn."

Sam pointed with the orange tip of his cigar. "What's going on down there?"

George made out three figures on the gangplank. He recognized one as Patrick, the Irish mess boy.

"Where do you people think you're going?" He bellowed out at them.

Patrick looked up with a grin and waved a slip of paper. "Begging yar pardon, General, sar. We have been given leave to go ashore by our darlin' Captain Blackstone."

116

George's jaw gaped. That horse's ass, Blackstone must have been drunker than normal to issue such a pass. "Be cautious in your dealings with these people," he called down, "we are far from Boston."

Patrick gave a smart salute. "Aye, aye, General, sar. They can't help but to be lovin' us for we shall be on our best behavior."

George muffled a laugh. "See that you are, and do not tarry on these hostile shores."

Sam muttered behind him. "I'm sure as hell not delighted to see them going out there tonight, sir."

"Well, your men are around to look after them if they get in a scrape." George knew that was a foolish excuse. He should have ordered those boys to stay on the ship and had it out with Blackstone later. He strained to see against the gathering darkness. They had scampered off and were gone now, but he saw something else.

"Is that one of ours, the one with the long duster coat and straw hat?"

"I don't make him out to be one of our men, sir."

"Odd, just standing there in the doorway. What's he up to?"

"Want me to go see, General?"

"No, wait, he's headed this way."

George heard Sam unsnap the flap of his holster. The figure approached the sentries at the gangplank and spoke to them. George and Sam left the bridge on the double for the gangplank, blue cigar smoke trailing in their wake.

The sentry reported as they clumped down the ladder. "General McClellan, sir, this man claims he has an appointment with you."

"Oh, indeed." George could well imagine the kind of appointment. A hand thrust into the folds of the duster coat, coming out with a gun or a dagger. He could imagine the words too.

Up the Confederacy! Down the Oppressor! Glorious death could visit in an instant. George felt a thickness constricting his chest but he forced himself to march right up to the man.

"Ah, General McClellan, I am glad to see you, sir."

A thrill of relief at the burring Scottish accent. George laughed and turned to Captain Grant. "Ah, at ease, Sam, and you can holster your piece. I know this man."

"E. J. Allen reporting , sir."

George could just make out the little Scotsman's button eyes twinkling in the shadow of the broad brimmed straw hat. George put out his hand. "Well, Pinkerton. I had about given up hope."

"It's a relief to be among friends again."

George observed the detective's wrinkled, stained duster coat. "Did you have a difficult time of it, old man?"

"I've lived to tell the tale, General. What more could I ask?"

In a few minutes they were both with Seward and Hamlin in the ship's salon. George made the introductions.

"Your Excellency, Mr. Pinkerton has performed excellent service for me as a railroad detective. He also guarded the safety of President Lincoln on his trip to Washington."

"Yes, Mr. Pinkerton," Hamlin, said with cordial warmth, "I've heard your praises sung by President Lincoln himself. What brings you to Charleston?"

Pinkerton gave a sharp questioning look at George. "Why, I've been working for General McClellan, sir. He gave me the assignment of scouting in the seceded States and told me to report to him here in Charleston."

"Did you have any chancy adventures along the way, Mr. Pinkerton?" Seward asked.

"There were some unsettling moments I wouldn't want to reprise, sir. One false word in Memphis and I would've found myself necktied to a tree with no floor to dance upon."

"But here you are, Pinkerton, safe and sound," George said with a come-along smile. "I had no doubt you would complete your mission. I just didn't know when."

"Yes, and you look tuckered out, Mr. Pinkerton," Seward said, kindly. "Would you like something to eat and drink?"

Pinkerton breathed a weary sigh. "Anything at all would be most welcome, sir."

"Well, I'll see what I can rustle up in the kitchen," Seward went off crabbing.

"Those feckless mess boys all went ashore tonight."

Hamlin cocked a bemused glance at George. "I must say, you are full of surprises, General. You neglected to tell me about Mr. Pinkerton and his mission."

"Oh, that way he wouldn't be embarrassed if I had got myself hanged as a spy," Pinkerton said with a cool laugh.

"Pinkerton? Pinkerton? Who's he? Never heard of him."

George ignored the jab. "I took it upon myself to ask Mr. Pinkerton to discover the true opinions and feelings of the South, Your Excellency. I'm paying him out of my own pocket."

Hamlin pulled up a chair, sat down and eyed Pinkerton with frank interest. "Tell me everything."

"Well, by way of preface, it's not just my report, Mr. President," Pinkerton said. "I dispersed three of my best operatives through the South. We communicate with each other by telegraph in cipher. Among us all, I think we've taken a fair and true sample of opinion and feelings among the people and the politicians as well."

"Tell me about the politicians," Hamlin said. "Especially Jefferson Davis."

Pinkerton's small face brightened. "I can help you there. Lucky enough I was able to place a plucky operative very close to President Davis, in service to his family. She is in this city tonight at the Mills House Hotel. I just stole a meeting with her." Pinkerton allowed himself to gloat a bit.

Hamlin knit his brows, perplexed. "A spy in his very household? Is such a thing honorable, sir?"

Pinkerton's head jerked back and his eyes popped.

George interjected before Pinkerton could say something stupid, "If she is serving the interests of our country Mr. President, that's honorable enough in my book."

"Is she a slave then?" Hamlin asked, troubled.

Pinkerton eased back with a satisfied smile. "Well, she don't consider herself a slave and neither do I, though I do have

119

false papers that say I own her. I hired her services out to the Davis family when I was in Montgomery."

George barked a laugh and clapped the detective on the back. "Who else could plant a slave-spy in the Jefferson Davis household?"

"Thank you, sir. I knew you'd like it."

"Well, we are in a kind of war already," Hamlin said. "I suppose I must get used to such distasteful things."

"War can put arduous strains upon one's moral structure," George said. He hoped he didn't sound too preacherish. Pinkerton shot a raised eyebrow.

Hamlin sighed, still uneasy. "Tell us what you've found out, Mr. Pinkerton."

"Well, sir, I traveled myself down to Nashville, thence to Memphis, to Montgomery, and then made my way here. Went by the name Leroy Desmond, made out to be a Britisher in the cotton trade which led to plenty of political discourse as I had hoped it would. My other operatives covered New Orleans, Saint Louis and Atlanta and points between. We had planned our routes and our hotels so that their telegraphs came to me at the right time and place. Lots of cotton pricing and family matters discussed, don't ya know? It's a pretty fine code if I do say. Invented it myself."

Bill Seward came in from the kitchen carrying a tray.

"This is all I could find in the cold cupboard," he said. "We had it at supper and it was pretty good." He placed a plate of yellow cake and sliced fruit in front of Pinkerton, then poured a cup of coffee.

Pinkerton grinned up at him. "Why, thank you Mr. Seward. This is prime service indeed."

"That's what they say about me, ya know. As Secretary of State, I make a dandy waiter."

"Mr. Pinkerton is about to tell us what he found in the South," Hamlin said.

Seward wiped a crumb from his sleeve and sat down. "As the stalk of corn said to the farmer, 'I'm all ears.'"

Pinkerton cleared his throat and took a sip of coffee. "Ah, that's good. Well, gentlemen, as I traveled I could see changes in public thinking clear as the seasons shift. First, right after Lincoln died, they were whooping like Indians. War it would be and no doubt on it. A British traveling man had best say nothing against it. Rambunctious they were, guns everywhere, marching about, yelling and screaming. Their blood was up! They still hated Lincoln even after he was dead." Pinkerton held up and waved a stubby finger. "A sea change took place when you, Mr. President, announced you were coming here to Charleston. That was a stunner to 'em."

"Oh, you don't say?"

"Yes, sir." He paused to chew a bite of sliced apple. "People were utterly shocked, didn't know what to make of it. Last thing in the world they expected of you."

Hamlin nodded to the Secretary. "Mark up that one up, Seward. You predicted as much."

Seward squinted and cocked his head. "But they're still down on us, aren't they?"

"Well, yes and no. There is great curiosity as to what will happen when you meet Davis, Mr. President. They knew Lincoln would never have done such a thing, prideful as he was, and I say that as one who loved the man. But, gentlemen, here's the bedazzler. Mr. President, do you realize the effect your arrival had the other day? That march you made up Meeting Street? What it did to opinion in the South?"

Hamlin shrugged. "Today we saw the New York and Washington newspapers. They didn't think much of it. Some said I made an ass of myself and got what I deserved."

"Never mind, them, sir," Pinkerton said with some urgency. "In the South you were almost, well, I should not say a 'hero' exactly, but they saw that you marched bravely amid all the catcalls and flying vegetables. There is a kind of sullen respect for your courage all over the Confederacy and even some wishful talk that you might not use military coercion on the States. That is the talk among the people. As for the politicians ..."

"I am no hero to them."

"No, Mr. President, they fear you."

"Fear me?"

"Yes. They fear that you may doom the Confederacy."

Hamlin's eyes narrowed. "Well now, you have my interest."

"What I mean, Mr. President, all my operatives tell me, and I confirm it. Davis leans toward a civil war to pull and hold the South together."

Hamlin's jaw tightened. "War to unite the South."

"Exactly, sir. We all know there is distrust between the peoples of the sections, North and South, but that is nothing compared to the jealousy and animosity between these politicians of the Confederacy. Jefferson Davis will attempt to hold them in line but they are ready to turn on him like a pack of wolves should he falter. Secession has been like a poison brain tonic for some of these people. Brings out the worst in 'em, you know?"

Hamlin said, "How true. What you would have me do then?"

"Do nothing, Mr. President. Give the fools enough time to stew and fester in their own juice and they will split like a rotten tomato. Do nothing to give them an excuse for war. Even now, Jefferson Davis carries a message on his person from a close and trusted advisor. It states and I quote..."

He pulled out a small, tattered notebook. "You must throw blood in their faces, and soon, or the whole Confederacy will be gone up. Hamlin may be harder to provoke than Lincoln, but you must do it."

Hamlin stood up, his face coloring at the mention of his name. Pinkerton snapped the book shut, "I say, dodge war now, sir, and this whole rotten Confederacy will die of its own incoherence. And that's the opinion of me who's been among 'em, and someone else as well." Hamlin asked the unspoken question with a lift of an eyebrow.

Pinkerton said, "Last night found me in Montgomery at the hotel barroom celebrating my upcoming departure which is the

122

best thing that can happen to you in Montgomery. Well, I was joined, quite unexpectedly, by a high-falutin official of the Confederacy, a little fellow just so high, looks like a boy with a bad case of fever scars on his cheeks. In my honor he ordered up the drink of my homeland. Then a curious thing happened. This man, when he sat down, was Vice President of the Confederacy. But the more Scotch whiskey poured down our gullets, why, damned if he didn't transform into a Union man."

Seward snorted and grinned. "Don't tell me you were drinking with that peanut, Alex Stephens?"

"I was indeed, sir, Alexander Stephens himself. Spent the evening with him 'til there was no more evening. Near missed the early train this morning by a hair. You see 'tis easy for a Scotsman to pass for English in Montgomery, Alabama. I was so convincing I near started to despise myself."

"Stephens is honorable," Seward said, "and well respected, even if he's the tiniest man I ever laid eyes on. In Congress they used to call him the Giant Dwarf."

George spoke up without thinking. "Didn't he make a strong argument against secession in the Georgia Legislature last winter, just before they went out?" He caught a curious look from Hamlin.

"That's exactly what he told me, sir," Pinkerton said to George. "He even quoted that speech. 'The greatest curse that can befall a free people is civil war.'"

"Then why is he the Vice President of the Confederacy?" Hamlin asked.

"He gave it all his best," Pinkerton said, "but when Georgia went out he felt bound to go with his State. Reluctantly."

Hamlin grunted. "Reluctantly. Of course. The State comes first with these people. Did you learn anything else from him that may be of help to us?"

Pinkerton flipped pages in his notebook. "Understand I was a might jangled by the distilled malt of my homeland. By the end words was gettin' slippery. Oh, here 'tis." He read: "Two kinds of secessionists he says there are. The mad dogs, which is the ones here in South Carolina, forever lookin' for an excuse to secede. Full of hatred they are, but a small minority. Then there's what he called the canny ones. Their motto is: 'We can get a better deal outside the Union than in it.'"

Pinkerton glanced up from his notebook. "You see to them, secession is more like a withdrawal from a sour venture. They hope to forge a deal, then pop themselves back in the Union like good lads. Stephens is one of these. He thinks there's room for compromise, but then he is the most anti-secessionist Confederate I met in all my travels. If it was up to him and they'd all be back in the Union tomorrow, kissin' the stars and stripes."

Hamlin rubbed his chin, looked at Seward, but said nothing.

"I liked the little fella," Pinkerton said. "He's got grit. Oh, and another remark he made that stumped me. Perhaps you'll interpret it. He said if Davis couldn't be the President he wanted to be, he got to be the president he could be. Said it with a big wink like I was supposed to be in on the shenanigan."

Hamlin looked the question around the room. "Any thoughts?"

George cleared his throat. "Your Excellency is aware that I am a member of the Democracy."

Hamlin made an impatient sound. "Yes, yes, we all know you're a Democrat, General McClellan."

"I believe I know what Mr. Stephens may have been referring to."

George waited to see if Hamlin was going to be riled.

"Go on," the President said.

"I have heard stories from some of the New York and Boston men of my party. They say that Jefferson Davis made a bid to be considered as a nominee for President three years ago. They said he was like a leopard changing from spots to stripes, even made some speeches favorable to the Union in Massachusetts."

Seward let out a shrill chuckle. "Well, by golly, I do recall that now. Didn't take much notice of it at the time though. I twigged the sea air had rusted his wits."

124

"I was told," George said, "by men who know, that he seriously desired the presidency, and made his wishes known."

"Presidency of the United States?" Hamlin asked, his face a marvel of astonishment.

"So I was told, Your Excellency," George shut his mouth. He would say no more unless asked.

Hamlin pursed his lips. "So the Confederacy came along making him the President he could be. Well, it's an intriguing hypothesis, I suppose, but I don't see it does us much good."

George didn't know whether to be relieved or irritated. Davis had wanted to be President. It seemed an important idea to him, but why?

Hamlin stood up, went to Pinkerton and placed both hands on the man's diminutive shoulders.

"It's getting late and I know you're tired," he intoned in his politician's rumble. "Thank you, Mr. Pinkerton, on behalf of the United States of America, for your brave service. General McClellan, I shall see to it that you are not out of pocket in all this, even if you are a Democrat."

Then he dismissed them.

When McClellan and Pinkerton had gone, Hamlin slumped back in his chair and gazed dreamily into the lamp light. No answers there. He began idly fingering a napkin.

Seward strolled by, juicily munching on a leftover slice of orange.

"Well, Bill?"

"Well, Mr. President?"

"What in God's name went on here tonight?"

"We met a brave man who gave us commendable service and we are obliged to General McClellan for bringing it about."

Hamlin threw the napkin to the floor. "McClellan gets my back up, always proclaiming that he's a Democrat, yet loyal to the Union. As if we're supposed to be grateful."

"I am grateful," Seward said. "So many of these army officers are going South. Don't forget, Han, whatever happens, we're going to need the McClellans and the rest of the Democrats."

"Oh, I know, I know." Hamlin rubbed his eyes, felt a headache waiting in the wings. He thought of Ellen, missed her healing touch, then put the memory aside for later. "Do you believe that cock and bull story about Davis seeking the Presidency?"

"Yes," Seward said with sober dignity, "I do. I believe both the cock and the bull."

"Then you're too gullible. What do we know about Pinkerton, after all, except that his services are for hire? And what do we know of McClellan really except that he is a Democrat, sympathetic to the South like Anderson and the rest. Perhaps we were given a message tonight from Davis himself, or from Alex Stephens or God knows who. Fact is, I don't trust anybody fully."

"Well, I must say, you're in a foul temper tonight, Your Excellency. Come, let's mosey up on deck and have a smoke, if you'll trust me not to stab you in the back with a butter knife."

Hamlin rose and wiped a hand through his hair. "I need to sleep, Bill. What's more I need to think, and can't do both." He stopped and grinned. "Ah, but it is a comfort to know that I am such a hero in the South to people like Alex Stephens." He intended that to get a laugh from Seward and it did.

"Say, there's a good story about him they tell," Seward said. "One of his enemies in some argument came up to him and said, 'Why, Alex Stephens, you scrawny little runt, you're so tiny I could eat you.' And old Alex says, 'That's right. You could eat me. Then you'd have more brains in your belly than in your head.'"

Laughter echoed over darkened Charleston Harbor as Hamlin and Seward emerged on the upper deck.

Hamlin came to his cabin door, placed a hand on the brass knob. Maybe it was the cool air or the darkness that helped, but he felt his lawyer's mind clear with thoughts coming more freely. He wanted to talk some more.

"Suppose you tell me this if I am to believe Pinkerton. In these months that I am to wait for the Confederacy to flounder and die by its own incoherence, our Union of States must continue to flourish. What, pray tell, should be our policy while we wait for this bad old Confederacy to die and go to hell?"

"Build up the Army," Seward said with authority. "Wait and watch along the border. Be ready for anything. Let the mails go through, collect as much customs at the ports as you can, but make no contentious moves. Oh, and one more thing. The fuse to the bomb is lit right here in Charleston, and we must throw water on it. Pull the troops out of Sumter."

"When?"

"Right now, right this minute, send 'em up to Fort Monroe and wait for Davis and Company to fold their tents."

"And get impeached when we get back to Washington?"

"Take the chance."

"Easy enough for you to say. So, you believe Pinkerton?"

"I do."

Hamlin paused to think. Davis as a candidate for President? Odd idea. Yet, McClellan knew the high flown Democrats.

"Do you think that was a true message concerning Davis? Did McClellan have it right?"

"Makes sense to me," Seward replied. "I know Jeff Davis. He would relish being President. So would his wife. So would I for that matter."

"Well, you might yet have your chance, Bill." Hamlin wondered if he was giving away too much. "I'm beginning to think I'm the wrong man for this job." Ah, well, the truth felt easier in the friendly darkness. He opened his heart. "Lately I've thought I shouldn't have come down here at all. Doing so, we gave legitimacy to these people, and for what? They won't buckle under, no matter what Pinkerton says. We're going to have to come down here with force, I see it now. Lincoln knew that."

"I'm not sure about Lincoln," Seward said. "The man was a mystery. But I tell you this, on the day he died he had not yet decided what to do about Sumter. Hold on or let go, that was the debate in the cabinet that day. Me, I was always for letting go." He waved at the harbor. "God damn it, Han, it's just a pile of bricks out there."

"I know that, Bill. I lean your way, believe you me. I don't want war, but how can I just allow these people to run wild in insurrection while hoping they'll regain their senses?"

Seward gave a resigned sigh. "Then what are we doing in Charleston, Mr. President?"

Hamlin waited to answer, finally faced it within himself. "Trying to accomplish the impossible?"

Seward's stark, wrinkled face was deeply etched in the lamplight from the portholes, drained of all laughter now. "Then it looks like maybe we just came down here to smell the orange blossoms before we have to smell the gunpowder."

* * *

George was back on Morris Island, that sun-blasted beach. The sky was blue, the wind was hot and he was stretched out on a picnic blanket, sipping cold wine and watching naked Mary Chesnut straddle the tube of the Blakely gun. She rode her black mount with zesty pleasure, her cheerful breasts heaving, her white thighs radiant and flexing.

A perfectly natural and healthy exercise. He would like to see Nelly do that.

Mary Chesnut grinned down at him. "Why I declare, General, I think you have a capital idea! Oh, my, yes, yes! Did you just think of that?"

Having Nelly ride the gun? Oh no, she was talking about the idea he had just explained to her, his way to avert the war. "I did, Madam, but I fear President Hamlin will reject such advice. He warns me to stay out of politics."

"Oh, pish and tish," naked Mary exclaimed, all breathy. "Tell him about it. Convince him. You can do it!"

"I appreciate your encouragement, Madam, and may I compliment you on your noble body as well."

"Oh my, it's so very nice to be appreciated, general. Thank you for your gracious remark. Would you care to mount up and ride with me?" She leaned back with an open, inviting smile, and he caught sight of the secret shadow between her legs.

128

Sharp pounding rattled the cabin door. George lurched awake.

"Who's out there?"

"Captain Grant, sir."

He fumbled in the darkness, found a match and struck it to the lamp.

"Be right with you, Grant."

He splashed tepid water on his face, got his shirt on, looked for his pocket watch, found it. Still the seductive dream echoed. How Mary Chesnut's imposing, rounded bosom contrasted with his wife's delicate little nipples. He started to button his trousers and felt the hard character of what Nelly called his 'manly sword' standing at erect attention. Decorum. Discipline. Control. Wash away the shameful dream. Duty awaited outside the cabin door.

Yet, there was something in it about Davis. Some idea he had. What was it? He opened the door, holding the lamp up and away.

"Yes, Sam. what is it?"

"Trouble, sir."

Well, of course, trouble. What the hell else would bring this man to his cabin at two and a half in the morning? But the simple dignity of Grant's grave, square face claimed respect, so no acerbic retorts.

"Go on."

"That Irish messboy, Patrick. Remember we saw him go ashore?"

"Yes."

"He's been killed."

George felt a kick in the stomach. "How?"

"At a tavern, as you might guess, sir, they got into it with some of the local patriots. Just a fist fight at first, they took it out in the alley."

"How was he killed?"

"Beaten with clubs, shot through the heart. My men heard the commotion, got there too late to save him, but they recovered the body. He's laid out in the storage room on the bottom deck."

George stepped to the rail, gripped it, took a deep breath of dank harbor air. Keep your mind clear. He could make out the ghostly light of Fort Sumter piercing the blackness of the harbor like a fading star. He was surprised that he could feel hatred for an insensate, masonry object.

"Can we know who did it?"

"I have my Lieutenant out and looking into that right now, sir. The other two boys have told me the circumstances. It don't seem to be an official killing, just some local, drunk uglies got into a fight with 'em over Fort Sumter. Would we give it up, or no."

"And I'm sure Patrick contended we would stay there til hell freezes over."

"That's about it, sir."

Shouldn't have let him go, George told himself. He felt the full blast of guilt.

"I am going to dismantle that idiot, Blackstone, limb by limb," he said.

"I'll help, sir."

"Has he been informed?"

"He's locked in his cabin, and won't come out."

"Oh, delightful. What if we have to get away from here in a hurry? Do we swim?"

"We're prepared to break down his door with an ax, sir."

"Not yet. Does President Hamlin know?"

"He's down below with the body, sir. He requests your presence."

"All right." George started, then paused. "Sam, do you think there is any danger we may be attacked? Perhaps it was an official killing."

"If they do attack, sir, we're ready. My entire company is on alert and under arms. Two platoons drawn up on the wharf and the third in reserve on deck."

"Good. Stay alert."

* * *

130

He found Secretary Seward in the passageway outside the storage room. Wearing a faded dressing gown, Seward looked badly wrung out, his eyes glossy and red tinged.

"Morning, General. Bad business."

"Yes it is. I'd say we've taken our first casualty of the war."

"I did like that young man, so chipper and cheerful he was. Full of life." Seward shook his head. "Full of life no more."

"Yes, very sad. If you'll excuse me, sir, I understand the President wants to see me." He paused. "Are you coming in as well?"

Seward's cheeks puffed a breath. "Nope, I've been told to wait out here."

George struck two sharp knocks on the door, then stepped inside the storage room to witness a stark tableaux. Lit by a single oil lamp, Hamlin stood in rigid stillness behind the corpse of Patrick Riley. The body had been draped with the national flag. As George moved closer he saw brown blood stains from the head had seeped through staining the red and white stripes.

"General McClellan, at your service, your Excellency."

For a long time Hamlin said nothing. His face was half hidden in shadows, but glistening tear streaks could be seen on his cheeks. Finally he shifted slightly, his eyes still locked down on the body. Only his lips moved.

"I have a question for you, General." Another drawn out pause. "In the event of war between the States, what do you think would be the ultimate outcome?"

George felt himself clinch at the impossible question. Every bit of training, experience, and mental habit called for him to equivocate with great caution. He was ready to lecture of unknown circumstances and unpredictable results then stopped cold. Hamlin was glaring at him with hard eyes from a bottomless depth. They wordlessly revealed that on this particular night, in this smothering makeshift morgue, the President did not wish to hear evasive quibbles. George ignored the voices of a thousand "ifs" that screamed in his mind.

"The Federal Union would ultimately prevail, sir."

"Would it be a long war or a short one?"

This was all wrong. If only they could be seated at a table, a cool bottle between them instead of a corpse.

"Sir, would you be more comfortable up on deck? Or in the salon perhaps?"

With contained intensity, Hamlin restated his question, louder this time. "Would it be a long war or a short war? Answer me!"

George deliberately took a moment. As the youngest cadet at West Point, he had never gotten used to being yelled at, though his friends shrugged it off. He smiled inwardly remembering his classmate, Tom Jackson of Virginia. They could yell in Tom's ear all day and he still looked like he was in another world.

Probably was. But now, think, then speak.

"I know the Southerners, sir, from West Point and later in the Army and the railroad business. I have always liked them and enjoyed their company. They have some admirable qualities, loyalty to family and friends, and to their native States. And they have some not so admirable qualities. They are hot tempered, quick to be insulted, and eager to fight. Sometimes they don't think so well. They are, all in all, a little bit crazy, but should they become involved in a war with the central government, they would fight to the death. Especially if we came down here. They would look on us as foreign invaders of their homeland. It would be a long war."

"In that case, how many causalities could we expect?" Hamlin pressed on, his anger cooled, but still intense.

"From both sides, sir?"

"Both sides are Americans, General." Hamlin's eyes were wild. He hissed exasperation. "How many Americans would die in such a war? Total?"

George had to draw the line. "That is impossible to predict."

A shout. "Try! Make the effort!"

George closed his eyes and imagined himself a flying god with the whole country stretched before him, the Eastern coasts to be blockaded, the Mississippi to be controlled, the central

States, Kentucky Southward to Tennessee, the key cities, Richmond, Atlanta, New Orleans to be conquered and occupied, and between them the railroads, the mountain barriers. He saw armies marching, cavalry ranging, battles flaring over all the land, then made his godlike estimate, then doubted, then doubled it.

"It could run well over three hundred thousand, your Excellency."

Hamlin's face went white. He clutched his stomach, reached down and tipped a white pine ammunition box on its side and sat on it. "Three hundred thousand you say?" A husky whisper, weighted with dismay.

"A guess, sir, but knowledgeable, based upon what I have seen in Europe."

Hamlin took out a folded handkerchief and pressed it to his lips, his eyes shut tight. He let out a soft groan.

"There is one principle of war, Your Excellency, always true, and that is it's unpredictability. When war is loosed, no man can forecast the outcome. But as a general ..." He stopped. The President wasn't listening.

"Three hundred thousand," Hamlin rasped. Suddenly he stood up, reached down and gripped the edge of the flag and ripped it away from Patrick's battered face. Shock. Staring eyes, purple bruised flesh, bloody broken teeth. Shock. George flinched back at the sight.

"I have a son, Charles." Hamlin's voice was distant. "He wants to write books. If we have a war," Hamlin said, with a father's pride, "Charles will be first in line to enlist, and my heart will break with fear."

"Yes, sir."

Hamlin gazed down at Patrick. "They should have cleaned him up better," he said gently. He reached with a trembling hand and closed Patrick's eyes. "Though, you must be used to seeing dead bodies, General, in your line of business."

"I have never become used to it." George felt tears welling but turned away to wipe his eyes. When he turned back he saw that Hamlin was back on the pine box, his head in his hands, his fingers distractedly clawing through his hair.

He looked up, his voice distant. "If we have a war, General, there will be many Patricks, and boys like Charles, on both sides, and most will have a mother and a father, sisters and brothers. I see many a hometown funeral. I hear many a parent's curse."

"Yes, sir."

"And all these boys who die, like Patrick here, all will be Americans. All will be my boys." He laid his hand softly on Patrick's forehead. What are we to do, General? What are we to do?"

George thought back to the shameful embarrassing dream of Mary Chesnut on the cannon. He had said something to her, but he was really speaking to himself in the way of dreams. He saw Jefferson Davis' face and the idea that came back to him now, risky and extreme, even dangerous, something he must never mention to Hamlin. It was not his place to engage in politics. Keep your mouth shut, George.

"Sir, permission to speak on political matters. Though I know you have told me not to..."

Hamlin waved a hand. "Oh, go ahead. Is this George McClellan, Democrat I am about to hear?"

"George McClellan, citizen, sir. It has to do with Mr. Davis." There was still time to back off. "You may find this idea presumptuous or even repulsive ..."

"Ah, I can hardly wait to hear it."

George spoke carefully as he outlined his suggested strategy. It still sounded crazy, like a terrible mistake. When he was finished, Hamlin let out a noise midway a grunt and a strangled laugh.

"You have your nerve, McClellan, to ask me to do such a thing."

"You are the only one who could bring it off, sir. With some grand gesture..."

Hamlin glared at him. "I don't know whether to give you a medal or place you under arrest."

134

"Well, your Excellency..."

"Quiet. Let me study this over. You ask me to do the unthinkable."

"Then it will come as a surprise to them, sir. Won't it?"

George saw a smile conquer Hamlin's face. "Yes, he would be surprised all right. Oh, yes, that's putting it mildly. Tell Secretary Seward to come in. I want him to hear this."

Seward's eyes popped when he heard it. "By, God, I thought my plan to get us into a foreign war was crazy enough. But this takes the cake." He frowned at Hamlin. "You're not actually considering doing it are you?"

"I don't know. Am I?"

Seward's fingers brushed the stubble of beard that was emerging on his chin. "Let's get up on deck where there's some fresh air. This place is hot and it stinks too."

"We stay here," Hamlin said. "Patrick is a party to this discussion. He can't help it if he smells bad. Now then, tell me, Bill, how would Davis respond to such a thrust?"

Bill Seward found another ammunition box, sat down on it. "Well, sir, it would be exactly like planting a bomb in his brain and lighting a match to it. What happens when a bomb goes off, General? Can you likely predict the results?"

George looked at both men. They were actually considering his proposal, the fruit of a sinful dream.

"I think he might go for it," Hamlin said, more to himself. "That's what scares me. He might actually bite on the hook."

Bill Seward peered at George. "You see, General, you've just proved to me that you are no politician, and could never hope to be one. No politician would dare do what you suggest because it goes against the grain of all our instincts."

Hamlin's voice took on a new energy. "All right, suppose the bomb blows up in our favor. We still have to resolve our position on slavery, here and in the territories."

"You know my solution on that one," Seward said.

"I know, Bill. It's a utopian plan to say the least, but it could work, given a chance."

"See here, Han, if he takes the hook in the first place, he's going to be looking for a way out on slavery. Agreed?"

"Yes."

"We'll accommodate him, give him the escape hatch. Because suddenly slavery's going to look a lot less important to him. I'll sell him on it, Han. You set the first hook and I'll reel him in. We talk fast and get out of town before he knows what hit him."

George felt his jaw gape. He closed his eyes and there was sweetly smiling Mary Chesnut on the cannon tube. "Why I declare, General, they're going to try it!"

"Predict his reaction," Hamlin said to Seward.

"He will be tempted," Bill Seward said, "if he is convinced you are sincere and not just trying to sell him a bag of dead cats."

"Whatever I propose will be sincere," Hamlin said.

"Then I'll back you all the way. Just remember they may hang us both from a lamppost when we get back to Washington."

"We'll worry about that lamppost when we come to it." Hamlin said, unsmiling, as he slowly drew the flag up over Patrick's battered face. "All my boys," he whispered. He stood silent for a long time, then turned to George.

"General, do you want a war? For promotion, for fame and glory?"

George's answer was sure and ready. "No, sir, I do not."

"Bill, do you want a war between the States?"

"Worst thing that could ever happen to us, your Excellency," Seward said, coldly somber.

Hamlin remained statue still, his eyes closed, his lips moving soundlessly. Then when he opened his eyes and spoke, George saw a transformation which made him seem to grow larger.

"I have made a decision, General. Give up hope of sleeping any more tonight. You are going to be busy."

CHAPTER ELEVEN

George squinted up at the rolling gray clouds overhead. The cold morning light at sunrise on the Charleston wharf predicted showers to come. He clutched soft bread wrapped around a chunk of charred bacon, put it between his teeth and chewed hard, then took a sip of hot coffee, strong enough to melt horseshoes. Amazing what you can stomach when you're tired and hungry enough.

He had been up and active all night. Hamlin had ordered the Vanderbilt on a trip through the darkened harbor to Fort Sumter. Delivering this order allowed Sam Grant to break down Captain Blackstone's cabin door only to find that officer flat on the deck, an empty bottle clutched to his chest. A disgusted President Hamlin had promoted Ensign Filmore to brevet Captain of the Vanderbilt. That young officer had stepped up to command of the bridge and proved himself with distinction.

Meanwhile George took passage on the harbor guard boat, a trim little side paddled steamer called the Nina. When the guard boat Captain heard the purpose of the trip he responded with instant, cheerful cooperation. The trip was a short one, only three-quarters of a mile to a scrubby little island in the harbor named Shute's Folly. On it was the old half-moon shaped masonry fort completed in 1811 and known as Castle Pinckney. Its garrison consisted of a veteran Sergeant named Jake Skillen and his fifteen year old daughter, Kate.

The Skillen family was not impressed or thrilled at the midnight visit of the acting General of the Army. In fact they grumbled loudly when George issued their orders, but years of obedience would not reverse in an instant. Bitter or not, they had quickly packed their small household and joined George in the Nina for a trip to Fort Sumter. George hoped that no daughter of his would ever roll her eyes with such disgust or voice such caustic insults.

Now on the wharf at six and a half in the morning, the Vanderbilt was getting up steam for its final run to Fort Sumter. Acting Captain Filmore strolled up displaying a new confidence.

"Good morning, General," he said. "We're about ready to cast off. Will you be going with us on this trip?"

George thought it over. He would not really be needed at Sumter. Better to stay here on the wharf with Sam Grant's company in case of any trouble. He eyed the shuttered ice cream stand. He could lie down on one of the outdoor tables and grab a few winks.

"I'll stay here, Captain Filmore. By the way, congratulations on your skills of midnight navigation. Is it true you threw Captain Blackstone overboard by the President's order?"

Filmore snapped to rigid attention. "I'm happy to report that Captain Blackstone is recovering from his indisposition."

"Ah, is that what you call it in the Navy?"

Filmore put a fist to his mouth and cleared his throat. "What do you think of the President's decision, sir?"

George allowed his eyelids to droop closed. So easy it would be to fall asleep on his feet, and now this boy Captain wanted to jaw over policy. "Just see to your duties, Filmore. There will be plenty of time to talk on the voyage to Washington."

"Yes, sir, it's just that some of the men are bitter, sir. About Patrick of course, but also about the President's action. That's why that bacon you're eating is burned to a crisp."

"Morning General. Morning Filmore." Sam Grant joined them, chock full of good cheer and munching a bacon sandwich. "Say this is the best bacon I've tasted in awhile," Grant said. "Somebody finally cooked it right. The coffee's good and strong too."

Filmore saluted, turned away and marched up the gangplank of his ship.

"What's got him riled?" Sam asked.

"Oh, we're all tired and out of sorts. What about your men, Sam, are they feeling rebellious?"

138

"They'll do as ordered, sir."

George looked around, confirmed they were alone. "What do you think, Sam?"

Grant pulled his pistol from its holster and inspected it for correct load. "Smart move," he said, under his breath.

George nodded. "Agreed. We're due at the hotel at nine and a half. We'll take one of your platoons with us for security. If you need me for anything I'll be over by the ice cream stand."

Captain Grant brought his heels together and saluted smartly.

George found the same table where he and Mary Chesnut had lately conversed. He unfolded his body on its hard planks and closed his eyes with relief. It felt good as a feather bed. He wondered what dreams might come.

* * *

President Hamlin and his party arrived at the Mills House ballroom later that morning to find Davis and Benjamin looking dour and uneasy. After some hesitant, polite small talk, Davis shoved his coffee cup aside. "I have a response to your proposal of a national convention, President Hamlin."

George studied the President. Amazing how his whole demeanor contrasted with his irate behavior of the day before. Hamlin now seemed to have a ballast of contentment centered within himself, a sign of the relief he felt with the decision made. He glanced at George with a trace of a smile and a gentle nod that said, "Here goes." Then he replied to Davis. "Before you do that, sir, may I claim the floor for an announcement?"

About to speak, Davis was interrupted by a boyish-looking Captain who appeared at the door, his gilt trimmed, gray wool uniform fresh from the tailor's shop. George guessed that the young officer was wearing the costume of rank for the very first time.

"President Davis, sir, I have an urgent message from General Beauregard, sir. He requests I await your reply, sir."

139

Davis snapped up the offered envelope and nailed the Captain with a crinkled glare from his one good eye.

"Easy now, Captain," he said. "It's not the end of the world is it?"

He was about to rip the seal when Hamlin stopped him.

"Do not read that. Let me tell you what it contains."

Davis sighed. "Very well."

Hamlin gathered himself, but before he could speak a new sound broke through. All recognized it at once as the rattle-clack of military drums. Troops were on the move somewhere.

Hamlin raised his right arm in a proud gesture. "Those are our drums you hear, Mr. Davis. The drums of the Fort Sumter garrison. They have landed on the Battery and are marching up Meeting Street. They will be here momentarily."

Davis' face went white with alarm and rage. Judah Benjamin jumped to his feet, his eyes darting fearfully. He shouted at Hamlin. "How dare you, sir? What treachery is this?"

Hamlin waved dismissal. "Oh, calm down, gentlemen. We are not making an attack. And you, young man, put that sword away before you stab yourself in the ass."

George saw that the young captain had indeed drawn his blade and was shivering it uncertainly.

Playing the role of grand host now, Hamlin gestured for the others to join him on the iron balcony that overlooked Meeting Street. George, John Hay and Seward all crowded in behind them. Major Anderson and his men could be seen in the deep distance, guidon's fluttering, arms swinging, bayonets glinting, feet moving in perfect step and alignment, marching up the street, their band, tooting out the old Cavalry song, "Gerry Owen."

Davis was red in the face. "What is the meaning of this?"

Hamlin pointed a stiff index finger toward the marching men. "There is your gesture, sir. I have ordered the removal of our troops from Fort Sumter. I believe that is what the captain's message makes reference to."

Davis ripped the envelope and read. "It does, sir." He turned to Benjamin with a questioning look. George saw a man unable to grasp and totally at a loss for something to say in the face of unexpected, unwanted success.

Benjamin could only shake his head.

"This afternoon they will sail with us for Fort Monroe," Hamlin added pleasantly. "It should be a fair day's journey what with the sun breaking through."

Davis made a rasping noise, finally regained his voice. "Have you totally evacuated Fort Sumter?"

Hamlin pursed his lips and shook his head. But there was a twinkle in his eye.

"No, sir," he said, "we have not. The garrison now consists of a gunnery Sergeant and his fifteen year old daughter, Kate. She is quite pretty if a bit too spirited. Her father, the Sergeant, will run up the national colors every day. Kate will learn to blow the bugle. It is still our fort, after all."

"Yet it offers no military threat," Seward put in, "unless your men cower at one pretty maiden and a fat old Sergeant."

Hamlin spoke with composed authority. "I seek now a reply in kind, not of words, but of action. Disperse your troops. Send them home, sir, where they can engage in more productive activities than filling sandbags and getting drunk every afternoon."

Davis' face betrayed a mind clearly racing over contingencies and probabilities. "Why should we do that?"

"Why? May I remind you, that as we stand here, comfortably speaking with each other as gentlemen on this day, no shots have been exchanged."

Davis licked his lips, glanced another unspoken question at Benjamin who was still frozen silent.

"What real, lasting harm has been done?" Hamlin spoke on, building his oration. "None, yet. A few rump conventions of turbulent, vindictive men have caused their States to 'secede' as they phrase it, from our Union. The people of these States were not consulted. Their votes were not counted before launching this adventure. As I stated yesterday, some property has been

141

illegally seized. It can easily be returned to the custody of its rightful owners, the people of the United States. Hear me, Davis, I'm saying you can still go back. It's not yet too late."

George glanced a worried look at Seward. Was this a bag of dead cats? But Seward's face glowed with confidence.

Jefferson Davis, his eyes lowered, turned away from the balcony and walked slowly into the ballroom. He eased himself into a chair and placed his fingers on some pages before him then began to absently shove them back and forth.

Hamlin followed, moving quickly, pounced across the table and gripped Davis' arm. "The President of the United States," he said, "does not intend to call out the militia to suppress a rebellion or to coerce a state in its adherence to the Federal Union, for sir, there has *been* no rebellion. No State has seceded for that action is legally impossible under the Constitution."

Hamlin stepped back, regarded Davis, alert for a response.

Seward snorted a laugh. "In other words, what you're saying, Mr. President, is that some politicians of these seven states got together to do themselves a little play acting?"

Judah Benjamin stroked his chin and emitted a small chuckle that for once seemed genuine. His eyes danced between Davis and Hamlin.

George held his breath watching the unspoken exchange between these men.

Davis raised his hand as if to reserve time for himself while he conjured up his next statement.

"Of course you would not call out the militia," he said deliberately, as if musing to himself. "For should you do so, you would lose the border States. Virginia and North Carolina would immediately secede before they would provide troops for such an evil purpose as military coercion. Kentucky and Tennessee as well."

"We agree on that," Hamlin snapped back. "Let's see what else we can agree on."

Davis' eyebrows were knit in concentration. "We both need the border States."

"That is true."

Davis sucked in his hollow cheeks. "You really do not intend to go to war?"

"I choose not to answer that," Hamlin said. "I must reserve all rights and options. But do take note of the fact that we evacuated Fort Sumter this morning, on our own hook. Is that an act of good faith? I answer myself and say it is, sir. My cards are flat out on the table. Now, I want something from you to match."

Judah Benjamin leaned over the table and quickly whispered. That done, Davis leaned back and eyed Hamlin warily. "I will tell you something now that I probably shouldn't. I have been advised by men I trust, that our cause must have bloodshed to prosper and survive. I have been told that I must, to quote, 'throw blood in their faces.' Otherwise the Confederacy will fall apart, as pro-Union sentiment arises and asserts itself. I must admit, sir, that your refusal of military action will evoke favorable Union sentiment among some of our people, especially in the border States."

"In other words," Seward said, "if you can't provoke us into shooting at you, your cause is gone up?"

Davis pursed his lips and cocked an eye at Seward. "You have a way of getting at things, Billy. Always have."

Hamlin pressed his attack, his voice rising point by point as if summing up before a jury. "No actions have been taken that cannot be easily revoked. No cannon ball has yet left the tube, except by the unfortunate actions of that maniac the other day. Only one man has died so far in this conflict, a likely young Irishman who had his whole life before him, killed by cowards here in Charleston." Hamlin's voice trembled with honest feeling. "We have brought his body to this place, as testimony to our resolve. Step outside and observe."

Davis and Benjamin rose with no real enthusiasm and followed Hamlin to the balcony. From there they saw Patrick's flag draped body mounted on a horse drawn artillery caisson, guarded by Anderson's men as they came to a halt at the hotel yard.

143

Hamlin stepped between them and spoke doggedly on. "So I say one has died and that is one too many. General McClellan tells me that if we have war, many more young men will die. They will die by the hundreds of thousands. Each of those lives is precious to me for each is an American. And those lives should be precious to you as well, Davis."

He paused, then placed his arms around their shoulders, and spoke again in a new thoughtful tone as if inspiration had just flamed within him.

"Why I tell you, gentlemen, I firmly believe that the man who is seen to defuse this crisis might, at some future date, be rewarded by a grateful Nation with the highest office of the land." He locked eyes with the astonished Davis and squeezed his shoulder. "I admonish you to look to it, sir."

Hamlin left them on the balcony and went to the food table where he poured himself a glass of iced water. George had moved close to his side. Hamlin looked dead ahead and said in a side-mouthed whisper. "I planted the hook. Let's see if we reel him in."

Davis and Benjamin stood rooted for a moment, then began actively whispering at each other. The clock in the corner ticked. Out on the street the troops waited at ease while a crowd gathered.

George watched Jefferson Davis conferring intently with Judah Benjamin. Something had energized the President of the Confederacy. The one good eye lit up. Lips twitched. Then an eyebrow went crinkling, as if Davis was in a losing fight to maintain a poker face. Something powerful in him was striving to break loose. Hamlin had landed a Sunday punch.

Finally, Davis came off the balcony and confronted Hamlin. "You cannot," he said, wide-eyed, "promise me the Presidency."

"Well, I suppose that is so," Hamlin said hurriedly, flicking that inconvenient point aside. He took another sip of water taking the time to think, than placed the glass carefully on the table.

"But consider practical politics," he said, his voice refreshed. "The South would vote for you certainly. Oh, there

144

would be grumbling, no doubt, from the croakers and the firebrands, but the mass of the people would follow you. In the North, they would see you as the savior of the Union and reward you with their votes. I would, of course, make some speeches in your support. You would be remembered as the man who saved the Union, while I will be a mere footnote in history as Abraham Lincoln's Vice President. But I won't mind. Indeed, I make this solemn pledge to you now, sir, that should you denounce and disband this mad-dog confederacy of yours, I will back you under whatever party banner you should choose to run."

"And I am certain that Billy Seward here will endorse my commitment and make a similar pledge of his own." Hamlin turned to Seward. "Isn't that so, Bill?"

Seward looked elated enough to burst into song. "Right you are, Mr. President."

Davis shot a severe glance at his partner. "Well, Judah, what do you say to this lunacy?"

Benjamin lifted his hands, an open gesture of acceptance. "Well, what would you have me say? It is the best bargain offer, the best negotiating ploy I have ever heard of in my whole life. Only an idiot would refuse."

Jefferson Davis pondered. "I could never run as a Republican," he said with high dignity.

Hamlin gave a shrug. "Naturally."

Davis looked to Benjamin who slowly nodded. "Take it," Judah Benjamin said. "A good attorney always knows when to settle."

Jefferson Davis studied the honest face of Hannibal Hamlin. What a wrenching effort if must have been for him to make this offer. But it wasn't over yet. They must get down to the nut of it all.

"There is yet issue of some concern to us," Davis said. He paused to allow himself the beautiful vision of himself and the lovely Varina, strolling down the stairs of the President's Mansion to greet an assembly of dignitaries. Varina would glow and surpass them all. With effort, he put the thought aside. Back to business.

145

"What will be your position on the question of slavery?" he asked. Strange that the question had once seemed so crucial. He caught himself. Well, of course it was crucial and must be addressed.

"We will obey the laws," Hamlin said with warm assurance. "I will even back the constitutional amendment which passed Congress in February. It enjoins Congress to keep hands off your domestic institutions."

"And in the territories?"

"Under my administration you may take your slaves wherever you choose, Davis. Even bring 'em up to Maine for all I care."

Had Hamlin completely taken leave of his wits? Lincoln had been most adamant against slavery expanding into the territories or the free States. It had been his keystone position and that of his party and one of the chief causes of secession.

Davis turned to Benjamin. "He is being entirely too amenable, for a hard shell Yankee abolitionist. What is up your sleeve, Hamlin?"

"Only my own arm."

Davis squinted, baffled, searching for the hidden answer. "You have always been an enemy of slavery. I have heard you, hour upon hour preaching your abolitionist creed. You do not change on a whim."

"I have not changed," Hamlin said. "I hate human bondage and I propose to take action to set it on the road to extermination. But legally and constructively. Indeed, I intend to show more respect for your property rights than you have for ours."

Davis felt a dead weight upon his chest. The sunshine dream of the Presidency was fast fading. Perhaps it had been but a sweet opium dream, too good to be true.

"Exterminate slavery and respect our rights? That is double talk, sir, of the worst kind." Davis said it sharply, slapping himself awake to cold reality. They had tried to take him for a fool. "We've come right back to the same impasse that split the Union."

146

"Not at all," Seward said with a chuckle, then quickly scratched some numbers on a scrap of paper and passed it to Davis. "What if I offered you that figure for each and ever one of your ...uh ...servants? Cash or notes secured by the Central Government?"

Davis looked at the number and let his lips twist in a ironic smile. "I would snap up your offer and think I was doing business with a blithering idiot."

"And what if, after I had purchased your servants, I issued them their freedom papers, guaranteed by the Federal Government? Have I violated your property rights?" Seward folded his arms and waited, confident as a river-boat gambler with five aces.

Davis frowned, letting the revelation sink in. So that was it. Compensated Emancipation, the old untried ideal. Even Lincoln before his death had made a passing effort to institute the practice in the border States. The more slaves purchased and freed, the higher the price for the remaining slaves, eventually driving down and destroying the slave economy through impossibly high prices. The big buy-out. It was one of those bizarre ideas, often theorized but never yet put into practice.

Now he heard the murmur of a crowd assembling on the lawn of the Mills House. He felt himself compelled by some outside, unknown force of energy to move to the window and be seen. A cheer came up at him. He held an arm out to them, a feeble wave.

What was he doing here? Down in the front edge of the crowd he saw his precious Varina standing with Mary Chesnut, both women grinning up at him like schoolgirls on holiday. Ah, well, if this was an opium dream he would relish it fully.

Judah Benjamin joined him at the window and touched deft fingers to his shoulder. "Take it," Benjamin breathed softly in his ear. "Take the chance. Once in a man's lifetime. Give Hamlin his victory. He'll have enemies in Congress who will seek to impeach him for giving in to us."

"That's how they will see it?"

"Oh, dear, yes. They'll accuse him of betraying the Union. Compensated Emancipation is despised by the black Republicans. It will cost too much, and we sinner slavers get the money. They will fight him over it hammer and tongs. Only you can save him and be the hero of the day by bringing our seven States back into he fold to support him. Don't you see he is staking everything on you?"

"But our people will accuse me of selling out as well. They have always suspected me of being a secret Unionist."

Benjamin patted him on the back. "And now, my dear fellow, you shall prove their fears well founded."

"What will you want out of this, Judah? Vice President?"

"Secretary of State."

Davis frowned deep lines. "I just don't see it. He cannot buy out all the slaves. Where will they ever get the money?"

"Who knows? Bonds? Loans? Squeeze the damn rich abolitionists to put their money where they preach. Anyhow, let that be his worry. Slavery is a dying system and will be gone one way or another by the turn of the century. We all know that, but for now, short term, we have received our guarantees of non-interference in the territories. We could never have hoped for such a concession from Lincoln. Take that back to our people and proclaim victory. Those who said we could get a better deal outside the Union were right. End of debate." Benjamin's smiling eyes danced.

Davis felt his stomach roll over. "A golden opportunity?"

"I think so."

"They will hate me," Davis said, and in saying it found he didn't care.

"Some will hate you. In the North some will hate Hamlin."

"They may try to kill me," Davis said, testing his own courage.

"They might," Benjamin replied a little too casually. "Listen Davis, this is in no way a sure thing for either one of you. I am merely advising you to seize the moment, and take the chance!"

Davis let his eyes sweep the room. Young John Hay was speaking head to head with Billy Seward. Both men looked happily relieved. General McClellan was conferring with a blunt-looking bearded officer, his hands gesturing importantly. Hannibal Hamlin sat a small way apart, composed and staring off into some unknown.

Davis took a deep breath and made his decision. The Presidency. It would please Varina so. Well, no, he checked himself. That would not be the entire reason. It would fulfill Jefferson Davis as well, crowning his life and career. He would be a hero President of the United States of America.

And yes, they had to be United, by the Almighty, he saw that clearly now. No more of this poisonous secession sickness. It had too long festered right here in the heart of South Carolina. Root it out. He himself had nearly fallen victim to it. He stood up and squared his shoulders as the statesman-warrior he knew himself to be. He would deal sternly with these people if necessary. The Constitution would be upheld when he was President of the United States, and no State would be permitted to back out.

He walked up to Hamlin and thrust out his bony hand.

"When you get back to Washington, don't forget this agreement." Davis said.

Hamlin gripped his hand and looked him in the eye. "When I get back to Washington, there will be a move to impeach me from some of our more ardent Republicans. Dissolve your Confederacy and get your representatives back to Congress post haste where I can expect them to vote in my acquittal. Do we have a deal?"

"We have a deal."

"You all heard that," Hamlin said to those present.

"I reckon you may want to be quiet about this," Seward said from the side of his mouth.

"Bill, I am fifty-one years year old and I have never yet done anything to be ashamed of," Hamlin said. I don't propose to start today. There is nothing I have said in this room that I would not say to the whole American people. I merely lit up the fire of patriotism in Mr. Davis here. And now let us go down to the piazza and address the crowd."

Davis and Benjamin led the way to the piazza, walking quickly, their heads close with eager whispers.

Hamlin hung back with Seward. The President regarded his Secretary of State with a raised eyebrow.

"I predicted he would bite on it."

Seward cackled. "Three cheers for ambition."

"Remember we have a deal, Billy. I will be true to it and I expect you to go along as well."

"Ah, well, to retire as a country lawyer. There are worse fates, are there not, Han Hamlin?"

"Indeed," Hamlin spoke solemnly. "Civil war is a worse fate."

* * *

George scrambled down the stairway to arrive on the piazza well ahead of the rest of the party. He strode out on the shaded porch, anxious to observe the mood of the crowd with an eye to safety. At first glance they seemed unthreatening.

"Yo ho hoo, General McClellan." A lilting contralto cut through the chatter, and there was Mary Chesnut glowing like a princess in a smashing pink satin dress. With her was another dark-eyed, raven haired woman with a face that was at once dignified and pretty. Mary Chesnut fluttered slightly in deference to her.

"Mrs. Jefferson Davis," she said with a graceful hand gesture, "may I present General George McClellan."

Varina Davis radiated pride of place seasoned with a cool tone of amusement.

"I have heard so many complimentary opinions about you, General," she said in a voice rich with the sweet syrup of Mississippi. She cast a side smile at Mary Chesnut. "Can't exactly recall where though."

Mary Chesnut blushed and George who blushed back, recalled the unmentionable.

Suddenly, Varina Davis was all business and her voice went to a lower pitch. "I hear we have reached some kind of accommodation or understanding with your people."

"So it would seem, Madam."

"Well, glory be for the blessing then. My husband was not looking forward to a war between Americans I assure you, General. But for awhile there it seemed the only way out for the poor old South."

Mary Chesnut pointed at Hamlin. "I feel sorry for that man," she said. "Even now in Washington they are building the cross and sharpening up the nails for him."

"I hope you exaggerate, Mrs. Chesnut," George said. He bowed to Varina Davis. "An honor to meet you, Mrs. Davis. If you'll be so kind as to excuse me, I have some matters to attend."

Mary Chesnut waved him off. "Oh, you men, always on the scurry hither and yon with your great affairs."

"The curse of our gender, Madam." George tipped his cap and bowed his way out, watching Varina Davis smile smugly at Mary Chesnut. Don't ever get those two mad at you, he thought, as he worked his way over to Sam Grant who was standing with Major Anderson. He exchanged salutes with the two officers.

"Good morning, Major Anderson."

"Good morning, General, what a fine day!" Anderson's yellow teeth bared in a grin as he leaned over to George and whispered with whiskey breath, "I never thought the President would have the guts to do this."

George nodded. "He is a man full of surprises. And high courage."

"My boys are just relieved as hell to be out of that brick pile except for that damned abolitionist, Doubleday, who is going to pout from now to doomsday. But you know and I know, General, if they had ever started firing on us, Fort Sumter would have been our tomb."

George looked over the crowd. "Quite right," he said absently. "By the way, Sam, has anybody seen or heard of Mr. Stanton since last night?"

151

Anderson looked blank.

George explained. "A member of the President's party, Major. He was considerably upset by today's course of action."

"That's putting it politely," Sam said. "Yelling and screaming and foaming at the mouth, calling the President a traitor. No one has seen hide nor hair of him this morning though."

"I for one hope he has disappeared for good," George said, cheerfully. Can you imagine how he would be in a position of power?"

"Would probably have himself a fatal accident," Sam observed.

George's eyes swept the crowd. "Keep your men on the alert, Sam. Anything can happen. Mr. Davis and President Hamlin are going to speak. I don't know what they're going to say or what the crowd will do but remember our first duty is to protect the President."

"Which one?" Sam asked.

George considered. "Both of them."

Jefferson Davis was now gesturing for the crowd to hush.

"This should be interesting," Sam Grant said, but George had walked away. He had just seen something he didn't like.

From the shaded Piazza, Davis addressed the expectant gathering. "My friends, my dear South Carolina friends, may I have your attention." He was pleased to hear his voice carry out over their heads with loud and commanding authority. "You all hear me now." The crowd cheered. Davis scanned their happy faces. Obviously the news of Sumter was out.

He held up his arms, waved to settle them down. Finally when he felt the moment right he launched into a speech, unwritten, unplanned, unexpected.

"My dear friends, this is a grand day for South Carolina, a grand proud day for the South ..."

"And the United States of America," Hamlin growled in his ear.

"And the United States of America," Davis said. "I am proud and pleased to announce that an arrangement has been

152

reached between myself and the Honorable President of the United States. Certain guarantees to our benefit have been proposed and I have accepted. The Confederacy has accomplished its high and noble purpose, to guarantee the rights and respect of the South. Having accomplished that righteous purpose, it is no longer needed, and so on my return to Montgomery I shall recommend its dissolution and a return of our seceded States to the bosom of the Union."

The crowd was shocked into silence, then some curses and cries came back. "No! Never South Carolina!"

Davis raised his hand. "South Carolina is free to do as it pleases. And further, since the central government has removed the military threat from Fort Sumter, I hereby order General Beauregard to disperse and return our brave soldiers to their families."

The crowd was babbling now, confused, muddled. Was this good or bad? Should they cheer or hiss? With their emotions balanced on the head of a pin, how could Davis nudge them over?

"Traitor to the South! Traitor to the cause! Cursed Yankee bootlicker! Taste cold steel!"

George had been a split second too late. Mad old Edmund Ruffin erupted with a shriek of ugly curses, lowered his sharp pointed iron pike and charged up the steps of the piazza, his wild, hate filled eyes burning into Jefferson Davis. George had lunged after the lunatic, but too late, tumbling, picking himself up, yelling to the troops.

"Stop that man!"

No one was near enough. Edmund Ruffin lunged his deadly pike at Jefferson Davis' heart. Reacting fast, Davis got himself twisted away so that Ruffin's blade ripped into his right shoulder, shredding cloth, skin and bone. Davis screamed as his knees buckled and he slumped and slid back against the wall of the hotel.

Blood all over the place. George and Sam Grant got to Ruffin, fell on him, grabbed, punched and kicked him into a quivering heap. George looked down at the would-be assassin.

153

"Sam, this is one for the record book." His breath came in gulps. "He just tried to kill two Presidents in two days!"

"Takes his politics serious," Sam said.

The soldiers hauled Ruffin away, half dead.

* * *

For Hannibal Hamlin, it was the moment God sent.

Years ago as a boy in Boston studying law, Hamlin had discovered the theatre. He would sneak away whenever his studies allowed and buy a cheap ticket in the remote upper rows. From there he would study the movements, the spoken arias and grand gestures of the great actor-managers of the day. He saw men move with the assurance of gods, voices and gestures seeming to command the world. Hamlin stored it away, and gave it back to himself in the tight privacy of his room.

"Friends, Romans, Countrymen ..."

And now he put it to use. With half an eye on the crowd, he bent over the crumpled body of Jefferson Davis. He lifted the body partially upright just as Varina Davis came hurtling down on the other side, her mouth working in silent sobs. Hamlin placed one hand atop Davis' head, and raised his other hand to heaven and unleashed an actor's vocal hymn.

"Friends, fellow Americans, countrymen and my dear people of South Carolina!"

The crowd was frozen. He had them. Now hold them.

He felt the words thunder up from his gut. "See to what depths this terrible hatred has driven us. Hatred, blind, pig-headed hatred, sick poisonous hatred from both sections of our beloved country, has very nearly ..."

He saw a sketch artist reporter from Harper's Magazine flashing his pencil over his drawing paper. The sketch would be turned into printing plate and circulated over the country. Hamlin deliberately held his hand upright and still, a gesture to Heaven, as the sketch artist recorded it all with slashing strokes.

"... nearly split our dear country into vicious factions in horrible civil war. My friends, we must not let this happen, and

154

I know I speak for that fallen hero, that bleeding fount of courage, Jefferson Davis, when I say, we must not let this happen."

He looked down at Davis' eyes which were glassy, half open. He bent down as if to listen, nodded, frowned.

"Jefferson Davis may be breathing his last, right before your eyes."

Varina Davis let out a wail. Mary Chesnut was now at her side, hugging her shoulders. A doctor pushed through to the wounded statesman.

"But I know he wants you to hear the words he just spoke to me."

Hamlin raised himself to his full height. "He said: THERE MUST BE BUT ONE UNITED STATES OF AMERICA. One America, my friends, not a bloody war between fathers and sons, brother against brother, State against State. For we are all Americans, all Americans, and we must not be enemies, but friends."

A sudden fright. Would they know he was quoting Lincoln? Oh, well, keep going, keep it up, keep it loud.

"We must not kill each other! We must not open our great nation to foreign adventurers because they think us weak and easy pickings if we war among ourselves. No, no, my friends, never. Never! Never let that happen! Hands off, French tyrant! Hands off, English King and Dukes! Hands off" ... he strained to think of another foreign villain ... "Mexican bandits! This is our America standing forth strong and united. The United States of America! That's God's name for us! You have just seen Jefferson Davis spill his life's blood in the cause of our great and blessed Union. Let us go forth, with no less a dedication to that great cause! No more secession! No more Americans killing Americans. No war! No war! No war!"

The crowd took up the chant. Hamlin knew they were his. George began to clap his hands in time. Sam Grant joined in, as did Major Anderson and his men. George caught an arched eyebrow and a lazy, knowing smile from Mary Chestnut as she helped attend to the wounded Davis. George walked up to her, lifted his cap and bowed.

She brushed fingers to her lips, her eyes locked on him. "A capital idea, General."

George gasped. Was it possible? Had they shared the same secret dream?

Part Two

The World of War

"The old Southern doctrine of extreme State-Rights, including that of secession, would reduce the Union to a mere rope of sand, and would completely paralyze the general government, rendering it an object of just contempt at home and abroad."

General George B. McClellan, *"McClellan's Own Story"*

Just received a telegram from Halleck stating that Pope and Burnside are very hard pressed_ urging me to push forward reinforcements & to come myself as soon as I possibly can... Now they are in trouble they seem to want the "Quaker," the "procrastinator," the "coward" & the "traitor."

George to Nelly, August 21, 1862

CHAPTER TWELVE

September 17, 1861

"Onward." George cracked the whip lightly and jostled the reins as he guided the buggy over the muddy ruts of the road. The horses, a willing, spirited team were a pleasure to drive, responsive to every gentle pressure. Unusual for a livery stable hire.

The early September weather in Georgia was ideally mild. His wool jacket felt about right. He whistled, flatly and off key, a Stephen Foster song, something about a racetrack.

Whistling ceased when he rounded a curve and saw his destination. What a grotesque jumble it was with its odd turrets and darkened porches. Rusty iron lettering arched over the entrance posts and named the place: "Whitaker's Asylum For Lunatics and Imbeciles."

The horses came to a sudden stop. George cracked the whip again across their flanks and the buggy rattled on through the gate and up the weedy driveway.

This place had few visitors.

He attached the horses to the hitching post and put on feed bags.

"General McClellan, I presume." The voice was raspy. The figure of the man who went with it was faintly visible on the shaded veranda.

"Doctor Whitaker?"

"At your service. Come in, sir, do come in." A cough. "You made, ah, good time I see, ah, from the depot."

George stepped up on the porch and touched hands with Doctor Ransom Whitaker, a pink faced, thick set man of sixty odd years who evidently suffered from some form of severe asthma.

"Right this way, ah, General."

George followed Whitaker into the dingy interior of the building, and after a passage through several hallways, found himself in a small office furnished with glass cased book shelves which displayed some seedy, long-ago-stuffed animals and birds. The walls were pale with little discernible color and were water cracked from ceiling to floor. Light retreated from the grimy window.

"Sit down, General, sit down. Make yourself to home."

George sat carefully on a cracked leather sofa.

"Now, ah, General McClellan, ah, I am honored that such a high member of the national government should pay us a visit." Whitaker caught his breath and recovered from the effort of the speech. "It's not so often..."

"I believe we have some business to conduct," George said crisply.

"Ah, indeed, sir. Ah, can I offer you a drink?" A bottle half full of murky fluid was on the desk, two glasses at the ready.

George felt his lips purse. "Regretfully I must decline, Doctor, but thank you all the same."

Doctor Whitaker coughed and hawked something into a rag. "Ah, well, sir, I never decline, heh, heh." He poured out a nearly full glass and took a deep gulp, then wiped his lips. "Would you care to stay for supper?"

George tried not to even picture that. "I have to transact my business and be on my way."

"Of course, of course, ah, an important man such as yourself," Whitaker said with a softly disdainful tone.

George remained silent hoping it would speed things along.

"You were with Hamlin at Charleston I believe."

"I had that honor."

"Ah, yes. Must have been most thrilling, eh? Jefferson Davis nearly killed by that uh, misguided patriot. Thank God he has survived, sir." Whitaker gave another wracking cough.

"Yes, thank God. It was a near thing. He came near bleeding to death ..."

"Some folks think Jefferson Davis was a traitor, sold out the Southern Confederacy for some kind of political deal with old Hamlin." Doctor Whitaker's eyes had gone hard and unblinking.

162

"Some folks think all kinds of crazy things," George said quietly, "as I'm sure you know."

"And now," the doctor paused, taking care to pour himself some more of the murky fluid, "old Hamlin and the government are buying up the slaves for big cash, lots of folks a' gettin' rich I hear."

"His plan seems to be working."

"Abolition by dollars, buying up the slaves, destroying the South, and Jefferson Davis going right along with it, for shame, for shame."

George crossed his legs and inspected the shine on his boots.

"Some of us down in these part call him a Judas to the South."

"They can call him whatever they like," George said. "At least we avoided a war."

Doctor Whitaker gave a sour grin. "Oh, Glory be, we avoided war. When maybe war was just what was called for. And I ask you sir, ah, now where is our honor?"

George didn't want to get into that hornets nest. Gratefully he sensed a presence behind him, turned to discover a bright faced Negro boy.

"I am not, ah, ready for you as yet, Albert," the Doctor said firmly. "Wait in the hall, please."

Albert bobbed his head and, still grinning, backed out of the room.

"That was my boy, Albert. I still own him, glory be. He, ah, will be assisting you in the arrangements."

George stood. "Shall we transact then?"

Doctor Whitaker shrugged. "I can see you are, ah, no political man."

"Just a soldier," George said. In Charleston he had touched politics and been lucky at it. It was a faraway dream, fading fast. Yes, he was just a soldier.

In a few minutes, their business concluded, Doctor Whitaker gave him the directions he needed. "Please enjoy the rest of your visit, General, but ah, make it brief if you please."

George nodded sharply. "Be assured, Doctor, I will."

He found Albert waiting in the hall and was guided to a certain room where Cump Sherman was sewing a button on a tattered shirt.

"Sherman?"

Gleaming blue-gray eyes darted up and drilled him suspiciously.

"It's George McClellan, Cump. You do recognize me?"

Sherman's mouth fell open and then cracked in a broad grin. "By the Almighty, so it is! What are you doing in this hell hole, Mac? Did they catch you too? Did you spill the beans?"

George shook out his handkerchief and wiped the chair before sitting down. "I was just passing through the neighborhood. Heard you were here, thought I'd drop in. How are you feeling, Cump?"

"How am I feeling?" Cump's voice was more strained than usual. "Well, now, I'm confined in a mad house run by a Doctor who ought to be an inmate. How the hell do you think I'd be feeling?"

George reached in to his coat pocket and produced a cigar. "Have a smoke?"

Cump's reaching hand trembled. "I haven't had a cigar in the three months I've been here."

George scratched a match and offered flame.

Cump's cheeks sucked in. He expelled a blue cloud. "Ah, the pungent elixir of life."

George licked the end of his own cigar and lit up.

"Mighty kind of you to come here like this, Mac. It's more than my brother, the big bug Senator has done."

"Why Cump, Senator Sherman has been burning up the telegraph wires with messages to the Governor of Georgia ever since it was known you were here. I saw him just before I left Washington. And Ellen too. She sends her love. She's been writing you almost every day."

"I've heard nary a word from any of them," Cump said, his eyes morose.

"I suspect the mail service is less than reliable at this place. How exactly did you come to be here?"

164

Cump sighed. "A long story, as the man says."

"Which I want to hear."

Cump got up and began to pace the narrow room gesturing with his cigar. "Well, it all began after the President settled that war scare business in Charleston.

George smiled. "Remind me to tell you all about it someday."

"Oh, yes, I knew you were in on it. Anyhow, a most unpleasant depressive mood came over me. Nothing new as far as that goes. Ellen claimed she understood and took the children with her back to her family in Ohio. As usual. I took a leave of absence from the street railroad company and got on the first steamboat headed down river. Meant to visit my old friends in Louisiana with some hopes of resuming my career at the military school there."

Cump paused, with a distant look. When the boat stopped at Vicksburg, Mississippi, something happened to me. I just had to get off and go gallivanting off to Atlanta."

"Why Atlanta?"

Sherman spread his hands, palms up. "It was a mindless thing that just took over, like some giant hand had grabbed me by the collar and marched me to the train depot. I had to be in Atlanta and that's all there was to it!"

George inspected the glowing tip of his cigar. "Well," he said, "you obviously arrived in good shape. What caused them to put you in this charming place?"

Sherman sighed. "Let us say that on the streets of Atlanta I was not myself."

"You were screaming at the top of your lungs that your army had conquered the city, or so I have heard. Is that true?"

"The fact is I have had an experience impossible to define or explain."

"Tell me about it."

"I shall in good time," Cump said, as he strolled to the open doorway and beckoned George to follow. "First, let me give you a little tour among the natives so that you'll begin to understand this place."

Cump led him into a large open room. Smudged sunlight filtered in through barred windows. The men gathered there were of all ages, their clothing unkempt, their hygiene neglected. Some pretended to read books that were not there while others stared off into empty distance. One old man was intensely "writing" with no visible pen or paper. An oppressive, putrid, animal odor filled the room. George tried not to breathe.

"My colleagues in the madman business," Cump said, with a sly pride.

George whispered behind his hand. "In my opinion, sir, if you weren't mad when you came here, this environment could drive you to that condition."

"Oh, you're catching on. Six more months in this place and I'll fit in natural like, just like that dammed crack-pot, Whitaker who is no more a doctor than that fly on the wall."

George looked around. As expected, he saw no attendants. It was time. "Come with me, Cump. We're going for a walk."

Cump pouted. "Not allowed to go out yet, not 'til exercise time."

"I said come with me." George put a rigid hand on Cump's elbow. They walked. At the end of a dark hallway there was a door exactly where George expected to find it.

"That goes to the outside all right," Cump said," but don't bother, it's locked."

"Trust me." George twisted the knob and the door opened. "Voilá, as we say in Paris. Follow on!"

Cump's face came alive with a dawning awareness.

Once outside, George stepped off purposefully across the scrubby grounds, dodging around bushes and trees.

"Delightful day for a walk, don't you think? Smell that air. Bracing. Look sharply, now, Cump. Keep up with me!"

"Where are we headed, Mac?"

"Where would you like to go, old boy?"

"Home to Ohio."

George raised his arms as he broke into a fast stepping jog. "I am the great magician. Home to Ohio we shall go. Pick up the pace, old boy!"

George found the back gate, his buggy waiting per the arrangement, the horses held by the grinning Albert.

"Good-bye, General Sherman! Make sure we don't see you here no more."

"That is my fervent wish also, Albert," Cump said. "I'm putting you all out of my mind like a bad dream."

"Yessuh, I'll tell Doctor Whitaker that when he wakes up."

Cump snarled. "May he never wake up."

George clicked the reins and broke the horses into a smart trot. "I trust you had no baggage you wished to take."

"I'm all the baggage I need."

They drove on a few miles in silence.

"Well, how much did it take?" Cump said, eyes staring dead ahead.

"Five hundred in gold," George said. "Your father-in-law provided."

"Five hundred? Is that all I'm worth? Half the price of a decent slave?"

"If you disapprove of the deal, I'll be happy to turn around and drive you back." Cump made a sound like a childish giggle, but said nothing more. Eventually he closed his eyes and dozed off.

CHAPTER THIRTEEN

They arrived in Atlanta, returned the buggy to the livery stable then crossed the street to the depot where George bought two connections for Cincinnati. As they sipped tepid coffee in the depot's "Quick Lunch" room, Cump fixed a gaze deep into his cup, then looked up at George.

"I still can't believe it, Mac. That was slick as grease through a goose. I'll be eternally obliged to you."

"You have lots of friends in the army, Cump. If it hadn't been me, Sam Grant was willing to come."

"Good old Sam. He was with you at Charleston I heard."

"He was my strong right arm. By the way, he told me you saved his life in California."

"Well, he had hard lines out there. It was he who pulled himself up out of the bottle. I only gave him sound advice."

Cump was momentarily silent, then said, "I realize I owe you an explanation for my behavior, Mac. In Atlanta, I mean. Once we're safely on the cars, I'll regale you with the whole story."

"Whenever you're ready, old man." George rustled the pages of the *Atlanta Journal*. They sat in private silence for a half hour until the train resounded into the station, bell clanging. Out on the platform George couldn't resist walking up to the huffing locomotive where he admired the precise valve gear linkage.

"I do love these big contraptions," he said with a grin. "I guess I'm just a railroad man at heart."

They boarded, and George was further delighted to find their car was a spanking new Chicago Pullman with the new fangled bed design that could be made up for sleeping.

"Imagine, sleeping beds on a train," he said. "It's going to be great shakes for the business."

The cars jounced and got underway, a process George always enjoyed. First the deep-throated chuff-huff-cuff of the engine, building slowly in pace and power, and then the easing back on the cutoff until the train was clicking along at "full chisel," as the engineers called it.

George relaxed back into the padded chair, felt the solid resonance of balanced wheels rolling true on steel rails. He estimated they were making a lively clip of twenty-seven miles per hour.

As the late afternoon sun tinted hills and trees outside the car window, he recalled the letters waiting on his desk in Washington. The directors of three great railroads were all biding for his services as chief executive. He would talk with President Hamlin about his resignation now that the threat of civil war had passed.

Unionist-Moderates now held a precarious power in the South. Though slavery was still technically legal, President Hamlin's policy seemed to be working despite the occasional outbreaks of violence and cries of frustrated rage from some of the Secessionist fire-eaters. That old wheeze, Doctor Whitaker for example. Of course no one dared call it emancipation or abolition these days. It was the *Federal Labor Redeployment Act* of 1861 which Jefferson Davis supported, true to the deal made in Charleston.

It was high time. George would resign his commission within the year and accept one of the offers. He and Nelly would move back to Chicago, or perhaps they might enjoy the sumptuous, worldly pleasures of New York City. It was pleasant to contemplate.

"Mac?"

Sherman's eyes radiated the wild desperation of a trapped animal. George reached over to touch his arm.

"What is it, Cump? You can speak freely now. We're going home."

Cump's cheeks puffed out a breath as he combed fingers through his spiky tufts of auburn hair. "Mac, there's a reason I went raving on the streets of Atlanta, and I'm going to tell it to you now. I don't ask you to believe me, but I'm afraid once you hear it you're going to want to ship me back to the crack-pot house."

170

George sat back, arms folded. "Not a chance. Now get on with it."

Cump sent glances darting all around, then moved his lips.

George put a hand to his ear. "You'll have to speak up."

"I said, 'there was a war.'"

"A war? Yes, where?"

Cump frowned, as if struggling with some wrenching interior force. Finally, with a shudder he blurted it out.

"The Union versus the Confederacy. Lincoln against Jeff Davis. It's happened already in some sort of other world, another place, but it has happened and I can't even begin to explain it, but in this other world there was a war between the States."

George nodded. "Ah ha. You mean you imagined how it would have been if there had been a war. Why, I've speculated on that myself, Cump, many times since Charleston. We all have."

"No!" Cump's voice cracked. Heads turned among the passengers. Cump looked more demented now than at the asylum.

"No, no, not imagination. Not a dream either. This is real, but a different kind of real, another world, another place. I don't know how it works or why, but Mac, I tell you I know it to be true. In this other world the war took place. Lincoln didn't die in March this year. Hamlin never became President, never went to Charleston. There was a war! I know because I was in it and so were you!"

George saw clear as sunrise why the judge in Atlanta had trundled Cump off to the asylum. Still he had no regrets for effecting the escape. The poor fellow would be better off in the care of his family.

"Yes, Mac, I see the skepticism writ plain across your phiz. You think me mad don't you?"

George weighed his reply. His doctor father, who loved to pursue "the science of the brain," had told him once about a theory of some European physicians called "The Talking Cure," where the patient was encouraged to discuss and expound on all the vaporous illusions that beset him. Somehow the mental poison was supposed to be expelled in the breath of conversation. As Doctor McClellan had said, "It may all be flap doodle, George, but it certainly could do no one any harm."

George reached into his jacket, produced two cigars and offered one to Cump. "I'd be most interested in hearing what you have to say. Always have had an exploratory mind. For instance, how exactly do you transfer to and from this other uh ... 'world' that you describe?"

Cump's hand clawed through his hair again. "Don't I wish I knew. Nearly as I can tell though, it's just something that comes over you. It just happens."

"Uncalled for? You didn't go into a trance or attend a seance or anything of that kind?"

Cump shook his head. "Mac, I tell you, one day I was running the street railway in Saint Louis, living content with Ellen and the children. I had read in the papers all about the conference in Charleston and the Hamlin-Davis agreement. I was pleased and disappointed all at once, you understand?"

"Yes. I understand exactly."

"Next thing I knew, I woke up, not in my neat little home in Saint Louis, but in a musty old army tent on a ridge above Arlington overlooking Georgetown. I looked out the flap and could see the unfinished capital across the river. It was Washington city. I was flabbergasted. I picked up my uniform jacket and found eagles on the shoulder boards! Glory be, I was a full Colonel in the Regular Army, commanding a motley crew called the Third Brigade of the First Division. I had three New York volunteer regiments and one from Wisconsin."

George frowned. "Volunteers! Hard people to control."

"Well, they weren't too bad for green troops. Except for the Sixty-ninth New York, all Irish of course, and you know how they are. So come to find out, it was July 16 of this year. We were getting our traps together, preparing to march out to do battle with Beauregard and Joe Johnston at a little crossroads about thirty miles South West of Washington."

"That would be near Manassas Junction."

"Exactly so," Cump bounced in his seat with excitement. "The very place!"

George fingered his mustache. "Well, what happened?"

"Why, we marched off to the fray which took place a few days later and became known later as the first battle of Bull Run after the little creek that runs through." Cump's face flushed with pride. "It was there, Mac, that I heard the bullets sing for the first time and I confirmed my calling. I found myself to be a true soldier who stands up under fire as well as the next man."

"That doesn't surprise me one bit, Cump. But what of the battle itself? Who won?"

Cump blinked. "Oh, that. Well, as I said, we had green volunteers, but we fought well all day in the sweat and the dust of July. Then, late in the afternoon, old Joe Johnston hit our right flank a mighty hard lick, and sorry to report, the boys started running, not mine of course. We fell back in good order and held on a ridge until relieved."

"Bully for you, Cump," George said, bemused to be congratulating Cump on a battle that had taken place nowhere but in his own fervid imagination. Odd how easy it was to fall into the rhythm of the thing. Still, it was interesting, and prompted questions.

"How did the war come about in the first place," George asked. "How did we get from Fort Sumter to Manassas Junction?"

"What started it," Cump declared, "was that both Lincoln and Davis got the same idea in their heads at once. For different reasons and God knows with different expectations, but one thing they had in common. They both thought that it would be a jim-dandy idea to get a war going."

George frowned. Somehow, as if hearing faint music, he knew all this. There was a phrase in French for it ...

"So they did," Cump said. "One played into the hands of the other. Davis determined in the name of Southron honor that he could not permit Lincoln to reinforce Sumter, so of course that's exactly what Lincoln had to go and do. If I didn't know better, I could swear they confabulated among themselves to get the shooting started. Lincoln and Davis had to drum up a war, each for his own purpose. They each had to strike a match in the powder factory."

George felt an odd apprehension of distant muffled drums. From Charleston he heard Pinkerton's words: *He has to throw blood in their faces.*

"Then Sumter was fired upon?"

Cump chuckled through a twisted smile. "April 12 of this year. For two days and nights Beauregard hit it with high and low angle fire. Bob Anderson hauled down the flag on the fourteenth and we were off to the races. Nobody killed, to speak of miracles. As you would expect, I packed my bags that night in Saint Louis."

He had to throw blood in their faces.

"But we know now," George said, "that Davis was looking for any excuse to start a war in order to hold his confederacy in line. If Lincoln had only shown some restraint."

Cump raised his hand. "All well and good, but that's not the way it happened in this world anyway. Next day, after Sumter fell, Lincoln put out a call for seventy-five thousand volunteers to put down the insurrection. Ninety-day men, sad to say. He called on all the states to contribute."

George's eyes bulged. "What? You can't mean it! All the states, the border states included? But that's damn foolishness. The border states were teetering between Union and secession. He should have known the response he'd get. Where was Seward to let this happen?"

"Beat's me," Cump said, "I don't know what was in Lincoln's mind either, but the border state Governors gave him the reply you might expect. They told him it was an evil thing he was asking, that they would not assist in military coercion of any sovereign state. What they really told him in legal language was to go piss in his hat. Then, just to make sure he got the point, Virginia, Arkansas, North Carolina and Tennessee all seceded. Kentucky declared itself neutral and crossed its legs, and Missouri got drunk." George puzzled it over. "It's true, as you say, it's almost as if both men wanted to start a war and so each did what would guarantee it. Lincoln calling up the troops lost the border states. Davis firing on Sumter must have inflamed the North."

"Oh, it did that," Cumb said, "raised a ruckus to put it mildly. The volunteers all fell into line to save the Union and the cry was *On To Richmond*. That's what got us into trouble. There was too much *On To Richmond* and not enough of a ready Army to accomplish that little job. But Congress wanted to see us fight and put a lot of pressure on Lincoln to make us go out and do it."

"Lincoln didn't stand firm against their stupidity?"

"He was new on the job, feeling his way like all of us. Anyhow, the Congressmen got paid back in kind," Cump said with a disgusted laugh. "A small mob of them followed us out to Virginia to witness a nice little battle. Came out all tooted up with carriages and picnic baskets of wine and stuff. The ladies were there too, bless 'em, in their pink summer frocks and their parasols."

"Idiots," George said.

"Uh huh. When we started falling back we got all mixed up with them. Awful to be in a stampede with terrified, drunk Congressmen and their wives. They clogged the roads all the way back to Washington."

George laughed. "Disgusting, the kind of people one is forced to associate with in a stampede."

Cump smiled and eyed him quizzically. "None of this seems familiar to you in the smallest way, General? Doesn't ring any bells with you at all?"

"Well, George struggled, "it's beginning to seem so." He tried to catch the flicker of indistinct memory that danced just beyond the border of his awareness.

"You know how it is," he said, "when you try to recall a dream?"

"Yep. The reason I ask," Cump said, his head cocked, "is because this is where you come into the picture in a mighty big way."

"By all means, go on then," George said, but with a growing unease. He felt some unknown overwhelming force bearing down on him.

Suddenly the memory broke through.

West Virginia, July 1861.

He was seated on a camp stool in his tent writing a letter to Nelly. The hot wind rustled in the trees and sent rippling dapples of sunlight and shadow across his table. He heard the troops drilling, those brave Indiana and Ohio boys, shouted orders and curses cutting in and out on the breeze.

Now he held a telegram and read the words:

> Circumstances make your presence here necessary. Charge Rosecrans or some other general with your present department and come hither without delay.
>
> Simon Cameron
> Secretary of War

He was back in the train facing Cump Sherman.

"You're remembering it!" Cump clapped his hands and let out a whoop. "I can see it! Glory be! I can see it by your face!"

"Yes," George whispered. "Very strange indeed ... I was in Western Virginia, those green mountains ... We had defeated ... Who was it? ... Garnett ... Killed him. Then I was called to Washington ...?"

Cump nodded. "That's right! You were put in charge of the whole goddamn Army! Lincoln was that desperate!"

George frowned. "Desperate indeed! I was the right man for the job. It was my destiny."

"Why, of course, Mac. I meant, they were desperate days. They feared the Rebs would march right into Washington at any moment. You were the man to save the whole shebang."

George squinted at him. "Then what are we doing on this train? Which is the real world, Cump? That world of war, or this one?"

"I've had time to give that a whole lot of thought, Mac, lots of time. Not much else to do in that hellhole asylum. Near as I

176

can figure, both worlds are real in some peculiar way we can't understand. Most people can't cross over between 'em. Can't or don't."

"Thank God," George said. Images, faces, panoramas of battle flooded and resounded through his mind. "It's as if suddenly I've come awake and remembered ... and remembered ..."

"That's right," Cump said. "That's exactly how it feels, and you can't tell anyone, and it can drive you crazy which is what happened to me in Atlanta, of course. Some gears and springs snapped loose up here." He tapped his forehead with two fingers.

George looked off into the muted orange twilight and allowed his thoughts to trail from his mouth. "Nearly a million casualties. I warned Hamlin but I never thought it would go that high. But tell me, Cump, which world is the dream? Both can't be real. Even if they are somehow, impossible as it is, you have to settle in one world or the other."

"That's right," Cump said. "It's the cutting back and forth between 'em that wears and tears on your mentality."

"But the war is over now, isn't it? It's about mid April, 1865? You are in the Carolinas ready to finish off Joe Johnston. Yet here we are in September of 1861. How could ...?"

Cump nodded. "Yep, that world of war is on a faster clock. I've just marched my army all the way from Atlanta into South Carolina. You can't imagine the hang-dog effect that had on the secession movement. I'm just waiting for Joe to surrender."

"My compliments on that march you made from Atlanta to the sea. A memorable achievement, sir. It will be recorded so in history I have no doubt, though I trembled for the risk you ran. I could never bring myself do that, leave my base and just plunge off."

Cump straightened his back, his face radiating satisfaction. "Much obliged for the compliment, General. It was a grand adventure."

George waited expectantly for Sherman now to return the compliment, to mention and praise his victory at Antietam creek. But the praise didn't come.

"So let me see now where are you at this point?" Cump said. "Still living in New Jersey?"

"That is our home of course," George replied, "but right now I see myself in a sunny garden in Rome at the Palazzo Barberini, writing letters under an olive tree."

"Ah, yes, I'd heard you were traveling abroad." Cump cast his eyes down.

"Don't be uneasy, Cump. We all know I am not the public figure I once was. Sunny Italy can soothe a man's blasted pride." George paused and looked intently at Cump. "Oh, all right, yes, I'll admit I was a fool to run for President against Lincoln. I merely wanted to explore discussions with Davis and company, yet Lincoln and his people made out that I would sell out the Union. It was grossly unfair. After all the bloodshed, I would never have compromised the Union."

Cump leaned back and inspected his cigar. "I know that, Mac. Politics is always unfair, and it just wasn't your game. 'Tis a witches brew right out of Shakespeare, politics and soldiering. First do one, then the other, like our old friend Sam Grant. He assured Lincoln he wasn't after his job, so Lincoln left Sam alone to do his, and now look at him."

George shook his head. "And now he'll probably be our next President. Sam Grant."

"Yep, it's a crazy old world," Cump said. "I wonder if or when I'm ever going back there. Or you? Or have we got us a choice in the matter?"

"I don't want to go back," George said, "not if I can help it. I did not do as splendidly as I might have hoped."

Yet something was tugging at him.

"Well," Cump mused, "in one world we had our war, and in this one we have our peace. The strangest thing of all, we can sit here and discuss it in a sagacious way. You know what else, Mac?" He chuckled. "It's a comfort to know that I'm not demented."

"Yes, hip, hip hooray."

Cump yawned, and stretched. "Yes, sir, a comfort." His eyes hooded over. "If you don't mind, Mac, I think I'll just nod off for a spell. So tired after all that's befallen me today. Later we'll talk more about the war, plenty for sure I want to ask you." He scrunched down in his seat, eyelids flickering closed. "Plenty I want to ask ..." Soon his mouth drooped open in a gentle snore.

But there was no sleep for George McClellan. Why did Cump have to wake up those memories? He would have been content never to recall that other life, dream, fantasy, whatever it was. Cump Sherman had questioned whether it was "real," but what difference did it make after all? It was real in their own minds which apparently were in perfect conjunction with memories vivid enough to weigh down upon him now, real enough to evoke gloom.

Were there others who lived in this counterpart existence? There must be. Was Nelly aware of it? Should he inform her? What about their other soldier friends of both sides? And what of Hannibal Hamlin? Was that good man mindful of the fact that he never became President, that he passed the time of war without much real duty or responsibility? Hannibal Hamlin had become so bored that he volunteered for duty with the Maine Militia and served as a private for a week.

Cump was snoring with noisy gusto.

George slumped in his seat. He could easily close his eyes and open himself fully to the memories. He brought himself up short. Did he want to? Wide awake now, he sensed that in the unknown governance of things he faced a choice. He could go back to that horrifying world of civil war or he could sit tight here and now, watch Cump sleep, safe in this comfortable railroad car, warmly lit against the night. The world of war would be gone forever.

Still the overwhelming emotional pull reached out to him. Hell yes, he wanted to go back, and he rationalized an excuse. Perhaps he could learn from it after all. He had been a soldier, and a good one. Once in Washington, however, watching

Lincoln, Stanton and the others and seeing how he measured up to them, a new fever struck. Politics. Fatal word.

He closed his eyes. Go back. Learn your hard knock lessons. Somehow he knew he could remember and relive, but couldn't change his locked in destiny. You can't attack Bobby Lee's center on the afternoon of September 17th no matter how much you might want to, he told himself. Relive the great adventure at least to see where it had gone wrong. It would be good for his character, make him a better man for the experience, or was he just going back for the bloody throbbing excitement of it all? Know thyself, George. He smiled inwardly, sat back, closed his eyes, and let the images flow freely.

In Western Virginia he had been a bold success, smashing the tattered ranks of the Secesh, killing their general, saving the district for the Union. That mission deftly done, Lincoln had called him to Washington to set things right following the Bull Run calamity.

Lincoln.

The name and the memory creased his brow. Lincoln, the mysterious, the ridiculous, the deadly. He saw again that shadowed, jagged face, the distant, haunted eyes. Abraham Lincoln was the towering magistrate who settled the fates of men and armies. At first his admiring friend, later his enemy.

Could he really say that Lincoln was his enemy? Political adversary, yes, but Lincoln the man had always been cordial to him, even sympathetic, joshed easily, and called him by his Christian name. Still, Lincoln had also been tolerant of his real enemy, and was influenced by him. George felt a surge of cold rage and a shiver of distaste as he mouthed the name of that virulent adversary, the treacherous Secretary of War, Edwin McMasters Stanton.

"But, ah, in the beginning," George felt his lips whisper the words that led his thoughts. In those golden days of late summer 1861 it had all been so splendidly ripe with promise.

In that world of war, July 30th, 1861, George sat at his desk in Washington City and wrote to Nelly:

I went to the Senate today, and was quite overwhelmed by the congratulations I received & the respect with which I was treated. I suppose a half a dozen of the oldest made the remark I am becoming so much used to. "Why how young you look___& yet an old soldier!" It seems to strike everybody that I am very young. They give me my way in everything, full swing & unbounded confidence. All tell me I am held responsible for the fate of the nation, and that all its resources shall be placed at my disposal. It is an immense task that I have on my hands, but I believe I can accomplish it.

I pray to God that I may be endowed with the wisdom and courage necessary. Who would have thought when we were married, that I should so soon be called upon to save my country. I learned before I came on they said in Richmond, that there was only one man they feared & that was McClellan.

Who also is your devoted husband,

George

He wiped the pen carefully and replaced it in the inkwell, arched his back and allowed his aching lower body a small respite. After eight stiff hours in the saddle inspecting the defensive works building up around Washington, it was sweet relief to sit on a pillow and pour out his heart to Nelly.

He knew these letters to his wife would accomplish two ends at once. Sharing his life with his beloved Nel was a pleasure and a privilege. Also these transcriptions of his daily activities, his immediate perceptions in these historic days would be most valuable in that future time when he would write his memoirs.

The chief lesson he was learning was the simple, human vulnerability of politicians with Lincoln as prime example. After knowing the President as an ordinary railroad lawyer, it was clear that the man was no more than a good natured political drudge, severely overmatched in the current national emergency. How evident it was that he, George McClellan, stood no worse and certainly a great deal better than those "great men" who governed the nation. He could easily see himself as President, or even, as some had suggested to him, a sort of dictator who would step in to subdue the secession crisis, and then, humbly, like George Washington, abandon his powers and retire from the service of his country a beloved and respected hero. He was eager to explore these ideas with Nelly when next their heads touched the same pillow.

He sighed, yearning at the thought. But first Nelly must give birth to their child in Cincinnati come October. Then God grant she would be well enough to join him in Washington soon after.

He rubbed his tired eyes. Yes, he did enjoy the taste of glory, as what man wouldn't? But these first desperate days in July after his arrival had tested his courage. He found only about fifty thousand of infantry, and one thousand of cavalry plus a few pieces of artillery. It was in fact a sham Army, more a demoralized mob. Though there were a few sound units commanded by reliable professionals such as Cump Sherman, the bulk of the Army was absent from duty and drunk in the muddy gutters of Washington. No defensive fortifications had been built, the camps were located haphazardly without regard for defense and no training or drill was being conducted. No roads were picketed or patrolled by cavalry.

Washington was wide open to Joe Johnston's Sesech Army and the sour smell of oncoming defeat tainted the air. George had changed all that in a matter of days.

CHAPTER FOURTEEN

The house at 1520 H Street along Lafayette Park had been built in 1818 within sight of the President's Mansion. A sturdy, three-storied red brick federal, it was locally known as the Cutts-Madison house after its builder, Richard Cutts and its most famous one-time occupant, Dolly Madison.

On a cool October evening in 1861 it was the home of General George B. McClellan, who sat alone at a table in the downstairs front parlor that he used as a work room. He was paging through the draft of a proposed examination for field officers. The room was generally lit by hissing gas fixtures, but he used a kerosene student lamp for close reading.

He frowned over the examination. What is the range of a twelve-pounder? How many wagons to supply a regiment? If only there were a question that could foretell a man's performance in battle, a test that could predict bravery. An officer with perfectly polished brass and a clean starched shirt could know all the answers to these paper questions but freeze in the face of enemy fire.

He tapped his pen. In a way his daily, probing patrol actions served as a testing for officers and men to see how they behaved under fire. His taut lips relaxed into a cautious smile at the thought of his pickets relentless pop-popping small arms to keep old friend Joe Johnston awake in his tent down in Manasses.

Joe's considerable army sat positioned West and Northwest in an arc from Manasses to Leesberg, Virginia. When George had first arrived in Washington in those sweltering, horrible days of July, he had lived in terror at the prospect of immediate attack. He had confided as much to Nelly in a letter when he said:

"I am in a terrible place here." Now he believed his army strong enough to resist Joe's attack.

Probably.

He heard arrival noises in the entry hall and the familiar voice with the prickly, back country twang. "Good evening, sir. Is George in?"

The muted voice of his assistant adjutant made a respectful not quite audible reply.

George stood up, put the examination paper in its folder. He lifted his jacket from the back of the chair, put it on and buttoned up the brass. A glance in a mirror, a hand through his thick, auburn hair and he was ready to meet the President.

The door opened. His adjutant stood at attention. "The President is here, General McClellan."

George strode forward, hand outstretched. "What a pleasant surprise, sir."

"You ought to quit being surprised by now, George, much as I'm over here. Hope it's not too late this time. You busy?"

"Paper work as usual, your Excellency. I welcome a recess."

Lincoln sauntered into the parlor looking lanky and bemused as always, his white duster coat flapping at his knees. He carried a book with his finger tucked in the pages and pointed with it at his companion.

"I brought along my secretary, George. You remember Johnny Hay. High time he got a dose of military wisdom. Had to drag him away from a party of rosy cheeked damsels, I'm afraid. My, but weren't they disappointed."

George sat down and glanced at his adjutant who was awaiting refreshment orders. "Yes, he said, smiling, "I've heard that Mr. Hay can sniff out a company of hoop skirts at a hundred miles range. May I offer you coffee or tea?"

Lincoln declined with a wave, but John Hay spoke up. "Tea with lemon, cream and three sugars," then turning to Lincoln, "You know, Mr. President, I much prefer your company to that of any rosy cheeked damsel in hoops skirts or out of."

"Ah, then you're a great deal stranger than I gave ya credit for, Johnny," Lincoln said as he folded his angular limbs into a chair. Now then, George, what mischief were you up to before this untimely interruption?"

"Working on ways of testing our officers, your Excellency. As you know we're training them in classes, but I want to find out what they've learned." He opened his folder and passed the draft examination to Lincoln who put on wire framed eyeglasses and cocked his head back to read. After a few moments of study, Lincoln handed the paper back. "Sound idea, this testing of their knowledge," he said.

"War is dangerous business, sir," George said, "and we must make professionals out of amateurs."

Lincoln nodded slowly. "As fast as we can," he said, eyes glinting over the lenses. "As fast as we can, eh George?"

"As fast as is humanly possible, sir," George leaned forward to underscore his point. He smelled what was coming.

Lincoln cracked his wide toothy grin. "Why you know, I could answer many of these questions myself what with all the studying-up I've done. Maybe I'll make myself into a general yet, just like old Jeff Davis."

"I wasn't aware that President Davis was a general."

"Oh, he's not. Just thinks he is, the way he bosses all his people. And by the way, George, it's not a good thing to call him 'President.' He's not President of anything but a band of rump States that imagine themselves out of the Union. They're not. Never were, and never will be. Just call him Jeff Davis for that's all he is."

"I'll remember that, sir." George hated being lectured like a schoolboy.

Lincoln took his glasses off and began absently polishing the lenses. "I had visitors today, some of our friends in the Congress. They were curious as to when we may expect aggressive action from our boys in blue, this astonishing army you've assembled. I told them I would ask you."

So the attack was on. "That's just the point, sir, it's not an army yet, not at all worthy of that appellation."

"Ah, I see." Lincoln pursed his lips in and out. "Well, but you can understand their confusion, can't you George? They see these grand thrilling reviews you put on over across the river. I don't mind telling you I enjoy watching them too, and so does

Bill Seward when he can stay awake. Indeed, sir, they are mighty impressive, all those men by the thousands marching in sturdy ranks, bayonets glinting. I know you must be rightly proud of them, George, and for us that don't know any better, it damn well looks like an army."

"It is an army in the making, sir. Those reviews are part of its training."

"Ah, well now there's a question. What does an army learn from all that marching up and down?"

"Many things, sir, primarily the habit of obedience to orders as in any drill. Most of all the parades give a lift to their morale. The band music stirs them, and they see their comrades by the tens of thousands, it comes home to them most decisively that they are a part of something far greater than themselves. It gives them a confidence in themselves and pride."

Lincoln was silent for a moment, allowing John Hay to get a word in. "I see your point, General. These parades boost what the French would call *esprit de corps*," which was briskly pronounced with a nasal accent that would have roiled the stomach of any Frenchmen.

George flickered a smile. "I couldn't have said it better myself, Mr. Hay."

Lincoln looked with open amusement at Hay, then said, "Well, George, you're the boss of the army, that much is certain. You train them. March 'em up and down, 'espree decore' and all that stuff. Just let me know when you intend to use them, and how."

"I will, sir."

"There's just one other thing, George." He glanced at Hay. "Would you give us a minute, Johnny, thank you kindly."

John Hay rose promptly and offered his hand. "I don't know much about military matters, General McClellan, but it's a relief to walk the streets of Washington without tripping over a dead drunk soldier. I thank you for that." He left the room, smoothly closing the door behind him.

Lincoln leaned forward, hands on his knees, both feet flat on the floor. "You had a fine long lunch today with some upper crust Democrats from New York State I hear."

"That is true, sir. They're old friends, and we are all members of the Democracy." George locked eyes with Lincoln. He knew what was coming and determined not to give an inch.

"The terrapin stew was merely adequate, but the champagne was excellent. You should have joined us."

Lincoln chuckled. "I wasn't invited, for I would have been about as welcome as a tit on a bull. You often have such lunches and dinners as well with your Democrat friends I hear."

"I do, sir, on occasion."

Lincoln eased back in his chair, seeming to relax. "It's a mighty confused and conflicted party you belong to, George, running three candidates for President at once. It was the thing that got me elected with forty percent of the vote. Without that, probably Judge Douglas would've been elected, and we'd have no secession, and you'd still be in Cincinnati running your railroad." He smiled kindly. "Remember back in Illinois when I was debating Judge Douglas? You rode on his campaign train and I heard tell it was your main job to keep him sober. And I must say, George, you were more often successful than not."

"I've always liked Judge Douglas," George said. "I voted for him."

"Oh, my yes, so do I like him, though I must confess I did not vote for him. Truth to tell, George, I feel mostly comfortable with you Democrats in many ways. Of course I come down a little bit harder on slavery maybe."

George was silent for a moment. Lincoln's opinions on slavery varied widely according to who he had talked to last. His solutions to the problem had ranged from deportation to limited compensation to God only knew what.

"This war, as I see it," George said, carefully, is not about slavery. It is for the integrity of the Union."

"Well, George, I couldn't agree more, but in politics, ya see, sometimes one thing get mixed up with another, and outlooks change." He frowned slightly, then said, "You're so busy here,

187

George, that you have to sit up by lamplight catching up with your duties. Might I might make one little suggestion?"

"Of course, your Excellency."

Lincoln's eyes glinted, his normally relaxed mouth was firm as if it had never smiled. "You are a Democrat, but you are also a soldier. Could it be that you spend a little bit too much time bein' a Democrat, and should maybe spend a little more time bein' a general?"

George felt his cheeks flush. He locked his lips down hard for he knew any words that came out now would only "aggravate the aggravation" as his mother-in-law would say.

Lincoln cocked his head, eyes widened. "Oh, now there I see I've made you angry, George. Damn, but that was the last thing I intended." He reached out and laid his large hand on George's arm. "What I meant to say was this ..." He gathered his thoughts. "You and I, we know our particular fields of endeavor, you as a soldier, and me as a politician. I only meant to suggest we stick in our own bailiwicks, you and me, and thereby do the most good for the country. And then, George," Lincoln raised and waved a long spatulate tipped finger, "when the time is right, I will give you every support you may need for a plunge into the lake of politics." The President looked off thoughtfully. "Although some would call it more a mud hole I suppose."

George took in a deep breath. "I will give every consideration to what you have said, Your Excellency." Did Lincoln actually take him for such a fool? Lincoln would support him as a Democrat? His party mentors had warned him to never trust Lincoln, and he judged it sound advice.

"Is there anything else I can do for you, sir?"

Lincoln squinted at him. "Well, yes, George, I wanted to ask you your opinion of something I read in Clauswitz's *Principles of War* which I found mighty interesting." He flipped the book open where his finger had marked it and began to read:

"Generally we are not nearly as well acquainted with the position and measures of the enemy as we assume in our plan of operations. The minute we begin carrying out our decision, a thousand doubts arise about the dangers which might develop. A feeling of uneasiness, which often takes hold of a person about to perform something great, will take possession of us, and from this uneasiness to indecision, and from there to half measures are small, scarcely discernible steps."

Lincoln looked up from the book. "What do you think of that, George?"

"I am quite familiar with Clauswitz," George said, "but not that particular passage."

"Then he goes on to say:

Not only are we uncertain about the strength of the enemy, but in addition rumor and all the news we obtain from outposts and spies exaggerates his size. The majority of people are timid by nature, and that is why they constantly exaggerate danger. All influences on the military leader, therefore, combine to give him a false impression of his opponent's strength, and from this arises a new source of indecision."

George waited for Lincoln to make his point.

"This got me to thinking, George. This fella, Pinkerton, the detective, he's in charge of all your estimates of enemy strength. He gets the stories from all the prisoners and spies and then he estimates to the high side all the time doesn't he?"

"He is following my orders, your Excellency. I do not propose to be surprised by enemy strength. I believe Joe Johnston to have in excess of a hundred thousand men opposing us in Virginia. If I err it will be on the side of caution."

Lincoln rose, his face stark white and abruptly drained of energy. "Very commendable, I'm sure, George." He offered his long, bony hand. "Well, then, good night. I hope I haven't said anything to put your nose out of joint, George. I run off at the mouth sometimes, and my brain don't get a rein on my tongue until I'm back in the barn."

George pushed a smile. They were both worn out from their long days, and there would be another like it tomorrow. "I know the feeling sir," George said as he walked with Lincoln to the door. "Say goodnight to Mr. Hay for me."

When Lincoln had gone, George mulled over the encounter. His eyes fell upon two red and white signal flags propped in a corner. Lincoln's rambling commentaries were a type of signal not difficult to decode.

He looked beyond the flags into the immediate future. He would go on building up his army, zig zagging around his Congressional enemies, the Republican radicals, getting along respectfully with the strange, double talking Lincoln. Then in the early spring, with his army a sharp honed sword, he would mount his grand thrust Southward, the water route to the James peninsula, slashing through Yorktown and Williamsburg and then on into Richmond, where his overwhelming force would demonstrate to the Sesech the indomitable resolve of the Union. Perhaps then they would not even make the charade of a fight. They were not fools after all. Seeing clearly that their cause was hopeless, they would sue for peace and accommodation with probably some agreement on gradual, compensated eradication of slavery by the turn of the century.

The Union would be saved, and the lives of hundreds of thousands of young American men would be spared. George McClellan, as savior of his country, would be rewarded with Lincoln's job in 1864.

He took a final sip of coffee and smoothed his mustache with a napkin. It was a sound plan, not perfect, but then no plan is perfect.

CHAPTER FIFTEEN

Early afternoon, a day in November, 1861, near Fairfax Virginia.

A column of blue uniformed Federal troops marches down a muddy country road, National and Regimental colors fluttering in wintry sun. A clatter and thumping of hooves is heard from the rear of the formation. Sergeants shout orders to split the men left and right, clearing a pathway on the road just as General George McClellan and an attending officer gallop along the interior of the column kicking up mud clumps. George holds his short-billed soldier's hat aloft above his head giving it a twisting, twirling flick of the wrist in acknowledging the yells and cheers of the troops.

"Hooray for Little Mac," they shout.

He leaves the troop column and gallops up a small hill, the other officer following.

"You see that, Fitz?" George says, his voice energized from the ride and the cheers. "Throughout the Army they know it's me because of the way I flip my cap. No other officer is permitted to do it that way. I think I'll take out papers at the patent office."

George sees his old friend, General Fitz John Porter, do something quite uncharacteristic. Fitz smiles, almost laughs. Nelly always claimed that Fitz John's visage was a model of that famous old literary knight, Don Quixote. Behind her hand she would affectionately call him "The Knight of the Woeful Countenance."

Sternly dignified, Fitz John Porter is one of the team of officers that George has assembled to lead the Army of the Potomac. Mostly friends from West Point and the railroad business, they are loyal, competent and mostly members of the Democratic party.

George loosens the reins on Dan Webster, and the horse shifts forward and noses deep into the long brown grass, chomping whatever he can find. A gift from railroad friends in Cincinnati, the glossy black Dan Webster is strong and intelligent.

"What's on the program here, Fitz?"

"A full brigade attack, sir, the Third Brigade of Baldy Smith's Division, General Hancock commanding. The objective is that line of woods. Two forward regiments attacking, the third in support."

George concentrates on the scene unfolding before him. He plays his field glasses over the two front regiments which are now rolling off the road and into battle formations. He picks out the rippling colors of the 7th Maine, the 49th New York with the 33rd New York in reserve, the standard two up and one back attack formation.

George turns in his saddle. "We're missing a regiment here aren't we? Where's the 77th New York?"

"General, your question will be answered shortly."

"Ah ha. Playing games today are we, Fitz?"

Fitz say nothing, his Woeful Countenance restored.

George scans the attack once again. The regiments shift into double time, their tightly packed ranks keeping good alignment, their mounted officers well posted for control.

"Go my lads, go. So far so good," George says as he looks back at Fitz. "What happens when they hit the woods?"

"They won't hit the woods, sir."

Off on the hard right flank of the attacking regiments, a mass of men suddenly pops up out of a field of tall grass, a surprise apparition of a thousand ghosts in raggedy browns and grays. They level their rifles and break into a run with an Indian-like screech.

"Ah, ha," George shouts. "All right, boys, get around, get around and meet it."

Shouted orders from the field below and the two attacking regiments smoothly swing to the right changing their front to meet the new threat. The volume of rifle fire rises from the initial pop-pops to a steady roar.

"We're all shooting blanks today, I trust," George says.

"Let us devoutly hope so sir," Fitz John Porter says. "We're right in the line of fire from that 'Sesech' regiment, which is the 77th New York. Haven't heard anything whiz by yet."

George says, "All right, Hancock, let's see what you do with your reserve now."

Porter waves at a fast moving officer on horseback behind the regimental lines. "There he is, sir, he's bringing it up."

"Ah, yes, but let's see what he does with it. What would you do, Fitz?"

"I'd still be worried about those woods. This flank attack could just be an amusement."

George nodded. "Right on the nail, Fitz." He studies Hancock's movements. "Keep 'em going toward the woods, General."

"He's not doing it."

Hancock is now moving his reserve regiment to the right rear of his two engaged regiments. George watches a moment then shifts his glasses to scan the woodline. "Damn it, look at that! Any fire from those woods now is going to take two regiments in flank, until he gets the reserve regiment to wherever the hell he's going with it."

"Looks like he wants to use it to come around and attack the 77th."

George snorts in disgust. "That's exactly what he's doing and it won't even be a full flank attack. Look, he's going in at a forty-five oblique. He's going to end up blocking the field of fire of the 49th New York. He'll be over committed and still open to attack from the woods. What a cock-up, as the British say." George tightens the reins on Daniel Webster. "I'm going to have to talk to him, Fitz. Let's go."

They find General Hancock Scott after the mock battle. His handsome, well framed face is dripping with sweat. He rides up to George and salutes.

"My compliments, General Hancock!"

"Thank you, sir."

"Good sharp response to the flank attack, but I don't like the way you handled your reserve. Should have kept them marching on toward the woods. We'll be going against people like Tom Jackson who likes to lurk in woodlines and pop out at the most inconvenient moment, just when you're having your tea and cookies."

"Sir, I agree," Hancock exclaims, his breath still coming in hard puffs. "Had it been up to me, I would have moved the reserve regiment forward and hooked up with the Seventh Maine, formed a ninety degree refused line that covered both the woods and the flank attack."

"Well, why the hell didn't you do it then?"

"Orders, sir. General Smith made up this exercise, and he told me exactly what to do."

George barks a laugh. "Hah, the Army is still the Army! So Baldy Smith told you to do that? Well, let it be a lesson to you, General Hancock. In the future you just do the opposite of whatever Baldy Smith tells you, and you'll come out fine."

A grin. "Yes, sir, General McClellan."

"Another principle that's served me well through my career, Hancock, always try to operate as far away as possible from your superiors."

Hancock, not sure how to respond, nods and wipes the sweat away from his trim mustache.

"Seriously, Hancock, you have a nice flair for handling troops. Good sense of ground too. Keep it up, we'll have an army yet, if the damn politicians will allow it."

"Yes, sir. I'm glad it's you has to deal with them and not me."

"You have your hands full with Baldy Smith. Now then, I want to address the men. Gather them around that knoll. Face them about so that I have the wind at my back."

With nearly four thousand troops tightly assembled around the knoll, George guides Daniel Webster up to the front ranks. Hands reach out to pat the horse on his flanks. Some respectfully touch George's boots in their stirrups.

First he shouts. "Can you hear me back there in the rear?"

They tell him they can.

"Soldiers, your General is proud of your efforts today. My compliments to the 77th New York on your scruffy Seceshedness. You outdid the rebels with your yell. I just hope, for the sake of your comrades, that you don't smell like 'em too."

Laughter, whoops and hollers.

"Mock battles can be good training, and I must complement General Hancock and General Smith for the superior handling of this exercise."

George jerks reins and gives a "Whoa-Boy," to Dan Webster who is side stepping, making it known he wants to be elsewhere.

"Now then, men, let me tell you what your General has planned for you! More drill, more training, and next Spring when the roads are dry, I'm going to take you on a trip down South. I can't tell you the exact route, but I promise you we'll cause some sleepless nights in Richmond. We're going to go down there, boys, and we're going to kick the Secesh in the hind side of their paints and drag them by the scruff of their necks back into our Glorious Union, whether they like it or not!"

Big cheers.

"We'll teach 'em that they can't steal eleven States from the United States of America without a firm protest from The Army of the Potomac!"

Hoorays for Little Mac!

"Remember men, we're fighting as Christian soldiers for the Union. We don't destroy property and we don't mistreat prisoners. They are fellow Americans, some our friends and brothers. As for Slavery, we leave that up to the politicians. We're not going down there to free the damn slaves! Of course if some of them get free on their own hook and want to dig trenches for us, well I won't boot them out of camp."

"They can have my shovel, General," a voice erupts from the crowd.

George lifts his hat and twirls it three times above his head.

"Bully for the Third Brigade," he yells as he slaps Dan Webster with his knees and breaks him into a quick trot and then a gallop.

The Third Brigade comes back with a Bully Cheer for General McClellan.

CHAPTER SIXTEEN

On an evening in early December 1861, George stirred himself awake and remembered with a start that he was at the home of attorney Edwin Stanton. Outside the gaslights of H Street still made radiant halos in the fog. He shook his head and then made out the shadowed figure of Stanton himself sitting in a gently rocking chair by the fireplace. The lawyer's oval eyeglasses glinted in the yellow-orange light of the embers.

"You must excuse me, Stanton." George noted with some chagrin that the papers he had been reading had fallen to the floor. "How long was I asleep?"

"Twenty minutes or so." Stanton's voice was warm and comfortable. "Nothing to be concerned about, General. You need and deserve the rest."

George had forgotten his pocket watch. "What time is it?"

"Half past ten."

"I should be on my way." He felt vaguely guilty at being away from Nelly and the baby.

"Have another brandy," Stanton said. "The Long-armed one may still be roaming the streets looking for you."

"Ah, no thank you. It was the brandy put me to sleep."

"Plus the secure quiet of this room, and the fact that you know you are in the presence of a friend who will not dog you as to when the Army will move next."

"True. It is most peaceable here. I told Nelly I come to your house to dodge browsing Presidents."

"Hah," Stanton shot a laugh. "The browsing gorilla you mean."

George smiled within himself. Stanton's wit could be a bit caustic at times.

"Yes, I know you must be careful," Stanton said. "You hold high office, and I do not. I enjoy the sweet luxury of plain speech." Stanton began to polish his glasses. "You know,

General, I've been thinking, we have much in common. We are the both of us high flown egotists. We, the both of us, see the stupidity, the corruption of this administration. Surely you take my meaning. That we are superior men is a fact, is it not?"

"Don't flatter me so, Mr. Stanton. I may be tempted to believe you."

"But, surely, General, you must realize that you have at your command sufficient force to rule this nation? Why you could march your great Army right to the White House this very night, arrest the President on whatever pretext you choose, and then march the other way up Pennsylvania Avenue to the capital and dissolve Congress at gun point. You would be the man of destiny, General. The savior of your country. The mobs would cheer."

George considered the tone of his reply. Stanton's idea had to be the result of brandy and high spirits. "History teaches us that the dictatorship game is a dangerous one. Why, I hear they often end up getting hung, stabbed or exiled. Besides which, Nelly would never stand for me being a dictator."

Stanton stared into the fire, his lips in a sardonic twist. Finally he snorted a hollow laugh. "Hah, Nelly! That's a good one. But seriously, General, if I can't tempt you to be dictator, perhaps you can give me some sound advice."

"Be happy to. I am full of brandy and sound advice."

Stanton reached over to George's glass with the bottle. "Here, have a little more. Let's drain this as the true men we are."

The brandy bottle clinked on the edge of George's glass and he did not object. The darkness of the room, the heat of the fire and Stanton's good fellowship was softly enveloping. He would forgive the silly talk about dictatorship.

"As you may know," Stanton said, more briskly now, "I have been doing legal consulting work for Mr. Cameron at the War Department. You heard the one about Cameron didn't you? Someone said Cameron was a thief. Lincoln said, no he wasn't for he would never steal a red hot stove."

George laughed with a polite restraint. Simon Cameron had given him friendly support and little trouble. "I could not confirm that of Mr. Cameron," George said.

"Oh, it is only a joke, I imagine, and I am not adept at telling jokes. But there is trouble concerning Mr. Cameron. He has gotten himself into a corner with Lincoln over his proposal for arming the niggers and putting them in uniform to fight alongside white men. The Long-armed One of course will have none of that."

"It could be a grave mistake," George said, with a chuckle. "If you arm them, who knows which way they would shoot?"

"Why of course," Stanton said, "who would want such a thing except a John Brown abolitionist? In any event the word has come to me from good sources that our estimable President is thinking to rid himself of Cameron, pack him off to Russia as Ambassador."

"Ah, a chilling thought," George laughed, then took a deep sniff of the fragrant brandy. Bless the French for inventing this stuff.

Stanton now rose up from the rocker and transferred himself to the sofa alongside George. "My question, General, is this. Would such an appointment meet with your approval?"

George was momentarily lost. "What appointment?"

"Oh, myself as Secretary of War. Didn't I mention that? The President, I am told by those who know, is giving it serious consideration."

George perked up and gave Stanton a good fellowship slap on the knee. "Why, that would be bully by me, old man. What a team we would make."

Stanton nodded with gratitude. "Thank you for your confidence in me, General, I am much obliged for it."

"When do you estimate the change will take place?" George asked.

"Within the next two months I expect. Say nothing of it."

George put a finger to his lips.

Stanton smiled thinly.

"Well now," George said, "since you asked my opinion, I shall ask yours in a matter that has been of some concern to me." He heard the brandy slowing his speech, but he knew he was making perfect sense.

"Some weeks ago, before Nelly came to stay with me, I attended a wedding of one of my officers. At the evening reception the champagne flowed and flowed, and then flowed some more deep into the night."

Stanton nodded and listened.

"Well, eventually I made my way back to my house. Guess who was waiting for me in my front parlor office."

Stanton grunted. "The Long-armed Phantom of the night? I think he must wander the streets so as to avoid the horror of an encounter with his wife in a dark room."

"John Hay, his secretary, was with him," George continued carefully. "I saw them waiting as I came in. I managed to get upstairs to my bedroom, threw some water on my face, and then decided I would just close my eyes for a minute."

"Very wise I'm sure."

"Well, I don't know about that, for the next thing I knew the room was lit by the sunrise, I was still fully dressed, my boots were on, and the old rooster next door was crowing."

Stanton gave a sharp laugh. "Ah, ha, and was Lincoln still waiting for you downstairs?"

"I was mortified. I learned later that my aide had told Lincoln I had gone to bed, and he left. Now, my question is this: Lincoln has made no mention of the incident. He is as friendly as ever and so is Mr. Hay. Should I bring up the matter and apologize? Or should I better let it go unspoken?"

"Is that all you're worried about, General?"

"I was quite embarrassed."

"Worry no more. Lincoln has a thick skin. He's no doubt forgotten the incident by now, as should you. It would be best if you never mention it to him."

George nodded and stood up. "I must take my leave now, Mr. Stanton. Thank you for the interesting talk, the good advice, and the sanctuary. Not to mention the excellent product of France."

"We Democrats must stick together, General. Perhaps between us we can be an antidote to the imbecility of this administration."

George felt a surge of affection for this odd, gruff talking man. He controlled the urge to hug him as he would a brother.

"Help me to dodge the politicians," George said.

"I am ever your loyal friend," Stanton replied, his voice mellow.

* * *

Alone now, Stanton resumed his seat by the fire and mused on the gullible McClellan who he could manipulate like a child. Lincoln, he knew, had been hurt and insulted by the General's behavior that night and expected an apology. John Hay had been furious as he told him about it. It was so easy to fool the young Napoleon, hardly a challenge.

All his life Stanton had made a purposeful science out of lying. He had found that men, and women for that matter, would swallow any prevarication as long as they are told exactly what they yearned to hear. Thus to George McClellan he had disguised himself as a responsible, old-line Democrat full of the ancient dirge about state and property rights and the dangers of overly strong central government. He had even listened with feigned sympathy as McClellan preached on about the virtues of Christian war.

He thought of the Southern states. How like foolish, petulant children those Slavers had been to create their "revolution." They had been the power of the Federal Government from the beginning and could have gone on controlling Congress, Supreme Court and Presidency for as long as they pleased aided by their allies in the North.

And yet, astonishingly, they had thrown it all away, split their party in three, succumbed to the rantings of their own madmen, and allowed themselves to be spooked into secession

201

only because Abraham Lincoln, that ineffectual, blathering, ape-man had threatened to look cross-eyes at them.

Stanton snorted. If only those idiotic Slavers could get a close glimpse of the President, they would all come galloping back into the Union, rightfully convinced that he was no threat to them. Lincoln, he saw now, had won the election only because his opposition was divided, and because few men of any consequence had ever met him. The Abraham Lincoln who the Southerners viewed as the devil in long pants was nothing but a fictional creature constructed out of the feverish rantings of whimsical newspaper writers and rumor mongers. The real Lincoln was little better than an old fashioned Democrat wearing the Republican party label who would sell out the anti-slavery cause in an instant if only Jefferson Davis would lead the erring sister States back into the Union. He had publicly said as much. Then the Democrats would step back into power, and slavery would endure for another fifty years.

Well, we can't have that. The destruction of slavery was of course the will of God, which happily and conveniently offered the political opportunity of a lifetime. The South was there, fat, witless and ready for the plucking. Their leaders had stupidly blundered themselves into this civil war, opening fire on the symbolic flag at Fort Sumter. Lincoln had been forced to respond with the only action in the range of his narrow imagination. Call out the troops.

That little outrage led to the secession of four more States, and today's pretty mess.

Well, war. So be it. The loyal Unionist-Democrats like McClellan would be useful for fighting it, and then they could be disposed of.

Traitors, we will call them.

The Republicans would benefit for the next hundred years. Stanton smirked. Should he become a Republican, join his friends Chase and Wade and the others in the party of Emancipation? No, it would be better and useful to remain as that oddity, a cooperative 'Democrat.'

With the war settled, they would take over the riches of the South, take the land and free the slaves, who in unending gratitude to the Republican party would vote it into office for the next hundred years. That fool Lincoln, all he could think of was shipping them to Africa or South America, or the disgraceful dream of compensated emancipation. Imagine, actually paying the Slavers with public funds to free their poor woolly victims. Sickening.

No, the only way to destroy the slave drivers and unleash four million dark Republican voters was by flaming, brutal, all-out civil war, no quarter given. The South must be punished for its sins and eradicated. He and his friends would then pick up land which would be open for the taking from the bankrupt Slavers. The votes of the docile, grateful niggers would be theirs as well. But the war must be stretched out, extended in violence and brutality, until there was no hope for the kind of peaceful settlement that men like McClellan dreamed of.

McClellan. He must not be allowed to take Richmond this year, for it might well lead to an unwanted, premature settlement. As War Secretary Edwin Stanton could see after that little matter.

The war would end when he and his friends in Congress decided it would end. Then they would get rid of the soft-hearted Lincoln who would no longer be of use to them.

One of their own must then be President, a man who would not be afraid to be cruel to the South. Where could they find such a man? Why, perhaps a good old 'Loyal Democrat' who had served the Union with distinction as War Secretary?

It was all God's will.

CHAPTER SEVENTEEN

Washington, January 12, 1862

They were back in Mexico, the two of them manning a lone artillery piece. The sweat smeared face of Captain Bobby Lee grinned at him, swabbing out the tube, ramming the ball home against the powder bags. Fire! Recoil. Aim the piece!

"Come on, Mac. Move!"

"Blow 'em up, Bobby."

His lips were sticky, as if glued together. As the war scene faded, a cherished face appeared framed in an uncertain light.

"George, can you hear me?"

"Nel?" What was she doing in Mexico?

"You were having a fever dream, shooting up Mexicans with Bobby Lee."

Of course. He knew where he was now.

Nelly's cool hand moved from his forehead down to his neck. "Your nightshirt is soaked, darling, I'm going to get you a clean one."

"What day is it?"

"Sunday."

"What date?"

"January 12th. Do you know the year?"

"I think I still remember that. Good Lord, Nel, I slept a day away. But at least the floor has stopped rolling and you are lovelier than ever. I am either on the road to recovery, or have I died and you're an angel?"

Nelly gave the husky laugh he loved. "Angel indeed."

He tried to swallow. "Water, please."

She poured a glass from a pitcher that tinkled with a lump of ice.

George pulled himself against the pillows. "Never get the typhoid fever, lady mine, even if someone tells you it's fun."

"Ah, I'll be careful then."

"Is it snowing still?"

"No, it stopped finally." She went to the window and opened the velvet drapes. "See? The sun is out. Oh, George I was so afraid." She strained to keep the tears out of her voice. "The doctor said you might die."

"Cheerful fellow. Let's have him shot."

Nelly sat on the edge of the bed and smoothed his hair. George caught her hand and squeezed it. "I long to kiss you, but my mouth tastes like the Potomac at low tide."

"I'll get your toothbrush. Now darling, I hate to tell you, but that creature is downstairs, claiming there is some meeting you must attend. I told him it was out of the question."

"Who? Lincoln?"

Nelly wrinkled her nose. "No, the one I love and respect so much."

"Stanton? What does he want?"

"For you to go to the President's house with him. I've tried to shoo him off, but he has planted himself down in the parlor. Insists he must see you."

George swung his legs out of the bed and felt the sharp tingle of cold floorboards. "It must be that important then. I'll have to see to it, Nel." He peeled away his nightshirt. "Help me dress."

Nelly pursed her lips.

George broke into a small laughing and coughing fit. "Oh, don't give me that sour apple look. It must be an emergency. Good God, are the Sesech attacking the city? Did Joe Johnston get off the pot?"

"George! Such talk." She poured warm water from a pitcher into the wash bowl and wiped his face. "As I gathered from the creature, it's just a meeting President Lincoln is holding with some of your generals."

"What?" George bellowed, and dropped the sock he was trying to put on. "With my generals?" He quickly finished dressing, and feeling only slightly dizzy, made it down the stairway with Nelly holding on at his elbow. Meeting his generals? What sort of game was Lincoln playing now?

At the foot of the stairs he hugged her close.

206

"Are you sure you can do this?" she asked.

"Yes. I think I have to. Don't worry."

"Get back soon," she said. "I'm making white bean soup with ham."

"Ah, that will surely cure me."

Nelly walked into the parlor with him and preached at Stanton who rose as they entered.

"Now then, sir, I advise you, General McClellan is far from completely well. Look after him, and do not let him stay out too long or get overtired. You hear me, now?"

The man with the gray wire beard smiled, flashes of light filling the ovals of his spectacles. "Mrs. McClellan, I shall take care of him as if he were my own brother."

George saw Nelly's lips twist. Why did she so unreasonably despise this odd but true hearted man?

Once outside and in the carriage, the blast of January cold staggered him despite overcoat, cloak, and gloves. Sun blasting off the snow banks stung his eyes. Should have worn his smoked glasses.

Stanton settled beside him in the carriage, and soon the driver had it crunching its way through the sloppy gray residue of mud, gravel and snow that coated the street.

"What's going on, Stanton?"

"The President has been consulting with some of your generals." Stanton said in tones of gravity. "They are counting on your death, and are already dividing among themselves your military goods and chattels."

"Faugh! Do I look like I'm dying to you, Stanton?"

"Thankfully, no."

"Who is attending these 'consultations' as you call it?"

"General McDowell, I believe, and General Franklin, and also General Meigs."

George controlled a flush of anger. McDowell he could understand, that darling of the Radicals, the numskull who had lost the battle at Bull Run. He would love the opportunity to show off. Meigs, the well respected supply officer would merely be following orders.

But Bill Franklin, his most loyal friend? That worried him.

"Then today," Stanton continued, "there will be Secretary Seward, Secretaries Chase and Blair."

George ran through the names. Blair, the Postmaster General, was a West Point graduate who came from that touchy border state, Missouri. A supporter if not exactly a friend. Seward, the smooth talker, he had never been able to figure out, but Chase, the Treasury Secretary was a high browed Ohio abolitionist. Some weeks ago George had tried to get Chase on his side by hinting at his plans for the army's main attack. The ploy had proved worthless. Chase had lined up with his radical enemies in Congress.

"What a cast of characters," George fumed. "Positively Shakespearean. And by what excuse has Lincoln called my generals?"

"Because you are supposed to die," Stanton said with a touch of impatience.

"Ah, that would be a popular move on my part, no doubt."

"And nobody knows any of your plans." Stanton glanced sideways at him, his breath puffing white in the cold. "Even I have not an inkling of what you intend to do, or when."

"Not an inkling, eh? That's good." George clapped his gloved hands, starting to feel a little more chipper at the prospect of conflict. He had been in bed too long.

Stanton suddenly coughed explosively and trailed off in a series of wheezes. George recalled the man suffered from asthma. It must have cost him to come out on a day like this. Presently Stanton recovered. "I felt it was imperative that you put in an appearance at this little gathering. Just barge in like Jesus risen from tomb and scare the piss out of the apostles."

George shifted uneasily. "No need to bring our Lord's name into it." He would ignore the vulgarity.

"Oh, of course. Very sorry. But I have other news, which I hope may perk you up."

George felt his mind drifting. "What is that?"

"The President came through and is about to appoint me Secretary of War, but as I told you before, I shall not accept if I do not have your blessing."

"Why, that is good news, Stanton. I certainly do approve."

Stanton's faced glowed magenta with cold and pleasure. His breath billowed in clouds. "Thank you. Thank you. I am most humbly grateful."

Once at the President's house, Stanton insisted upon remaining in the outer hallway while George attended the meeting.

"After all I have not been invited," Stanton said. "I do not officially take over until next week, and Tom Scott is in there representing the War Department. So I'll just wait here and say my prayers til you're finished and then I'll see you safely home to your good wife."

George steadied himself, opened the door with its familiar squeak and entered Lincoln's office. He first sighted the green wallpaper and recalled Cump Sherman's true comment as to how ugly it was. No one had seen him yet. He slammed the door behind him. Wake up, boys! The sound snapped all faces around in a comic reaction.

The corpse had just walked in.

There were his Judas generals. McDowell's eyes bulged, but Bill Franklin smiled broadly. The courtly General Meigs showed bemused interest. The politicians, Chase, Seward, Blair and of course Lincoln were all frozen in shocked befuddlement. Tom Scott, that level-headed railroad man, looked pleased.

Lincoln recovered first. He unfolded his arms and legs out of his rocker and ambled over with an extended hand.

"Why, General McClellan, what a delightful surprise, sir. I know I speak for all of us here. We were so very worried about you and the state of your health."

George nodded politely to the President and to everyone in the room, then took a seat at the table between General Meigs and Secretary Blair. "Glad to see you up and about, General," Blair said in a low voice.

"This meeting is a matter of some interest to me," George replied under his breath as he surveyed the room. Chase, Seward and Lincoln whispered among themselves until Lincoln looked up.

"General McClellan, I was afraid your health might be so impaired that you could not continue in your duties. With that in mind, I invited General Franklin and General McDowell to give me their views as to what the Army ought to be doing. I even said, joshing, that if you weren't going to use the Army, I might want to borrow it for awhile."

No one laughed except Lincoln. George locked eyes with the President, hardly able to control his flaring temper.

"So we were just about to hear from General McDowell, when you came in," Lincoln went on, smoothly. "He is going to tell us what he would do in your place."

McDowell's alarmed glance darted from the President to his Commanding General. He swallowed, tried to smile, but his lips went all wrong. "I'm just following orders, sir. I was directed to make this presentation by the President."

"Then I think you should proceed," George replied. He glanced a raised eyebrow at Bill Franklin who gave back an embarrassed shrug with the unspoken message: "This wasn't my doing."

George felt a new wave of fever as the petrified McDowell made his highly qualified recommendations. McDowell, it seemed, was all for an attack on Joe Johnston at Manassas. Brilliant! Repeat the mistakes of the past. Attack them straight ahead, right into the teeth of their strength, where they're most prepared for us. Then grind on to Richmond in the bloody overland route. As McDowell rambled, ducked and dodged about his plan, in severe embarrassment, standing before a map on an easel, George saw that Seward was nodding in agreement, as was Chase.

Idiots!

Franklin, when his turn came, spoke briefly in favor of a water route to the James peninsula. So, he was still a friend, and God bless him.

When both generals had finished, Lincoln called for comments. There were none. All looked at George. General Meigs leaned over and whispered in George's ear, "They expect you to speak now, General."

George looked at the well meaning Meigs whose big, round face showed concern. He whispered back. "I am not going to reveal my plans in this meeting. Lincoln can't keep a secret. He will tell his boy Tad, and it will all over Washington by nightfall and in the *New York Herald* tomorrow."

George closed his eyes and felt the room tilt. Why was he even bothering to explain himself to Meigs? The headache was coming back, and with it the chills. To his horror he felt his bowels knot up and grumble. Thankfully there was an indoor commode room across the hallway, but it would be an undignified retreat.

"Are you still feeling unwell, General McClellan," Seward inquired in a kindly voice. "You look green."

Before George could answer, McDowell cut in. "I meant no offense in my presentation, General McClellan." Then a sideways glance at Lincoln. "I was ordered to give my opinions and did so."

George sighed. "You are entitled to have any opinion you please." He wished McDowell would sit down and be quiet.

Again Lincoln and Chase were urgently whispering to each other. George felt moisture running down his back. This trip may have been a mistake. He put both hands on the table to steady himself.

Suddenly Chase was speaking in his strident, nasal voice. "General McClellan, as I understand it the purpose of this meeting is for you to describe your plans in detail, that they might be submitted to the approval or disapproval of the gentlemen present."

"I wasn't aware that was the purpose of this meeting," George said. "If so, it's entirely new to me." What the hell was Chase talking about?

"Well," Chase said, with building agitation and a side glance at Lincoln, "that's the way it is. So you had just better get on with your explanations."

George folded his arms, slumped back in his chair and aimed a disdainful look at Chase. Open fire. "Sir, I understand that you are the Secretary of the Treasury. I do not recognize the Secretary of the Treasury in any manner my official superior. You have no right to question me upon military affairs in my charge. Only the President and the Secretary of War have the right to interrogate me."

George turned away and said quietly to Blair. "Do you think any of that penetrated his numb skull?"

"No, but you've just made an enemy for life," Blair, said with a small chuckle.

Chase, red faced, whispered with Lincoln who then turned to Seward and whispered some more. Lincoln then looked up at George with his most winning smile. "So it's up to me, is it General? Well, so be it. I think you'd just better go ahead and tell us what your plans are."

George got to his feet, gripped the back of his chair, comforted by the thought that Blair and Meigs would catch him if he fainted.

"Mr. President, if you have confidence in me there is no call to entrust my designs to the judgment of others. But if your confidence in me is so slight that you require these other learned gentlemen to fortify and approve my opinions, well, then Your Excellency, it would be wiser to replace me."

"No, George, I don't mean to replace you."

"It would be wiser to replace me with someone fully possessing your confidence. I tell you, gentlemen, no general worth a damn ..." He looked at McDowell with open contempt. "No general worth a God damn would submit his plans to the judgment of such an assembly as this, where some of you are incompetent to form a useful opinion and the others of you are incapable of keeping a secret."

George felt his knees weaken. He braced himself, one arm on his chair and the other on the table. He had to stay on his feet.

"The Secretary of the Treasury and His Excellency both have a general idea of what my designs are. Therefore I decline to give any further information in this meeting unless you, Mr. President, issue an order in writing and assume responsibility for the results."

George lowered himself into his chair, his body trembling.

There was a heavy quiet in the room until Secretary Seward popped up, buttoned his coat and laughingly said, "Well, Mr. President I think the meeting had better break up. I don't see that we are likely to make much out of General McClellan."

"Well, then, let's adjourn," Lincoln said, a bit annoyed that Seward had jumped up first. As the others gathered to leave he came up to George and shook his hand. "You take good care of yourself now, General. I hope you don't mind me thinking about borrowing your army for awhile."

"Perfectly understandable, Your Excellency. But if you'll just trust me in military affairs, I'll free you from all your worries and troubles. I promise."

Secretary Chase walked by pointedly not speaking to George.

In the hallway, he found Stanton awaiting him. "Well, how was it?" the lawyer asked.

"My arrival had very much the effect of a shell in a powder magazine."

"Hah," Stanton exclaimed. "Boom!"

"A big boom," George said. "Everyone was embarrassed, and rightly so."

"Well, we must get you safely home to your warm house. We'll talk more later."

George laid an unsteady hand on Stanton's shoulder. "You are a kind and decent friend, Stanton. You were quite right. The blade was out and they were preparing to plunge it in me, the hypocrites. I tell you, my days of trusting in Lincoln are over. He told me he just wanted to 'borrow' the army if I wasn't using it. Can you imagine the gall of the man?"

Stanton shrugged with an air of resigned sadness. "Well, we have always known what he is, haven't we?"

George steadied his wavering legs. He willed for his bowels to hold out until he reached home.

"I'm relieved and pleased that you will be the new War Secretary, Stanton. It will be a pleasure to work with a man I can trust.

CHAPTER EIGHTEEN

New York, April 6, 1862

Sir William Russell left the ship's rail and hurried back to enjoy the warmth of his cabin. He'd seen quite enough of New York harbor as it faded away under a lowering cloudscape. The prow of the ship was pointed for England, thank God. The United States of America, tearing itself apart in bloody civil war, was stimulating enough for a visit but he was happy to be going home.

Yes, and how splendid it would be to walk peacefully on public streets without being insulted and pointed out as a object of common scorn. Whatever years were left to him, whatever his accomplishments or honors, he would forever be known in American lore as that disdainful Englishman, "Bull Run Russell." His only crime had been to report the simple truth about the conduct of Federal troops in that first great battle in July of last year. He told how they had run.

Americans didn't like to hear about that.

Russell sat at the tiny desk in his cabin and shuffled through his notes and papers until he found the notebook with his rough reportage of his last interview with General George B. McClellan. He would fill the days of the voyage with polishing and editing this despatch so that it might be published upon his arrival in London. It would still be timely.

He perused his notes.

April 1, 1862, Alexandria, Virginia, late afternoon, at the Potomac docks, jam packed with transports for the great invasion thrust to Richmond. Someone calling it "The Footstep of a Giant." Not bad. Use it.

Saw General Mac on board his headquarters ship, the Commodore. A well furnished stateroom with shaded deck overlooking the bustling fleet. Constant noise, yells, shouted orders, units marching burdened with baggage, too much confusion in the constant loading and boarding of guns, men, horses, more baggage, supplies and just plain 'stuff.' Masts of ships everywhere. A forest of masts? McClellan looks on what he has wrought with unconcealed, almost childlike pride. Once he excused himself to go scampering down on the wharf to straighten out a tangle of horses being boarded. He came back with a wry grin on a smudged face, said he bet no British general would have done that.

Quite correct, I told him.

Says he had to wrestle with Lincoln and Stanton to get approval of this invasion. They live in quaking fear of a Secesh attack on Washington, and Mac had to assure them city would be safe, would leave enough troops to guard it etc., etc. Guard the valley to the West as well. As if Confeds would be fool enough attack here while their own capital city is threatened.

Mac worries, (better word, "fusses") over every detail, which is of course a result of not having an effective staff. His old father-in-law, General Marcy, nominally Chief of Staff, is well meaning but not cruel enough. Aides dash in and out on this mission or that. Somehow it all gets sorted out, so perhaps am too critical.

General Mac says he will depart for Fort Monroe, Virginia, within the hour. I offer constructive criticism, tell him Federal army looks too luxurious by far. He is taking a small printing press to make bulletins to the troops. He is taking two balloons for spying on the enemy and a small chemical factory in wagons for gassing them up. He is taking endless other wagons heavy with telegraph wire. All units will be busy telegraphing jolly greetings to each other it seems. More wagons pregnant with photograph equipment for making maps, and so on and on etc. I fancied he would take a gun factory from Pittsburgh if it could be gotten on a ship. As to guns; endless varieties, from siege pieces and mortars so heavy I fear they might sink the boat. Once they get to Virginia, some of them will require railroad track to be laid before they can move.

Never in my whole experience have I seen such a rich army.

Looking upon all these marvels or modern warfare, I said: "This is just the sort of war in which the general who moves lightly and rapidly, striking blows unexpectedly and deranging communications, will obtain great results."

He took my advice with a ready laugh. He thinks his big guns will make all the difference. "Can't have too much artillery," he says All in all, General Mac charming and friendly to me as ever. I recalled to him our evenings last fall spent in designing this grand strategy. He cheerfully said if he failed in this invasion, he would see that I got all the 'credit.'

Told him that I was going home because of my difficulties in getting a pass from Stanton. "If I am not to be allowed to cover the war, then what am I doing here?" I asked quite reasonably.

He told me I was "damn lucky" that Stanton didn't arrest me. Said, "It is well known that Bull Run Russell is a friend of General McClellan. So be glad that Stanton only denied you passage, and nothing worse." I believe he is truly disappointed that I am not to be allowed to travel with him to the Peninsula. I shall miss the attack on Yorktown and the battle for Richmond.

McClellan puts up a jolly front, but he told me the situation with Lincoln and Stanton has become nearly intolerable. (Note the word "nearly.") I told him many a general would have resigned when he was demoted as Chief General and learned the fact only in a newspaper story. He acknowledged my concern, clearly moved, but loves his Army of the Potomac so much (too much I think) that he will put up with the humiliations and insults inflicted. "Who will lead them and take care of them if I am gone?"

Thought to myself, there will always be another greater fool for glory out there ready to take his place when the ax falls. And it will. Only a matter of time.

He told me that on March 8th at a private meeting in the President's office, Lincoln came right out and called him a traitor. Mac (naturally) jumped up, lost his temper and demanded Lincoln take it back, which the President did with much sputtering and backing down, merely reporting what was being said by some in Congress and so on, blah blah blah ...

"Now, don't get me wrong, George," in that snuffling twang, of his. Yet I have sympathy for the President too, all pressures falling on him, a son recently dead, a wife as mad as a bedbug.

Appalling how free and easy Americans are with that fatal word, 'traitor.' They 'sling' it too much.

Mac says Stanton had professed to be his friend right up to the time be became Sec. of War. Then as they say, the roof fell in. I had warned him of Stanton. Better still, his astute little wife had warned him as well. He should have listened to us.

Fit this story in. Lincoln only a few days before had taken one whole division away from him for purely political reasons. They were Germans from St. Louis, had to be sent to Missouri's Political General, Fremont in West Virginia. Mac says he took it with good grace in hopes of soothing relations with Lincoln, who actually came down to the ship and apologized for the 'necessity.'

I know some Generals who would have tossed Lincoln in the stinking harbor, and not apologized for the 'necessity.'

Mac quote, for possible use: "Lincoln has got the idea he knows war. He only knows books about war." Don't quote him directly.

A thought not to be uttered. Yet. Mac may be too soft, kindly, humane. Says he cries when he sees dead bodies of his men. (Who would admit such a thing?) Fear he may try too hard not to lose. War demands deaths.

Big secret: Mac is obsessed with the idea of success without winning battles. Says he will attempt to open up negotiations with the Confederates once he gets his vast, monster establishment to the edge of Richmond. His theory is they will be so frightened of all his big guns, his printing press and his balloons etc., that they will quiver and quake and want to open discussions. Must be secret because Stanton would foam at the mouth in fury if he knew of it. Told Mac not to expect a "rip roarin'" success. I know these Southrons.

In parting he placed in my care a last letter to his wife for me to mail. He knows that if it goes through regular army channels, someone with the initial S. will read it.

I shook his hand, looked him in the eye, and wished him success. I know we will not meet again in this life.

Left General McC. with mixed emotions. He is a finely tuned soul, perhaps too fine. War demands a certain brutishness. Which thought led me to explore around the port of Alexandria, which in turn depressed me even more. Once a sleepy little village on the Potomac, it is now a 'full blast' military town with all the slime and smell of corruption one would expect. It is common knowledge here that one general is so fond of prostitutes they are now called by his name. 'Hookers.'

He is said to be a capable general in his off moments.

CHAPTER NINETEEN

Camp Abraham Lincoln, Savage Station, Virginia. Midnight, June 27, 1862

They gathered around a blazing pine cone bonfire, Keyes, Heintzelman, Sumner, Franklin, Porter, all Corps Commanders of the Army of the Potomac. The fire burned in the front yard of General George B. McClellan's headquarters, a mile south of the Chickahominy River and ten miles east of Richmond.

George stood apart from the group and gazed unblinking into the flames. Moisture dribbled down his back, just as another drop ran down his forehead and dripped off his nose. He dabbed his face with a damp handkerchief, feeling both hot and cold, signs of the fever coming back. At least the fire kept the buzzing swamp insects at bay.

He squared his shoulders. It was unacceptable to be sick again. He took a deep breath to steady himself, knowing he must soon brace this band of Generals and soothe their raw nerves.

Something made him look to his left. There was the haggard, dirt and sweat streaked face of Fitz John Porter whose woeful, haunted eyes regarded George then looked away. Poor old Fitz had taken a brutal hammering today, holding out for most of the daylight hours in a strong position north of the river on a dusty farmyard knoll called Doctor Gaines' Mill. The Sesech had finally flanked him and broken his lines only in the red and dusty sunset, sending Fitz and his whole Fifth Corps reeling in retreat to a tight perimeter around the bridges over the Chickahominy River. The Secesh, themselves bloodied enough for one day, had backed off into the darkness to pick up the moaning wounded and the silent dead.

Fitz John Porter's Fifth Corps had been the vulnerable right flank of George's army, out there 'floating in the air' anchored to nothing, as it faced the defenses of Richmond. It was only going to be a matter of time before he took Richmond in his own well planned and methodical way. But time ran out. Bobby Lee had sortied forth from his defensive works, looped around and attacked from the northwest bloodying and finally breaking the Fifth Corps.

Who was it he had to thank for the weakened condition of his right? Lincoln and Stanton. Give Lincoln the benefit of the doubt; perhaps it was merely bookish ignorance, but with Stanton it had been his characteristic vindictiveness or even worse. Well, he intended to send those two gentlemen a telegram tonight that would set the record right even if he died in the forthcoming battles. He owed that much to history, to Nelly and his baby daughter.

The Corps Commanders were unusually quiet tonight, not a good sign. Some sipped coffee and some swigged champagne from sweating green bottles. The ice to cool the wine came from U. S. Navy gunboats anchored ten miles to the south in the James River. Fitz John Porter, not normally a drinking man, took a long pull from one of the green bottles as he conversed intently with Nelly's father, the calmly dignified General Randolph Marcy.

George needed a few more moments alone. He stepped away from the fire, composing and rethinking the words he would speak. To see where you are, consider where you've been. He had managed the army to this place, within ten miles of its goal, Richmond, heart of the Confederacy, despite near criminal lack of support from Washington.

At Yorktown, his first objective at the eastern tip of the Peninsula, he had been criticized for taking a month to get past it, a month spent moving up and digging in his big guns, preparations for a siege. Lincoln had told him on April 8th to "break the enemy lines at once." George wrote to Nelly: "I was tempted to reply that he had better come down and do it himself."

The delay had paid off. Just when all his giant mortars had been set up within 1100 yards of the Secesh entrenchments, the wily Joe Johnston had pulled out without a fight and skedaddled for Richmond. It was George's first "bloodless victory," as he had called it in a letter to Nelly.

From there they had cracked through Williamsburg, with his fighting generals, Hancock, Hooker and Kearny leading the way. George telegraphed Nelly that they were doing pretty well for a "Quaker Army."

But all the way to Richmond, Stanton had continued to undercut him. If only McDowell's Corps had been with them as planned and promised. But McDowell, scheduled to come down overland to reinforce the Fifth Corps, had been held back to protect Washington from the perceived threat of the dreaded Tom Jackson, that rampager of the Shenandoah Valley.

George drifted away from the orange flames and into the darkness of the pine woods. Were they facing defeat? Or was it opportunity? He felt too tired to think. He sat down on a log and began writing again in his message book, continuing the telegram he had begun earlier, the plain truth intended for War Secretary Stanton:

"If we have lost the day we have yet preserved our honor & no one need blush for the Army of the Potomac. I have lost this battle because my force was too small. I again repeat that I am not responsible for this & I say it with an earnestness of a General who feels in his heart the loss of every brave man who has been needlessly sacrificed today. I still hope to retrieve our fortunes, but to do this the Govt must view the matter in the same earnest light that I do -- you must send me very large reinforcements, & send them at once."

George let out a breath. There was so much more to say. He stood up and walked a few steps deeper into the piney woods. His foot tripped on something and he stumbled, nearly falling face forward.

"What the devil? Who is that?"

"Sorry, sir." George saw in the faint glimmering light that he had almost fallen over the extended boot of one of his aides, a boisterous young Cavalry Captain.

"What are you doing down there, Armstrong, trying to break my neck?"

223

A lanky, blue uniformed figure surged up out of the darkness to face him.

"No, sir.   Beg pardon, sir."   George Armstrong Custer brought himself to attention as much as he was able, his pale, raw boned young face swaying in the firelight that glinted off his thick blonde hair.

"I was jush... I was just..." He held up a mostly empty green bottle. "...enjoying some refreshment, Genel McClellan, sir, and a little rest."

"Well, you did some hard riding today, Armstrong. I reckon you deserve some refreshment."

"Ah, begging the general's pardon, shur ... sir." Armstrong frowned with effort, getting his words straight. "Is it true what they say, that we're retreating?"

"Faugh! Who says we're retreating?"

"I observed we ... got beat today, sir," Custer said, his blue eyes sad above his drooping mustache.

"Nonsense. We're going to move south of that infernal river to consolidate our position and change our base. They still teach the importance of a secure base at West Point, don't they Armstrong?"

"Indeed they do, sir. Or so I heard from them who went to classes."

"Well, pay attention tonight and you may learn something of soldiering despite yourself."   George turned away then remembered something else.   "By the way, Armstrong, you caused me some embarrassment today."

"Me, sir? How was that?"

"Remember that message you brought me? Your eyewitness report of the battle. You said the Secesh looked to be retiring about three p.m.?   It caused me to telegraph General Porter to pitch in and give chase to them."

"Yes, sir."

"If your report was correct, Armstrong, then tell me who was it that drove the Fifth Corps back up against the river? Ghostly phantoms?"

Armstrong raised his right arm in a carefully crafted salute. "Most apologetic, General." With his left hand he lifted the champagne bottle and poured the bubbly stuff over his head.

George snorted a laugh. "Better on your head than in your belly, eh, Armstrong? Well, we all make mistakes. Even myself on occasion."

"You, sir? Never! Why, what a thing to say!"

"Just make sure you're ready to ride at first light tomorrow."

"Ready to ride this instant, General. Always ready to ride. That's what Libby likes about me, haw, haw!"

"At ease, Armstrong."

"Libby thinks it funny, General, you calling me Armstrong and all, but I explained to her how you said we can't have two Ghorsh ... two Georges in this Army."

"I trust she approves." George moved back to the group around the fire with Custer trailing, their boots crunching in the dry grass.

"Oh, she approves, yes, sir. Sometime she calls part of me Armstrong too. Guess which part."

George ignored that one and raised his hand for silence.

"I'm ready to learn shum ... something, General," Armstrong whispered from behind. His voice and body exuded compounded odors of sweat, horses, champagne and the cinnamon which he liked to wear in his hair.

"Back away, Armstrong, and see you don't fall in the fire. You would cause an awful explosion."

"Yes, sir, General McClellan, sir." Custer sat down with a jolt.

"Give me your attention, gentlemen. First of all I want to commend General Fitz John Porter for his courageous stand today up at Gaine's Mill. I know you all join me in that."

There were nods and muttered affirmations, some hand clapping. "Good for you, Fitz. Well, done, old man."

George's voice took on added authority. "You managed your command with great skill General Porter, and held out gallantly all the day. I regret that I could not send you more reinforcements because we were under heavy pressure on this side of the river. When I asked for reinforcements to shore up your position, each of our Corps Commanders here told me by telegraph that they were hard pressed and expecting to be attacked at any time."

More agreeing nods from the Corps Commanders. Yes, yes, it was all true. The Sesech had been threatening mayhem all day on their front lines.

"Since about seventy-five percent of our Army is here, south of the river, I thought it prudent to hold our positions here. Indeed General Hancock has just beaten off a strong attack this evening at Golding's farm."

"That's too bad, General," Fitz John Porter said, his voice hoarse from a day of shouted orders. "My men thought we were holding out north of the river so the rest of the army down here could push on into Richmond."

George felt a flair of annoyance. Why would his friend Fitz say that? "Well, it wasn't to be, Fitz. Let's not be concerned about what might have been. We have to face the facts."

"Yes, sir." Fitz John Porter's eyes were downcast. "I've been facing facts all day, sir, about fifty thousand of them trying to kill me. How many of you, other then Hancock, were actually attacked today?"

There was no reply from the other Corps Commanders.

"Do you think we let you down, Fitz?" There was silence.

"I make no further comment, General McClellan. You sent what help you could, I suppose."

"Yes, I suppose I did." George fumed, but forced a composed front.

"Very well, gentlemen, let's examine our situation."

He paused. What were the facts? He commanded an Army of a hundred thousand, perhaps, facing a hundred and eighty to near two hundred thousand led now by the very capable Bobby Lee, assisted by Tom Jackson, A.P. Hill and other 'old friends.' This band of fellow West Pointers had just wiped out his right flank. They were now in a position to sweep down across the Chickahominy River, cut his supply line to his base back at White House Landing and threaten his whole army.

"Of course we all know why General Porter was left in such an untenable position today," George continued. "The irony of it is remarkable. General McDowell, with thirty thousand men, was held back from reinforcing us to guard against Tom Jackson's threat to Washington. So what happened? Wonder of wonders, Tom Jackson came sweeping down here today to attack us, while McDowell stayed up at Manassas, sucking his thumb, guarding Washington, by order of the President."

From across the flames George caught a warning look from his father-in-law, General Marcy.

But the Corps Commanders had been sparked by his speech. They murmured, shook their heads, some laughing sourly. Bill Franklin said: "What I want to know is how do you suck your thumb when it's already up your ass?"

"McDowell could find a way," Old Bull Sumner said.

They laughed too loudly.

"God save us from our political masters," George bellowed into the fire, giving full vent to a weary day of frustration.

He looked at General Marcy, nodded with a tired smile. Don't worry, I'm okay.

He pulled out a set of papers from his inner blouse pocket. "Gentlemen, I have been planning something for over a week now. When I saw the threat developing on our right, Tom Jackson coming down from the valley to attack us, and knowing the kind of aid we might expect from Washington, which is to say nothing, I determined that it might be necessary to give up our whole right including our supply base at White House Landing in order to save this Army."

"What do you proposed to do, General?" It was Fitz John Porter, his voice firm again, his way of apology.

George smiled at Fitz. "Study these maps, gentlemen. They were prepared by our engineer survey squads and reproduced by our photographers. I'll warrant these roads you see depicted here are accurate to within fifty yards."

Bull Sumner, the veteran, sixty-year-old commander of the Second Corps gave a growling laugh. "We're all over the Secesh on maps anyway," he announced. "We found out last

227

month from prisoners at that Seven Pines fight, they don't know horse shite about these roads around here, where they go or where they come out."

"An advantage for us," George said, "and I intend to use it. Now then, note your positions and routes of march are marked in red ink. We will move South along the Quaker Road, a fighting flank movement, to this place on the banks of the James River, Harrison's Landing, just east of where the James River forms a turkey neck. It's a wide flat and open area where we can dig in and be protected by the direct fire of the gunboats."

Murmured comments from the Corps Commanders as they studied their maps.

"Tonight we move this headquarters back to Dispatch Station. General Keyes, your Fourth Corps will move south with all its trains. You will cross White Oak Swamp and take position down here at Malvern Hill. It's a damn good piece of ground, men. I've surveyed it myself. We can hold it strong, and don't forget down there we'll be within range of the gunboats."

"The big boomers," Captain Custer said approvingly from down in the grass. "And all the ice we need."

George side glanced Custer then turned to Fitz.

"General Porter, you will follow right on after General Keyes. Generals Franklin, Sumner and Heintzelman will cover your movements from the positions indicated on your maps. Then they will pull back in the order given. Questions?"

There were plenty, but their spirits were up now. "We can do this; we can fool Bobby Lee."

"He'll think we stampeded to the East. They'll be looking for us there."

"Good move, General."

Old 'Bull of the Woods' Sumner summed it up: "They'll be looking for us to zig and instead we shall zag."

Bill Franklin caught George's eye with an encouraging wink. "It's not such a bad idea, Mac," he said. "We'll hold em off as long as you need to get those trains by."

"Speaking of trains, we can't take everything with us," George said. "It's too bad but we'll have to burn and destroy what we can't carry. That includes the railroad from White House. I have our engineers working on a scheme to blow it up and the locomotives too."

With more details, questions, give-and-take, the meeting ran on until nearly two a.m., when the tired Generals went back to their units.

George retired to his tent with a fresh bottle of champagne to finish the telegram he had started. He took a swig, and told an orderly to send for the telegraph operator on duty. He pulled off his boots, took another drink. Those cowardly curs in Washington had sent him to Richmond, without any real intention of letting him take it. That was plain enough.

He rubbed his eyes, too tired to write more to Nelly. He found the copy of the telegram he had sent her earlier in the evening.

Camp Lincoln 8 PM June 27th, 1862: "Have had a terrible fight against vastly superior numbers. Have generally held our own & we may thank God that the Army of the Potomac has not lost its honor. It is impossible as yet to tell what the result is. I am well but tired out. No sleep for two nights & none tonight. God bless you."

Poor Nel would be worried when she got that. He would telegraph her more tomorrow if the Secesh hadn't cut the wires by then, and if he was still alive. He swigged more from the green bottle. It was getting warm and flat, needed more ice.

The telegrapher appeared at the tent entrance. George waved to him.

"Come in, Captain. I'm composing a telegram to be sent to Washington in cipher."

"Yes, sir."

"Have your code book ready. I'll have it for you in just a few minutes."

"Yes, sir."

He placed his message pad on his folding desk and wrote by the light of a single candle: "I shall draw back to this side of the Chickahominy & think I can withdraw all our material."

Then some choice words about the President, and his judgment. If I had only had ten thousand more men, George mused. No. More than that were needed. Fitz was attacked by sixty thousand. He scratched his chin with his pencil. How to make those idiots in Washington understand? When they refuse to understand.

The quiet of the night was broken by a sudden a commotion outside his tent, men's voices, horses jangling up. His guards gave rough challenge.

A messenger? George stood up in his stocking feet. An orderly stuck his face in the tent flap.

"Yes?"

"Sir, General Heintzelman is here with General Kearny and General Hooker. They request a meeting with the General Commanding, sir."

George stepped outside his tent and felt a warm, damp breeze slap his cheeks. There facing him in full uniform were two of his best fighting Generals, Joe Hooker, Commander of the Second Division, and Phil Kearny, Commander of the Third Division, both components of General Sam Heintzelman's Third Corps.

The dull and stoic Heintzelman hovered. Clearly this wasn't his idea.

Joe Hooker was impressively tall and square-jawed handsome with thinning sandy hair, his face dominated by a hawkish red veined nose. He had served in Mexico and been a farmer in California before the war. George liked 'Fighting Joe' as the newspapers were now calling him, despite the fact that his eyes were set too close together giving him an untrustworthy demeanor or that he was often sidetracked by his love of hard drink and soft women. Worst of all, he was a friend and ally of Treasury Secretary Chase.

Phil Kearny was a character right out of a stage melodrama. Sprung from a family that had left him independently wealthy,

Kearny played the military profession with the passion of an artist. He had fought in Mexico and left an arm there, but that never stopped him. He would ride his horse full tilt with the reins clutched in his teeth. Before the war he had lived grandly in Paris with his common law wife, a society belle of New York. To keep up his soldierly skills he joined the army of Louis Napoleon and fought battles in Italy. He dressed and lived with French flair, his soldier's cap tilted crisply over one eye. Phil Kearny feared no man, always spoke his mind without restraint, and he totally despised General George B. McClellan.

George looked down and noticed he had forgotten to pull his boots on. Ah, let it go.

"What can I do for you, General?" George returned two good salutes and a casual wave from Phil Kearny who swayed a bit.

There was an edgy silence.

"Good evening General Hooker, General Kearny." George studied their faces. They had their wind up about something and they would not be shy in letting him hear about it.

Kearny spoke up first. His thin oval face, large bulging eyes and a pointy French style goatee all caused his men to say he looked like a devil.

"General, we hear that you intended to retreat south. That's of no consequence to us, of course. You can do whatever you want, but we request permission to fight our two Divisions into Richmond and release our prisoners. There are upwards of fourteen thousand of our boys in jail there."

"You think you can fight through their lines? I doubt that, General."

"They are fake lines," Kearny exploded. "Lee took the bulk of his army up North for the attack today. The lines down here in front of Richmond are papier-`mâchié! Oh, they marched and yelled and made out they were about to attack us all day, but it was just play acting by that clown MacGruder. He pulled the same trick at Yorktown, made you think he had a hundred thousand men, and you took the bait."

"I've had no confirmation of that," George responded sharply. "Mr. Pinkerton said they had a hundred thousand. General Porter from the balloon saw no cause to deny it. I brought up our guns and played it safely. There are five to ten thousand of our men alive tonight because I did so."

"He fooled you at Yorktown and he fooled you here," Kearny steamed on. "We could have taken Richmond today on this side of the river. I guarantee it. Let us take our divisions in, we'll give you Richmond, make you out a big hero." Kearny staggered, then righted himself.

"Sir," Hooker said, "he's right, I'll vouch for him. Let us fight our divisions into Richmond. We'll yell out if we get into any trouble!"

"Of course you'll yell! Even if you get to Richmond, how long will you hold out before Bobby Lee and Dutch Longstreet kick you out with heavy losses? I tell you gentlemen, when one of us goes to Richmond, we'll all go."

"Let's all go then," Kearny yelled at the top of his lungs. "Cut out this treasonous retreat you're fostering on us. Let's go at the enemy, not away from them!"

"General Kearny, you're in no condition for reasoned discourse."

"Yeah, General Mac, sir. What's that I smell on your breath? It ain't rosewater."

"Control yourself, General Kearny."

"Why don't you let real soldiers fight, you big bucket of chicken shite!"

George turned to Hooker. "General Hooker, my ears just failed me."

"Yes, sir, sorry, sir," Hooker said. "But we feel strong about this. We could do it, sir. Just give us the go ahead."

"No, and that's final."

"Why won't you fight?" Kearny ranted. "Why the hell won't you fight? I tell you men, we are being led here by a burnt-out impostor posing as a General. He has no talent as a general. He is nothing but a great spoiled child. He is a military

232

imbecile. He is incapacity personified. He is either a traitor or a coward, take your pick. I say both!"

George turned to Heintzelman. "General, your man is out of his mind."

"Yes, sir, very sorry sir," the distraught Heintzelman said, wringing his hands.

Kearny was screaming, sputtering, stomping in a circle, a grotesque Indian dance, his empty left sleeve flapping out. Hooker caught him as he nearly topped over.

"Get him back to his tent, Hooker. He should not have come here in that condition."

"Yes, sir, General McClellan. Pardon his choice of words, sir, but he is not himself."

"Oh, faugh, Hooker. He is entirely himself, and you know it."

Kearny went at it again. "Why don't you court martial me, you craven impostor? Go ahead, court martial me!"

"Because I need a fighting soldier, you blathering son of a bitch. Now get out of my sight, Phil and get some sleep before I lose my temper."

Kearny seemed to run out of air. He blinked, then sat down carefully on the ground.

Hooker tried to contrast himself, speaking with reasoned dignity. "Sir, I still say, with all due respect sir, give us the go ahead and we shall take Richmond, sir."

Kearny scrambled to his feet and glared at George. "We would do it, sir. I would do it, as my name is Phil Kearny and I'm a soldier. Just give the order, sir. Begging your pardon if I got a little out of line back there."

That was enough of too much. "I prefer it when you're true to yourself, Phil. Never mind the empty apologies. Now goodnight gentlemen, though it's nearly morning Report to your commands, get some sleep." George turned on his stocking foot heel and went into his tent. There awaiting him was Allan Pinkerton.

"You heard all that, Allan?"

"I did, General. Disgraceful language."

"Oh, that's just Phil Kearny. Damn it, they think it is so all fired easy to take Richmond."

"Not with a hundred thousand of the enemy ready and waiting on us south of the river, sir."

"That's what you make it?"

Pinkerton nodded with heavy certainty. "That's what all my detectives tell me."

"This change of base is the only move I could make, Pinkerton. I have no other choice."

"Looks thataway, General."

George sat at his desk, picked up his pen. "Excuse me for a minute while I finish writing this love note to our gallant Secretary of War."

Pinkerton guffawed. "Give that horse's ass a big kiss from me. Got any more champagne?"

George pointed to an ice bucket. Then he wrote in his message book:

I feel too earnestly tonight -- I have seen too many dead & wounded comrades to feel otherwise than that the Govt has not sustained the Army. If you do not do so now the game is lost. If I save this Army now I tell you plainly that I owe no thanks to you or any other persons in Washington -- you have done your best to sacrifice this Army.

George showed what he had written to Pinkerton who said, "That's telling the truth, sir. Let 'em have it."

He ripped off the message sheet and handed it to the waiting telegraph Captain.

"Encode and send this, Captain."

The Captain scanned the message, then looked up wide eyed. "Are you sure this is what you want to say, General McClellan?"

"What kind of a question is that? Do you have authority, Captain over what messages I send or do not send? Do I have to get your approval?" George put his face an inch away from the Captain's nose, West Point style.

"No, sir."

"Then send it, God damn it! Send it! We may all be dead tomorrow!"

CHAPTER TWENTY

Turkey Bridge, Virginia June 30, 1862, 7:00 p.m. Telegram from George to Nelly

    I am well but worn out__no sleep for many days. We have been fighting for many days & are still at it. I still hope to save the army ... Goodbye dear Nell & God bless you.

July 1, 1862, Telegram, Abraham Lincoln to General McClellan:

    It is impossible to re-enforce you for your present emergency. If we had a million men we could not get them to you in time ... Maintain your ground if you can; but save the army at all events ...

July 1, 1862, Telegram, General McClellan to Adjutant General Lorenzo Thomas:

    Another desperate combat today ... If it is the intention of the Government to reinforce me largely, it should be done promptly, and in mass. I need fifty thousand 50,000 more men, and with them I will retrieve our fortunes ...

July 2, 1862, Telegram, Abraham Lincoln to General McClellan:

    Allow me to reason with you a moment. When you ask for fifty thousand men to be promptly sent you, you surely labor under some gross mistake of fact ... All of Fremont in the valley, all of Banks, all of McDowell not with you, and all in Washington, taken together do not exceed, if they reach sixty thousand ... Thus the idea of sending you fifty thousand, or any other considerable force promptly, is simply absurd ... If you think you are not strong enough to take Richmond just now, I do not ask you to try just now. Save the Army, material and personal; I will strengthen it for the offensive again, as fast as I can.

July 2, 1862 Telegram, General McClellan to Abraham Lincoln:
I have succeeded in getting this Army to this place on the banks of the James River ... As usual we had a severe battle yesterday and beat the Enemy badly, the men fighting even better than before. We fell back to this position during the night and morning. Officers and men thoroughly worn out by fighting every day and working every night for a week. They are in good spirits and after a little rest will fight better than ever ...

Letter, George to Nelly , July 4, 1862
We have fine weather today, which is drying the ground rapidly ... I am ready for an attack now___give me 24 hours even & I will defy all Secessia ...

Message from General George B. McClellan to The Army of the Potomac, Camp near Harrison's Landing, Virginia, July 4th, 1862
Your achievements of the last ten days have illustrated the valor and endurance of the American Soldier. Attacked by vastly superior forces and without hope of reinforcements, you have succeeded in changing your base of operations by a flank movement ... the most hazardous of military expedients ... Your conduct ranks you among the celebrated armies of history. No one will now question that each of you may say with pride: I belonged to the Army of the Potomac.

Letter, George to Nelly, July 8, 1862
It is terribly hot and has been for the last two days___but we manage to worry through it ... We are strengthening our position daily___the enemy waiting for something or other a few miles off ... I have written

a strong, frank letter to the Presdt___if he acts upon it the country will be saved ...

How I long to see you in the midst of my troubles. The thought of you has been an immense consolation & support to me. How perfectly happy I shall be if God sees fit to permit me to be with you once more. I will never leave you again if it in the power of humanity to avoid it. No rank, no wealth, nor honors can reconcile me to absence from you.

Letter, George to Nelly, July 9, 1862

... His Excellency was here yesterday and left this morning. He found the army anything but demoralized or dispirited___in excellent spirits. I do not know to what extent he has profited by his visit__not much I fear, for he really seems quite incapable of rising to the height of the merits of the question & the magnitude of the crisis. I will enclose with this a copy of a letter I handed him, which I would be glad to have you preserve carefully as a very important record.

I thank you a thousand times for your kind and loving sympathy ...

Telegram, General McClellan to Abraham Lincoln, July 12, 1862

... Rain ceased and everything quiet. Men resting well, but beginning to be impatient for another fight.

I am more & more convinced that this Army ought not to be withdrawn from here___but promptly reinforced & thrown again upon Richmond. If we have a little more than half and chance we can take it. I dread the effects of any retreat upon the morale of the men.

Letter, George to Nelly, July 13th, 1862

It is a little hard that I cannot see my own baby or her dear Mother ... I wish indeed I could see her, & *somebody else too ...*

There never was such an army, but there have been plenty of better generals ... In no battle were we repulsed. We always at least held our own on the field if we did not beat them.

I still hope to get to Richmond this summer___unless the Govt. commits some extraordinarily idiotic act___but I have no faith in the administration and shall cut loose from public life the very moment my country can dispense with my services ...

So you want to know how I feel about Stanton & what I think of him now? I will tell you ... I think that he is the most unmitigated scoundrel I ever knew or read of; I think that ... had he lived in the time of the Savior, Judas Iscariot would have remained a respected member of the ... Apostles & that the magnificent treachery and rascality of E. M. Stanton would have caused Judas to have raised his arms in holy horror ...

I may do the man injustice__God grant that I may be wrong___for I hate to think humanity can sink so low ... He has deceived me once___he never will again. Are you satisfied now__lady mine? I ever will hereafter trust your judgment about men ... I remember what you thought about Stanton when you first saw him___I thought you were wrong___I now know you were right. Enough of the creature___it makes me sick to think of him!

Letter, George to Nelly, July 17, 1862

... I agree with you that a certain eminent individual is 'an old stick'___& of pretty poor timber at that. I confess that I do not at all appreciate his style of friendship. The army did not give him an enthusiastic reception___I had to order the men to cheer & they did it very feebly___this you can keep to yourself ... It may well be that I have made great mistakes, that my vanity does not permit me to perceive ... I did have a terrible time during that week___for I stood alone without anyone to help me___I felt that on me rested everything & I felt how weak a thing poor mortal erring man is! I felt it sincerely & shall never I trust forget the lesson___it will last me to my dying day ...

Letter, George B. McClellan to William H. Aspinwall, July 19th, 1862

I have reason to believe that General Halleck is to be made Commander in Chief of the Army ... & I think I detect ... symptoms of further changes. I can get no replies from Washington to any of my dispatches___I receive no reinforcements & no hope of them is held out to me;___the game apparently is to deprive me of the means of moving & then to cut my head off for not advancing ... I am quite weary of this ...

Looking forward ... my main object in writing to you is to ask you ... to see whether there is anything I can do in New York to earn a respectable support for my family___I have no exaggerated ideas or expectations, all I wish is some comparatively quiet pursuit___for I really need rest ...

Letter, George to Nelly, July 20th, 1862

... I see it reported in the evening papers that Halleck is to be the new General in Chief. Now let them take the next step & relieve me & I shall once more be a free man ... I hope Halleck will have a more pleasant time in his new position than I did when I held it ...

No position can ever temp me into public life again___my experience in it has been sad enough ... But one useful lesson I have learned ___to despise earthly honors & popular favor as vanities___I am content___I have not disgraced my name, nor will my child be ashamed of her father ... I shall try to get something to do which will make you comfortable ...

We should lead hereafter a rather quiet & retired life___it will not do to parade the tattered remnants of my departed honors to the gaze of the world. Let us try to live for each other & our child ...

Letter, George to Nelly, July 22, 1862

... Be very careful what you telegraph & tell your father the same thing. *I have proof that Stanton reads all my private telegrams.* If he has read my private letters to you his ears must have tinged somewhat ...

Letter George to Samuel L. M. Barlow, July 30, 1862

... Halleck remained but a few minutes ... & saw nothing of the Army___departed just as wise as he came ...

I get no reinforcements and no information___until Halleck came I had no word from Washington, since he left I have received nothing. I know nothing, absolutely nothing as to the plans & intentions of the Govt___

Telegram, General George B. McClellan to General Henry W. Halleck. August 4,

1862 Your telegram of last evening is received. I must confess that it has caused me the greatest pain I ever experienced, for I am convinced that the order to withdraw this Army to Acquia Creek will prove disastrous in the extreme to our cause___I fear it will be a fatal blow ... Clear in my conviction of right ... I entreat that this order may be rescinded.

Malvern Hill, twenty miles southeast of Richmond, August 7, 1862

Top of the tree.

George could climb no further among the thin upper branches. Bracing his boots on a precarious limb, he swept the area with his field glasses. Nothing to be seen at first, but then a glint, a movement in the shadows, the flash of a hat in a rustling bush, a rush of birds. He listened and heard a distant cough, a metallic clank, a horse's shiver, and then an oppressive silence, menacing in itself.

Barely visible signs and traces.

A voice from the base of the tree. "How about it, General? See anything?"

He waved to the man on the ground to be quiet and scrambled back down the tree trunk, scraping his hands on the whacking branches. He landed hard on the grassy stubble, nearly lost his footing.

"Steady there, General." Joe Hooker grabbed for his elbow. "Well, sir, what do you think?"

"You're right, they're down there," George said. "Waiting."

"What strength do you estimate?"

"At least a division, probably more." Or even more than that?

George returned his field glasses to their case, then wiped his face with his neckerchief. Damnable heat. Damnable flies. Damnable Virginia. He looked out at Hooker's wary men in loose formation in the grass, some stretched out asleep in the blazing morning sun, their rifles ready at their sides.

Strange to be back here on Malvern Hill, site of their greatest victory of the campaign. How did it ever get to be called a 'Hill?'" It was merely a gently sloping piece of ground, only sixty or so feet above sea level, topped by a large open plateau which he estimated ran about a mile and a half in length and three quarters of a mile wide. The 'Hill' or whatever you wanted to call it, had served admirably last July 1st as the final defensive line in the change of base movement. Here they had aligned their artillery wheel to wheel and masterfully blew apart a series of enemy attacks. The next day George pulled the Army back to Harrison's Landing.

Now here they were again on Malvern Hill with two Infantry Divisions under Hooker along with cavalry and artillery supports. Hooker had taken back the hill two days ago, easily brushing aside the small enemy force that had stood guard here.

George had joined him here yesterday and had spent the night, sleeping on the ground wrapped in an old horse blanket.

And now Joe Hooker awaited his decision.

George fingered his mustache. He was torn with contradictory urges. The aggressive Federal movement to recapture Malvern Hill had put Bobby Lee on the alert. He had sent troops to the area, perhaps in division strength. Signs of their build-up were showing in the swampy woodline a mile away. So fight or back off? Obey Halleck's orders from Washington to retreat? Or push into Richmond?

"Permission to speak, sir?"

George found the tin cup of coffee he had been drinking before he climbed the tree. He sipped it. Cool and gritty, but still potent.

"Go on, Joe," he said.

"Sir, as a soldier I think that order to retreat from here is the stupidest goddamn thing I've ever heard of. We're only twenty miles from Richmond where we stand under this tree. Halleck wants you to pull back to a position seventy-five miles away, after marching seventy miles to get there, and then go after Richmond from there. It is fucking insane."

George smiled with a rush of warm feeling for this vain, prickly man. "Hooker, for once I can't fault your bad language. You are right on the nail."

"Well, sir, having agreed to that, I would point out that you can't comply with your withdrawal order if you are engaged in a raging battle. Now can you?"

"True."

"Well, sir, I say go for Richmond. I can open the fight right here and now while you bring up the rest of the Army. You know the old saying, General, you might as well be hanged for a sheep as an old goat."

"I'd prefer not to be hanged at all, Joe."

He saw the red faced Hooker struggle with his feelings, wanting to say more. "Ah, I know what you mean. I'm in trouble enough with our masters in Washington. What's one

242

more battle to them? Why I might even be defeated or killed, the best of all possible worlds."

"It would take pressure off of Pope in Virginia," Hooker said, ignoring George's bitter remark. "Lee's been moving North going after Pope on the belief you won't attack Richmond."

"And now we've caught his attention once again."

"Damn right, General. We thrashed him on this hill a month ago. We can thrash him again."

George pondered, weighed, considered. General John Pope was the new darling of Stanton, Chase and the anti-McClellan clique in Congress. He was their boy of destiny now sitting at Rappahannock Station, Virginia, with a patched up group of marginal units calling itself The Army Of Virginia. Tom Jackson had been detached from Richmond and was going after John Pope who was starting to get nervous. George was to pull away from Richmond, and come back up to reinforce Pope. That was the all-wise plan of the War Department. But Hooker was right. They couldn't pull back if engaged in combat at Malvern Hill. It was an enticing proposition.

"All right, Joe. I'm going back to headquarters, but I'll give serious thought to your recommendation. You'll have my decision this afternoon."

Hooker's cold blue eyes were searching. "Sometimes sir, it may be best for a soldier to just go ahead and act without thinking."

George paused with a curious frown, then called for Dan Webster to be brought up. The two officers exchanged salutes. As he rode off George thought over Hooker's peculiar remarks. "Act without thinking?" It sounded like something young Custer might say.

* * *

Deep in the heat of the afternoon, George stood alone next to the gangplank of the Hospital Ship Columbus. A parade of stretcher bearers and walking wounded made shuffling, stop-

and-go progress past him. General Halleck had ordered the sick and wounded to be shipped off as a first step in the big skedaddle.

"Thank you for your honorable service," George said softly again and again, as the wounded made their halting, painful way past him and up the plank to the ship.

Men on stretchers with limbs missing, lifted their heads and saluted.

Men on crutches hobbled by with respectful greetings and stiff smiles.

"Proud to have served with you, General McClellan."

"Don't let them get you down, General. We'll be back."

One man in a stretcher held on to his hand and squeezed hard. "Say General, I'm the lucky one, escaping from all this heat and the flies."

"You are indeed," George said, holding on with both hands. "It'll be cooler out on the water. Why, this ship is so fast, she'll beat us back to Washington in no time flat."

"That's good. I never seen such big flies. Nothing like them in Ohio, eh General?"

"That's one of the good things about Ohio, soldier."

The man muttered something to himself, his voice drifting off. "I didn't need that extra leg anyway."

George's father-in-law, General Randolph Marcy joined him on the pier.

"Nothing new from Washington, General. The wire's restored, but they say Halleck has left the office for the day. I got off that message you sent from Malvern Hill, Enemy under cover in strong force. Then I threw in that we could be in Richmond in five days if we got reinforced."

"We'll hear nothing back from them you know," George said as he pulled the bill of his cap lower against the setting sun. He was tired of all the mental struggle with Halleck, Stanton and Lincoln. He dismissed them from his thoughts and concentrated on the wounded, greeting each man with fond respect.

General Marcy stood awhile watching in silence until the last of the invalids had passed by them. Then he sighed.

"It's good to be back from Washington and in the company of soldiers again. To see honorable men, with honorable wounds."

"I appreciate your going to that hell hole as my ambassador, Dad."

"Ah, well, George you did me a favor. It was sure nice to see Mary and Nelly again. But otherwise I'm afraid I didn't accomplish much." Marcy looked troubled. "I better confess to you right out, I said a stupid thing to President Lincoln."

"He hears stupid things all the time."

"Well, I told him if we didn't get proper reinforcements down here we might have to surrender this Army."

"Hah! You said that?"

"Got him pretty upset, George, and that's an understatement."

"Let him be upset. Did you just make that up on your own?"

"I regret I spoke without thinking, but damn it all, George, I wanted him to see the seriousness of our situation."

George thought back to Hooker this morning. Act without thinking. Perhaps it's the new vogue, even his good old father-in-law was doing it.

"I tried to patch things up between you and Stanton too," Marcy continued. "I may have done some good, I don't know. Last month when his baby died, he said he much appreciated the sympathy note you sent him. Nelly sent one too."

George looked at Marcy with open affection. "We are civilized after all, Dad. The poor baby couldn't help who its father was."

"Stanton claims he is forever your loyal friend. Always was. Ever will be. Regrets any misunderstanding. Etcetera, etcetera."

"Yes, watch out for that etcetera."

"He also said an interesting thing. He is so loyal to you that he would lie naked in the street gutter and allow you to stand on him."

George took off his cap, wiped his wet forehead, and squinted in disbelief. "You can't be serious."

"He said exactly that. I wrote it down."

George felt his stomach lurch at the appalling image. Were they all going mad in this heat?

"Excuse me for a moment, Dad."

He walked up the plank to shake hands with the Captain and some of the attending doctors.

"Take good care of my boys," he told them, loudly, with authority. "See they get plenty of ice." Then he rejoined General Marcy on the pier. "Let's adjourn to my tent for a drink. Speaking of ice, we still have a few cool bottles."

General Marcy licked his cracked lips. "No arm twisting required, George."

As they walked the dusty street of tents they passed close by General Phil Kearny in close conversation with several officers. Kearney, who pretended not to notice George, was saying: "Up the hill! Down the hill! Up the hill. Down the hill! I tell you we're commanded by a great spoiled child."

General Marcy bristled at the insult, but George pulled at his arm.

"Don't let Phil rile you." He aimed a cool look and a rigid salute at the group and walked on.

"I talked with Hooker after he got back from Malvern," Marcy said. "He was disappointed, to say the least."

"And disgusted and bitter and all the rest. But, I couldn't do it, Dad. Put our men at risk in an ad hoc battle, with no reinforcements coming? And disobeying the order to retreat? Well, I couldn't do that either."

"I know, George. I know. Respecting the orders of knaves and fools is the soldier's lot."

"There are two generals who would agree with you on that."

They arrived at George's headquarters tent. All four flaps were rolled up to catch any scant breeze. A large gray masonry jar full of water hung from a tent pole, supposedly to cool the air. For some obscure reason the jar was called a 'monkey.'

George sat down on a stool and reached into a tub of iced water to pull out the last green bottle of champagne.

"We'll celebrate your return to God's country," he said, passing the bottle to an orderly for serving.

George took off his uniform jacket and General Marcy did the same. Their shirts were dark with sweat.

"George, I'm afraid the knives are out for you in Washington. I talked with a lot of others beside Stanton. Johnny Hay was helpful even if he's no friend of yours."

George looked thoughtfully at the 'monkey.' "You know, Dad, the man who can cobble up a device to cool air, why he will make a fortune. What an invention that would be! I'm a fair engineer, and I'm going to have to do something or other."

"Son, do you want to hear my report or not?"

George sat on his cot and pulled off his boots. "Speak your piece, sir."

"That letter you gave Lincoln is all over town. They say it is your opening gun in your run for President."

"Faugh!"

"That's how the politicians see it, George. You tell Lincoln how to conduct Christian war, soft on the South, anti-confiscation, the Union as it was and all such Democrat talk. What are they going to think? I told you it was not a real good idea to write that letter, and worse to hand it to him."

"It was the expression of a concerned citizen."

"I'll not get into a pissing match with you, George, but as I see it you're a soldier first."

George hated to be at odds with Nelly's father. "I picked the wrong time to give it to him," he admitted.

"You sure did. Anyhow, let's talk soldiering. I saw the great General Pope at the President's reception. What a blatherskite! Wants to hang all the slave owners. Thinks are a nice enough man, but too soft for civil war, and when the hell are you going to get your army up to help him out because if Jackson comes after him, he's going to be in a hell of a scrape, I tell you sir ... Humph, humph."

George broke out laughing, held up both hands. "Stop, stop, that's too good an imitation!"

"Yep, well, seriously, I'm afraid the game will be to put the blame on you for whatever happens to Pope. I just smell it coming. Halleck is already telling everybody you're dragging your heels in evacuating from here. And then when Pope gets whipped, it'll be all because you didn't get your army back in time to save him."

"Ah, it's so easy to turn a great army around in the face of the enemy and load it on boats and sail blithely away." George stood up, walked over to the monkey, scooped some water and splashed it on his face.

"Don't shoot the messenger, George."

George lifted his champagne bottle. "To the Commanding General of the Army."

"May he get exactly whatever he deserves," Marcy said with a sour smile.

George thought of the sick and wounded he had just sent off. "To hell with Halleck and all the rest." He raised his glass. "God bless the men and boys."

CHAPTER TWENTY-ONE

Washington, September 1st, 1862

Early that morning George rode into Washington City from his camp at Alexandria. Amiable guards at the Potomac bridge waved him on even though he didn't know the password of the day.

Who would bother to inform General McClellan of the password?

He arrived at the massive, red brick War Department Building, dismounted and looped Dan Webster's reins over the hitching rail. Fifty yards off to his left the President's Mansion imposed its compelling presence, columns glinting in the sun. George wondered if the two guards at the War Department entrance would stop him with a challenge or allow him to pass.

Was he friend or foe?

He drew off his tan Italian leather riding gloves and mounted the steps, striding with all the authority he had left in him. The guards snapped to Present Arms, and one of them, a Sergeant with a deeply lined face gave him a winking grin.

"Ah, good morning to you, General McClellan," the Sergeant said with a lilt of Irish song in his voice.

"And a good morning to you Sergeant, and you too, Corporal. At ease."

Two rifles moved as one and clanked to Parade Rest.

George smoothed his mustache. "Well now, are you men keeping good order here at the War Department?"

The Sergeant looked straight ahead, his chest thrust forward. "Doing the best we can sir, to prop up the Union against the forces of stupidity."

"Then your work is cut out for you, Sergeant. I fear the forces of stupidity have long occupied this building."

"You said, it General." The Sergeant turned and looked him in the eye. "And they did their damndest work when they pulled you away from Richmond, sir."

George wanted to hug the man. "I can't disagree with you there, Sergeant. But, as they say in the Army, orders is orders."

"Yessir. Beg your pardon for inquiring, sir, but will you be back in command any time soon do ya think?"

"Not likely, Sergeant. I command that part of the Army of the Potomac not sent off to General Pope. Since all has been sent, I am left in command of nothing -- a duty I feel fully competent to exercise."

"Don't let the scalawags get you down, General. I was privileged to be with General Hancock at Williamsburg, ya know. Near got killed to death, yet here I am."

"It seems to me, Sergeant, that General Hancock was privileged to be with you. Carry on."

"Yessir."

George felt ten feet tall as he ventured through the great brass trimmed door into the sacred precincts of Edwin Stanton & Co. For some odd reason the place always smelled to him of overcooked cabbage. Or was the aroma merely Stanton's presence playing tricks on his mind?

He mounted the stairway to the second floor and followed the old familiar click-clack noise to the telegraph office, a handsome wood paneled room that had once been the library. Now, though a few rare books still remained on display in glass cases, Stanton had changed these rooms into a communications center. Shortly after becoming Secretary of War he preemptively removed all telegraph operations from George's authority and transferred them here to the War Department where he could easily supervise and control everything that passed over the wires.

It had been George's first sign of trouble.

The operator on duty, his young face taut in concentration, took no notice of the visitor and went on tapping his key.

"General McClellan." A brittle, nasal voice from behind.

George turned. "Why, Colonel Sanford. Good morning."

Colonel Edward S. Sanford, former President of the American Telegraph Company, and now Military Supervisor of Telegrams, was a tall, studious looking man. He was also a loyal Stanton ally.

He ignored George's offered hand.

"Is there anything I can do for you?"

George studied the man. Sanford had the air of a imperious store clerk who suspected shoplifting. "Nothing in particular, thank you. I'm to meet General Halleck. Have you seen him?"

Colonel Sanford paused before replying. "No."

"Anything new this morning from General Pope?"

"The wires to Centerville are down again."

"Why, has that wild man Jeb Stuart been up to his old mischief?"

"Mischief is hardly the word for it. General Pope has apparently suffered a defeat at the old Bull Run battleground."

"A defeat? Well, they certainly do take the joy out of life."

Sanford's voice dropped to a near whisper. "You may jest sir, but we hear that the situation is serious."

George was immediately shamed at his childish sarcasm. He pictured torn bodies that had once been his soldiers, dead on the ground in their regimental ranks, yellow sunlight washing over their stillness out on the rolling hills of Virginia. Killed by that idiot, Pope.

"Major Hammerstein of my staff came back from the field at three this morning and gave me a full report," he said. "It's a big stampede. General Pope is trying to stop it and hold at Centerville."

"I suppose we can only hope and pray for the best," Sanford said.

"Yes. Hope and pray."

Sanford wore an introspective frown. At length he said, "I have something to tell you, General McClellan. It's been bothering me all summer. Honor demands that I inform you."

"Well, come on then, Sanford. Honor must be served." What new calamity, he wondered.

Sanford cleared his throat. "On the twenty-seven of June, more correctly at two thirty a.m. on the twenty-eighth of June you sent a telegram to Mr. Stanton and by implication to President Lincoln as well."

"I remember that terrible night."

Sanford raised himself to his full height. Ah, here it comes, and not a chance in the world it'll be enjoyable.

"In that telegram, sir, you made an accusation, and I quote: 'If I save this Army now, I tell you plainly that I owe no thanks to you or any other persons in Washington -- You have done your best to sacrifice this Army.'"

George fixed the Colonel with a level stare. "I should be flattered, Sanford, that you memorized my words. Indeed, I wrote it, and I sent it. I meant it. What is your point?"

"My point is I did not approve of your message."

"You did not approve?"

"I did not deem it an appropriate statement to the Secretary of War, or the President. I thought it was treasonous."

"Who the hell cares what you thought?"

Sanford blinked, but stood his ground. "Therefore, I deleted that offending sentence from the translated cipher message. It was treasonous and insulting to the President and the Secretary. I thought you must be drunk or in a state of panic or both."

"Oh, I see. You have God-like powers then?"

Sanford's eyes held on him a moment, then shifted.

"You took it upon yourself to censor me, to soften my bluntness? You were afraid that I might cause injured feelings? Is that it, Sanford? Why, what a humanitarian you are!"

George found he had crumpled his gloves in his right hand and was pounding them into his left palm. Easy now.

"I wish," he said, "that you could have been with me on the Peninsula the night I wrote that message. I wish you could have seen the sights I saw and know the disquiet I felt, responsible for the lives of a hundred thousand men, and the enemy trying to kill us all." He lowered his voice. "It's so simple to follow war from the comfort of this room, Sanford. No blood and no shock of battle here, just coffee and sweet cakes."

252

"I have no interest in your justifications, McClellan," Colonel Sanford said. "I did what I knew was right. Now I've informed you of it."

George shuffled through a few choice, insulting retorts. But why bother? This obnoxious civilian in uniform was not his true enemy. No wonder that Lincoln and Stanton had never responded to his accusation. Should he in fact be grateful to Sanford? His mind pulled both ways on that one.

"Good day, Sanford," he said at last. "I'm glad you were able to unburden yourself of this terrible secret. But I'll worry the next time I send a message to this office. I'll just have to grit my teeth and hope you are not in a censoring mood."

A voice from the doorway: "I heard you halfway down the hall McClellan." Henry W. Halleck, Commanding General of the United States Army, shuffled into the room. "What are you abusing Colonel Sanford about? Only I am permitted to abuse Colonel Sanford."

George realized with a start that Halleck was serious.

"Just a private matter, General Halleck." Sanford said as he flashed a strained conspiratorial smile at George.

"We were telling some old railroad stories," George said.

Sanford gave Halleck a worried look and made his escape.

Alone now with Halleck, George observed that the Commanding General was really quite an imposing figure. Tall and strongly built with a bulging forehead, framed by fuzzy gray hair, his regular army nickname had been 'Old Brains.' His sturdy presence was contradicted, however, by his vague, watery blue eyes. There was talk that he was a victim of 'The Chinese Habit,' an overuse of opium.

There was the time when Halleck commanding the Union Forces in the West, had ordered Sam Grant arrested for not answering telegrams fast enough. Grant later explained he'd been out capturing two Confederate forts.

Now this same Henry W. Halleck was titular boss of the United States Army, but in essence a nervous front man for Stanton. Halleck, with the spirit of a loyal clerk following

253

orders, had now taken all of George McClellan's Army away from him after ordering the retreat from Richmond.

"What are you doing here, McClellan?"

"Sir, we arranged a meeting by telegraph last night."

A look of wonderment, eyebrows bobbing up and down. "Oh, yes. I forgot." Halleck made a huffy noise. "I didn't forget exactly. Everything slips my mind these days. I really need some rest."

George waited. Halleck looked at him, glazed eyes going wider as if rediscovering his presence. "What exactly did you come to talk about?"

George brought himself to attention. Make it formal.

"General," he said. "In my opinion we're facing a crisis. Pope has been whipped. I have the word from the field if you'd care to hear it. Something must be done immediately."

Halleck had a characteristic habit while under stress. He would cross his arms and vigorously scratch his elbows. He did so now.

"Oh, stop standing there like a damn nutcracker, McClellan. At ease. At ease." Halleck stopped scratching his elbows, but started rubbing his nose. "I'm not at all convinced that Pope has indeed been defeated in the technical sense," he said. "A temporary reverse, perhaps. In his telegrams he says he has survived a day of hard fighting but that he is all right."

"He said that? He is all right?"

"Words to that effect. Maybe he ought to hold at Centerville and we should push all we have to reinforce him there. I haven't decided yet. It's hard to know what's going on out there."

"Sir, it's easy to know what's going on. We send troops out and they get chewed up, killed or captured like General Taylor's Brigade, three days ago."

"Yes, yes, very unfortunate."

"You told me to send them. Yesterday we had a Squadron of the Second Regular Cavalry captured by Fitzhugh Lee just three mile West of Fairfax Court House."

"Yes, yes, I got your telegram on that."

"The enemy is getting between us and Pope."

"Oh, yes, yes, I know what you think, McClellan, leave Pope to 'get out of his own scrape,' as you said. The President saw that message you sent me, by the way. He didn't like it; thought it most ungenerous of you."

"General, I meant by that phrase that the defense of Washington should be our first priority. We can't keep sending troops out to Pope. He has a bad habit of getting them killed. In the technical sense."

Halleck pursed his lips, wagged his head. "I'm still not at all convinced that he has been in fact defeated."

"What would it take to convince you? Why not go out into the field and discover for yourself? I'll accompany you. As Commanding General, sir, and with respect, I suggest that you go out there and command."

"Easy enough for you to say, McClellan, and don't use that belligerent tone with me. I'm not Colonel Sanford. I won't have it."

"Sorry, sir, if I sounded brusque."

"Look here, McClellan, I have a million details and the whole army to attend to here, so I can't be gallivanting out to Centerville on your whim. I just don't have the time. Besides, what if I were captured?"

"That would be a terrible blow to our cause, sir," George said, suppressing a laugh.

Halleck paused, sniffed, scratched his elbows. "Tell you what. I'll send Colonel Kelton out. What do you think of that? He can render me a report."

"Kelton is an excellent choice, sir. I'll go with him if you wish."

"No, no, no, General Pope doesn't want you interfering. Anyhow, I have something for you to do here."

"Good, I want to discuss that with you, sir. My position here is very tenuous and awkward ..."

"Yes, yes, never mind that now. I have here a message from General Pope we received early this morning before the line went down. Listen to this:"

I wish to report the unsoldierly and dangerous conduct of many brigade and some division commanders of the forces sent here from the Peninsula. Every word and act and intention is discouraging and calculated to break down the spirits of the men and produce disaster.

George saw red fury, controlled it. General Marcy had warned him that he would be blamed for Pope's failures. He said, "I trust General Pope made similar complaints to General Lee?"

"Yes, yes, we all agree you're a master of sarcasm, McClellan. Now I want you to send a message to those friends of yours who are with General Pope. Tell them to support him loyally and without complaint, that means Porter, Franklin, Sumner all that crowd that are so thick with you. This directive comes from the President."

"Inform the President that I will comply. I'll go home now and start working on the message. You'll have it this afternoon. But I'll need something from you in return."

Halleck's eyes narrowed. "I don't make deals about orders, but what is it you want?"

"An official position, General. I am hung up here, neither fish nor fowl. I have been doing my best to assist you in this crisis, but I have no office, no real command."

"Yes, yes, McClellan, I have been hearing that same complaint from you ever since you came up from the Peninsula. I have passed your requests on to the Secretary and the President." He raised his palms, a helpless gesture. "They answer with silence. What am I to do?"

"It will help my message if I can tell my friends that I occupy some position of trust here in Washington," George said.

A cloud of anxiety played over Halleck's face. He reached for his elbows, clearly worried over Stanton's furious reaction if General McClellan were actually to be given some authority. Did Henry Halleck have the daring to take that responsibility?

He did. "Tell your friends that you are ... uh ...." He waved a hand, a vague gesture for anything or nothing. "You are in command of ..."

George leaned forward.

"In command of The Defenses of Washington?" Halleck looked a wide-eyed question at George. "You think that will do?"

"I am honored, sir."

"Very well." Halleck looked at the floor with a vague wave. "You're in command of the Defenses of Washington. Let's hope for both our sakes that Mr. Stanton never finds out about this."

George came to attention and saluted. "Yes, sir. Let's hope."

For once, perhaps the only time, Henry W. Halleck and George B. McClellan exchanged understanding smiles.

A few minutes later while leaving the War Department, George caught sight of the enemy emerging from the President's Mansion. The enemy had his head down and carried several crinkled papers in his right hand as he walked along with quick little steps, his lips mumbling. He glanced up and saw George in his path.

George almost laughed. "My word, Stanton, you looked like you've just found a fly in your soup. It's only me, your good old friend the harmless General."

Stanton recovered enough to offer him a perfunctory nod and a good morning, his lips contracted in a distasteful grimace.

George was in no particular hurry either to speak or to leave the scene. He shifted his weight back on his boot heels and occupied the center of the gravel pathway.

"What brings you, here?" Stanton asked. "I thought your camp was across the river in Alexandria."

"Conference with General Halleck this morning. The military situation, you know."

"Oh, yes. Very bad, very bad what little we know." Stanton eyed him with seething distaste. "You're not nosing around here hoping to see the President are you? Because he doesn't want to see you. If you have anything for him, go through me or General Halleck. You understand?"

"I have no particular business with the President." George felt a warm comfort descend over him. The longer he stood there facing Stanton, the better he felt. His gracious, courteous presence was driving the Secretary of War to pinnacles of discomfort. How delightful.

Stanton looked at him, shifted as if to walk around him, then halted. He produced one the papers he had been carrying and waved it in George's face.

"I want to show you something, just so you can't contend that I went behind your back. It is a draft of a letter to the President that I am circulating to the Cabinet for signature."

"Why, what a thing to say, Mr. Secretary. Our intercourse has always been freely open to the best of my knowledge." Interesting to see how long could he go on trading slimy hypocrisies with Stanton who was a master of that game.

"Just read this, McClellan."

George took the offered paper, and read:

Mr. President, we the undersigned feel compelled by a profound sense of duty to the government and people of the United States, and to yourself as your Constitutional advisors, respectfully to recommend the immediate removal of George B. McClellan from the command of any army in the United States.

George glanced up at Stanton whose face was now a frozen mask. He continued reading:

We are constrained to urge this by the conviction that after a sad and humiliating trial of twelve months and by the frightful and useless sacrifice of the lives of many thousands of brave men, and the waste of many millions of national means, he has proved to be incompetent.

Suddenly the paper was gone, snatched from his fingers.

"I've decided I don't want you reading this." Stanton folded the paper and put in away. "It is for the President."

George grinned warily. "Oh, well, I got the key point of the message." He said no more, wishing thoughts of murder could make good the deed.

Stanton's face brightened. "I must say one thing to you, McClellan. Some advice. You have been bombarding General Halleck with requests for new command, for clarification of your official position, all that military flim flam. You even told us you wanted to go out and join Pope so you could get shot and die with your old regiments. I must say that was a tempting notion, but General Pope would have none of it. So we decided it was best to let you to stew in your own juice and gnaw on a file, as the saying goes."

George thought of his Plebe days at West Point and the deliberate cruelty of the hazing. Stanton would have been good at it.

"So, to ease your mind as to your future prospects, General McClellan, there are none. There never will be any. You are a cooked goose. If I were you, I would hop right down to the Union Station and buy myself a connection to New Jersey or wherever you decide to make your residence."

George remained silent. Stanton grinned. "Well," he said, "I must be on my way. Give my regards to your charming wife."

"Doesn't it concern you," George said carefully, "that the rebels may be about to take this city?"

"Oh, of course it concerns me, General, and we're taking measures against it. But I would rather see them take this city, than see you back to command even one squad of American troops. I don't trust you. Never did. Never will. Do we see eye to eye?"

"Perfectly," George said.

"Good day then, General McClellan."

"I'm ready to take you up on your offer, Stanton."

"Offer? What offer is that?"

"Why, last month when my father-in-law was up here from the Peninsula, you told him what a loyal friend you were to me. Remember that?"

"Yes, go on," Stanton said, not happy.

"You said you were so loyal to me you would lie naked in a gutter and let me stand on you? You remember you said that, Stanton?" Stanton's face passed through a variety of colors in the space of an instant, from white to purple to greenish gray.

"Haven't you ever said anything in the heat of the moment that you lived to regret, McClellan? Anything at all? Perhaps something like: 'You have done your best to sacrifice this Army?'"

Stanton flashed a grin of hate, turned sharply and crunched off down the gravel pathway.

CHAPTER TWENTY-TWO

Washington, September 2, 1862

George was enjoying a solitary breakfast at his home on H Street. He would have to compliment the cook on these fresh eggs in butter, the hot toasted bread and salty Virginia ham. Even if his staff was reduced to one elderly Sergeant and a Negro cook, he wanted to take care of them. He sipped the coffee. Strong and hot. Even Sam Grant would approve.

There's a thought. Perhaps he would write today to the successful General Grant who just might have a job available for him as a corps commander.

"May I get you anything else, General? Some more coffee?"

The old Sergeant had appeared soundlessly and now stood at the ready. George glanced down and saw that the man was wearing faded red slippers.

"Coffee? Yes please, Sergeant."

The shaking cup clinked in the saucer as the coffee was poured. On second thought, why bother Sam with idle hopes? George B. McClellan would never be allowed to serve as a corps commander or as a mess sergeant. Stanton would see to that. This grizzled character who was slopping coffee all over his saucer had a brighter future in the army.

"You've heard about our latest stampede, Sergeant?"

"They're calling it the Second Battle of Bull Run," the Sergeant said distantly with a sigh. "I thought the first one was bad enough."

"Yes," George said. "God rest the men and boys who died there."

"Our poor country," the Sergeant said in the morose tones of an undertaker presiding over a client. George looked up and met the Sergeant's pitying eyes.

"You can wait in the kitchen, Sergeant."

261

"Yes, General."

"I'll be finished soon."

George was left alone with a warm breakfast and cold regrets. He was finished now. At age sixteen he had been the youngest cadet at West Point, and then it had been a grand odyssey; mortal combat against Mexicans and Indians, studies in Europe, articles published, inventions that bore his name, command of a gallant army and now a career blown up in his face at the unlikely age of thirty-five.

He applied blueberry jam to a piece of toast. Think now, where would they live? Nelly had loved Cincinnati, but the best opportunities in the railroad game were in New York or Philadelphia. And there was baby May to think of. What would be best for her? He had to get a job; that was primary. He would write again to Barlow, Belmont and his other friends. He would try not to sound desperate.

Or could he pen his memoirs? He was a competent writer. Yes, but he had no large success to relate. Readers want generals who win battles, and as he had admitted to Nelly in a letter, he had "not done splendidly" before Richmond.

Damn it all, he had been pulled back from Richmond against every instinct of his character. He should have taken it, orders or no. He should have told Hooker to make the attack after the fatal directive from Halleck to retreat.

Admit it, McClellan, your courage failed you there. He remembered a doddering old pugilist he had met once. He was like that man who had taken one too many punches to the head, always talking of the matches he should have won.

He heard the front door open.

"George?" An unmistakable voice called. "Are you up for visitors yet?"

He got up and went to the entry hall. "Your Excellency. Good morning." Some far-seeing part of him had been expecting Lincoln.

"I'm at breakfast, sir. Will you join me?"

·

"No, thank you kindly, George." Lincoln was accompanied by a silent and twitchy General Halleck. This is the last place he want's to be, George thought.

Lincoln unfolded his lengthy self into a chair. "Well, maybe a cup of coffee," he allowed.

George gave instructions to the Sergeant. There was a stroke of silence. Lincoln eyed Halleck, who shrugged and began playing with a spoon and fork.

Lincoln let out a dejected sigh. "George the bottom is out of the barrel. You know what I mean?"

George studied Lincoln's lined, weary face and felt a wave of brotherly affection. "I've heard you use that expression back in Illinois when you thought our court case was going wrong."

"I did, yes," Lincoln said. "It's a useful saying, George. Gets at the heart of things." He drummed his long fingers on the table cloth and glanced at Halleck who had begun scratching his elbows. "Stop that, Halleck. You drive me to distraction with it."

General Halleck stopped scratching, folded his arms and held still. But his eyes were busy.

"George, I'll get right down to it. I don't have to tell you what's happened to our Army over the last few days. They are falling back to this city in disorder."

"I know," George said.

"I've just talked with that Colonel Kelton who we sent out yesterday. He told me what happened. That horse's ass, Pope, let Jackson get around behind him. Jackson wiped out all our supplies at Manassis Junction, burned up what his men couldn't eat, drink or steal. Then he took up a strong defensive position behind an old railroad grade just to the North. From there he ambushed us. Pope made a series of unsupported attacks that just wasted men. Worse, he ignored Longstreet on his left until it was too late."

George listened with interest. Lincoln knew how to boil down complex facts, and he loved to play the military critic.

"Pope thought Jackson was retreating, which he wasn't. Meanwhile McDowell got lost and disappeared. Worse luck, he

263

turned up again. Then Longstreet launched a big attack with massed regiments. Our 5th New York held against them until it was near wiped out. Those brave New York boys, they died to give Pope time enough to retreat to Henry Hill and make a stand."

George inclined his head in sympathy. Lincoln had it boiled down right.

"Bad business, George. Bad business." Lincoln's eyes were tear filled. He took out a smudged handkerchief and blew his nose. "All those brave boys. I fear Washington may be lost."

"Really?"

"Mr. Stanton thinks so. He has even ordered the armory emptied, all our arms and ammunition shipped to New York, so Lee don't get 'em."

George felt his jaw drop. He couldn't roar with rage. He couldn't grab a sword and run over to the War Department to stab Stanton through the heart. He had to get a grip.

He did. "I don't think that was the correct thing to do, your Excellency."

"Well, that may be, George. It comes to the point of my visit. I want you to take command of our whole damn Army. Save Washington if you can, then go after Lee's force. Will you do it, George?"

George shoved his chair back and rose to attention. Destiny should be met standing on two feet.

"You have only to give the order, Your Excellency."

"I'm giving it. Take charge of the Army, George. Fit it up, organize it, shake up the commands, but make this city secure. Than take right after the rebel Army and destroy it." Lincoln stood now and laid a hand on his General's shoulder.

"You think you can handle that?"

"You're talking to the right man, Mr. President."

Halleck spoke up now, croaking with anxiety. "We think Lee may not come after Washington right away. There is a possibility that he has disengaged at Centerville, and may be headed up toward Maryland or even Pennsylvania or God knows where."

Halleck's watery eyes widened. "Or he might turn around and attack Washington from the Northwest. Or he could head for Harrisburg, Baltimore or even Philadelphia. He can raise holy hell with us any number of places, and we don't know where he'll strike next."

George frowned, then cocked an eyebrow at Lincoln. "Why he might even attack Springfield, Illinois."

Lincoln slapped his knees and yelped a laugh. "I don't suppose it's that bad yet. But nearly." Lincoln wiped his eyes, then in an instant lost all merriment. He nailed George with a questioning stare. "You have anything further to say, General McClellan?"

"Thank you for this expression of confidence, Mr. President. The city will be saved."

"Don't thank me, George. It was all General Halleck's idea."

Halleck's head snapped back in amazement.

Lincoln gave a broad wink. "At least that's what I'm going to tell everybody in the Cabinet." Again Lincoln paused. "You're sure there's nothing else you wish to say to me, George? Perhaps in private?"

Of course. The President was probing for any conditions he might demand.

He was tempted. Eliminate Stanton and Halleck. Be General of the Army again. Get guarantees of a free hand from Lincoln. He was in a position to dictate, but be cautious. Here at this breakfast table he had already regained considerable power. Well and good, but what if he were to go out and smash Bobby Lee, send the Sesech Army reeling back to Richmond? George felt a surge of pressure in his chest, his breath caught short. He would then truly be in a position to dictate to Lincoln and the government.

"Your Excellency, I attach no conditions to my acceptance of your order. I will serve the country unconditionally. I trust you to treat me with your usual fairness."

Lincoln paused, his mind racing to digest this odd and unexpected circumstance. Then he offered his hand.

"I should say then, we have a deal. Go to it, George."

Shortly after Lincoln and Halleck left, George stepped out onto the small marble porch to light a cigar in celebration. He was immediately startled to see two troops of cavalry perfectly aligned, their uniforms shimmering blues and golds in the mild September sunlight. They gave a rolling deep-throated cheer when they saw him. An officer dismounted, marched up the steps to the porch and saluted.

"Congratulations, General," Captain Armstrong Custer said, with a toothy grin. "I knew they'd have to come after you to get 'em out of their scrape."

"The news is out already?"

"You know me, General. I slip about and find out things before they happen. The rest of the staff is on its way here too, fast as they can hop."

George felt a stirring new energy in this crisp September weather. He had his Army back. "Good, Armstrong. I have immediate use for you. Take a patrol down to the armory. A certain government official issued an order to ship all the guns and ammunition to New York, and I want it stopped."

"New York? Much good they'll do us there. What lunatic would issue such an order?"

"Need you ask?"

Custer shook his head in disgust.

"On your way, Armstrong! Don't let them ship a single ball or powder bag."

Custer doffed his hat. "Consider it all undone, General."

* * *

Upton's Hill, Four miles West of Washington, September 2, 1862, Five p.m.

General Pope and General McDowell were walking their tired horses side by side when they encountered George and a few orderlies coming from Washington on the Fairfax Road.

Pope waved a listless salute. "Why hello, McClellan. What brings you here?"

266

George did not return the salute. "I'm out looking for my Army, General Pope. Heard it was around here somewhere."

Pope was grimly silent, his jaw trembling, his face pasted over with amber colored road dust.

"Say there, McDowell. You look sick," George said.

McDowell, his expression frozen with fatigue, raised his right hand then let it flop.

"Feel sick," he said.

"That firing off to the right," George said, "any idea what it might signify?"

"Why I reckon that would be General Sumner in contact with the enemy." Pope's voice had the detachment of a bored spectator. "He commands the rear guard in that direction."

McDowell's glassy eyes nearly came alive. "I suppose you've heard the news about General Kearny," he said.

"I did," George replied crisply. "A sad loss to us all."

Pope showed a small spark of interest. "I wonder about you saying that, McClellan. He was no friend of yours I hear."

"He was my prime strategic advisor." George hoped the shade of Phil Kearny was somewhere near enough to enjoy the jest.

"They got him just up the road from here," Pope said blandly. "Damn fool rode into Jackson's lines in a rainstorm. They called on him to halt and surrender. He cussed them out and rode off. That's how he got shot in the ass."

McDowell snickered. "A true soldier's death."

George wanted to slap McDowell with a glove. "I'm going to see what the shooting's about," he said.

"Do we have your permission, General, to proceed into Washington?" Pope's voice was edged with scorn.

George cast a long, thoughtful stare at the two disgraced Generals. "You can both proceed anywhere you wish, boys. Or to nowhere in particular."

He dug his heels into Dan Webster's flanks and galloped off toward the sound of the guns. Topping a ridge he suddenly encountered a shabby looking column of infantry. The men

267

shuffled along, heads down with no semblance of order, pride or unity. They carried no National or Regimental flag.

"What regiment is this?" George demanded.

"Who gives a warm bucket of shite?" A surly Captain growled, not bothering to look up at the man on horseback.

A sword whistled over his head knocking off his hat.

"Look at me and come to attention when I address you, Captain, and clean up your language."

White-eyed shock at seeing a living ghost. "General McClellan. Pardon sir, I didn't realize! Men, come to attention."

"What regiment is this?"

They told him.

"What's the state of your ammunition supply?"

All gone up they told him.

"Killed and wounded?"

Forty percent, they said, including the Colonel.

"When were you fed last?"

Two days ago, some hardtack.

"When did you last sleep?"

They couldn't remember.

"Well, men, all that is about to change."

They blinked, then cheered and danced and hugged each other. The word spread back down among the limping columns. "McClellan's back! McClellan's back! Three cheers! Three cheers for Little Mac!"

The shouts and celebration laughter echoed in the ears of General Pope and General McDowell as they walked their horses to nowhere in particular.

CHAPTER TWENTY-THREE

George McClellan's house on H Street, September 3, 1862, 8 p.m.

They filled the dining room with cigar smoke and buzzing conversation. Space was tight, but no one complained. Senior officers occupied the few chairs available. Others squatted or sat on the floor while the rest stood in the doorways and along the walls.

George drained a glass of champagne, stubbed out his cigar and surveyed the room. They were all here, his friends, relatives, the commanders from the Peninsula, Hooker, Hancock, Sumner, Bill Franklin, joined now by loyal old "Burn" Burnside. There was Judge Key from Cincinnati, now a Colonel on his staff, Seth Williams who had been an usher at his wedding, Major Herb Hammerstein who had brought him the field report of Popes's debacle at Bull Run. Captain Arthur McClellan, his handsome younger brother was here along with his beloved father-in-law, General Randolph Marcy.

The old Sergeant shuffled up in his red slippers. "Should I open more champagne, General?" he asked in a rasping whisper. "They went through that last case in no time flat."

George smiled and held up a restraining hand. Someone, sounded like Custer, gave a haw haw in the midst of telling a story. Fitz John Porter was relating his dreadful experiences under Pope at Bull Run. Listening to him, and practicing their English, were the two French princes who served as volunteer aides, the Duc de Chartres and the Comte de Paris, pretender to the French throne. Their worldly-wise uncle, the Prince de Joinville, a former admiral in the French Navy, looked at George with an expressive raised eyebrow.

Yes, it was time. He raised his hands.

"Gentlemen! Gentlemen!"

The buzz died down into scattered whispers and finally silence.

"The gang's all here. Welcome to the new Army of the Potomac."

They clapped and cheered.

"Gentlemen, I have decided to split our forces. Part will remain here in Washington for defense in case Bobby Lee comes back this way."

"With his tail between his legs," Custer yelled.

"Bow wow," someone said.

George waited for the laughter to ease. "The second element I will call the expedition army. These units I will take out from Washington City, in a northwesterly direction, locate and attack Bobby Lee. When we find him there will be a great skedaddle on the part of the Secesh, I assure you."

They agreed, loudly, roughly, and with some salty language.

George pursed his lips and shook his head scoldingly. "Please, boys, you'll shock my delicate ears. Now then, Generals Sumner and Franklin, your Second Corps and your Sixth Corps had no heavy fighting in the Bull Run campaign, so I am sending you new regiments and additional artillery."

"We'll train 'em up in a hurry," sleepy-eyed old Bull Summer growled from his chair down front.

"You two will be coming with me in the attack army."

"Thank you, sir," Bill Franklin said with tense satisfaction.

"General Burnside, your Ninth Corps will be reinforced by a new division and the Kanawaha Division from Western Virginia. You will also be with me."

"I'll take anything you can give me, General, and proud for the invite to the party." Burnside was one of his oldest friends.

George consulted his note paper. "General Sykes, your division of regulars will be attached to my headquarters as a reserve."

Standing in a doorway General Sykes came to attention. "We are honored, sir."

George nodded and then went on. "General McDowell's Corps from Pope's army will be renamed as the First Corps, and

General Hooker, you are placed in command. I expect you to work the kinks out of them, Hooker. Make them hate the enemy as much as they hated General McDowell."

Hooker scrambled up from the floor where he had been sitting and saluted smartly. "That I will do, sir. I only wish General Kearny could be with us."

"So do I, Hooker. I'll miss his timely advice and his reticent manners."

This got the affectionate laugh he wanted. God rest your tortured soul, Phil Kearny.

"General Banks, I am placing you in overall command of the defenses of Washington City."

General Nathaniel P. Banks arose. A clear-eyed, former Congressman from Massachusetts and Speaker of the House, he was more politician than soldier, but he gave it his best. He replied now in the deep, rounded tones of his profession. "I will not fail you, General McClellan. Count on me, sir."

"Yes, thank you, General Banks. I trust you even though you are a Republican."

Banks joined in the laughter.

"Now, your old Corps, General Banks, I am redesignating as the Twelfth Corps, and I am placing General Mansfield in command. He is not here yet I see, but is on his way up from Fort Monroe. Now, as for the defense of Washington, I want General Sigel's Corps, and Heintzelman's Corps, as well as the balance of General Porter's Fifth Corps."

The German-born Sigel spoke in his ponderous accent. "We got us pretty chewed up, Mien General, attacking Tom Jackson, but we will do our damnedest if we is called on, sir."

"I know that, Sigel. That's why I want you to refit, rearm and rest your men. I'll get some fresh regiments to you as soon as I can."

"Yes, sir, thank you sir," Sigel said, his voice heavy with respect. "It's goot to see you back in der saddle again, sir."

"Sigel, it's goot to be back in der saddle. I'll count on all of you to help me stay there this time."

Whoops and cheers.

Later as the room emptied, the Comte de Paris hung back.

"My I offer commentary, mon ami?"

"Of course, Phillipe"

The young French nobleman flashed white teeth, his breath perfumed with the evening's champagne, his voice lowered to an intense hushed whisper.

"I do hear that you have no official orders for to take the field with this grand armee."

George dropped his voice to match his friend. "Ah, but Phillipe, I have Lincoln's wink as my assurance, whatever that's good for. They know I am going. They can stop me if they wish."

"But my comrade, George, they will let you go, and then if you fail, they will hand you a basket with your head in it. They will say you acted without having the ... what is the word?"

"Authority."

"That is the word."

"I am aware of all this, Phillipe, but my obligation is to the country and the Army."

The Frenchman wobbled a finger under George's mustache. "You have an obligation to cut Stanton's throat before you go on campaign. If you leave him here in your rear, his poison will turn Lincoln's head against you once again. Be warned by happenings of the past."

"I must chance that, Phillipe. If I can whip Bobby Lee and drive him out of Maryland, then I may be rid of Stanton and Halleck for good."

"I pray you are correct, mon ami." Phillipe stepped back, knocked over a chair, then gracefully allowed himself to drop to the floor where he stretched out on his back, his voice gurgling a sing-song chant. "Oui, oui, whip Bobby Lee."

"Are you all right, Phillipe?"

The Comte de Paris began to snore. George removed the empty glass from the Frenchman's fingers, sat down and pondered. Could he whip Bobby Lee with these patched-up forces he was assembling? The odds were long against him, but if he managed to bring off a great victory ...?

No, he could hear Lincoln's cranky voice in his imagination.

"But George, you didn't destroy him enough!"

CHAPTER TWENTY-FOUR

On the road to Frederick, Maryland, early morning, September 13, 1862

George rode at the head of the column with Brigadier General George Sykes, commander of the Division of Regulars, proud young men who would stand their ground and deliver accurate fire by the hour with parade ground precision. They were George's favorite troops. Proceeding side by side through the lush green hills of Maryland, the two Generals allowed their horses an easy pace, taking care not to raise dust in the faces of the men marching behind them.

George pressed a black and white checkered handkerchief to his brow, then wrapped the cloth around his neck. He glanced over at his companion. "Good campaign weather, Sykes. A little sweaty, but I welcome the dry roads."

"Beats rain and mud any day, General." Sykes a laconic, forty year old professional, was modest with words, but long on soldierly common sense.

Rocking gently in the saddle, stretching his legs against the stirrups, George allowed himself a small moment of satisfaction.

So far his plan was working. In those first frantic days of September, Lee's Army had been reported to be in many places, but no location was certain or confirmed.

Halleck was in a stew. "Lee could be anywhere," he moaned, "could disappear at will and then appear out of nowhere, perhaps at Baltimore or, God helps us, Philadelphia."

When George had soberly agreed and warned that the eerie Stonewall Jackson might even pop up at the President's dinner table unannounced, Halleck had just looked at him bug eyed. George knew he should restrain himself, even though Halleck was such a tempting target, but finding Lee was going to be difficult. Then one night George had tossed in a worried sleep

273

and dreamed that he was on a rain-swept London street, looking in a shop window, searching for a gift for Nelly. Shoes, gloves, a dress? Then he saw it, a shimmering blue Chinese fan. He came awake and scratched a note. He would send out his three major units from Washington in three wings, in a broad fan formation instead of the conventional column. If any wing met the enemy the other two wings could quickly converge on the fight.

The right wing under Burnside consisted of Hooker's First Corps and Jessie Reno's Ninth Corps. They would cover Baltimore. If Lee veered that way, the right wing could block him or at least give chase, nipping at his rear.

The left wing, Bill Franklin's Sixth Corps and an extra division under Couch, would patrol to the Northwest closer to the Potomac and would meet Lee head-on should the Confederate commander double back to strike at Washington.

George assigned himself the center of the fan with Sumner's Second Corps and Mansfield's Twelfth Corps as powerful striking force, backed up by General Sykes' Regulars. If Lee went North for Pennsylvania, George would follow and attack his rear, with his right and left wings converging to pitch in with him.

As his eyes swept the countryside ahead, he reviewed what he knew so far. Off to his right Burnside, Hooker and Reno had found no hint of the enemy, even after sending cavalry probes as far North as Westminster. Baltimore appeared safe for now, and so he had yesterday ordered that right wing of the fan to shift to the West and converge on Frederick, Maryland, where Lee had last been reported. The first of Burnside's troops had entered Frederick late yesterday afternoon and were greeted with joyous celebration.

Meanwhile off to his left, Bill Franklin and his Sixth Corps had been picking up steady evidence of the recent presence of Lee's troops. More important, the Federal's own cavalry commander, General Pleasonton, was daily running up against small units of Secesh cavalry blocking the roads. They would appear, fire a few warning shots then retreat, performing that classic function of cavalry, screening the movement of the main units of Infantry. Most reports and his own intuition now told him that Lee had probably moved West over the Catoctin Mountains, a heavily wooded North-South range that cut through Western Maryland.

"Well, Sykes, I'll bet you a donut we're going to have to cross those mountains to get at Bobby Lee. What do you think?"

Sykes unscrewed a canteen, wiped his lips and took a minimal gulp. "No bet, General."

"He knows we're coming after him." George said. "Maybe he doesn't want to fight us for some reason or other." He meant to provoke a laugh, but Sykes didn't buy it.

"Oh, he'll fight, General, as soon as he finds the time and the ground to his pleasing. He'll turn and fight us, don't worry."

Sykes was sounding too gloomy. "You know I talked with my detective, Pinkerton, last night."

"Yes, sir, I saw he was in the camp."

"He just got back from Frederick. Says the citizens gave Bobby Lee a pretty hard time when he was there."

Sykes looked dead ahead. "Glad to hear it," he said.

"He says Bobby Lee had been reading too many Richmond papers all about how Maryland wants to secede. Thought he was going to be welcomed as the great liberator. Hah! The folks just turned their backs and held their noses. One of them said the damned Secesh looked like a pack of starving wolves and smelled worse. Apparently they were polite though."

"Southerners are always polite, sir," Sykes said, "right up until they slide the blade in you."

"You sound like a man who knows."

"Spent some duty time in Florida, sir. Almost as bad as Virginia."

George wondered. Could anything be as bad as Virginia? The thought reminded him of the ever-nervous Halleck back in Washington. "General Halleck," he said, "keeps warning me in every telegram that Lee is going to turn and strike back at Washington. He says we're being drawn out here as a *ruse de guerre* to get us out of the way."

Finally a smile from Sykes. "Say, that's mighty impressive, sir. General Lee using a French thing on us?"

George barked a laugh that was heard a hundred yards back in the column. "Yes, by God, a French thing. We should be honored, eh, Sykes?"

"Rider coming in, sir."

"Yes, I see him."

Laughing to himself, George trained his binoculars on the lone galloping figure who was raising a dust trail and coming right at them. Was it Custer? No, the image looming in his glasses was another young man. A few minutes later as the rider pulled up to them he turned out to be a lad with red hair and freckles. He ought to be in school this fine day, George thought to himself.

A salute with a dusty gloved hand. "General McClellan, sir, Captain Custer sends his compliments and a message."

"In writing?"

"No, sir. I am to repeat."

No surprise there. Custer hated to write. "Very well, repeat away, Lieutenant."

"Captain Custer reports: Nine o'clock this morning. Farmer reports main body, Jackson or Longstreet, moved West on National road away from Frederick two days ago. Encountered squadron-size cavalry screen this morning ten miles West of Frederick. They retired without a fight. Climbed a tree and observed dust from marching infantry in Turner's Gap passage over South mountains. Could be a rear guard setting up shop. End of message, General."

"Have you had anything to drink, Lieutenant?"

"I'm dry, sir."

"My escort has some good well water we drew this morning. See the Sergeant Major when we're through."

"Yes, sir. Thank you, sir."

"You have anything to report personally, Lieutenant?"

The young man squinted into the morning sun. "Well, no sir. Captain Custer said it all I reckon."

"Where does he think Lee is going?"

276

A puzzled look. "Uh, well that wasn't in my message."

George put his right hand to the young man's shoulder. "What's your name, Lieutenant?"

"Albert Lundy, sir."

"Very well, Lundy, you talk with Captain Custer don't you? On the ride?"

"He talks, sir. I listen."

"Well, what's he saying? Did he express any personal opinion?"

"He expressed some strong political views, sir, and used very insulting language. He's down on the administration, and I'm a Republican from Connecticut, sir."

"Ah, Lundy, you disappointment me. Here I was hoping to escape politics for awhile and enjoy a nice peaceful battle out here in Maryland."

"Yes, sir."

"But before we can have a battle, Lundy, we have to find the enemy. Now, does Captain Custer have any idea where General Lee might be going?"

"Oh, yes sir. He thinks they may be headed up to Gettysburg."

"Thank you, Lundy. Get yourself some water."

General Sykes had already opened up the map.

"Interesting," George said. "Custer has a knack for smelling out things." He gestured with his fingers over the small block markings that depicted Gettysburg just over the Pennsylvania line. In that one small town there was a major junction of roads, one up to Harrisburg, another over to Philadelphia, and a third that ran southeast to Baltimore. There was even a road back to the Potomac that could support a retreat.

"If I were Bobby Lee I'd be interested in Gettysburg."

"Worth a look," Sykes said.

After Lundy had filled his canteen, George gave him an order for Custer. Probe up toward Gettysburg.

"Tell him to keep off the main roads. Observe, but don't be observed. Come back this evening and report. I'll be camped just South of Frederick."

277

Lundy saluted. "Yes, sir. Hope we find 'em, sir."

"Be careful what you hope for, Lieutenant. He's not authorized to open a battle, be sure you tell Custer that."

"Yes, sir."

George made himself frown severely at the young Lieutenant. "Stay alive, Lundy. You're more useful to me that way."

Lundy saluted and galloped off while George whispered, "God be with you, boy."

A half hour later the column topped a small ridge and there a mile off was the compact city of Frederick, Maryland, drowsing in the morning sun.

"Seems peaceful enough," Sykes remarked with reserved skepticism.

George opened his binocular case. He focused the lenses and spied the picket company strung out well in front of them, patrolling through the rolling farmland, looking for trouble and finding none. He raised his circle of vision up to take in the town itself.

"Well, our flag is flying from the top of the courthouse, Sykes. That's something I like to see."

It was the Fourth of July and all other holidays in one for Frederick, Maryland.

George led their parade march down Main Street where gathered crowds cheered with lusty relief, just as they had the day before when Hooker and Burnside arrived.

But this was a special, joyous greeting for General McClellan, commander of their 'liberators' from Washington. Bands tooted patriotic hymns and marches. Ladies waved handkerchiefs. A little girl in her best pink dress dashed out into the dusty street and thrust a garland of roses over Dan Webster's neck. George patted the horse. "Hope you don't mind the smell of roses, old fella."

General Sykes jingled up alongside smiling. "My wife will never believe this," he cried over the music and the cheers.

"Makes one feel rather Roman, doesn't it, Sykes," George shouted as he tipped his cap to everyone in sight.

"Sure beats hell out of Virginia," Sykes called back.

"At last we're getting the reception we deserve," George shouted. "Down in Virginia we were the brutal invaders. Here we're the good old army boys, come to the rescue."

The dusty, sunburnt troops following behind them were in high spirits too, having all sorts of good things thrust upon them, cool water, milk, pies, candies, sandwiches, beer and wine. Some of the bolder ladies would rush out and kiss them on the cheek.

"Thank God, you're here, boys," the citizens yelled as they waved their star spangled banners.

"Go get those rascals, McClellan!"

"Run them stinking damn seceshers out of Maryland!"

George was shocked to see a red faced, squalling baby thrust up at his face for a General's kiss.

A field South of Frederick, Maryland, September 13, 1862, 11:30 a.m.

George inspected his headquarters tent which had just been erected in a sweet smelling patch of beaten-down clover. Situated upon a gentle knoll, it caught a cooling breeze from the West over the Catoctin Mountains.

He took off his cap and shook out some stray pink blossoms. He would enjoy describing the celebration festivities to Nelly, how well they had been received by the men and especially the ladies of Frederick.

But now, to work. He had to sift the reports from Pleasonton and Custer, the wild outbursts of panic from Halleck, the lies of prisoners, the excited estimates from the citizens of Frederick. Somehow he had to puzzle out the true location of Bobby Lee's army and its intentions.

"Grass smells nice, don't it, General?"

George turned. "Oh, hello there, Pinkerton. Just the man I wanted to see."

Pinkerton prided himself in going and coming on his own whim, bragging that he might turn up anywhere at any time like the ghostly Tom 'Stonewall' Jackson. Always a crafty dresser, the detective was turned out today in a spiffy gray tweed suit with a rounded derby hat tilted low over his eyes.

"Our friendly enemies took right good care of this camp ground when they were here it looks like," Pinkerton observed with a squint.

George was immediately curious. "Which unit camped here?"

"D. H. Hill's Division, they skedaddled over the mountains I suspect, with the rest of them."

"The question is, what will they do next?"

Pinkerton had an air of confidence. "We'll find out soon enough, General. My men are out like bloodhounds. It's hard to move a hundred and twenty thousand troops around without somebody noticing."

"Do you still stand by that strength estimate, Allan?"

"One hundred and twenty thousand at least," Pinkerton replied with calm certainty. "Could be more."

"Oh? How do you see that?"

Pinkerton unfolded a map and stretched it on the grass. "Halleck keeps complaining to us there are large units of the enemy been spotted here, South of the Potomac, and he's near pissing his pants fearing they are primed to attack Washington. But, what if they are on their way here from Richmond to join up with Lee?" Pinkerton's brown eyes danced and glinted with the troubling idea. "Why, sir, you could be looking at the business end of a hundred and fifty thousand guns or more when you catch up with him."

George felt his stomach tighten and twist. "We'll be lucky to have ninety thousand all up and ready," he said, almost whispering, as if he didn't want the word to float out on the wind.

Pinkerton shrugged with a broad expression of concerned sympathy. "My numbers don't lie, General."

George sighed. Yes, Pinkerton had a way of conjuring up dark clouds of doubt even on sunlit mornings. But better to be prepared for the worst.

"Well, now, what have we here?" Pinkerton pointed at two officers who were walking purposefully in step toward them.

George recognized Colonel Silas Colgrove, Regimental Commander of the 27th Indiana. With him was Colonel Sam Pittman, Adjutant to General Williams who was the temporary commander of the 12th Corps.

The officers arrived at the headquarters tent and saluted.

"Sir, may I present Colonel Colgrove of the 27th Indiana."

"I know the Colonel," George replied, cordially returning a salute. "At ease, gentlemen." He looked curiously at the Indiana colonel, a short man with an egg-shaped head topped by thin, close cropped hair. Colgrove, in George's opinion, was the finest kind of citizen soldier, a man of few words, clear thinking and resourceful on his own hook. He was not an officer who would come around to pester the Commanding General without cause.

"General McClellan," Colgrove spoke up, "one of my men, Private Mitchell of D Company found a certain paper on our new camp grounds." Colgrove was obviously proud of his Private Mitchell. "I immediately took it to our Corps Commander, General Williams, who agreed that you ought to see it."

George accepted the paper but continued to listen to Colonel Colgrove.

"As you may know, sir, our camp ground was recently occupied by General D. H. Hill's division of the rebel army. The document you are now holding was discovered in an envelope down on the ground. It was wrapped around three cigars."

George sniffed the paper before reading it. "Pretty good cigars."

He unfolded the paper. Attached was a covering letter from General Williams which said in part: "This is a document of interest and also thought genuine."

George began to read, and stopped breathing. When he had finished he looked up at Colgrove with a broad smile. He turned to face Pittman. "What do you think, Colonel? This is signed

281

by Colonel Chilton, Lee's Adjutant. You served once with him, didn't you?"

"Yes, sir. Before the war. We were stationed in Detroit." Pittman paused, then gave his verdict. "That looks to me like his true handwriting, General."

George controlled a surging excitement. "Are you positive?"

"Positive, sir. I believe it to be genuine."

George slapped his left hand on the paper making it crackle. "I've seen copies of Lee's orders before, obtained from prisoners. I can hear Lee's voice in this one."

"If that document is genuine, General," Colgrove said, "the Lord has shined good fortune on our cause."

George looked into Colgrove's sturdy face. "Colonel if this document is genuine, then I have just been issued a lifetime supply of good fortune with a red ribbon around it. If I can't beat Bobby Lee with this paper in my hand, I'll be willing to go home."

He handed the paper to Pinkerton who began to read.

"Thank you, gentlemen," George said, "and my compliments to General Williams and to Private Mitchell. Be assured I'll make proper use of this."

While waiting for Pinkerton to finish he reviewed to himself the high points of the document. Yes, it was an actual copy of a marching order from Bobby Lee. Issued on September 10, Special Order 191. They left Frederick on September 11th.

> *To Maj.-Gen. D. H. Hill:*
> *The army will resume its march tomorrow, taking the Hagerstown road. General Jackson's command will form the advance ...*

It was as if he had been allowed to open up the enemy commander's skull and peer inside. Lee was dividing his army, sending Jackson and two other units to Harper's Ferry with a side trip to Martinsburg, West Virginia. Another unit to Hagerstown, Maryland. No threat to Washington or Baltimore.

After capturing Harper's Ferry, it appeared he was going North through Hagerstown on his way to Pennsylvania.

> *Gen. D. H. Hill's division will form the rear guard of the army ...*

You should be more careful with copies of your orders, Dan Hill. So here it was all laid out for him on a platter. Lee's Army was split all over the map, as much as twenty miles apart, with only Longstreet's Command and the wagon trains drawn up at Boonsboro on the other side of the Catoctin Mountains. Boonsboro was the closest town to the Union Army's present position.

> *Each regiment on the march will habitually carry it axes in the regimental ordnance-wagons, for use of the men at their encampments, to procure wood etc.*
> *By command of Gen. R. E. Lee.*
> *R. H. Chilton, Assist. Adj.-Gen.*

George paced as Pinkerton continued to read. He would send Bill Franklin to relieve the siege on Harper's Ferry. The National Road going through Turners Gap in the mountains appeared to be either open or lightly defended. He would concentrate the balance of his forces there tomorrow and attack.

Pinkerton glanced up from his reading with a smooth, wolfish grin. "Why, this makes it almost too easy, General. Where's the fun in that?"

CHAPTER TWENTY-FIVE

A mile east of Turner's Gap at the base of South Mountain, September 14, 1862, 5:00 p.m.

Dan Webster was not quite himself. He stood calmly with no stomping of hooves, no frantic lunges at the tempting green grass. Only his ears twitched occasionally at the familiar booming noises that echoed from the West. Perhaps Dan Webster had caught the mood of the figure on his back who sat erect and still in his saddle.

Horse and rider occupied a small knoll alongside the National Road just before it thrust through the pass at South Mountain, about ten miles to the West of Frederick. Topping a thousand feet above sea level, South Mountain of the Catoctin range ran in generally a northeast to southwest direction. The National Road, also known as the Hagerstown Pike, cut through it at right angles about four hundred feet below the crest. A few miles east of this passage was Boonsboro, Maryland, now occupied by Bobby Lee's depleted forces.

This defile through the mountain was known as Turner's Gap. George had studied it on maps and, as usual, it was different seeing it 'in the flesh.' The rising terrain all around was irregular, rocky and wooded, cut by ravines, thick with undergrowth. At the upper levels a handful of cultivated fields and clearings were marked by rough rail fences and stone walls.

Not an ideal place to fight, George told himself as he watched the smoke of battle envelop the tops of Turner's Gap. Jesse Reno's Ninth Corps was attacking up and around the left or south side of the gap, while "Fighting Joe" Hooker's First Corps was pushing up the from the right. Earlier that day George had made a deal with Hooker who hated the nickname that journalists had pasted on him.

"Whip the Secesh at Turner's Gap, and I'll never mention your famous nickname again, Joe."

"That's be fine with me, General. I'd welcome being known as plain old Joe Hooker. That thing they call me, why, it makes me sound like some kind of Mexican bandit."

"Wouldn't that be 'Fighting Ho Zay'?"

"Haw! Even worse," Hooker had bellowed with a twisted grin.

"Anyway, General Hooker, whatever your cognomen, I want you to take your three divisions off to the right, pick up an old farm road that goes to the top, and then cut to the south and try to flank Dan Hill or whoever is up there in the wrong uniform."

"Jesse Reno's attacking on the other side of the gap I take it?"

"Correct, though he got here a little ahead of you."

"We'll catch up, General."

And so he did.

George shaded his eyes against the low sun cutting through the gunpowder haze. He could just make out the troops swarming up the mountain, firing as they climbed, their discharging rifles making a mass of flickering firefly lights. Distantly the whirling whiz and whump of artillery echoed back to him. Good work, Jesse Reno, and you too, 'Fighting Joe.' God bless the men and boys. All they ever needed was a fair chance to prove their worth.

He turned to survey the scene in front of him. Here the long, undulating blue line of troops marched past him on their way to join the battle, the coming sunset illuminating their individual faces.

He wiped moisture from one eye. How he loved them.

He pulled his short billed soldier's cap lower over his eyes, a dashing, serious military look. He heard some scattered cheers and greetings, but made no acknowledgment. Act as if there were no cheers, as if he was all alone here on Dan Webster. But as he continued to stare at them his right arm made a decision of its own. It came up slowly and stretched, his index finger pointing out at Turner's Gap, pointing at the smoky haze and the pinpoint lights of battle ahead. He held this position stationary, arm outstretched.

Just pointing.

The troops broke into a roar of yells, cheers and whistles at the sight.

A pretty good pose for a statue. Or a painting.

McClellan points the way.

He wondered if there were any newspaper sketch artists nearby to catch it. Ah, well, his arm was getting heavy, but the troops loved it. He would hold the pose for a while more. He could easily repeat it for an artist after the war, if he survived without being killed by the enemy or his own government.

Telegram, General McClellan to General Halleck, Headquarters Army of the Potomac Beyond Middletown, Maryland, September 14th, 1862, at 9:40 p.m.

> After a very severe engagement the Corps of Hooker and Reno have carried the heights commanding the Hagerstown Road.
>
> The troops behaved magnificently. They never fought better. Franklin has been hotly engaged on the extreme left. I do not yet know the result except that firing indicated progress on his part. The action continued until after dark and terminated leaving us in possession of the entire crest.
>
> It has been a glorious victory; I cannot yet tell whether the enemy will retreat during the night or appear in increased force in the morning. I am hurrying up everything from the rear to be prepared for any eventuality.
>
> I regret to add that the gallant and able General Reno is killed.
>
> G. B. McClellan

Written Message: Captain George Armstrong Custer to General McClellan, about midday, September 15, 1862 from Keedysville, Maryland.

> The enemy is drawn up in line of battle on a ridge about two miles beyond Keedysville. They are in full view. Their line is a perfect one about a mile and a half long. Longstreet is in command and has forty cannon that we know of.

The Pry house, one mile southeast of Keedysville, Maryland, Sept. 15, 1862, Five p.m.

George guided Dan Webster in a trot behind Armstrong Custer's horse. They turned right off the Boonsville Pike and made their way up a sloping, tree-lined dirt lane that ran for about three hundred yards and ended at a neat grassy lawn. Centered there was a prosperous looking oblong, two-storied, red brick house.

Nelly's father, Brigadier General Randolph Marcy came out on the porch and waved his hat at them.

"Hello there, General. Welcome to your new headquarters."

George dismounted, happy to arrive, always comfortable with his fine looking Father-in-law. He offered his hand. "Good to see you, General. You look well."

"I'm just fine, George. Well, what do you think?"

George let his eyes play over the house and the surrounding area, inspecting in detail. "Nice looking place."

"Well, this is fertile country. I believe the owner has done rather well for himself."

"Who is the owner?"

"It's a Mister Philip Pry. He's taken his family into Keedysville for their safety. I told him any damages here would be paid for by the central government. I didn't say exactly when."

George nodded absently, slapped his yellow gloves against his palm. "I hate to take over private property," he said, continuing to scan the area. "Makes me feel like some damn confiscating Republican."

Marcy laughed. "If you'll step this way, George, I'll show you the chief advantage of the place."

They walked West from the house about thirty yards and found themselves on an overlook that offered a wide, arcing view of a shallow valley. A dull, rust-colored creek twisted through it.

"Highest ground in the area," Marcy said, proud as if he'd built the hill himself.

"I should say so. Who found it?"

"Who do ya think? I'm still a pretty good scout even at my decrepit age. At least I know good ground when I see it."

George grinned easily and patted the older man on the back. "Decrepit, faugh! You'll still be scouting Indians when I'm long gone." He took out his field glasses and began a careful scan. "You are to be commended, sir."

Marcy dug into his coat pocket and unfolded a stiff white paper. "The John Wilsons made us a map this morning, showing some roads, and elevations," he said mentioning their two topographical engineers, both named John Wilson.

George grunted. "John M. and John W. I'm surprised those two could get together on anything. Well, let's see what we have."

"All right," Marcy said, pointing from map to landscape, "this here creek to your front meanders down from Pennsylvania. It's called the Antietam, moderate flow, maybe five feet deep at the maximum, twenty to thirty feet across. Off to your left is Sharpsburg. You can just see the church tops. Now then a mile to the north of town is a shallow ridge along a wood line, stone outcroppings. Got it? That's the far woods."

"Oh, I've got it all right. Yes, sir, there you are you little devils. They look about centered on that stubby white building."

"That's a church, if you can believe it."

George lowered his glasses and called over his shoulder to Custer who was lounging near the house with some other aides. "Say, Custer, they're still out there. Why didn't you run 'em out of Maryland when you found them?"

Custer jumped to his feet. "Me against their whole Army, General? Why, that would have been most unfair to them."

George chuckled under his breath. He liked Custer but feared his wildcat lieutenant would not survive the war. He continued his inspection for some minutes.

"That patch of woods nearest us could be useful to mask an attack on their line."

"Yep," Marcy said, "we're calling it the Near Woods. Now that other wood line up to the north is designated the North Woods."

"Hah! Those Wilson boys have a way with names. Tell me about the bridges."

"Three of them. About a mile or less north of here, the Upper Bridge, plain stone but plenty usable with a ford nearby. Right down here to the left of us is where the Boonsboro Pike crosses the creek, can't quite see it for the trees. The Boonsboro Pike is the main road you turned off to get here. It heads straight into Sharpsburg."

George felt his chest tighten. "It goes two ways, General. That could be a line of attack from them to us. They could move out of those woods, masked by the ridge."

"That's possible. May I give the General a word of advice? Keep your center strong, George. Keep your reserves in tight right here where you can get at 'em. You never know what those sonofabitches are going to try."

"I know."

"Now then, the third bridge," Marcy continued his lecture. "It's about a mile and a half below the center bridge, called Rohrbach after the farmer down that way. It connects to a road running northwest into Sharpsburg."

George let out a breath. Another road into Sharpsburg. Control that two-road net and you control the town and the battlefield. He was about to announce his thought to Marcy when guns opened up from the enemy lines. They were quickly answered by a battery of the Second United States Artillery positioned near the center bridge. The federal battery had just delivered two quick counter-battery shots at the enemy guns, tearing up the area with both ground and air bursts. As the smoke cleared the enemy guns retired into the wood line.

"Accurate shooting," George said. "Send my compliments to Captain Tidball." He clicked open his pocket watch. "Well, General, the troops are still moving up. The roads are clogged. I haven't even begun to place them where I want them. The light is fading. I say it's too late to put on an attack today."

"Why make an attack at all?" Marcy clearly had a notion to sell. "We hold good ground here behind the creek. Make him come at us, and then let her rip. Remember what we did to them at Malvern Hill? We've got the same artillery with us. We could do it again right here."

"Highest ground on the map."

"Yes, sir, George, think on it, Bobby Lee is always prone to attack. I say it's his fatal weakness. It'll do him in someday."

Another flight of shells passed, swishing off to the right. "I know," George said. "Nothing I'd like to do better, General. But I'm carrying an order from the President, received today by telegraph. Can you guess what it says?"

"Destroy the rebel Army?" His son-in-law nodded with a tight smile.

"But gol dang it, George, that's what he always says. He doesn't know what he's talking about any more than Mother Marcy's cat."

George put an arm around the older man's shoulders. "Father Marcy, my job is hanging by a thread. I am going to have to be aggressive here to satisfy those hounds in Washington. Lincoln liked the result at South Mountain, but he wants more. I talk in his one ear, and Stanton and Halleck talk in his other. You know how it is."

Marcy breathed a tired sign. "I know how it is, son."

"Let's start thinking about how we're going to attack these people."

* * *

On a hill overlooking the Rohrbach Bridge, 600 yards southeast of Sharpsburg, Maryland, September 16th, 1862, 10:00 a.m.

George sat Dan Webster under the spreading shade of a lone oak tree. He brought up his field glasses. The graceful, triple-arched stone bridge curved and shimmered in the viewing circle. He tilted up and scanned the hills on the opposite side of the creek. Good defensive position for the Sesech. He moved the vision circle further up and right, catching the two church steeples of Sharpsburg proclaiming their connection with God.

He had been up since before dawn and considered hitting Bobby Lee's position this morning, but the pearly ground fog had been too thick. Just as well. He could use the extra time to move up more supplies, lay in more artillery, and just plain think through his plan. Everything had to be exquisitely poised and set.

He lowered his glasses and looked over at Brigadier General Ambrose Burnside who sat his horse a few yards off, his head nodding, either lost in a world of his own or asleep.

Burnside was a big man with an impressive, balding forehead. He wore his bushy whiskers in a peculiar outgrowth running from his ears to his lower jaw where they linked up with his mustache in a curving pattern. His busy dark eyes always seemed to be suspiciously searching for some distant good or some immediate threat. George had known and liked the man since their West Point days, and he had once happily roomed with "Burn" and his wife for some months when they both worked for the railroad in Chicago.

But Burnside could be trouble as a military commander. From day to day he could be either too rashly bold or too nervously timid. George hoped Burnside would have one of his bold days tomorrow.

293

Two flaming white puffs of artillery smoke from the enemy lines interrupted his meditation. All day Bobby Lee's gunners had been randomly potting away at the Federal positions, and George's artillery would answer back. The game had been going on since yesterday afternoon. Now the shells passed well overhead making their own particular sound signature. These were the rare whoosh-whiz variety that indicated an English gun. They exploded in an empty field well beyond them.

The impact snapped Burnside alert. His voice had a tone of detachment.

"I must discuss a certain matter with you, General McClellan," he said.

George shifted in his saddle and saw they were out of earshot of the other staff officers who stood in conferring groups well behind them.

"You can call me Mac when we're in private, Burn."

Burnside walked his horse to stand aside Dan Webster. "This is official, General McClellan."

"Oh, ho." George puffed out his cheeks. "Okay, what is it, General?"

But he knew what it was.

"Have my actions been unsatisfactory to the Commanding General?" Burnside inquired, his manner and his voice rigid with formality.

"You were slow getting up to Turner's Gap, General Burnside, and you blocked the road for General Hooker's advance. But we discussed that yesterday. I spoke sharply to you then because I felt it proper and necessary, but now the matter is forgotten."

"If it's forgotten then why did the Commanding General take General Hooker's First Corps away from me?"

"Because I want my two top generals on both flanks in this attack. Hooker on the right, and you here on the left with Cox's Ninth Corps. It's a position just as critical as Hooker's I assure you, Burn."

"Hooker has two other Corps in his attack. I don't."

George slapped his knee with a glove. "Damn it all, Burn, you sound like a whiny child. Now just cut it."

Burnside's face colored and his jaw quivered as he gazed out at Sharpsburg across the sluggish waters of the creek. "Is the General aware that I have been offered the command of this Army on more than one occasion by the Secretary of War?"

"Everybody knows that, Burn."

"Is everybody aware that I turned down his commission out of loyalty to you, sir?"

"I assumed as much from one of my oldest and closest friends. But I also heard that you didn't believe you were capable of commanding such a large Army and told them so. On that score I back your judgment."

Burnside swiveled around to face his commander. His lips were a tight line under his bushy whiskers, his brooding eyes glistened. "Loyalty cuts both ways, Mac. Someday they're going to ask me again, and I just might say yes."

George took off his cap and wiped his forehead. It was really quite a pleasant aspect from here on this hill overlooking the sun washed farms in the valley. Poor people. Who could have predicted that the war would hurricane through their placid world in this tiny corner of Maryland. Sad to think of what they would do to Philip Pry's beautiful farm.

He looked at Burnside and spoke in a mild, almost dreamy way. "Someday they'll get rid of me, Burn, when I have served their purposes and they feel safe in doing so. Then they are going to go looking for a commander they can control. I would hate to think, Burn, that my old friend, would fall into that trap."

Burnside's voice was distant. "Is it your intention to give battle tomorrow, General McClellan?"

George had to smile. Ah, let it go, let it go. George tried to match his friend's primly starched up manner of speech. "It is indeed my intention, General Burnside, to bring General Lee to battle tomorrow at daybreak."

"Then do you have any orders for me, sir?"

"Well, as a matter of fact I do, Burn. Tell General Cox to be prepared to attack tomorrow morning across that bridge in whatever strength necessary to carry it, and then to continue the attack by the right oblique, guiding on that near church spire at Sharpsburg." He pointed.

"I understand, sir."

"I am going to coordinate your attack with Hooker's. We'll put Bobby Lee in a vice."

"I understand, sir. His three corps attack, and my one corps attack."

Ignore the jab. "That's right, Burn. Don't go until you receive my order." George wondered what else he could say next to the puffed up, deeply offended Burnside. There was only one last thing. "Take good care of yourself tomorrow, Burn."

Burnside's pout cracked and gave way to a dispirited grin as he raised his right hand in a careful salute. "You can count on me, Mac."

George said, "That's good, Burn." He turned Dan Webster away and dug in his heels. The two friends did not shake hands.

CHAPTER TWENTY-SEVEN

Later that day George accompanied Hooker as that officer took his First Corps across Antietam Creek and into its attack position three miles North of the enemy's left flank. Hooker's normally blotched face was lit up more than usual in the smoky afternoon sun. A breath of whiskey floated between their horses.

"I'll open up on 'em, General. But if I get stopped, don't you dare leave me hanging out there. You hear? If they start chewing me up, give me supports when I yell for 'em."

"You shall have them," George pledged. "I'll put Mansfield's Corps across the creek by the time you attack. Remember, Joe, you command the field, despite seniority."

"Well, all right, but make sure Bull Sumner knows that. Is he coming across the creek today? By God, I wish it was anybody but him. He nearly got me and Phil killed at Williamsburg, sitting on his ass and leaving us in the lurch. And who's this Mansfield with the Twelfth Corps? Hell, he just got here. You're sure I can count on him?"

Hooker was wearing all his nerves outside his uniform today. "I haven't decided when to commit Sumner," George said, "probably tomorrow morning, but I'll need him to reinforce our center until I'm convinced it's secure."

"Hah! So you don't want weird Tom Jackson popping up on your flank, eh?"

"Exactly so. As for Mansfield, he's an honorable old soldier. He'll do his duty. But you're the one I'm counting on to whip them, Joe. Live up to that unspeakable nickname of yours."

"Let it remain unspoken," Hooker replied with a gusty laugh.

"Well, I've been called worse," George said. A simple statement of fact.

They were approaching a tall, waving stand of trees. Dimly in the far background to their left George could see the edge of the Confederate line marked by flags, campfires and glinting artillery.

"I'll leave you here, General Hooker. Be sure to stay in close touch with my headquarters. Set up a signal flag station on the best high ground you can find."

Hooker snorted. "I will, General. And tomorrow I'll drive 'em into the damn river." He frowned. "If they don't kill all of us first."

George reached across between their horses to lend a steady handshake. He then faced Dan Webster around to the East, flipped a quick salute and dug his heels into the eager animal. Joyfully, Dan Webster got to do what he loved best, run like fury with George along for the ride. As horse and General streaked along the endless stream of marching blue ranks George twirled his cap at them.

> They bellowed cheers that fell into a pattern,
> "Our George! Our George! Our George!"
> Drummer boys picked up the beat.
> "Our George! Our George! Our George!"
> The bands joined in.
> "Our George! Our George! Our George!

Their bright young faces flashed by him. If only he could save their lives, all of them. Not one of them should die. He turned his eyes away from them as the tears streaking down his cheeks became cold slivers in the wind.

* * *

The Pry House, September 16, 1862, 9 p.m.

George strolled over thick grassy lawn of Farmer Pry's home headed toward the overlook. Behind him he could hear the clink and chatter of his headquarters staff as they finished their supper.

He looked out into the forbidding darkness and felt a light, misty drizzle on his cheeks. Careful, don't fall over. He had ordered that no camp fires burn tonight.

Bobby Lee was not shy about showing up his position. There he sat, two and a half miles off, his Army arranged in a defiant line of resistance, his back to the Potomac, his fires sending out a clear message. "Here I am, Mac. Come and get me, and see what fatal surprises I have in store."

George had eaten only a few crackers and some watery bean soup, no wine. Yet his stomach and bowels were already wrenched and grumbling. Perhaps a little brandy later, in order to sleep.

From this elevation the last of the gray-pink Western sky now had faded. Below in the valley of the Antietam, the two facing armies seemed to heave and breath in unison in the misty dark. Through the fields and the mysterious woods and on into the enemy lines, the night was alive with movements felt but unseen, the clanking noises of artillery and wagons, a stray crack from a picket rifle, a shouted challenge, a melancholy howling dog.

He knelt down, tried to pray. No words came. Strangely, without knowing why, he bent forward and put his nose to the grass, breathed in the deep, wet smell of the soil of Maryland. Oh, God, it would be nourished by blood in the morning.

By his decision.

He rose up, brushed the dampness off his knees. Silly thing to do. He saw Nelly's face, experienced the perfume of her hair, felt the spreading pressure of her breasts. No, put those thoughts away. By this time tomorrow the results would be known. He would either be victoriously alive or beaten and dead in his boots. He had no wish to live beyond defeat. Whatever the outcome, Nelly and his little daughter would bear his name with honor.

He went to his tent at the edge of the lawn. Opened the flap. A dim candle burned within. He would close his eyes for a short while. He would put out some cavalry to look for Tom Jackson. It wouldn't do to be surprised.

* * *

Bobby Lee sat ready and erect behind his small fold-up desk. With every sense alert, he pushed the candle off to the side so that the flame did not block the sight of his visitor who sat shadowed in a corner of the tent. He was tempted to grab the candle, shove it up and forward to illuminate the man's face. But no. What would that tell him? Temper your nerves, sir, he advised himself as he idly stroked a finger through his beard. War was the art of the unexpected. You weighed all known factors and elements of a situation before making a decision. But somewhere in your recipe you always allow room for the unexpected.

Tomorrow the Corps of 'Mr. F. J. Hooker' would come storming down from the North. He would meet that threat and whatever else George McClellan threw at him. Such was his duty and he enjoyed it perhaps more than a man should. He recalled a well-worn thought. It is good for us that war is so terrible, else we should love it too much.

But this visitor? Who was he and what was he doing here? He was indeed the unexpected multiplied to new powers. Lee looked down as his poor bandaged hands, still bluish and purple from the accident. Fingers wrapped in the reins. Horse bolted. Still painful, but he was able to pick up a pencil and tap it on the desk as he digested the visitors opening remarks. He neither believed or disbelieved, but sometimes you can restate what another man says, and it will lead somewhere else.

"So you say that General McClellan firmly believes me to have one hundred and twenty thousand troops up with me tonight?"

"Once A. P. Hill and Tom Jackson join you from Harper's Ferry tomorrow," the visitor said.

"Ah, yes, well perhaps he's right in believing such a thing." A smile tempted his lips, but he disciplined his coldly neutral expression.

The visitor scoffed impolitely. "You'll be lucky to have fifty thousand up for action tomorrow. You know it, and I know it."

Lee was silent. An intriguing thought that was. Give him a hundred and twenty thousand men and another Tom Jackson, why sir, he could conquer the world.

The visitor rose to go. "Just thought you'd like to hear the news," he said indifferently. "Take it for whatever it's worth to you."

"Hold your horses, sir. You are in a military camp unauthorized. I can have you held under close arrest at my whim. Further, I can have you shot or hanged for a spy. So don't be in such a hurry."

The visitor breathed a long sigh, then sat down again and waited. "Before you hang me, can I have a cup of coffee?"

Lee called to Major Taylor who was just outside the tent. He ordered a cup for himself as well. Even lying, turncoat, untrustworthy men such as his visitor sometimes know the truth and speak it. Though he hated spies, this one had missed his Army's actual strength count by only ten thousand. May as well see what else he could learn.

"This is the first war," Lee said, "where both sides read the same newspapers and trade 'em back and forth. We know all about General McClellan's adversity with the administration, how they have undercut him, depriving him of the forty thousand man reinforcement he was to receive when in front of Richmond."

"That was your man Tom Jackson in the valley. Stonewall farts and Lincoln's ass goes tight. They were terrified he was going to attack Washington. That why they withheld McDowell's Corps."

"That was merely their excuse, sir," Lee answered with conviction. "Had they really wished to reinforce General McClellan's movement on Richmond, it would have been done."

"You may be right there, General." The visitor showed he didn't care much one way or the other.

Lee went on, driven by pure curiosity now. "McClellan made a brilliant move south when I attacked his weak right flank, fooled me entirely for two days. He had us chasing ghosts. Then when we finally attacked at Malvern Hill, I must admit they handled us quite roughly. Some thought they could've walked right over us into Richmond. But General McClellan chose to pull back to the James River. Then they left him hanging in front of Richmond, denied his request to cross the James River and strike at Petersburg. Now that would have made us most unhappy, sir. Petersburg is the key to Richmond as you must know."

"See here, General, I'm just a messenger, I'm not up on this military strategy stuff. I've never even heard of Petersburg."

Lee waved him off. "Then, here's what I will never understand. Incredibly they pulled him back from that fine lodgment he had, threatening Richmond, took his army away from him and gave it to Mr. John Fool Pope. Why, sir, we could not believe our good fortune. With Richmond relieved, it allowed us to march up here and give Mr. John Fool Pope the punishment he so richly deserved. Which in turn allowed us to invade Maryland. Our luck ran out when Lincoln woke up and gave the Federal Army back to McClellan."

The visitor grunted. "What do you want from me, General Lee?"

Major Taylor came in with two tin cups of coffee. He waited while Lee sipped his.

"Enough sugar, sir?"

"Perfect, Major Taylor. Thank you so much."

When Major Taylor had retired, Lee said to his visitor, "Now then, in light of all I've said, what I really wish to know, sir, is this: Do we of the Confederacy have some highly placed benefactor in the Federal War Department? Surely this series of events would cause one to suspect as much. You do see my point?"

The visitor snorted an unkind laugh. "You don't have a friend in the War Department. You've got something better. See here, General, the people I work for have an enemy, and it

302

ain't you. Beg pardon for saying so, but you are just a high flown gentleman who roves the countryside with a rebel army. No, their prime enemy is the General across the creek tonight. That's why I dropped by to give you some useful information on him. Do ya see it now?"

Lee sipped his coffee, the good Yankee stuff, rich with brown sugar, taken from Mr. John Fool Pope's supply trains.

"Can I be getting along, now, General?" his visitor asked.

"Major Taylor!" Taylor was immediately present. "Put this person under close arrest until further notice."

"Oh, no. Oh, shite! I told 'em this'd happen. Oh, shite!"

"Major Taylor will show you where you'll be staying. You'll be our guest for a few days. And be advised I do not like vulgar language in my presence. Good night, sir."

Major Taylor drew his revolver, took the sputtering, despairing visitor by the arm and led him away.

General Lee sat quietly for some minutes then bowed his head.

"Oh Lord," he whispered. And he went on with a reverent prayer of thanksgiving to God who had given him the wisdom to turn down command of the Federal Army when they had offered it to him.

Then he said a small prayer for the General across the creek.

CHAPTER TWENTY-EIGHT

The Pry House, September 17, 1862, 7:00 a.m.

He had napped a little in the evening, woke then and stayed up the rest of the night, planning, making sure, worrying. One by one his staff had nodded off. Two hours before dawn he went to his tent and crumpled face forward into a dreamless sleep.

Now he kicked his legs and rolled up and off his cot. He stood up, wavering. He forced his eyes to remain open. Cold morning light shown through the cracks in his tent. He allowed himself to realize what had awakened him. It was the smattering crack of rifles, the opening notes of Joe Hooker's symphony of small arms on the right with artillery as a rumbling underscore.

He had slept with his trousers and underwear on. Water was in the pan. He splashed some on his face. He undid his buttons and urinated on the grass floor of the tent.

Ahh.

He pulled on his boots, buttoned up his blouse and stepped outside. An aide handed him a steaming cup of coffee. He took it thankfully.

The first scattered shots had now blended into a fused rumble of combined fire, as thousands of rifles crackled as one.

Both sides going at it.

He sipped his coffee and tried to remember which of his bright young men had given it to him.

He walked west and joined Fitz John Porter at the overlook.

"Good morning, General," Fitz shouted, his voice straining against the background din. He was standing, arms folded, next to a group of six telescopes tied to wooden fence posts. Each was aimed at a different point on the battlefield which was now gradually emerging out of the yellow morning sunrise. Fitz looked like some morbid pitchman at a carnival.

"Yes, sir, step right up and see the world of war. Only cost you a few thousand lives."

George jerked his head in response. Didn't feel like talking yet. He took another biting gulp of his coffee and looked to the sky. Night clouds were breaking up fast in a fair wind. Across Antietam Creek, two miles away thin ground fog swirled and flashed with glints of rifle fire from massed formations of blue clad men moving forward.

George took a thin breath, found no air in it. He tried again, relaxed his constricted chest, breathed in deeply and slowly. Take it easy. Be orderly in your thinking. Everything depends on you.

He looked through a telescope, found and focused in on the action.

"It's a well-trained army, Fitz. Good discipline under fire." That sounded about right, just what a general might say.

"Indeed it is, for the most part," Fitz said matter-of-factly. "The green regiments are falling over their own feet of course, no drill, no training. But for the most part, you can be proud of them, General."

Well trained? He had said that? How could he or anyone train these massed lines of men and boys to go forward into the enemy's storm of fire? How could any man ask another to do what they were doing right now before his eyes, marching in dressed ranks, through barnyards and woodlands, through orchards and gardens, through a ripe, waving corn field where green stalks were being cut down, and the men who marched there were cut down with them.

And through it all they carried flags of the Nation, flags of their States. The flags would waver, sometimes fall, then onward again.

Even in the cool of the morning, he felt a tingle of sweat break out on his brow. Good God, he had nothing to do with any of this.

Did he?

Those troops chose to face the odds of certain death for some clandestine cause of their own. But what? The answer came to him, clear as tinkling crystal. They were all insane. Then a horrible recognition. More sweat. Who had made them insane? Worse, there was still a kind of terrifying beauty in what they were doing, a beauty he recognized and appreciated and made him touch his tongue to his dry lips. This beautiful insanity then was his profession. Yes, he saw that. He was supposed to be skillful at it.

Was he?

He turned away from the scene to collect himself, and there was John M. Wilson, one of the two topographical engineers by that name. The Wilson boys.

He remembered where he had ordered him last night. Speak now, voice low, authoritative, calm, in the way of generals. "Good morning, Lieutenant Wilson. How are things on the left with Burnside and Cox?"

"I was there a half hour ago, sir. No activity to report except light sniper fire from across the creek. Nobody hurt yet, but the enemy has a lot of rifle pits dug in on the hill opposite. It'll be hard going when they attack. Do you want me to deliver the order now, sir?"

George considered. This was good. A rational, deliberate order was required. Chess game. Move required. He would think on it.

"No, not yet," he said. "I want to make sure that General Franklin is up with his Corps from Pleasant Valley before releasing General Burnside."

He felt like a juggler. He was outnumbered according to Pinkerton, and Lee could strike back at any point. He had to be ready. Everywhere. For anything.

"Yes, sir," Lieutenant Wilson said. "Should I stand by here for your order?"

"Yes, Wilson, stand by." A smile. "Have a cup of coffee, but stay close."

All right now. The idea was to press Lee on both flanks at once, keep him from shifting troops to meet the attacks. Was it time to send the order? Probably. But should he really wait 'til Bill Franklin comes up? Depends on how Hooker's attack is going. He would have to return to the telescope and find out.

Something else first. He walked up to another young officer who wore cavalry yellow shoulder boards. He gripped the man's elbow. "Ride south on the road to Pleasant Valley and locate General Franklin. Find out when he will arrive here."

"Yes, sir," the Lieutenant said with a big grin, "and I'll be careful not to start a battle without your permission, sir."

George looked up in surprise. Oh, yes, it was the red-headed Lieutenant Lundy from Connecticut.

"Looks like I've managed to start one myself, Lundy. Where's Captain Custer this morning?"

Lundy gave a languid wave at the battlefield. "He's out there somewhere, sir, trying to win the war all by himself." He spoke with resignation, like the father of a wild adolescent.

"On your way, Lundy. Stay alive."

"I know, sir. I'm more valuable to you that way."

Franklin had been unable to save Harper's Ferry, a lost cause from the beginning. George had warned Halleck about the vulnerability of that difficult place, wanted to evacuate the town and save the ten thousand troops there. Halleck had blocked the idea. Well, anyway, it would be good to have Bill Franklin and his 1st Division Commander, Baldy Smith, join him here at the party on Antietam Creek.

George walked back to the telescopes, anxious to see how the attack was going. Fearing to see how the attack was going.

Someone had brought an armchair out of farmer Pry's house. It was there by the telescopes inviting him to sit and he did so. A sharp spring raked his back.

"See anything, Fitz?"

He clutched the arms of the chair. Think about nothing. Listen.

"Enemy's come out of the woods, sir, right near that little white church, forming ranks in a North axis, seems to be counter attacking."

Yes, to be expected. Lee, Jackson, Longstreet and the rest will never submit peacefully. Hah! Peacefully! George felt his teeth grind.

"I spot the Texas flag," Fitz called out. "That would be Hood. Taking a beating they are." He moved the telescope a notch right. "So are we."

Finally George cleared his head. Found a cigar and lit it. He stepped up to a telescope and trained on the critical area in front of the Far Woods.

Men were dying and he couldn't help it. He was their general and he couldn't help it.

He made the call. "Looks like Hooker's attack has been blunted."

"I concur," Fitz said. "Look over to your right. That would be Mansfield and the Twelfth Corps moving up in support. Lot of green regiments in that Corps." Meaning lots of ill trained boys will be murdered by Lee's veterans.

George stepped back, forced the next thought. "Now then, where's Sumner and the Second Corps?"

"Sumner is here somewhere, sir, awaiting orders," Fitz said, just to remind the General of what he must know already.

A buzzing in his head. Yes, of course, he remembered now. He had not yet committed Sumner's big Second Corps. No threat had developed here in the center. Yet. It was time to do so.

Was it?

He turned around and called to the gathered staff on the lawn. "Where is Sumner?"

An officer stepped forward. Came to attention. With a salute. It was Captain Sam Sumner who served as his father's aide.

"Sir, compliments from General Sumner. He's in the outhouse right now, but he respectfully requests permission to cross the creek and join in the fight. We've been ready to go since dawn, General."

George returned the salute, took one last moment to reconsider.

"Tell General Sumner, when he's done, to cross Antietam creek and coordinate with General Hooker who is in command of the attack."

"I will convey your order, General McClellan. Do you wish to give me a written copy of your order for General Sumner?"

"No. Just tell him to do it, and remember Hooker's in command of the field."

Captain Sumner saluted again and trotted off to the rear of the house with the good news.

It was 7:20 a.m.

George returned to his telescope, played it over the field and found only smoke and confused movement of men, horses, artillery. Were they winning? Were they losing? He had told Hooker to stay in touch. Where were his messages? He took a pull on the cigar. Tasted of ashes. That farmhouse on fire. Did we do that?

"What do you see, Fitz?"

"Can't quite make it out," Fitz John Porter muttered from the corner of his mouth. "Looks like our boys are up to the white church. Lot of casualties though."

"Can you make out any regimental colors?"

"I think it must be the Twelfth Corps. Holding on. They're going to need Sumner's help."

So it had been the right time to commit Sumner. No written orders. Keep the record vague. Written orders often turn up in court-martials.

The Pry House, 8:00 a.m.

He would wait no longer. He ordered Lieutenant Wilson, (John M.) to deliver the attack order to Burnside. "Attack across the bridge, move on Sharpsburg immediately upon receiving this order." Wilson mounted up and moved off at a gallop.

The Pry House, 8:55 a.m.

Fitz Porter had gone off to his own Fifth Corps headquarters just south across the Boonsboro road.

Two attacks had fallen apart on the right. The fields in front of the Far Woods were smoking, strewn with bodies, horses and men, broken guns, splintered rails, tattered flags. Some of the Twelfth Corps troops had gone into the Far Woods and not come out. George had stopped looking through the telescopes.

He stood alone smoking his third cigar. Hateful taste.

A signal corps Lieutenant was at his side. "Sir, a flag message from General Hooker's headquarters."

"About time."

The Lieutenant read from the message pad. "'General Mansfield dangerously wounded. The work goes bravely on.'"

There was a poet at the signal station. It looked to George that the work had stalled at the Far Woods. Now where was Sumner?

"Lieutenant, take a message for General Sumner, by flag to the North Woods station."

"Yes, sir," with pad, ready to write.

"Be careful how you advance. Fear our right is suffering."

The Lieutenant was off. A Sergeant replaced him. "Sir, fresh message from the right."

George took the paper. It read: "From Major Hammerstein: General Hooker is wounded in foot. Driving the enemy. Sumner coming up. General Mansfield is killed."

"Sir," the Sergeant said, "we just got another quick message about the same time this was coming in. It confirms General Mansfield is dead. Says we hold the field at present. Asks for all the supports you can give. That's from General Williams, sir, took over the Twelfth Corps. I'll get you a written copy right away, sir."

"Thank you Sergeant. Wait and I'll give you a reply. How's our visual contact with the flag station?"

"Perfect, sir. It's back beyond those North Woods, well out of the smoke. We're zeroed in on each other with our telescopes real good, sir."

George turned away, shut his eyes and thought hard. He had nothing left to send to the right. He would keep Porter's Fifth Corps still in reserve in the center. That was his ace. Franklin would be up soon with his Sixth Corps. Where would he put it?

"Take this reply to General Williams." He paused. "Hold out. Sumner with Second Corps is coming."

He hoped Sumner was coming. A rider rode fast up the lane. He'd lost his hat. Red hair glinted in the sun. Lundy. He brought his horse right up to the edge of the overlook and dismounted.

"Sir, mission accomplished. I met a courier coming up from General Franklin. Spoken message for General McClellan. Says he's a mile and a half away from here. Marching strong. Ready to polka."

George grinned. Ready to polka? What had gotten into the habitually dignified Bill Franklin?

"Did the courier know anything about the attack on the bridge?" It had been an hour since his order went out.

"Don't know anything about that, sir. He didn't mention it."

"Very well, Lundy. Good riding." He turned to another officer waiting nearby. "Colonel are you ready?"

"Ready, sir," Colonel Delos Sacket, said. A serious, forty-year-old West Pointer and Inspector General of the Army of the Potomac, Sacket was George's favorite courier-representative for occasions when messages were crucial.

He spoke slowly to Colonel Sacket, biting out each word. "Tell General Burnside he must move his troops across the Creek, push forward vigorously without delay and secure the heights beyond. Stay with him until you see it's done, then report back to me."

Sacket repeated the order and was off.

Had he waited too long? Or was Burnside simply late making the attack?

He joined General Marcy out at the overlook.

"How are you this morning, George? Thought I'd take a break from my chores in the house. How are things going."

"Things are going not too well, but not too badly. I can't seem to get it through to Burn on how important his attack is."

"It's in a bad location for command," Marcy stated. "No visual contact for flags."

"We should have laid telegraph wire down there."

Marcy shrugged. "If we had any." He studied the battlefield. "Looks like they're holding on by their fingernails, George. Lot of dead and wounded, theirs and ours. Ah, what's this I see? Take a look, George, coming out of the Near Woods."

He looked. It was Sumner and the Second Corps, officers and men riding and marching with parade ground precision, flags flying, long tightly dressed lines rolling over the ups and downs of the farm land. Moving on a southwesterly line toward the Far Woods."

"Beautiful looking attack formation," Marcy said with quiet respect. "Marching to hell or to glory as the saying goes." From somewhere out there could be heard the wail and the rackety drums of a distant band.

The Pry House, 10:00 a.m.

General Hooker was brought up to the Pry House in an ambulance wagon.

George left the overlook to go inside and see the wounded General placed on the parlor sofa.

Hooker's eyes flickered open, caught sight of George. "We were driving them, General," he said in a breathy mutter. "Driving them." His eyes went white, his lids fluttered. "Why the hell didn't you send Sumner? They started chewing us up."

"Sumner's out there now, Joe. He's making a big attack." He reached for Hooker's shoulder, a gentle touch.

"Can you get out of my way, General, please?" the doctor grumbled, as he started cutting away shreds of sock from the mangled foot.

313

Hooker's eyes rolled as his head fell back. He was unconscious.

"Will he live?" George asked.

"If we can stop the bleeding," the Doctor said without glancing up.

Suddenly Hooker was awake and screaming. "Save my foot! I need my damn foot!" They had to hold him down until he rolled back into unconsciousness.

George turned away and left the house. He met Custer on the lawn.

"Well, Armstrong, what's the report?"

"They tried to cross that bridge two or three times by now, General. Got shot up pretty bad. They're bringing up artillery to fire point blank. Snipers in rifle pits across the creek, not too many but real effective. You've seen that bridge, General?"

"I was there yesterday. It hasn't changed over night has it?"

"No sir," Custer answered literally, "but a narrow road leads up to it along the creek, then after it crosses the creek it doglegs to the right. Enemy is posted above the road and the bridge. Very difficult position, sir. Glad I'm not trying to cross it."

George looked over to the telescopes. Porter was back and observing.

"Come with me, Armstrong." They joined Porter.

"What do you see, Fitz? How's the attack going?"

"Trouble in the woods, General. Looks like they're catching a flank attack on their left. Pulling back. Not good. Not good."

George looked through the telescope. "Shite," he said. It was a word he seldom used.

He stepped back. Think.

Fitz Porter was silent and so was Custer. They made no hint of movement.

"Custer!"

"Sir?"

"Ready to ride?"

"Always ready to ride, sir."

"Baldy Smith's Second Division of the Sixth Corps is stationed on the Boonsboro road. They just got here a half hour ago. Ride down there and tell General Smith to move to the right behind the Near Woods and lend support to General Sumner. Repeat."

"General Smith. Move to the right behind the Near Woods, and lend support to General Sumner. Want me to guide them there, sir?"

"Yes. As fast as you can make it, Armstrong. Go!"

Custer was off and running for his horse.

George looked at Fitz John Porter. "It was very pretty attack wasn't it?"

The Pry House, 1:30 p.m.

George was munching on a ham sandwich when Colonel Thomas Key rode up with the news that Burnside's Ninth Corps had stormed the bridge. Key was another old friend, a judge and politician from Cincinnati. "They're across and moving slowly on Sharpsburg," he reported, clearly proud of his adventure as a courier in battle. Colonel Key had carried with him an order relieving Burnside if he did not act promptly.

"Should I tear up the order?" Key asked.

"Save it," George said. "We may need it later."

He regretted now the other order he had sent to Burnside through one of his aides:

"Take the bridge even if it costs ten thousand lives. Take the bridge." He couldn't believe he said that.

"Looks like we've done well in the center," Key said.

George felt the corners of his mouth turn up. We? Give a man a uniform and he loves to play General.

"Yes," George said, one soldier to another. "General Richardson broke through. Killed a lot of them in a sunken road. See it out there? He got stalled, then wounded. He's at the house here now, our hospital for Generals. I replaced him with Hancock."

Colonel Key nodded approval. "Excellent choice, sir."

315

George allowed his stressed nerves to ease a little bit. "That's good news about Burnside," he said. At last. He sent John M. Wilson to keep an eye on Burn's progress.

The Pry House, 2:00 p.m.

George was back with Fitz Porter. He glanced behind them. "We are collecting quite an audience."

"Beware, there are some reporters among them. I saw Smalley of the New York Tribune."

"Smalley's all right," George said. "I may talk with him when I get back from the right."

"You're going down there?"

George looked out over the settled battlefield. Nothing much happening now. "I've been getting contradictory messages from Bill Franklin and Sumner." He paused. "You still think Lee's counterattack will come right here at our center?"

"I'm sure of it," Fitz said. "That's why I've been planting artillery around the center bridge."

"Well, I think it may come on our right. Bet you a donut. That's why I want to go down there and straighten things out."

Fitz John Porter gave a stern salute. "Don't forget to duck, sir," he said, his long woeful face giving no hint of humor.

George rounded up a few aides, including Custer, Hammerstein and John W. Wilson. As they splashed across Antietam Creek at the north ford, they began to encounter the human debris of the battle, walking wounded and 'helpers,' able-bodied men assisting the wounded on their way to medical aid. As usual there were too many helpers.

That's how it is, George thought. Some men stood up in battle, and some didn't. Most men fired their weapons. Some didn't. They would often just keep loading never firing, jamming and ruining their weapons. The best officers were the one who could get most of their troops to shoot.

There were a few shouts and greetings from the stragglers as he rode along. An idea came to him, both thrilling and frightening. He would try it out on Bill Franklin when they met.

As they neared the battle scene, with its bitter smell of burnt powder, bodies started to appear, some still twisting, making pitiful small noises. They guided their horses around them. George looked and turned away, felt his stomach roll. Bullets whizzed in the branches, and now and then a shell burst rocked the ground. Lieutenant John W. Wilson easily guided them to the eastern edge of the Near Woods. Here a rough breastworks had been thrown together out of logs and dirt. He found General Sumner behind it hunkered down on the ground yelling at Bill Franklin who was giving as good as he got. Sumner's eyes were wild with shock and frustrated anger. His hands and legs trembled as he rose to salute the Commanding General. There was blood on his forehead, but no wound visible.

George hunched over as he approached the pair. The breastwork was none too high. Bullets snapped branches overhead. Nice to be short sometimes.

"Gentlemen, control yourselves! What kind of example is this for the troops!"

"My troops don't care." Sumner's voice was wavering, too high pitched, stressed to the cracking point. "My troops don't care," he screeched again. "Because they're dead mostly. What the hell do they care?"

He made a curious huffing sound, straining for breath. George feared he might have an apoplectic fit.

"Sit down here, General Sumner." He guided the old man to a tree stump. "Rest. I'll be back to speak with you in a minute." George turned his back on the old man and faced Bill Franklin. "Where's his son?"

"Wounded. Off the field."

George thought of the eager young man in the early morning sunshine.

"All right, Bill, tell me all about it. You still ready to polka?"

317

Bill Franklin grinned with white teeth that stood out against his wiry auburn beard. "I have fresh troops here," he said, snapping out the words. "They're rested from their march and ready to go. We've already driven up just short of the white church with two regiments of Hancock's brigade and Baldy Smith's third brigade. They got counterattacked, but they're holding out there behind a rise of ground. And I had two brigades of Slocum's division all lined up ready to hit that wood line, but General Sumner here just countermanded my order."

"I see."

Bill Franklin tried to level his disgust. "He is senior on the field, but I think it's a mistake. Another thing, if we don't go for the wood line, then we ought to make an attack at that little hill." He pointed it out, a very small rise of ground about fifteen hundred yards to the northwest. "They have artillery up there doing us wrong. We take it and we can enfilade those woods. We could shoot right up their back door, General. My boys can take it."

George raised himself carefully and looked over the edge of the top log, his first close-in view of the morning's battle scene. Franklin's report sounded a lot like a waiter offering a tempting menu of possible attacks.

He looked at the mysterious Far Woods. Something bad lived there. It had nearly destroyed Sedgwick's division this morning when it went in as part of Sumner's attack. Who's there he wondered. Jackson? Longstreet?

One way to find out.

"Here's an idea, Bill. We could gather the remnants of the three Corps that attacked this morning, pull 'em all together with your divisions, and go for those main woods. Big attack. All or nothing."

Franklin was interested. "Who's going to pull them together," he asked.

"Time to earn my pay, Bill. They would cheer, fall in and follow me, I'm sure of it."

Franklin's face lit up. "Sure, rally round the flag! Wave our swords, lead the charge. You do that, Mac, and I'll be right behind you!"

George laughed. Were they both going crazy? "Ah, the old Scotch blood is up, I see."

"This is the big one, Mac. We've got to win here! Got to push 'em in the river. I'm all for it, Mac. Let's ride to glory!"

Suddenly Sumner was with them. "Bah, you young fool," he shouted. He spat a great wad of something yellow right at the polished toes of Bill Franklin's boots. "You'll both be dead heroes. I tell you these three Corps are played out, and you, General Franklin, should not be wasting your strength in attacks. Be ready for them when they counterattack. They're coming, I know it. Mark my words, sir. Mark my words."

George gestured for silence. "Give me a few minutes."

He sat down against one of the logs of the breastworks, facing to the rear. What a place for a moment of meditation. He looked up with his field glasses and could make out the gleaming red bricks of his Pry House headquarters. Its hill dominated the field. He wondered if anybody was looking down on him through the telescopes? He gave a jaunty wave up that way, just in case. Yes, General McClellan was last seen waving like an idiot just before the blast killed him.

It was time now to think clearly. It was a tempting image, leading the charge, rallying the troops. Of course he would not live to enter the Far Woods.

Seductive idea that.

Death. A brief pain, a fall off his horse. Nothing to it. Then a hero's funeral, muffled drums. And aren't we sorry now for all the awful things we said about him? He could hear the ponderous music as they rolled his flag draped coffin to the cemetery.

The happiest day in Stanton's life.

Death. Terrible pain, long day's dying. Horror.

No more Nelly. No more little May. No more food, wine and languid days in the sunshine. Perfumed air. Sweet music. No more thrilling runs on the railroad.

319

Someday this war would end. School children would study illustrations of McClellan's famous 'Charge at Antietam.' Flags fluttering, he points the sword. This way men, onward!

The late General McClellan.

Nelly, tear streaked, all in black accepting the medals from a grateful Nation. Lincoln's creaky voice dedicating a soldier's cemetery here on Antietam Creek. And think of all the boys who would die with him.

He stood up and walked up to Franklin and Sumner who stood awaiting his decision.

"Burnside has broken through on the left. He's making good progress according to reports. I want you gentlemen to dig in and sit tight, wait for developments. We may yet attack today, Bill."

Franklin's face was blank and white. "Yes, sir."

Sumner did not smile.

The Pry House, 4:00 p.m.

Colonel Key was waiting for him as he dismounted. "News from the left, sir. General Burnside was moving on Sharpsburg . . ."

"Yes?" He saw from Key's face that the news was bad.

"Sir, an attack was made on Burnside's left flank by rebel troops coming up from Harper's Ferry. Reported to be A. P. Hill's division."

A. P. Hill? His roommate at West Point, a class behind him. Ambrose Powell Hill. Delicate health. Ambrose Powell Hill. Once Nelly thought she was in love with him. Wears a red shirt in battle they say.

"Where's General Porter?"

"Believe he's down by the center bridge sir."

George rode off, thinking of Ambrose Powell Hill.

Next to the Center Bridge, 4:30 p.m.

George was conferring with Custer, Sykes and Porter. Custer was agitated. "Sir, I got me a prisoner up near their center, squeezed him a little, told him if he talked I'd let him go.

320

He talked. He claims they are all shot up in their center, dead out of ammunition. They're just standing by their flags for pure cussedness. Sir, I just rode up there, nearly through their lines. All they could do was yell insults. I was safe as in Libby's arms. Their center is soft as a cream puff, sir."

"I agree, sir," General Sykes spoke with intense conviction. "I recommend an attack with the Fifth Corps here in center and the Sixth Corps in support on the right."

"That is improper, Sykes," Fitz John Porter stormed in red faced anger. "You can't recommend an attack with my Corps! Only I can do that."

"Beg pardon, sir," Sykes responded, not backing down. "It's just that I agree with Captain Custer, sir. I think they're worn out for the day, and we should take advantage. With all due respect, that's my opinion. I stand by it."

George shook his head. "I wish I could believe that, Sykes. I just don't know, and since I don't know, I lean to the side of caution."

"Rightly so, sir," Fitz Porter snapped, glaring at Sykes.

"It's been a long hard day for all of us," George said. He thought of poor old Burn who had just called for more supports in his fight with A.P. Hill. George had sent a battery of artillery, told him he had no infantry to spare. He had to hold his infantry to meet the counterattack both he and Fitz believed was coming. On the center or on the right.

George had told Burn he must hold the bridge at all costs. He feared it was the end of their friendship.

Custer was talking again. Porter argued back. George noticed that Smalley, the reporter for the New York Tribune, had followed him down here from the Pry House. He was standing a few yards away, listening.

George walked over to confront the reporter. "Could you hear our discussion, Mr. Smalley? Should I repeat it for you?"

"Anything you could offer me, General McClellan, would be most appreciated." His voice was molasses smooth, his manner respectful to the point of comedy. Smalley had learned how to talk to Generals.

"I understand you were with Hooker on the attack this morning."

"I had that honor, sir. Thrilling. I hope my humble words may do it justice."

"That was a brave place to be," George said, with respect. "This has been an awful battle, perhaps the worst of the war." He wondered what exactly he wanted to say to this man. "Our losses were heavy. So were theirs."

"General, I'm leaving for Frederick in just a few minutes, hope to get a telegraph wire to New York."

George listened.

"I'm saying in my lead sentence that the sun is going down on an uncertain field, something like that. Do you see that as accurate?"

George gave a small shrug. "You're the reporter, Mr. Smalley. Just be sure you give credit to the bravery of our troops today. If you don't, I'll come looking for you with a club. I don't care what you say about me."

Of course he cared.

"I heard a little of the discussion, General, just sort of floating on the wind. Some want to continue your attack I take it? Some think Lee will still counterattack?"

"And I get to make the choice, between," George said, laughing a little. Why was he talking with this man? Yes, he was tired and a little drunk from the emotions of the day. So many dead, so many wounded and dying, and he wanted to laugh and cry at the same time. That would never do. He saw with relief that the sun was low in the west.

"Can you give me your thoughts, General?"

What a question. "All right, Smalley, I'll give you my thoughts. But put them in the mouth of somebody else, you understand? We never had this conversation."

"What conversation?"

George paused, took in a breath. "It's very tempting to think of an attack. I have the Fifth Corps right here in the center, fresh and ready, and much of General Franklin's Sixth Corps off to the right. Perhaps Captain Custer is correct in his view. Their center is about to give out. We could storm through and crush them, push them into the Potomac. Tempting proposition? Indeed it is. But what if Custer is wrong? What if General Porter is right, and we will soon see a massed attack coming out of those woods."

"Just like at Bull Run?" Smalley nudged.

George gave him a pointed look. "I'm not John Pope," he said.

He looked off toward the little white church. "We don't know what forces they have in those woods. All day long we have sent units in, and they get chewed up and spit out. I don't know what they have in reserve behind those woods. Do you know Smalley?"

The reporter shook his head, his pencil flashing over the page of his notebook.

"The man who is supposed to know, Mr. Pinkerton, has gone off today, looking for one of his operatives who turned up missing. But here are some things I am sure of," George said. "I am sure that I command the only organized Federal resistance between here and Baltimore or Philadelphia or Harrisburg, Pennsylvania. I am out here with a rope around my neck, on the verbal authority of the President. On the authority of his wink. If I make a mistake and let Lee get around me, it will be discovered, Oh great shock, why I never had the proper orders to lead this Army. General Halleck will testify to that on the Bible. So will Mr. Stanton. Even worse, what if something happened to President Lincoln? His replacement would be Hannibal Hamlin, my worst political enemy."

Smalley nodded. Kept writing.

"I am walking the canyon on a tightrope," George said. "Is that enough for you, Mr. Smalley?

"I may not be able to use all of that General McClellan. There's some pretty strong stuff."

"Pretty strong stuff?" George guffawed. "Pretty strong stuff?"

He closed his eyes, bent over laughing, then coughing. His head went light. He wavered. Couldn't get his eyes open.

Sounds of voices faded. He felt a shift in the earth under his feet, something changing, wavering, moving in a push-pull motion. Eyes still closed but not asleep, he knew he was feeling the regular side to side motion of the train.

He opened his eyes. Night had overtaken them.

The passenger car was lit by dim oil lamps that threw pale yellow highlights slashed by deep shadows. Across from him Cump Sherman still sprawled, his arms and legs at odd angles from his torso, his mouth wide open, rippling a gentle snore. George shook his head. Had he been speaking aloud to Cump from that alternative world of war? He looked around the car. Their fellow passengers were nodding asleep or trying to read by the dim lamps. A man at the far end of the car sat with a blank expression. George turned back and saw Cump's bleak, dark eyes were open and fixed on him.

"Was I speaking to you, Cump, just now? Or was I dreaming? I was back on that ridge overlooking Antietam Creek with a reporter named George Smalley."

"Ah," Cump said, "the big fight at Sharpsburg. When you and Bobby Lee whipped and bled each other."

George squeezed his eyes and rubbed the bridge of his nose. "It's a shock coming back isn't it?"

"Yep. Always is. Just sit quiet for awhile, breathe deep, you'll be all right."

"I'm still angry up from the thing. You know, the worst trouble for me came in the aftermath. Lincoln could never understand that an army is worn out and depleted after a major battle. Mine had been through two of them in three weeks. We were not ready to fight on the next day, and neither was Bobby Lee.

"You crippled each other was the way I heard it."

"That's a fair statement. He backed off over the Potomac the night of the 18th, and I for one was very happy to see him go. Next day I sent two divisions under Fitz Porter across the river, and they got bloodied by A.P. Hill. I tell you, Cump, I was done fighting for awhile."

"Say, I know the feeling."

"Remember that July of next year when you and Sam Grant were taking Vicksburg? George Meade whipped Bobby Lee at Gettysburg. Or perhaps he just let Bobby Lee whip himself. Anyway it was a great victory for us. Fourth of July as I remember."

"Indeed it was," Cump agreed. "Sam and I celebrated."

"Yet the next day, sure as sunrise, Lincoln was after George Meade to 'destroy the rebel army.' Hah! That was his favorite phrase, as if saying it was next to doing it."

Cump laughed. "Somebody should have told him that an army after a battle is just like a man who's been with a woman. Worn out and depleted."

George, a little embarrassed, still laughed. "Yes, I should have gotten Joe Hooker to explain it to him."

Cump was just opening his mouth to speak when his chest bulged out and exploded, sending a shower of red wetness all over George's face.

Shotgun!

George felt the beginnings of the blast that would kill him tearing up his back. Smart attack he thought, two gunners coming down from opposite ends of the car, first one shoots Cump in the back while the second shoots me. The shock pushed him forward off the seat bumping into Cump's body which was pitching the opposite way. George struggled to reach for the tiny pistol he carried strapped above his boot. If only he could face one of the murderers and get a shot off, to die with honor, face to the enemy. But the second blast got him in the head.

It was all over. From somewhere his spirit heard the killers give a rebel yell.

"Dance in hell you, Yankee sonsofbitches!"

CHAPTER TWENTY-NINE

Hannibal Hamlin held open the door to his office with a gracious nod to his guest.

"Please, sit down, Mrs. Chesnut." He pointed to the red leather chair at the head of the table. "Make yourself comfortable."

"Why, thank you, Mr. President."

"Tea will be along shortly."

He watched Mary Chesnut peel off her white silk gloves as she settled in. Her roving glance took in the room. "So this is your office," she said with a tiny sniff of disappointment.

Hamlin grunted. "Not much to look at I'll admit."

She touched a finger to her chin. "Perhaps some different wallpaper would help. Make it brighter."

"You women." He forced himself to be jocular. "Ellen said almost the same thing, first time she saw it."

He strode over to a large oil painting that hung above the fireplace and held out his hand, palm open. "Well, this is what you came to see."

Mary Chesnut opened her reticule, extracted a pair of oval shaped glasses and perched them on the bridge of her nose.

"Oh, my word." She walked to the fireplace, her eyes locked on the painting. "It is so much more impressive in the original."

Hamlin looked out the window and saw the clouds were still hanging wet and gray. Gas street lights were being lit against the late afternoon darkness. He struck a match to fire up the small oil lamp on his desk. That's better. He was tired from the day's somber events. A nap would be welcome.

Mary Chesnut continued to study the art work in silence. The painting, which was officially titled "President Hamlin at Charleston," had been lithographed and reproduced in calendars and posters throughout the country. It had appeared in most newspapers, praised as exemplary patriotic art. Some had even called it: "The Painting That Averted The Civil War." Hamlin had groused when he heard that.

He and Bill Seward with some help from George McClellan had averted the war, not the durn painting.

Still, in his heart of hearts, he was warmly attached to the famous image. There he stood, President Hannibal Hamlin orating, "No War," his right hand up-reaching, his index finger pointing at heaven with his left hand a steady comfort on Jefferson Davis' bloodied shoulder. Hamlin saw that the sunlight fell across his face in such a way as to nobly mold his features. He supposed the artist had something to do with that, but it was the way he secretly pictured himself. There was a quiet tap at the door, and a servant entered with the tea tray. Hamlin told the young man to arrange things on the table. He took in his fingers a small slice of orange flavored cake thick with sweet white icing.

Tasted good.

Mary Chesnut detached herself long enough to pour two cups of tea.

"Why, I declare, it's a marvel," she said after her first sip, "how the artist was able to capture the moment so stirringly."

"A quirk of fate as to how that came about," Hamlin said. "The artist was on assignment from Harper's Magazine and had been recalled that day. Before he boarded his ship he followed the crowd to the Mills House, and so was on the scene when Mr. Davis was wounded."

"Well, I must say he did a stunning job. And I trust he does not flatter me too much."

Now for the first time he studied the other figures in the painting. Funny, he had never really payed attention to them before. Yes, there was Mary Chesnut herself, kneeling next to Verina Davis as they comfort her wounded husband. And cringing against the wall, it's that fool, DuBott, the hotel manager, useless in the emergency. Forgot all about him. Off to the other side there's General McClellan and Captain Grant, their faces straining as they wrestle to overpower the crazed old assassin.

328

The artist had obviously compressed many serial events into one moment in time. What a gifted young man he was, barely twenty-five years old, his signature painted boldly in the lower right corner: Winslow Homer.

"Poor General McClellan," Mary Chesnut said as she drew an embroidered handkerchief from her sleeve and touched it to her eyes. "So strange it is to see him there full of life, and here we've just come from his memorial service." She paused when he made no reply. "Your eulogy was quite inspiring, by the way."

Hamlin nodded slightly. The remembered gloom of today's service closed over him. The brave, young Mrs. McClellan, large with child, standing calmly in the drizzling rain listening to his words praising her dead husband, tears and raindrops blended on her pale cheeks. Then the glinting, polished coffin being loaded on the train for Philadelphia where the family plot awaited.

He heard Mary Chesnut's tea cup clink in her saucer and he chided himself for remaining silent too long, a poor host. He searched for a pertinent comment. "Mr. Stanton says they have traced the killers to Atlanta. He expects to make arrests soon."

"That is of some small comfort I suppose," Mary Chesnut said, distantly.

Stanton had proved to be a welcome surprise. Since their initial encounter at Charleston, the lawyer had transformed himself into an energetic and competent assistant. Hamlin had just rewarded him with the directorship of the new Federal Bureau of Crime. Edwin Stanton and his assistant, Pinkerton, seemed to have their fingers on everything that was going on throughout the country. He blinked, now suddenly aware that Mrs. Chesnut was speaking. For how long? Pay attention now. She'll be going soon.

"I would be just lost without my books," she was saying. "My secret ambition is to write one, but I never let on to James about it. Of course he's so wrapped up in his work down at the Senate, I suppose he wouldn't hear me if I told him."

"I think you should write, Mrs. Chesnut. You have an interesting way of stating things."

"Don't tell a soul." Her voice twittered. "But I do have an idea for a book. A very, very fanciful one and I shouldn't speak about it, but . . ."

"Oh, go ahead. Let's hear it." He took another bite of cake.

"Well." She composed herself. "Are you familiar at all with the works of Lucian de Rubempre' the French philosopher?"

"Afraid I'm not much up on my French philosophers, Mrs. Chesnut, I must ruefully admit."

She cocked her head, a finger to her lips. "More of a philosopher-poet I should say. Monsieur Rubempre' offers a most whimsical speculation. At each significant turning point in our lives, when we make an important decision, our existence at that point might split off into two different worlds."

"Two worlds?"

"Or more. Many more. For example, Mr. President, what if you had not made that trip to Charleston? She pointed to the painting. "What if, for some reason, you had decided against it? And what if, because you weren't there to stop him, Mr. Davis ordered General Beauregard to open fire on Fort Sumter?"

"We would have had a war, Madam."

"And perhaps we did! According to Monsieur Rubempre, that war took place. In another world."

Hamlin frowned. "You say every time we reach a turning point or fork in the road, a new world comes to be?"

"Yes. What if I had never met my dear James? I should be a tiresome old spinster in Charleston by now. Perhaps I am in some alternative world out there in the great void of the unknown."

Hamlin gritted his teeth and forced a pleasant, interested expression. He hated foolish talk like this.

"You, a spinster?" he said. Not a chance, Madam. Why you would have married that fine Judge Petigru." He listened to himself playing along with her feminine absurdity. French Philosopher, indeed. French Humbug!

"So, you see, Monsieur Rubempre's theory provides an excellent premise for fiction. I thought I might write a novel about the war that never was. A fanciful, imaginary account of a civil war between the states."

He stared at her suddenly lightheaded for an instant. He heard rumbling, muttering, unintelligible voices and muffled drums. He saw Lincoln's face sculpted in shining marble, larger than life. What was happening?

"Mr. President are you feeling unwell?"

"Oh, I'm perfectly fine, Mrs. Chesnut. A little fatigued." He composed himself with a smile. "That certainly is an interesting theory, I must say. But if true I'm afraid creation would be overflowing with different worlds, and I doubt if even the Lord Almighty could keep track of them all."

"Oh, it's only an airy speculation," Mary Chesnut said, a bit embarrassed now. "It's how philosophers occupy the hours between lunch and supper." She laughed at herself as well as the conceit, fiddling with her damp parasol. "Not to be taken seriously."

"Thankfully I am not a philosopher, Mrs. Chestnut. I am a plain man who must grapple with concrete cases, and in one world at a time."

"Well, if you don't mind a compliment, I would say you do very well with your grappling. I refer, sir, to your Compensation Plan. James and everyone else says it is a splendid success."

Hamlin felt a surprising wave of affection for this woman. "I am pleased that we are doing as well as we are, Mrs. Chesnut, beyond all expectations. Secretary Chase reports that funds to purchase Freedom Bonds are pouring in from all over the world, especially Great Britain. The Treasury is awash in cash, enough so that we are able to pay top dollar even for women and children and launch them on the road to liberty. The balance of funds not needed for purchase will be used for their education and welfare, if I can get Congress to agree."

"Buying off Slavery and good riddance. Cash beats guns any day, and folks are glad to get it. Why it's the American way. Don't those mean old Republican croakers regret now how they tried to impeach you."

"Some people are forever bitter, Madam, North and South. They were in love with the idea of pain and torment, and we managed to disappointment them."

"Yes, our pain and our torment. They'll just have to find someone else to hate I reckon, now that there are going to be no more evil slavers to persecute."

"They'll find an outlet for their rage, Mrs. Chesnut. People always do. For example the men who killed General McClellan in the name of Southern Pride." He shook his head. "Sickening."

"How true, how true," Mary Chesnut said, as she picked up her parasol and shook off some rain drops. "Well, I mustn't overstay my welcome. James may eventually notice I'm not home."

Hamlin strolled to the door with her, his fingers lightly touching her elbow.

She paused. "Seems selfish of me, I know, but I was counting on General McClellan to help me with my story. The military aspects."

Hamlin was lost. "Your story?"

"The war that never was, you know, as we were discussing?"

"Oh. Oh, my, yes. The French Philosopher." Was this woman never going to leave?

"We had talked about it a little at a dinner party, just before he went off to Georgia. He was quite charmed with the idea, said he would be happy to consult with me on it."

Hamlin wanted to let the silly subject drop, but he was betrayed by his natural kindness. "I may be able to help you, Madam."

"Oh?"

"Yes. There is very fine officer, well respected in the Army, former Commandant of West Point. Lives just across the river at Arlington. You've heard of him, perhaps. Colonel Lee?"

"Oh, my, yes. I've heard of Colonel Lee. All the ladies fall in love with him, they say."

Hamlin laughed easily. "Well, that is the risk you're going to have to take. I'll be glad to introduce him to you."

When Mary Chesnut had at last gone, Hamlin sat at the roll top desk sipping his cup of tea. He twisted the knob that turned the lamp flame down. Faces came to him, Lincoln, Bill Seward, poor dead Patrick, the messboy, Davis and Benjamin. He rubbed his eyes.

If there had been a war?

He thought of the arrogantly handsome Lee. Stanton had told him that Lee would have gone with the South. Hamlin's lip twisted. Let him fight his war in the pages of Mrs. Chesnut's outlandish "novel."

Serve him right.

Another face appeared. The proudly scowling George McClellan, that curious, edgy mixture of youth and wise maturity who had hesitantly sought to offer him political advice. How well it had worked out. Jefferson Davis was now one of the most staunch and outspoken guardians of the Union, as he quietly awaited his turn at the Presidency. He was even thinking, some said, of turning Republican.

So there had been no war.

He studied the icon of McClellan in young Homer's painting. Military men could have profited greatly from a civil war, but McClellan had been a soldier who counseled peace.

He asked himself the ancient question. Where exactly was George McClellan tonight? He remembered that they had a rambling talk of such things during the long hours on the voyage back from Charleston. McClellan thought that somehow God allowed us to keep on "working," as he put it. Perfecting ourselves, perhaps making up for our lapses and mistakes. Hamlin had pondered this. It was the kind of idea you might expect to hear from an older man near the end of life's voyage. Yet McClellan was only thirty-four when he died.

Hamlin attended church services like most people, paid lip service to the old myths of the afterlife. Within himself he

333

believed that death was the end of the line, though he hoped to be proved wrong.

He looked up at the painting: "May you find peace, George McClellan, wherever you are."

CHAPTER THIRTY

George found himself in Washington City, standing in the middle of Lafayette Park across from the President's Mansion. He walked and his boots made no crunch on the stone gravel pathway. There was no wind.

At the edge of the park stood a newsboy, a handsome lad of about thirteen, fresh faced, neatly dressed, smiling brightly.

"Good morning, General McClellan."

"Is it morning?"

"Yes, sir."

"Hmm." George studied the newsboy. He looked familiar.

"Do I know you?"

"Maybe, sir. You see a lot of faces in Washington."

"May I look at your paper just for a moment?" George would ordinarily have purchased the newspaper, but he somehow knew his pockets contained only Italian coins.

The newsboy handed him a copy of the *Washington Evening Star*. The date was April 14, 1865. The headlines showed he was back in the world of war or the remnants of it. Sam Grant had taken Richmond after Bobby Lee's surrender. Cump Sherman had cut his way up through the Carolinas and was pressing Joe Johnston to surrender any day now. George looked down at the newsboy with satisfaction. "We've won the war it seems."

"Excuse me, General McClellan, but may I ask you a question?"

"Yes?"

"It says right in this here paper that you are visiting in Rome, the town in Italy. How comes it you're here?"

George reflected and the answer came easily. "I was in Italy but I've returned. I had pressing business here."

"Oh," said the newsboy. "Well, that explains it."

George wondered what the pressing business was. He recalled being shot and presumably dead in the world of President Hamlin. But he wanted to make sure where he was now.

"Young man, I have been away for awhile. Remind me, who is President of the United States today."

The lad snickered. "Why Abraham Lincoln, of course. He beat you in the election."

"Ah, yes. How could I ever forget?"

The newsboy pointed toward a familiar looking house. "That's Mr. Stanton's home over yonder, you remember. You ought to stop by, say hello."

"Yes, we were friends once." Strangely enough, George did wish to see Stanton, but he also felt compelled to stay here with the newsboy. Something about the lad made him want to smile and laugh. There was no music but he felt like dancing. He narrowed his eyes and studied the boy. "I'm sure I must know you from somewhere."

A burst of laughter. "Why, father, I was wondering how long it would take you to recognize me."

"Father?"

"I'm your son, Max. I won't be born until November 23rd this year."

"1865?"

"That's right. You and mother conceived me on a hot day in Rome under most joyous circumstances."

George felt his face flush. "Please, son, a lad your age shouldn't mention such matters, especially with his father."

Max grinned showing a wide gap between his two front teeth.

This is a strange world," George ventured, "where a man can speak with his son yet unborn."

"There's a brainy professor here who likes to use big sounding words, father. He calls this the Transcendental Realm."

"That's a mouthful of a name, Max." He saw a loving cross between Nelly and himself in the lad's face. "Well, I must be off to see Mr. Stanton now."

"Be careful, father, and watch your step with that varmint."

"Hah! You're a wise lad for someone not born yet. Goodbye, son. I'll be seeing you."

Max laughed. "That you will, father."

It all seemed perfectly natural. He crossed the empty street and stepped up on Stanton's porch. The front door was an inch ajar. He pushed the door and entered the center hallway which smelled of stale cabbage. Still.

"Stanton, are you home?"

"Come in. Be quick about it."

The voice rasped back from the front parlor which was separated from the hallway by golden oak doors.

George rolled the doors apart and entered the parlor. Drawn curtains made the room dim. Stanton was sitting at a small desk, his back to the door. His wiry gray hair was untamed as ever.

"No, don't come any further, just stand right there," Stanton said. "I don't want to see your face." He coughed into a handkerchief. "Do you think it's so clever to be walking around in that uniform? I peeked out when you come up on the porch. For a moment I thought you were that scamp, McClellan come back to plague me. You even sound like him a bit, but then you actors know how to play with voices."

George was at a loss. Had Stanton finally gone mad?

"Not a good idea your coming here. Someone may notice." Stanton kept his back to the door. "But, since you're here, everything is arranged. The guard will not be on duty outside the box. The door to the box will not be locked. A peep hole as been cut in the door so that you may view the scene before entering. General Grant will not attend. Possibly got wind of something. The President's guest will be a Major Rathbone and his lady friend. He is a weakling and will give you no trouble."

Stanton blew his nose and coughed.

"Don't be fancy with the gun. Don't aim it through the peephole. Just open the door, wait for the big laugh. You know where. Place the gun to the back of his head. I mean be sure you touch the back of his head. Pull the trigger and that will be the end to all those funny stories."

Stanton chuckled and wheezed, enjoying his own wit.

"Your horse will be waiting in the alley. He's lean and fast, not one of those old cavalry clunkers. The Long Bridge will be open to you. The sergeant will be off duty. Do you have any questions?"

Before George could speak the front door opened and another man entered the room. George recognized him as the actor, John Wilkes Booth.

"What's he doing here?" Booth demanded.

Stanton spun in his chair, saw George and fell into a rapid coughing fit.

The actor's eyes popped with outrage. "Look here, Stanton, what's going on? I thought this was to be a secret meeting."

Stanton stumbled to the sideboard, thrashed and clinked amid bottles and glasses, finally found what he was looking for, took a deep gulp and collapsed into a chair, struggling to catch his breath.

George walked up to the actor and looked him over with curiosity. "I saw you play MacBeth once in Chicago, old man." He squinted at the memory. "Odd interpretation as I recall it, though my wife admired your costume."

"So you're as accomplished a critic as you are a general," Booth sneered, his jaws stiff, his teeth wolfish.

"You're planning to shoot President Lincoln are you?" George said, just to get the facts on record.

Stanton put his face in his hands. "Let me think. Let me think."

Booth, muttering under his breath, found a place on a sofa. He sat down and stretched his short legs. "So it's all off, I take it now that old 'Fighting George' is onto us?"

Stanton gestured for the actor to be quiet. He stood up and said to George, "I don't relish the necessity for this, McClellan.

I even grew to entertain a certain affection for the man. But he is about to give away the whole purpose and glory of the war. He says of the treasonous States. 'Let 'em up easy.' Oh, my yes, let 'em up easy. After all the treasure and blood they cost us. He will block every scheme we propose. He is against our taking their property. He will not let the niggers vote. So it was either impeach him or shoot him," Stanton said reasonably. "We had no grounds for impeachment." He shrugged and pointed at Booth. "This man wants to revenge the South and earn some money in the bargain."

"Death to the tyrant," Booth said, inspecting and flexing his fingers.

"If I had been elected President," George said, "would you have impeached or shot me too?"

"Hopefully both," Stanton said, distracted.

That settled, George pointed first at Stanton and then at Booth. "I hereby place the two of you under arrest for treason!" He bellowed in his loudest command voice: "Stand up and march!"

Booth's hand moved in a blur to his boot and flashed up a knife. Stanton waved him away. "No, no, you actors are so emotional." He looked at George with a poisonous smile.

"However will you arrest us, General?" He scoffed the title like a curse. "You have no gun and I see no army out there on the street."

"I will report you to the President," George said. "Soldiers will come for you! Be warned!"

"Report all you want," Stanton said. "You have no more creditability with him than a mouse. I've made well certain of that. He'll laugh at you."

George spun an about-face and marched out of Stanton's house. He felt his shoulders tense up for a bullet in the back. Having been shot so recently makes you sensitive. But no shots came, only insults.

"He'll not believe you," Stanton taunted. "He thinks you're a joke and an imbecile. And he's right."

The short walk to the President's Mansion was much the same as he remembered. At the door to the President's office Johnny Hay looked up at him startled.

"Well, look what the cat dragged in," Hay said.

"Good morning, Johnny," George said, his face composed in earnest purpose. "I must see the President."

"Oh." Hay's eyes were wide and mocking. "Must be sumpin' purty important to rate a visit from the great General." His tone changed. "Anyway, I thought you were still seeing the sights of Europe."

"Johnny, I have to see him. It's urgent."

Hay sighed. "Just a moment, I'll go and tell the Tycoon you're here. My, but won't he be thrilled."

George sat down, crossed his legs, jangled the Italian coins in his pocket and inspected his boots. They were perfectly shined. He reprised what he thought he knew. He was dead in the world of Hannibal Hamlin, apparently alive in this the world of war in Washington which felt entirely unreal. He had just met his son, as yet unborn. He was here to prevent the assassination of a man who had died in a riding accident four years ago. Strange. He laughed out loud at the thought. Strange? What an understatement, worthy of an Englishman.

Lincoln came rambling out of his office, right hand extended. "Why George, I'm so glad to see you. Indeed I am." He sounded sincere. "How are you, George?" George shook Lincoln's hand which felt crisp and dry. "I am as well as can be expected, Mr. President, under the circumstances."

"Well, that's fine, George. I had the mistaken notion that you were still in Europe. Obviously, you're not."

"No, apparently I'm here."

"Johnny said you had something important for me."

Just say it right out. "They're plotting to murder you, your Excellency. Tonight." "Oh," Lincoln said, his big lips in a thoughtful pout, "that reminds me of the old farmer who hit his mule in the head with a board. The mule says: 'Well, that got my attention.'"

"It's Stanton, Mr. President, he's got an actor ready to shoot you tonight when you go to the theatre."

"Stanton, eh? George, would you mind if we sort of conversed on the amble? I promised Mother we'd take a carriage ride this afternoon. She's out in the driveway fuming for me right now."

"Of course, Mr. President." He hadn't noticed a carriage when he walked up.

Lincoln headed for the staircase, George walking fast to keep up. "So let me see now, Stanton is fixing to send me to Heaven, as young Prince Hamlet would say."

"Indeed he is, Your Excellency. He has Wilkes Booth, the actor, ready to sneak into your box and shoot you in the head."

"That sounds pretty excessive, don't you think, George? An actor shooting me while I attend the theatre?"

They had reached the front door of the Mansion. Lincoln opened the door and took in a deep breath. "Ah, the sweet smell of Spring," he said, his voice joyful. "Ain't it wonderful? Happens every year, and yet it never fails to surprise me."

"Yes, the buds are out." George felt peaceful.

"Walk with me a bit here in the yard." Lincoln gave a wave to his wife who was seated in a carriage. "I'll be along in a minute, Mother," he called to her.

They strolled West toward the red brick War Department. "I've made this trek to the War Department often enough," Lincoln said. "I must know every pebble and blade of grass. Hung out at the telegraph office probably more than was good for me."

"That's where you used to send me those messages," George said. *Destroy the rebel army.*

"Hah! And you'd never do it."

"It turned out to be a lot harder that you thought. Sam Grant found out. It took him nearly a year and with your full support too."

"Ah, George, the war's over. Let's don't open old wounds. General Grant was a bull dog, bit Bob Lee right in the pants and wouldn't let go. He was a great general, and you want to know the best thing about him?" He looked down at George and winked. "He wasn't running for President like certain other people I could mention."

George was surprised to find the old resentments rising again here in the Transcendent Realm. His voice went hard. "I wanted to attack Richmond by going south to Petersburg. Halleck and Stanton wouldn't hear of it, pulled me out. Two years later Sam Grant did exactly what I had proposed to do. It was all right then."

"Now, George, what's the difference anyway? It all came out right in the end."

"Fifty thousand casualties, that's the difference," George said, flatly with a cruel intention.

Lincoln squinted. "What?"

"Sam Grant wanted to do exactly what I had done, take the water route to Richmond."

"He did say something about that as I recall."

"You wouldn't let him. You told him to take the overland route, fight his way down. He told you that would cost an extra fifty thousand casualties, didn't he?"

"I was determined to keep Washington secure," Lincoln said, his tone no longer friendly.

"Lots of fathers, husbands, sons, brothers missing at the supper table."

"George I always liked you, I honestly did, but I don't like you talking to me this cantankerous way. I am the President after all."

George felt all the old acid bitterness vanish. Gone. He blinked.

"I had to get that off my chest," he said dreamily. He looked around. Who was he and what was he doing here? Oh, yes, Stanton.

"You don't believe me, about Stanton. He said you wouldn't believe me, that I have no more credibility with you."

"General McClellan, I appreciate your concern, sir. I do indeed. That Stanton might plot to murder me is somewhat plausible, though I don't believe he would have the courage to

342

do it. Still, I'll admit he and his cronies would love to see me a goner."

Lincoln sat down on a bench under the branches of a knobby old apple tree. He waved an invitation. "Sit ye down, George, let's ponder this out." George eased himself down on the opposite edge of the bench. Lincoln gazed up at the fresh buds of the apple tree. "Sour apples always and few to the branch, but I still love to sniff the durn thing. Think I'll plant some when I get back home, apple trees I mean. George, do you ever have dreams that you remember?"

"Quite often, yes," George said. "I mostly enjoy them."

"My dreams are not enjoyable," Lincoln said, his distant eyes pondering. "My dreams are heavy with imperious meaning. It is as if I am an actor in a great Shakespearean drama. I hear about me loud voices, stirring pronouncements. Often I hear bells and clanging. I had such a dream last night, the arrival on a distant shore, the same dream that always precedes some great event."

"The end of the war no doubt," George said. Or perhaps getting shot in the head at Ford's Theatre.

"Yes, maybe so." Lincoln looked doubtful. "But the feeling of it was so chilled and unhappy."

"Father, will you come along?" Mrs. Lincoln called from the carriage. Cranky.

Lincoln continued to study the apple tree as he called back to her, "I will be with you in a moment, Mother."

Then he cocked his head at George. "You see, here's what I believe." Lincoln's liquid, sad eyes seemed to swallow him up. "I'm pretty certain you must be a ghost in a dream. Notice the odd coloration of the sky, the lack of everyday sounds."

"As in a dream," George said. "I've noticed that ever since I got here."

"Well, there you see," Lincoln said. "And where did you come from?"

"A most extraordinary and fantastic world, sir, one you could never believe in." Yes, it would be stupid and insulting to tell Lincoln about Hannibal Hamlin as President and how he had avoided the war.

"Well," Lincoln said, satisfied, "then you are a ghost, and I'm not obliged to heed your warning am I?"

"It does put me at a disadvantage I suppose."

"Ah, don't let that disturb you, George. Ghosts come to see me all the time. They are habitual to my environment." Lincoln clasped his long fingers around his bent left knee.

"Yep, they come to me, all ranks, Privates, Colonels, Generals. They seem to think that the first call of duty after death is to come and tell me all about it. Mostly they are friendly, not bitter much, although some are angry. They accuse me of being the fell agent of their demise, and what can I do but agree with them? They died at my bidding, to uphold a cause. The question is, was all the killing worth it? They like to discuss that one with me."

"What do you tell them?"

"Oh, well, I try to make out to them that it was all worth their lives. It's the same idea I give out in speeches and letters. Made a big thing of it at the Gettysburg cemetery speech. Lately I've been shoving it off onto God quite a bit as well. Must have been He wanted all this killing because Abraham Lincoln Esquire of Springfield, Illinois, certainly would never have done it."

Lincoln looked at George, his eyes pleading for some unknown mercy.

"Yes, sir, it must have been God urging me on. But even that's a defective excuse. A sham actually. Ya see I don't believe in God. In fact I strongly suspect it's a cold and empty universe. Maybe we're all the God there is in it."

George stared at Lincoln, uncomfortable in the moment. Where had all that laughing, confidant self assurance gone?

"I know Stanton was a trial and a terror to you, George," Lincoln went on. "But, by jinx, I needed him for the war, made good use of him. He was right for running that office. A son of a she-dog was needed there and so I installed him, thinking he was your friend, by the way."

344

"He had me fooled as well," George admitted with a smile. He felt pleasantly drowsy here under the apple blossoms.

Lincoln laughed. "Stanton. If I hadn't found him, I would've had to conjure him up. For I needed someone, George, who was able by nature to do cruel and vicious things." Lincoln sighed softly at that admission, then reached down and began unlacing his shoes. He took them off, then his socks. He wiggled his unhealthy looking toes, all discolored with corns and bunions.

"My feet would test the patience of a saint," he said as he walked a few steps in the grass. "Oh. Oh my, that feels so nice. I tell you, George, you may not believe this, but there is no act so overrated as sexual congress, or so underrated as feeling your toes in the grass." Lincoln glanced quickly at his wife waiting in the carriage. "Go ahead, George, try it."

George took off his boots and socks. The damp April grass was indeed a delight. Lincoln walked about stomping the earth, crinkling his toes in the green blades. "Boy oh boy, don't that feel fine?"

George was suddenly chilled and tired even in this "What's it?" dimension. He knew he was lying dead on the blood slicked floor of a railroad car in Georgia. This was the afterlife he assumed, but not as he had been led by preachers to expect. What was he doing here? He looked at Lincoln who was now lacing up his shoes.

"Got to be off and about, George. Mother is fit to be tied."

George sat down on the bench and pulled on his socks. He had one last question for Lincoln.

"Tell me, Your Excellency, was your offer a real one? Would you have kept your word?"

Lincoln's brow furrowed. He gave a suspicious grin. "I try to keep track of all my offers," he said intently. "Which one are you talking about?"

"Before the election last year you sent Mr. Blair to see me with a message. If I would call off my run for President, you would see to it I got reinstated as a General with an important command."

"Oh, that one?" Lincoln relaxed. "Oh, my yes, that was a perfectly real and valid offer, George. I meant every durn word of it."

"Would Stanton have allowed it?"

"I would have made him toe the line. Actually, now as I recall it, I had a nice little scheme cooked up. Boot Stanton to some foreign land as ambassador and then put you in as Secretary of War. Would've been a canny move, politically, linking up with a Democrat of your stature. You would have run that office right and with the support of the Army to boot."

"But could you count on me to be sufficiently cruel and vicious?"

Lincoln dismissed that with a wave. "You would have used those two killers, Grant and Sherman to do your dirty work."

George nodded. It made sense. "But I didn't bite," he said.

"Why not?" Lincoln said, openly curious. "I've always wondered."

"I didn't trust you."

"Me? Honest Abe?" Then Lincoln's face went somber. "Yep, too bad, you're not a politician, George. Then you would have known you didn't have to trust me. You see, I had to have a Democrat alongside me in that election. You turned me down, so I had to go do something that has shamed me."

The President finished tying his shoe and stood up.

"Yes sir, I had to get rid of one of the finest men, one of the most honorable statesman I've ever known. I dumped old Hannibal Hamlin off the ticket in '64, in favor of a drunk tailor from Tennessee, who just happened to be a Union Democrat. I am mighty ashamed of doing that, George. I betrayed Hannibal Hamlin. He took it like the gentleman he is, but I'll regret it to the end of my days."

"I've always respected President Hamlin," George said without thinking.

"You mean Vice President Hamlin," Lincoln corrected firmly.

"What?"

"You said President Hamlin. You meant Vice President Hamlin," Lincoln persisted.

"Oh, of course." George smiled. "Slip of the tongue." Slip of the worlds.

Lincoln eyed him with a sideways glance. "I always thought you were a tiny bit crazy, George. I mean that in the nicest way of course."

"Of course."

"Well, it's been grand seeing you again, George. Hope we will meet again under happier circumstances."

They shook hands, and George gave it one last try. "He's going to shoot you while you watch the play."

Lincoln gave a lazy smile. "Well, by jinx, that ought to keep me awake."

He started off then turned and waved as he joined his wife in the carriage.

Then he was gone.

George stood under the sweet smelling apple tree and realized he was hungry. Hopeful sign. Ghosts don't get hungry he told himself as he walked West two blocks to Wormley's Restaurant. The best caterer in Washington greeted him.

"Thought you was over the ocean, General. It is a pleasure and an honor to see you again, sir."

Wormley had a rich, freckled golden skin and a ready smile. Known as 'Wormley the Mulatto,' he had no Christian name, or at least none he admitted to. His white clothed tables were empty in the fast fading pink afternoon light.

"Do you mind if I sit here awhile, Mr. Wormley? You see, I just came into town and I don't have a place to stay."

"Extra rooms upstairs, General. You are always welcome at Wormley's. You can get anything you want here, and I do mean anything. You hungry? Got some prime fish stew on the stove."

"That would be perfect, Mr. Wormley. A big bowl, please, and some of those little crackers."

While Wormley tended the kitchen, George consulted with himself. Whatever this world may be, he remained a U.S. Army officer, pledged to defend the Constitution and his lawful

347

superior, the President. Actions change events. Perhaps he was sent to this particular world for a purpose. He would make a decision, take firm action, take the chance he had failed to take at Antietam. This time, in this transcendental world, he would ride to glory. He would save the President.

Wormley brought the richly spiced stew and served it to George with prideful style. It tasted delightful.

"Mr. Wormley, can you secure for me a six shot revolver pistol?"

The caterer gave him a knowing wink. "Why, in this town that won't be hard work, General. Give me a half hour."

Wormley disappeared into the darkened kitchen. A door slammed, then silence. George enjoyed the fish stew and found a glass of white Bordeaux had appeared near his hand. Ah, yes, he had come to the right place. In a hour Wormley was back with the revolver complete with holster. George checked the load and buckled it on.

"You gonna need some help, General? I can get you some men if you ain't particular about their skin tone."

"No, thank you, Mr. Wormley. This is something I must do alone."

Wormley's friendly face danced in and out in the early evening shadows.

"Don't you go gettin' yourself into any trouble now, ya hear, General?"

George barked a laugh. "Me in trouble, Wormley? Who ever heard of such a thing?"

After finishing a second bowl of stew and saying good-bye to Wormley, George walked the deserted streets to Ford's Theatre where he found the stage entrance in a side alley. A spunky yearling horse waited there, saddled up and ready. He pushed open the stage door and entered immediate blackness. His eyes adjusted, and he moved toward the gleam of the stage lights. He heard the mutter of performing actors and the answering laughter in the audience.

A gasp as he stepped on-stage. The actor, Harry Hawk, his face glistening with performance sweat, saw George and the six-shooter at the same time. His alarmed look said, "It's none of my business, sir, and if you don't mind, I'll be on my way." And he skedaddled into the wings.

George heard his own name drifting up at him from the audience.

"Why it's General McClellan."

"What's he doing here?"

"Is he an actor now?"

Nervous giggles gave way to held breath silence as George gazed up at the President's box. But the footlights in their reflectors blinded him. He moved a few steps to the edge of the stage. Now he could see a little better. Lincoln's side box was decorated with red, white and blue bunting. A portrait of George Washington hung just below the rail. Out of the darkness he could just discern the occupants of the box, Lincoln and his wife as well as a young woman and her escort, a bearded officer in army blue.

But, horror confirmed, there was a fifth figure in the box. Standing behind Lincoln was Wilkes Booth, his arm outstretched, a shiny thing in his hand.

Here George saw his duty. No doubts. No worried calculations. He raised the weapon and took aim.

The crowd screamed.

Booth's head was aligned in his front sight but then was gone as the gun barrel wavered. Footlights flared. His man-target came back again within the sight. George squeezed until white flash explosion and smoke wiped out everything.

The scene cleared. Lincoln was up and staggering, head titled back in pain and astonishment, his hand to his chest where crimson gushed and stained out over his white shirt.

Lincoln, eyes bulging, pronounced one astonished word. "George?"

He toppled forward, his long body draping over the rail of the box, his face upside down and nose to nose with the icon of George Washington.

Booth went wild. He leaped to the edge of the box, leveled the derringer, aiming high to compensate for distance, and screaming some muddled Latin, he shot George in the left knee.

I'm going down, George thought as his mind blacked out with pain, shock, anger and frustration.

The legal proceedings, conceived and directed by Edwin M. Stanton, were cruelly efficient. In less than a week the crippled George McClellan was arrested while still unconscious, indicted, tried, convicted and sentenced to death by hanging. John Wilkes Booth testified as to how he had discovered McClellan's plot only at the last minute and had rushed to the President's box to afford protection. The famed actor described his desperate efforts to save Lincoln from the madly vindictive McClellan.

"If only," he whimpered bravely from the witness stand, "if only I had arrived but a moment sooner." His voice quavered and broke, his head fell forward, his shoulders jounced with sobs. John Wilkes Booth was a national hero. He announced he would soon star in a revival of MacBeth.

No one believed George McClellan's bizarre tale accusing Booth and Stanton of the murder plot. Even his own lawyer rejected him and barely went through the motions of defense, embarrassed enough to be doing that.

Wormley was nearly lynched for supplying George with the gun.

On an overcast day in late April George was marched to a scaffold with a brown leather bag over his head. The noose was placed around his neck while a Presbyterian minister muttered some perfunctory prayers for mercy and salvation, then said, "May your bones fry in hell forever, George McClellan. There are some crimes even God cannot forgive."

Edwin Stanton awarded himself the honor of springing the trap-door. George reminded himself of the man in Sam Grant's story who said: "If it wasn't for the honor of the thing, I would just as soon skip it."

The trap door fell away, his feet danced on air as his body dropped and the rope went taut. George waited to be saved, to be shifted into yet another dimension, the next alternate world, to escape this sadistic humiliating terror. He felt the unrelenting, merciless choke of the rope, heard the burning jeers of the crowd as they witnessed his ultimate defeat. This was taking too long. Choking on his own tongue, he gurgled, "God help me!"

God is a three letter word with a hole in it," Stanton jeered.

Lincoln's words came back. "Maybe we're all the God there is."

And so in his final endless agony he called out the name of love, the only name he had for God in this life.

"Nelly, I'm dead yet I'm dying still! Nelly save me!"

He dissolved into a sheet of blinding light. An earthy, sweet perfume. A cool hand grasped his. The rope and the jeering crowd were gone. He opened his eyes in the olive and flower-flavored sunshine of Rome. Nelly was smiling, holding an iced bottle of wine and twin glasses. He told her what had happened, putting a hand to his neck and finding it thankfully sound.

Nelly poured the wine.

"That was a world you don't want to remember or explore any further my dear. I can't imagine how you stumbled into it when there are so many nicer worlds to visit. This one for instance."

"And which world is this, lady mine? I've lost track."

"Oh, this is the one you call the World of War."

"Then was Lincoln shot by Booth? Or will he be?"

"Sadly yes, it has happened I think," Nelly said. "We'll get the news here in Rome in a few days."

"Are we awake or is this still a dream?"

Nelly sipped her wine and stretched her arms. "Oh, we're as awake as we'll ever be. Isn't this breeze lovely? That aroma." She smiled sweetly. "You must stop being so literal, darling. There's so little difference between dreaming and waking."

"I'm an engineer and a soldier. My middle name is literal."

"I suspect," Nelly said, "that you explored that horrible world where you shot Lincoln just as an allegory to prove to yourself how blessed we are in this one."

"Allegory, eh? Remind me I never want to be caught in another one."

"This will be quite a pleasant life for us from now on, darling. The worst is over. May will grow up to be a lovely young woman. We will have a son named Max, and he will be Mayor of New York."

"By golly, I just met him as a boy selling newspapers."

"That sounds like Max. He'll be an enterprising lad."

"I'll warn him to stay out of politics."

Nelly laughed. "Can't. You'll be long gone."

"Oh, cheerful."

"We're all long gone eventually," Nelly said with a small shrug.

"So, my dear Miss Nel, you seem to a have memory that works backwards and forwards? Where did you learn this trick?"

"I'm your wife," Nelly said as if that explained it all. "You see, time is just God's way of keeping everything from happening at once." She laughed in that husky way that never failed to thrill him. "You don't want the past, present and future bumping into each other now do you?"

"That might be confusing." He squeezed her hand and gave up all hope of rational thought. Let Nelly lead the way. "Well, Miss Sees All Know's All, tell us our future and our past."

Nelly smoothed her skirts, took a sip of wine. "We were here in Rome when Lincoln was killed. We came back and lived in New Jersey. You made a lot of money in engineering and railroads. You eventually were elected Governor of the state.

"Ah, political success at last."

"Not like Sam Grant, thank goodness. He was elected President, but got into a mess of trouble with corruption and scandals. Cump Sherman was head of the Army for a long time and he stayed in touch. Then you died of heart trouble peacefully at our home in 1885. I was with you." She patted his hand.

"Sorry, Nel, I couldn't help it. Tell me, whatever happened to Stanton?"

"Oh, he died or will die in 1867. Rumor is he cut his own throat, but who knows? Some historians have tried to connect him with Lincoln's murder, but there is no real evidence, because Lincoln's son, Bob, burned certain papers."

"Good for Bob. Best for the country."

"Oh, don't sound so pompous. You just know in your heart he did it, George, the damned scoundrel. Anyway I went on living but lonely for you until 1915, when I died in Nice, France, which is not a bad place by the way. Every September 17, I celebrated Antietam day with a big party. Americans, English and French, they all came down from Paris. Once a famous novelist came. Henry James was his name. He told me he admired you and used a lot of big words.

"I should have led the charge at Antietam," George said wistfully. "I had the chance. I had the troops. I should have taken it. I should have taken that ride to glory."

Nelly gave him a sideways glance of annoyance.

"What's the matter dear alter ego? Why are you giving me that thunder cloud look?"

"We are going to settle this once and for all," Nelly said resolutely, and in an instant they were on Pry House hill overlooking the Antietam battlefield.

George groaned. "I never wanted to see this place again."

"The scene of your greatest victory?"

"How can you say that?"

"The history books say that, grudgingly, because they're slanted to favor Lincoln. But you did three things here, my man. Stopped Bobby Lee's first invasion of the North. And because of this battle, England and France dropped their plans to recognize the Confederacy. As for Lincoln, it gave him the credibility to issue the Emancipation Proclamation."

George scoffed. "He freed the Slaves we didn't control, but kept in bondage those in Union territory. Talk about hypocrisy."

"Some people can do good things with hypocrisy, George. It was the beginning of the end of slavery."

George put his arms around her. "My dear little abolitionist."

"Slavery was the real cause of the war. It took you awhile to see that. It was a poison the country had to vomit up."

"I still prefer Hamlin's method."

"That's just because it was nicer for Mary Chesnut and she made a lot of money," Nelly teased, but her eyes were not smiling. "I trust you've had no more of those disgusting dreams about her."

George let out a gasp. "Over there. Look, do you see him?"

Nelly turned. "Yes, I see him."

George was wide eyed, short of breath. "What's he doing here?"

Nelly strolled over to where Edwin Stanton stood, seemingly rooted to the ground like a rotten stump, his glasses fogged with moisture.

"He can't see or hear us, darling. He is serving a small eternity in another dimension as punishment for what he did to you after the battle."

George nodded. "That's only fair." He reached out and gave a rough tug at Stanton's beard. No response.

Nelly took his hand and pulled him away. "There's a rule here, darling. Don't play with the ghosts."

"Sorry. Couldn't resist."

They strolled through the National Cemetery, looking at the red stone grave markers. "Did you ever consider," Nelly said, "that here you were fighting one of the world's greatest generals, while at the same time you were opposing the cleverest politician that ever was?"

The revelation hit him. It was true. "I was lucky to come out with a head on my shoulders."

Nelly stopped and looked at him with love overflowing. "You held the line, George, until Sam Grant and Cump Sherman could come on and finish the job. You fought the good fight, and held the line. I am so proud of you, my general."

George blushed, kissed Nelly on the forehead. "I wonder whatever happened to Lincoln?" he said. "Any idea?"

"Lincoln? Oh, he was just passing through," Nelly said casually, "a creature from another world, tried humanity, didn't like it. Long gone. There's talk he haunts the White House, but it's really that actor, Booth, playing the role, as his punishment."

"My wife, the know-it-all," George said with happy pride. "Tell me what would have happened if I had made that charge out there from the Near Woods."

Nelly shook her head. No. Her lips were a tight line.

"Please."

"Oh, all right! You would've been shot through the head before you crossed the Smoketown Road." Nelly's voice was empty of feeling, her face strangely white now and drained of all its former joy. "I see you going over backwards off Dan Webster. Your cap falls and hits the ground before your head does. Armstrong Custer is shot dead trying to recover your body. The attack falls apart."

Colors and lights swirled around them. The earth tilted. Where to now, George wondered.

"And think," Nelly, cried, her voice fading in echo, "of all the brave boys who would have died with you."

CHAPTER THIRTY-ONE

Rome, April 14, 1865

A buzzing noise, a fly crawling on his nose. George swiped at it and opened his eyes to find Nelly asleep on his chest. They were naked in a tangle of perfumed sheets, a ladder of sunlight falling from lattice work shutters across their bed.

"Wake up, sleepyhead."

Nelly, eyes closed, stretched every muscle.

"Hmm, I just had the strangest dream about a dream," George said.

Nelly's eyelids fluttered. "Oh, dear, I don't like those. You never know when you're awake or what's real."

"Want to hear it?"

"Yup."

"I was in a world where Hannibal Hamlin was President and we didn't have a war."

"How pleasant."

"Yes, but I was killed there, and then somehow I shot Lincoln."

She licked a finger and brushed his lips with it. "Why, you naughty boy!"

"You were there too but of course it's all gone now. Oh, I remember, you were telling me you died in 1915 at Nice, and how you always celebrated Antietam."

Nelly rose up and pressed her loving breasts down on his face. "My good man, 1915 is a long way off."

George hugged her close and kissed the twin offerings.

"True," he said. "We may never get there. But right now we ought to get out of bed."

Nelly pouted and kissed him with serious intent. "Why?" she whispered.

"Dinner with the German Ambassador, remember? Best restaurant in Rome?"

"Oh, that old place. Nowhere near as nice as Wormley's." Her hand went adventuring under the sheets.

"Where's that manly sword?"

"Oh, no, please, darling we really have to get up."

"You care for the German Ambassador more than you do for me, Herr McClellan?"

"Maybe he'll offer me a job fighting the French."

"You don't want to fight anybody."

"Yes, I guess that's always been my trouble."

Nelly giggled and enveloped him with all her warmth.

"Darling, I really don't think it's possible," George whispered, "much as I might wish to . . ."

"Achtung," she shouted, thrusting the sheets to the floor and kicking her perfect legs at the ceiling.

"Achtung, Mein General!"

The laughed in each other's arms. All sad dreams forgotten.

CHAPTER THIRTY-TWO

He was a restless ghost, always dashing here and there, out and about, obsessively, furiously busy on his endlessly important rounds. He was after all, a man of weighty consequence.

Lincoln had called him 'Mars,' the god of war. He loved the title. His blustering voice had thundered like unto a thousand guns. He had stood at his lectern desk and issued blunt, hard, decisive orders that caused stupid generals to quiver with impotent rage.

His red brick War Department building was lost now in the dust of years. Yet he still made his rounds there, appearing in the corridors of the elaborate, angular edifice that occupied its old space. He was good at being a scary ghost. Took a certain pride. He developed a frightful, fang-like grin, eyes blazing through thick oval lenses with that magic, mysterious 'I despise you,' energy. He loved lurching out of night shadows, putting terror in the State Department clerks who worked there. Sometimes when they stopped screaming he held seminars for them in his specialties. Vindictive Plotting, Empty Hypocritical Moral Posturing, Bullying Argument, Insult (Basic and Advanced), Justifications For Murder, Most People Are Pigs And Need To Be Told What to Do, and other old favorites.

But that all faded away eventually, and he found himself in a melting void of a world in which unknown, time-empty years stretched behind him and beyond him, lost in a maze of chattering voices and melding images that faded in and out all around him like sputtering candle flames.

Once he saw Lincoln. The murdered President appeared to be exactly as he was in life, except that his features were blank and missing their old humorous animation. Lincoln looked at Edwin Stanton with stern eyes unblinking, then turned slowly, smoothly as if on a rotating platform, and Stanton saw the

359

smashed-in rear of Lincoln's head, all disrupted hair and bone mixed up in a bloody mush.

"You did this, Mars?" Lincoln asked with unmoving lips in his creaky, backwoods voice. "Thanks for the favor, old pard. Maybe I'll do you one someday."

Then he was on a hill. Heard wind blowing. Could not feel it.

He was overlooking Sharpsburg, Maryland and the dinky brown Antietam creek. Behind him loomed a run-down red brick house. He knew somehow that this house had once been George McClellan's headquarters.

A voice at his side, "Ain't so many of us left here anymore, Cap. Unusual to see a new 'un. Was you in the battle? Back for a visit?"

"No," Edwin Stanton said.

He had come to slowly realize that the horror and torture of being a ghost arose in your very own caring about your fervent lost loves and important spiteful hatreds and raging ambitions. To not care softened and blurred the pain. To not care was peace. He didn't know why he was at this particular place and he didn't care.

Or so he told himself, as he tried not to care.

"Yep, most of us have moved on," the voice rambled. "What's your business here, Cap?"

"I have no business," Stanton said, smugly. "I don't know why I am here. There is no 'why' to believe in." He stopped. The other ghost looked at him in that blank way of ghosts. Stanton had to say it, had to admit he cared just a little bit. "My dear old friend McClellan was here at this house during the battle, wasn't he?"

"Yes, this here was Little Mac's headquarters," the ghost soldier said, happy for the conversation. "Watched the whole doings from telescopes, he did, up there in the front yard."

"Ah, the great General," Stanton said with a reflexive sneer.

"He was our Commander," the ghost soldier said, his voice wistful. "He came and inspected us before the battle. He spoke

360

kindly to me, calmed my fears. He said it was normal to be afraid."

"Turns out you were right to be afraid," Stanton said with a joyful zing of cruelty.

The ghost soldier made no reply.

Stanton gazed out over the battlefield and raised his immaterial arms in an encompassing gesture. "This was the scene of a great victory in my war," he said.

"General McClellan's victory over General Lee?" the ghost soldier inquired.

"No, you simpleton. My victory over General McClellan. I did it here."

"I thought you was on our side. Your Secesh people generally hang out down by Burnside's Bridge." The ghost soldier shrugged his immaterial shoulders, thrust his hands into non-existent pockets and shuffled off singing softly.

"Come back you lump, I want to tell you about it."

But Stanton was alone.

For a long time.

One warm and smoky afternoon in September a famous politician came to visit. There were patriotic ceremonies with wind-whipped flags, band music and speeches.

Some grandstands had been set up on the wide grassy area adjoining the Battlefield Park Headquarters and Edwin Stanton as a long time resident, made his way there. The unspoken, unnamed rules under which he existed allowed him freedom to range over all the monument-studded battlefield. But he couldn't leave. "Just once," he grumbled to himself, "I'd like to meet whoever is in charge of this dimension."

The Politician himself as high guest of honor delivered a long rambling address. The ghost of Edwin Stanton stood in the busy crowd doing his usual good job of being empty air, and watched. Then a movement caught his eye. From the Politician a wavering transparent shape detached itself, a glowing intensified version of the great Politician whooshed over to Edwin Stanton and startled the veteran ghost.

"Hi there. Say, don't I know you?" the Politician's Essential Self said.

"I don't think you do," Stanton said. "Still there is something powerfully attractive about you. I like your white teeth and wavy hair. Perhaps you were one of my wives or lovers in some other lifetime."

"What?" The Politician's Essence was shocked. "What kind of pervert are you anyway? What's that stuff about other lifetimes?"

"I have heard we come back and live other lives," Stanton said. "It's a popular rumor among my kind. I don't know whether it's true or not. No one ever tells me anything."

"Hmm. This is a hell of a thing, ya know. To be talking with a ghost."

"Tell me, what makes the intermobiles run?"

"The what?"

"Those four wheeled contraptions you roll around in. Obviously they are driven by some kind of internal power source. I call them intermobiles."

"Pretty close, old man. Those are automobiles, gasoline combustion engines, that's about all I can tell you. I'm not much up on mechanics."

"When were they invented?" Stanton asked, just making conversation.

"Oh about, let's see, sixty, sixty-five years ago."

"This year is . . .?"

"1959," replied the Politician's Abstract Reality. "How do you think my speech is going?"

"I wouldn't know. What are you trying to say?"

"That I'm running for President, but not in so many words."

Stanton observed the proceedings. "You're getting a lusty response from the crowd."

"I know, I know." The Politician's shade was all bubbling and excited now. "I'm great with a live crowd, it's when I get on the tube that I come off looking like I've got a rail up my ass."

"Tube?"

362

The politician's Imperishable Spirit briefly explained television.

"Can you look into people's homes with this machine? Spy on them?"

"Well, no, it only works one way. They can see you, but you can't see them."

"Oh." Pity. The idea sounded promising. "I worked for a President who was very amiable with crowds. He would have done well with this television."

"Who was that? When?"

"Oh, a long time ago. You've never heard of him. His name was Abraham Lincoln."

"Holy shit! You worked for Abraham Lincoln? Why he's like a god!"

"Well, I wouldn't exactly call him that. Give him his due credit, he did establish the power of the Central Government over the States. He went after them with guns."

"Oh, well sure, we know that from history. The Civil War put the Federal Government on top of the States. That's why I want to be President."

Stanton was starting to feel at home with this man. "Do you hold office now?" he asked.

"Vice President."

"Oh," Stanton hoped his disappointment was not too obvious. "Is that office still what it was in my time?"

"Worse, probably. By the way, my name is Dick Nixon."

"Edwin Stanton, Secretary of War."

"Stanton? Why sure, I've read about you. Lincoln's hatchet man. What are you doing hanging out here?"

"Who knows? No one tells me. I do have a theory though. This was the scene of my greatest victory."

"Oh, right," Nixon said. "Stopped Robert E. Lee's invasion of the North. Blocked foreign recognition of the Confederacy. Gave Lincoln the political clout to issue the Emancipation Proclamation. That's all in my speech, The Historical Significance of Antietam."

"No, no, no," Stanton fumed. "That's all the same old bullshit they put in the history books. I'm talking about my victory over the true enemy, George McClellan."

"Tell me about it."

"After the battle here his Army was all shot up and depleted. Needed everything. We all understood that, except Lincoln of course. I held back supplies, but covered my tracks. Managed to stall McClellan here for over a month. One of the under secretaries investigated, discovered the 'mix-up' and I wasn't to blame. Meanwhile I was able to undermine McClellan with Lincoln, as usual. My God, but that man was so arrogant, I could make him do whatever I wished, and he would think it was his idea. Hah! He thought the sun in the morning was his idea. I advised him to fire McClellan for being 'too slow' and he finally did it in November. Simpleton McClellan gave up without a fight, naturally, and turned the Army over to Burnside, who promptly marched it to Fredericksburg and nearly destroyed it. But that's another story."

"Say, I'm really impressed," Nixon said. "Seems you were quite an operator."

Stanton whiffed a change in the atmosphere, a shift in the structure of his world. Something had popped. He knew he was free now to leave the Antietam Battlefield.

He got down to business. "Listen," he said, "let me work for you. I can deal with your enemies. I'm very good at it. The key is information, true information for your side and faulty information for your enemy."

"They call that disinformation now."

"Ah, so they've given a name to it?" Edwin Stanton had not felt so energized and just plain happy for almost a hundred years. "You have to do whatever is necessary. Break in, steal things, put people in jail. Use spies. For example, I had a man in my enemy's camp."

Nixon learned fast. "Ah, that would be McClellan?"

"Who else? I controlled his most trusted advisor, a detective who gave him consistently false estimates of the rebel's strength.

McClellan, that imbecile, always was ready to believe the odds were against him. My man convinced him of it."

"And that somehow played into your plans?"

"Why of course. We couldn't allow a Democrat to achieve a great victory. It would spoil everything. The Democrats were the true enemy, you know."

"Not the Confederates?"

"Oh, they were just the excuse for it all," Stanton's ghost laughed knowingly. "Let me tell you about the real Civil War sometime."

"I would welcome the education," Nixon said with a big smile. "Can you join up with me now? Or do you have to go on haunting here some more?"

"I am free to leave now," Stanton said. "It seems I have graduated."

"Well then," Nixon said with a husky chuckle, "Louie, I've got a feeling this is the beginning of a beautiful friendship."

What was he talking about? "My name's not Louie."

"I'll explain later."

So. He would go off with and work for this politician, Nixon, giving him the benefit of his wisdom. Somehow he knew that his soul would eventually return to the sweet material world, where there were three things he longed to do, drink fine wine, touch a woman's intimate softness, and pilot one of those speedy automobiles, preferably the kind with the open top. He wondered if he could do all three things at once.

* * *

Some years later Nixon did become President of the United States. After four and a half years of success, he fell victim to the worst political scandal in the Nation's history. Threatened with Impeachment, he became the first President to resign the office in disgrace.

Many members of his staff went to prison and wrote books while serving time. Though expressing their own points of view, they all did agree on one thing. President Nixon, they told us, had two clearly distinct personalities sharing the same body. One it seems was a virtuous man, sensitive and loving to his family and friends, a man of quiet good deeds who could feel sympathy for his political enemies, and leak tears at a passage of soulful Russian music.

The other was a lot like Edwin M. Stanton.

* * *

AUTHOR'S NOTES AND ACKNOWLEDGEMENTS

In the first part of this novel, 'The World of Charleston,' events depicted are speculative interpolations based on what history tells us about the characters in play. Certain people in this sequence are fictional. They are: Alexander DuBott, manager of the Mills House, his freeman bartender, George Washington, Captain Blackstone, Ensign Filmore and the crew of the Vanderbilt.

Mary Chesnut and her diaries are a strangely neglected subject for drama, film or novel. Maybe she came back as Margaret Mitchell and wrote *Gone With the Wind*.

The second part, 'The World of War,' depicts selected elements of George B. McClellan's experiences as commander of the Army of the Potomac. Two characters and their scenes are imaginary, Robert E. Lee's visitor on the eve of the battle of Antietam, and the red-haired Lieutenant Lundy.

Though I have found no prime source for George McClellan's meeting with his generals and staff at his home on the evening of September 2nd, it is likely that a meeting of this sort may well have taken place. The worries expressed by the Comte de Paris reflect George's own real concerns at the time.

George's letters up to and including Chapter Four are fictional. Thereafter his letters, telegrams and messages are selected excerpts from *The Civil War Papers of George B. McClellan*, edited by Stephen W. Sears, 1989.

George's speeches and interior monologues are my own invention based on what I know, believe and imagine about him.

366

His final adventure in the transcendental realm is a metaphor reflecting issues in the 'real world.'

In preparing this work of imagination, I have consulted the standard histories and commentaries of the period, plus the following special books:

The Life and Times of Hannibal Hamlin, by Charles Hamlin, 1899; *George B. McClellan, the Young Napoleon*, by Stephen W. Sears, 1988; *General George Brinton McClellan: A Study in Personality*, by William Starr Myers, 1934; *General George B. McClellan, Shield of the Union*, by Warren W. Hassler, Jr., 1957; *McClellan's Own Story*, by George B. McClellan, edited by William C. Prime, 1886; and *Report of the Army of the Potomac*, by George B. McClellan, 1864.

The Pry House still exists as part of The Antietam National Battlefield under the National Park Service. You can stand today on the same overlook where George conferred with Fitz John Porter. Two miles away you can still see the "Far Woods," behind the 'little white church.'

* * *

This book has had a long and rocky road through writing to publication, but there were friends along the way. Astute Editor David King was able to help me figure out exactly what novel I was trying to write, and then suggested the way to do it. Thank you, David. You are one of the best players in a demanding game.

Copy Editor, Joe Mott is to be commended for catching many a typo as well as questionable usages and a hell of a lot of other things.

As this novel developed I sent out versions of the manuscript to friends and associates. This role of honor includes William F. DeSeta, Dr. Elizabeth Lynn, Dr. John Y. Simon, Joe Weintraub, Marianne Kanter, Jackie Simon, Patricia Turbes-Mohs, Arnold Rosenfeld, Hal Thomas, Catherine Brashich, Ed Francie and John B. Sandwick. Thanks all for your helpful reactions and support.

Historians were consulted. They don't necessarily agree with anything in this novel, but the following were gracious to me: Dr. Joseph L. Harsh, Thomas J. Rowland, Dr. John Y. Simon, Stephen W. Sears, Dr. John Fairfield, and John J. Hennessy.

For guiding me through the mechanics of publishing I must gratefully thank Carmen Jacobs of 1st Books Library. Thanks also to: Mort Künstler, Jeff Lavaty and artist Sal Catalano for helping me obtain the fine cover graphics, to Gladys Gannon of Secretarial Services Unlimited for her patience and finely detailed work in preparing the manuscript, to Anna Samuel and Boris Moshkovits for the public relations campaign, and Sally Hertz for marketing advice.

Finally.

To the person who always has the first look, my friend and partner, thank you dear Patty for all these years of aiding and abetting.

ABOUT THE AUTHOR

John Grissmer has filled many roles. He has been an actor, professor of drama, film producer, writer and director, U. S. Army officer, playwright, business executive, theatrical producer and novelist.

Some years ago he pondered two questions. Was the Civil War truly inevitable, and had George McClellan been fairly treated by history? The search for answers to these questions led him to write *The Ghosts of Antietam.*

Currently a consultant and guest director in the Performing Arts Program at Xavier University, he has recently completed *The Perfect Game,* a musical play about the invention of basketball.

Printed in the United States
78540LV00001B/11